Ravenscourt

Samantha Ward-Smith

Published by Mabel and Stanley Publishing – Oct 2025

This is a work of fiction. Unless otherwise indicated, all the names, characters, businesses, places, events and incidents in this book are either the product of the author's imagination or used in a fictitious manner. Any resemblance to actual persons, living or dead, or actual events is purely coincidental.

This work contains some scenes of a sexual nature and domestic violence, which some readers may find distressing. The content has been kept to a minimum and is included to reflect the historical context of the period in which the story is set. Reader discretion is advised.

Cover design © Patrick Knowles

www.patrickknowlesdesign.co.uk

Image ©Shutterstock

For Judith and Linda

True Friends Are Great Riches

Prologue

The Westminster Gazette

January 1879

Tragedy Strikes Once Again at Ravenscourt

Sir Charles Pembrook, the prominent cotton merchant of Manchester, was found dead at his home, Ravenscourt, on 16th January. A supporter of free trade principles and an active member of the Exchange, he was warmly regarded for his enterprise, sound judgement, and an unwavering integrity in business.

However, the Pembrooks have endured mixed fortunes at the estate, which was built in the early 1830s by Sir Charles's father, Sir Thomas Pembrook. Sir Thomas's two-year-old daughter drowned in the lake whilst in the care of her mother, Lady Catherine, who not long after was committed to an asylum.

Sir Thomas later died of a heart attack in scandalous circumstances – too scurrilous to be reported here – at the house. Sir Charles's first wife, Lady Elizabeth, died at Ravenscourt after a short illness, emphasising the tragic memories the property held for Sir Charles.

Sir Charles had been suffering from illness in recent months, and it is believed he went to Ravenscourt to convalesce. He was accompanied by his wife of just under one year, Lady Arabella, who stands to inherit some of his wealth. However, the business and property, including the ill-fated Ravenscourt, will pass to his son, Matthew, and daughter, Sophia – his children from his first marriage.

Part One

Chapter One

Venice – February 1880

Years later, when Alexander allowed himself the memory of that first visit to Venice, he would recall the moment when he left the steamy bustle of the station. His body was stiff from the rattling, jolting train, and his mind was weary of the misery he had left behind in England. He eased himself into the waiting gondola, bobbing by the steps, and he reclined back onto the scarlet, velvet cushions as the early morning winter mist shrouded him.

The water lapped lazily against the sleek, black boat, with the slow rhythm of the pole pushing through the surface, hitting the unseen mud below, as they made their way through the narrow canal. Only the gondolier's harsh voice echoed off the enclosing walls, breaking the eerie silence. 'Beware,' he seemed to cry, 'I am coming.' The early morning fog slowly lifted, revealing Venice in all its famed beauty. Alex took in the vibrant, painted walls; tall, Gothic windows looking down at him with their ornate balconies; and the slimy water steps leading to large wooden doors of the Palazzos. A tired old woman, in a faded dressing gown, leant on a crumbling sill, smoking a cigarette, oblivious to their boat below. As they slowly progressed, Alex glimpsed little white bridges crossing smaller canals where people scuttled to and fro, hurrying to get to work. There were no tourists at this early hour who would have paused and taken their time, enticed by what lay ahead.

A pigeon, disturbed by the movement in the water, flapped upwards towards the weak February sunshine which began to tinge the walls pink breaking through the gloom, reflecting on the green sheen of the water. The faint odour of the canal tickled Alex's nose, repugnant and unsettling. Then suddenly they were upon the Grand Canal itself. The gondola rocked alarmingly as Alex gripped the sides of the low boat tighter, feeling the cold spray of water on his hands. But the gondolier, a capable expert, steadied them as they moved against the current. They avoided the numerous other craft traversing the main waterway of the city, but he could almost reach out and touch the succulent fruit and vegetables on the barges touting their wares to the hotels, the boarding houses, and the residents along the banks. Behind him in another gondola, Alex hoped, followed his valet, George, with all their tottering luggage. By now his senses were fully alert to the bustle that was happening around him in the city. The long journey from London temporarily forgotten and the arguments with his father pushed to one side as he enjoyed the vibrant life around him.

He laughed as the gondolier ducked to get under the Rialto Bridge then smiled as children called out and waved to him from above. He listened to the shopkeepers animatedly greet each other as the shops on the bridge began to open for the day. He marvelled at the magnificent Palazzos lining along the water's edge, each seemingly more beautiful and grander as they edged closer towards the hotel. He did not register the decay beneath the silken, green water – the rottenness of the city's foundations, nor the ugliness which tarnished its beauty. A beauty that was a façade, a Carnival mask covering the dark truth that nothing was as it seemed.

When they arrived at the Hotel Danieli, Alex stretched his long legs as he glanced up at yet another exquisite building with more of those Gothic arches, complete with sparkling windows, and intricate balconies. He was eager for some food, a hot bath, and most of all some sleep after an exhausting journey. The sleeping carriage of the train had not been as comfortable as he had expected, with the bed too narrow and too short to accommodate him.

'Alex! You made it,' an excited voice broke into his thoughts as he entered the large foyer. Before him stood a man he immediately recognised – a pleasant-looking, sandy haired young man, short in stature, with a rather magnificent moustache which framed his happy smile.

'Rupert Sydney.' He laughed. 'What gets you up so early?' Happy to meet his friend already but surprised at the hour.

'I've just returned from an all-night card game with old Carisbrick. Lost a fair sum, I'm afraid.' Rupert chuckled. 'Get checked in and you can have breakfast with me. You are just in time. George can get you unpacked.'

Alex completed the formalities with the effusive hotel manager, who was always amenable to revered guests from Britain's aristocracy, and he left George to manage his luggage. He joined Rupert in the elegant dining room, whose windows overlooked the enticing vista of the Giudecca Canal with its bobbing gondolas. Rupert had chosen a secluded spot, the table tucked away behind a decorative pillar and hidden by an abundance of fern leaves.

'It's good to see you, Alex.' Rupert looked at his friend, noting the tiredness in the dark eyes and the pain marring his otherwise handsome features. He seemed to have aged since Rupert had last seen him at Cambridge only a few months ago, before they had both been sent down for different reasons.

'I'm amazed your father still gives you an allowance to gamble with.' Alex shook his head. 'When you told me you were also coming here, I must admit I was surprised, but I'm relieved to see you.' He accepted coffee from the attentive waiter as they ordered their breakfast.

'I'm not like your kind, Alex. My father thought it was hilarious when I got sent down. My mother was the one with grand pretensions of a university education for her son – the merchant's boy.' Rupert smirked. 'Pa wants me to go into the business, so I've been sent here to look at some silks for him and to work with Roger Jobson, one of his old business associates. And in the meantime, he has given me a generous allowance and told me to have some fun.' As a plate of food was laid in front of him, he swished out his linen napkin, ready to attack his breakfast with gusto.

Alex wished he had his friend's freedom and the lack of constraint to be able to have fun. Of course, it was different for Rupert because he was from new money, so there weren't the same pressures for him in terms of securing a good marriage to continue the family line. And they were safer from scandal because Rupert and other families like his were ignored until people needed their goods or investment. Most of all, Alex wished his own father was more similar to Rupert's.

'You look like death, Alex. Has it been so awful for you?' Rupert asked, as soon as the waiter had departed. 'I was even more surprised your father allowed you to come here after all that happened. Thought you would be engaged at least to that neighbour of yours by now, and firmly put back in your stately place,' Rupert teased him.

'Oh, god, Ru, it's been bloody awful. He's sent me here to let the whole sordid scandal die down – his words, not mine.' Alex looked at the food on his plate, his appetite suddenly diminishing as he contemplated the last few weeks. 'Helen is a lovely girl. I've known her all my life, and our estates neighbour each other, so the match would be good for both families, but she doesn't excite me – I don't love her,' he conceded.

'Are we supposed to love our wives?' Rupert raised an eyebrow, wiping crumbs from his bushy moustache.

'I want someone who challenges me, who shares my interests, my desires, and my goals in life,' Alex ventured. 'Helen just loves horses, the country life, and being a good sport. She has no interest in reform even for women – her and my mother think it is extremely unseemly. But my father wants the marriage, and I have no idea what I can do about it.'

'Well, I suggest you enjoy yourself while you are here. It's fairly different to London – a lot more rich Americans, lavish parties, and of course the Carnival,' Rupert encouraged his friend, realising it was not the right time to discuss Alex's transgressions as he could see how it was still a painful subject.

'Oh, yes, George has become extremely informed about the Carnival, speaking to the train attendants and anyone who will tell him about it.' Alex grinned, happy to change the subject than have to confront the dreary future that lay ahead of him. 'He regaled me with stories about all the characters, which passed the time I admit, but I thought the Carnival wasn't the same as it had been before the wars?'

'Good old George, you are lucky with your man. He helped us get out of many a scape,' Rupert reminisced. 'I've been told the Carnival is definitely not what it was, but it's been revived in some form for the tourists. There are plenty of masquerade balls and people still love to dress as the Carnival characters. In fact, there is one such ball tonight at Palazzo Grimani and we are invited. Venice is agog that the Viscount Dundarran is in town, so I shall be riding on your coattails to secure all the best invitations,' Rupert said with a wink.

Alex baulked at the thought that Venetian Society already knew he was in town – how quickly news travelled. But a scandal such as his would have reached even these distant shores.

'I suppose I can't avoid the gossips, and you are right I should enjoy myself while I can,' Alex resolved.

Rupert had no concerns that they wouldn't have fun. His friend's arrival was already much anticipated even without the scandal that had followed him here. Alex was young at twenty-two, but heir to a considerable fortune and to the Dukedom of Ushington. Most of all he was attractive with his striking dark looks and the high-etched cheekbones inherited from his mother – a renowned Society beauty back in her day from what Alex had said. But Rupert knew there was so much more to his friend, the Viscount, than his pretty looks. He was indeed enthusiastic about reform, generous to those who knew him, and a thoroughly kind, considerate soul. He was also a loyal friend and took people at merit rather than by their social standing, which is why they had been able to forge such a strong friendship despite their different starts in life. But he was too kind, too trusting, and definitely too gullible, Rupert thought, which had got him embroiled in the scandal that brought him here.

The waiter came to clear their plates and pour more coffee, which they gratefully accepted.

'So, is it as debauched as they say it is – the Carnival?' Alex asked, leaning in.

'Not so far, I'm afraid,' Rupert laughed. 'Well, I guess if you are looking for such things, they are always to be found beneath the surface. The masks allow more mischief, but to be honest I have spent most of my time on the gaming tables so far instead of dancing and all that.'

'Ru, you never change, nor it seems does your luck.' Alex smiled at his friend. He had been relieved to leave England, and he was more than happy to be reunited with Rupert, whose company would definitely make Venice brighter.

'I'm afraid you are right on that.' Rupert sighed, draining the last remnants of his coffee. He glanced out of the long Gothic windows, watching the sun's rays rippling on the water beyond, signalling the day was starting in earnest. The dining room was filling up now and heads were turning in their direction, and Rupert was now ready for his bed having not made it there last night. 'Come, we both need to sleep; get some energy for tonight, for you are already being noticed. I'm sure soon enough every mother will be keen to introduce her daughter to you.' He grinned.

'They will be disappointed then, as the last thing I am looking for is a wife to incur my father's wrath further!'

'Well, yes, as you actually desire a bluestocking wife, you are unlikely to find one here, so your father's wishes will be safe on that count.' Laughing, they left the prying eyes of the dining room and sought the comfort and privacy of their luxurious rooms, where soft beds awaited them.

Chapter Two

That evening, rather than take the longer, more languid route by gondola, Alex and Rupert decided to walk the short distance from the hotel to the Palazzo Grimani. Alex was glad to stretch his legs and get some fresh air. He had slept deeply until lunchtime when his appetite, which he had lost at breakfast, had returned with a fury. He had partaken of a solitary luncheon in his suite, not yet ready to face the curious eyes in the dining room on his own. He had worked up the courage to take a brief stroll to St Mark's Square for his first glimpse of the Doge's Palace and the famous church with its prancing horses, before briefly joining the crowds in the bustling square with its colonnaded walkways and busy shops. He had not loitered, saving any further delights for another day; instead returning to the hotel to write letters home, confirming his safe arrival to his mother. Short, terse missives lacking the usual affection exchanged between them.

Now here he was with Rupert navigating Calle de le Rasse, a narrow street filled with revellers. Their masked faces, long black or red cloaks, and the flamboyant tricornes gave a sinister feeling to the place. Alex felt as if he had descended into Hades itself as the white masks with their beak-like chins and over-prominent noses glanced towards him, the staring eyes taking in his own maskless appearance and making him feel even more exposed. He had not been able to bring himself to wear a mask, hating anything on his face, which remained ever clean-shaven when all his friends sported the fashionable moustache. Rupert had indulged him, laughing at his well-known foible. Rupert himself wore a half-mask, claiming he preferred it to the full Bauta most of the revellers wore.

'You can hide behind a mask,' Rupert had tried to reason with Alex. 'No one would have a clue who you were.'

'I would prefer they know who I am than have my face feel so enclosed. You know how much I hate anything on my face. Plus, they will be gossiping about me anyway so I would rather confront it head-on.' Alex had been adamant.

The Palazzo was located down another side street and its dark, red doors opened into a large courtyard where loggias ran along the entire façade of the building. Classical statues adorned the loggias, which were covered in plant motifs with baskets of fruit and vegetables spilling abundantly onto the floor. Lanterns were strung up in small trees as further light spilled down from the rooms above, where the music of the ball interspersed with gay laughter and the clink of glasses. They were shown across the mosaic square to the imposing marble staircase which led up to the main reception or portego rooms.

Immediately, they were thrust into a dense throng of people wearing colourful masks with colourful costumes – here they found Arlecchino in his harlequin suit, the dastardly Captain Spezzaferro with his roguish whiskers, and Isabella in her red taffeta, Colombina coquettish behind her fan. Fiorinetta and Silvia were glimpsed amongst those who had only adorned themselves with the full Bauta or the half-masks, but their gowns were no less sumptuous. Occasionally, they spied the sinister plague doctor with his long hollow beak of a nose, his white-gloved hand clutching his staff. Here were the echoes of the old Carnival in the fading Palazzo Grimani. Alex felt the lack of his own mask now they had arrived at Grimani, and already worried he was the focus of much attention.

The portego was lined with portraits of the famous Grimani family, counting Doges amongst them. Rupert had explained en route how important they had once been in Venetian politics, although now the family lived on past glories. Already their glamour was fading, their power and wealth waning. But tonight, it would appear the Grimani still carried some influence, as most of Venetian Society and their esteemed overseas guests were out in force if the crush inside was anything to go by.

Alex was aware of masked faces turning his way, whispers behind gloved hands or bejewelled fans, nods of recognition in the crowd which made him blush crimson. Not only was he handsome new blood, but his family name – plus the recent scandal attached to it – seemed to pique everyone's interest in him. He was soon purloined by their hostess, a brittle, thin woman in a Colombina outfit, the Duchessa playing at the maid. She was overjoyed to be the first to welcome the infamous Viscount, and her party's success was now assured thanks to such a notable guest. She embarked him on a swirl of introductions, of small talk, of stealth-like hands stroking his arm as if to possess him. Rupert had quickly disappeared, tiring of the fuss, and now Alex could not have seen him if he tried among the sea of white masks.

Alex found himself in a small formal room off the main portego, talking to a group of masked women, all seemingly competing for his attention and laughing eagerly at his every word although he said very little. They pressed upon him endless information regarding the delights of Venice, the best shops, the best coffee places, and of course more invitations to visit their own Palazzos and their upcoming soirees as part of the Season's festivities. Eager to distract himself, he glanced up and discovered a beautiful ceiling covered entirely with fruit trees, flowers, and numerous birds. In one corner of the magnificent fresco, he spotted an owl carrying off a smaller bird, and he envied the unfortunate bird, wishing he too could be carried off away from the gabble of women congregated around him. The heat of the room pressed down on him and he swayed slightly, feeling it all becoming too much.

'Ladies, please excuse me,' he said with a bow and, giving no further explanation, abruptly turned away from them, pushing through the other guests, desperate to get away from the noise. He spotted a closed door at the end of the room and made his way towards it, hoping it was empty so that he could escape the maddening crowd if only for a little while. He eased open the heavy door and inside the room only a few lights flickered. As he closed the door behind him, the noise receded and in the semi-gloom he could see a few of the classical sculptures the Grimani family were famous for. He leant against the door and closed his eyes in respite.

He was startled by a polite cough and opened his eyes to find he was not alone after all. Sitting on a small, padded bench between two statues at the end of the room, which he vaguely recognised as Diana the huntress and Venus the goddess of love, was a woman. She had been shadowy in the faint light of the room but now, as he moved towards her and she gazed directly at him, he could see an incredibly striking young woman. Her face could have been sculpted by the man who had made the Diana next to her, and he was stunned to see such beauty.

'I apologise, my Lady. I thought the room was empty.' He was tentative now, aware of the impropriety of being alone with her.

'Please do not apologise. I too needed a moment away from the crowd.' She smiled politely at him as his eyes widened at the sound of her American accent.

Not a Roman goddess after all, he thought.

As Alex studied her further, it was as if she was a female version of himself. She had the same thick black hair as he, although hers was swept back into a fashionable bun with curls that framed her face, seeming natural and not made with artifice. Her cheekbones could have been etched from the same bone structure as his, but it was the eyes which mirrored his own the most – a deep brown colour which appeared almost black and edged with an abundance of lashes. Her skin too was pale, translucent even, and similar to him, she had faint dark circles under her beautiful eyes. There was an aura of sadness around her which gave an air of fragility. Then he noticed the black crepe of her dress, the lack of adornment which contrasted with the gaudy, colourful costumes of the other ladies and the heavy mourning ring on her gloved hand.

'Forgive me, you are in mourning.' He bowed his head at the realisation.

'Yes.' Her voice was soft. 'It is a year since I lost my husband, Charles. But I am now allowing myself to come back into company. Tomorrow I may even wear lilac, which is wrong of me apparently, but I can't bear black any longer, especially not in a city that is filled with so much colour.' She gave him a weak smile, although he could see her struggling to hide her emotions. 'My aunt insisted I come out tonight. My name is Lady Arabella Pembrook.' Alex thought he knew the name but could not place it.

'Alexander FitzOsbern, Viscount Dundarran, my Lady,' he said, reaching out and kissing her delicate, gloved hand. 'But you hardly look old enough to be a widow, may I say.'

'You sir are too kind!' She smiled. 'I am nearly thirty. I also have two stepchildren who are seventeen and twenty years old, would you believe?' She sighed quietly.

Alex was unsure of how to act around her or what to say in response. She broke the awkward silence by standing up and gesturing towards an open door at the far end of the room.

'Have you seen the famous Tribune room?'

Alex looked at her blankly.

'It's our host's most important collection and not to be missed,' she admonished, teasing him. As they walked towards it, he noticed she matched him in height, though she was far more graceful and poised. As they entered the room, he gasped.

'It's stunning, isn't it?' she whispered in his ear.

Suspended from the highly decorated ceiling was the most spectacular sculpture Alex had ever seen. A naked youth was clasped in the grip of a large eagle, who was carrying him upwards to the window which appeared high in the ceiling above them. Only the moonlight lit the room, making the sculpture eerily luminous. The rest of the collection was in the shadows, insignificant to the entwined figures. It was a masterpiece of theatre and sent a shiver down his spine.

'The abduction of Ganymede?' he asked in wonder.

'Yes, that most beautiful of mortals who was taken by Zeus, disguised as an eagle, to serve the gods. I find it sad how this gorgeous young boy was made to serve a much older man. Such is the way of the world. Art such as this is frivolous in my eyes,' she remarked.

There was silence as they both stood studying it for a few moments. When Alex turned at last to speak to Arabella, he noticed tears in her eyes.

'I'm sorry, I am banishing ghosts,' she said in a hushed voice, quickly wiping her eyes, and turning from the room.

Alex followed her, eager to speak to her and comfort her in her distress, but the door opened and an older, sharp-faced woman entered.

'There you are, Arabella. What are you doing shut away in here?' She paused when she noticed Alex, who quickly introduced himself.

'Mrs Harriet Burton, my Lord. Lady Pembrook's aunt.' She bobbed her head slightly in acknowledgement.

'A pleasure, Mrs Burton. I was keeping your niece company having stumbled across her when seeking sanctuary for a few moments and was about to offer her some refreshment if you would care to join me.'

'You see, dear Harriet; I was not shut away after all, simply making a new acquaintance.' Arabella beamed at her aunt.

'A friend, I hope.' Alex proffered his arm.

'A friend, yes, I would like a friend,' Arabella murmured.

The aunt smiled as they walked past her and braved the heaving throng of revellers. Alex noticed the room observe their entrance. Neither he nor Arabella were wearing masks, so it was obvious who they were to the other partygoers, and he was quick to sense the surprise evident behind the masks that surveyed them. Arabella bowed her head slightly as if to shield herself from their gaze.

'Come let us find those refreshments, and I would be honoured if you and your aunt would take supper with me.' He had an urge to protect the fragile widow clinging tightly to his arm as they moved towards the supper room, her aunt trailing in their wake.

As he settled them at a table and motioned to a waiter to fetch them drinks while going to ferry food himself from the buffet, Alex vaguely remembered whom Sir Charles Pembrook was. He had been a rich merchant with cotton mills in the north of England, but not someone Alex himself had personally made the acquaintance of. Merchants were rarely part of his social circle at his young age, until he had met Rupert of course, whose father's newly acquired wealth meant he could have an education befitting someone of their new social standing. Having been at Cambridge these past few years, Alex had not been abreast of Society's news, yet he had a feeling there was something more to Arabella's story which continued to niggle him. For now, he turned his attention to the present and getting to know the lady in question.

Rupert, walking into the salon, spotted his friend and was taken aback by what he saw. Alex and Lady Pembrook. *My, that is a surprise*, he thought.

'Alex, there you are. I thought you had left already, but I see you have made new friends.' Rupert smiled at the two women. 'Rupert Sydney.' He introduced himself to the ladies with a polite bow of the head.

'Rupert, meet Lady Arabella Pembrook and her aunt, Harriet Burton.'

'Ah, yes, Lady Pembrook, Mrs Burton. You travel with Mr John Burton and your stepdaughter, Sophia? My sympathies on Sir Charles's tragic death,' Rupert kindly offered his condolences as was customary.

'Did you know my husband?' Arabella's voice was tremulous.

'Yes, through my father, but before your husband's death they had not seen each other as much as they once did. Anyway, Alex,' Rupert changed the subject, reluctant to distress her any more as he noted Arabella plucking at her dress disconcertedly. 'I came to tell you I was leaving. There's a card game at Palazzo Barbaro with the American crowd. Are you staying?'

'You go ahead. Cards aren't my thing; I prefer the present company, and I am hoping Lady Arabella and Mrs Burton will allow me to accompany them back to their hotel to ensure their safe return.'

'That would be most kind, my Lord,' agreed Harriet. 'My husband would have accompanied us, but he suffers from gout, so he stayed at the hotel tonight with dear

Sophia and Arabella's companion, Mary. We have taken a suite at the Grand.'

Alex was grateful for Lady Pembrook's quiet company on the walk back to their hotel later that evening. She seemed to sense his need for peace after the crowded Palazzo and her aunt had followed her niece's lead. When he returned to his own hotel, he was overcome by an immense tiredness from the exertions of the evening. As soon as he got into bed, he quickly fell into a deep slumber dreaming of canals, masked revellers, and the cry of the gondolier, 'Beware, I am coming.'

Chapter Three

A few evenings later, Alex found himself seated between two young women – one a confident, eager American; the other a timid, blushing English creature who appeared as insipid in nature as much as the former seemed garrulous. Both grated on his frayed nerves.

The room was ablaze with candlelight, which reflected in the large, ornate gilt mirrors and off the vast amount of silverware on the table, which was overflowing with fruit and heavy-scented flowers – their scent adding to the heady atmosphere. Lady Lyborn, a leading English socialite who resided in Venice, certainly had fine taste in furnishing, but Alex wished the same extended to the company that she kept.

Rupert had secured his own invitation to this gathering thanks to his association with a desirable Viscount, who Lady Lyborn coveted to bring into her inner circle. Rupert was fully aware of his own worth, as was Alex, knowing he was always invited because his title brought added gravitas to these gatherings. He glanced sideways at the American heiress, who had been strategically placed on his right. He could not remember her name, although he had vaguely registered her loud, braying father. He was brash about his wealth, ensuring all knew of the dower price on his daughter's head. Alex suppressed a smile to himself, for even with all her fortune, she still would have not been worthy enough for his father and deserving of the family name. There were no crumbs to be gained at this table, when in his father's eyes, Alex was already promised to the Lady Helen.

The American heiress touched his arm daintily with her small, neat hands, eager to attract his attention. He realised he was being negligent with his manners, so turned now to speak to the sharp-faced girl. Her dark blonde hair was pulled back from her face into a tight chignon, which only emphasised her long nose and jutting ears. An unfortunate face perhaps, but she had the confidence of wealth in how she carried herself with her fine, expensive jewellery, and didn't seem to be aware of her limited intelligence. She would not lack suitors, but her father sought a title in any potential match.

Alex knew his type and how American money was transforming British Society. His father had been appalled when Lord Randolph Churchill, the second son of the Duke of Marlborough, had married Jennie Jerome in 1874. Her father, Leonard Jerome, was a wealthy financier, and his daughter's marriage seemed to spark a trend in American heiresses marrying into high society. The Duke of Ushington had disparaged these 'dollar princesses' and declared he would allow no such women in his family.

Alex and the American conversed briefly. He would not remember what they spoke about as they ate the fish course; the evening was superfluous in his eyes and tedious in its length.

'You must miss her,' a soft, timid voice addressed him. The English girl blushed to the roots of her dull brown hair when Alex looked at her. She blinked rapidly as if surprised at her own audacity of speaking out of turn. He found he had no reply to give the girl, but thankfully she had already turned to the man on her left, flustered with her own words which she had blurted out before she could stop herself. Alex knew of whom the girl spoke, and he was overwhelmed with a feeling of wretchedness knowing he could not outrun his past.

The waiters removed the final plates and the ladies, led by their indomitable hostess, retired to the drawing room to freshen up and then retrieve their cloaks and masks ready to depart on the waiting gondolas to take them to that evening's ball. Alex was eager to take his leave and forgo the port being passed slowly around the table among the remaining men. The fat cigars they chugged filled the room with clouds of smoke, and theirs was the inane talk of vain men vying over the worth of their fortunes, discovering whose wealth was bigger and therefore who had the most important standing. Alex caught Rupert's eye and recognised the same impatience, although he was probably longing for the gaming tables. Alex smiled at his friend's simple pleasures, albeit an expensive habit.

Finally, they found themselves on the narrow street outside the Palazzo, opting to walk the short distance to that evening's ball whilst the other guests had taken the black, sleek gondolas.

'God, that was tedious,' Rupert said while lighting a cigarette, savouring the quick relief it gave him. 'I was seated between two extremely snobbish, married matrons who were horrified that my family was in trade! Old as the hills too. Lady Lyborn obviously doesn't see me as marriage material for her younger guests.'

'You were lucky, believe me, Ru.' Alex shook his head ruefully. 'I detest being judged like one of my father's stallions, placed between two brood mares ready to mate. I wanted to blurt out how my father already has my future wife lined up and even if he didn't, he would not be eager to marry me off to either of those girls.' Alex paused, thinking how distasteful his father would find such a prospect. 'For a start, he abhors Americans, finds their wealth vulgar, and shudders at the idea of new money in his family. The other girl he would have for dinner – can never abide shyness and simpering. Yes, I know – father is indeed a contradiction. Doesn't want an outspoken woman yet hates one with nothing to say.'

Rupert laughed again and pitied his friend's family obligations, especially when he knew Alex's relationship with his father was rather strained. He had not minded his hostess' snub with the seating arrangements, preferring instead to concentrate on enjoying his meal rather than having to perform to would-be wives. The matrons' hostility towards him had meant he had enjoyed the feast set before him and could dine in relative peace.

Rupert was happy to be in the company of his friend, and Alex was keen to have some time without the whispers, the demands for dancing, and the flirtatious smiles of young ladies desperate to snare a Viscount. They strolled leisurely for a while in St Mark's Square, which was packed with Carnival revellers, jugglers, and other such street performers, being in no rush to get to the ball, as the music from Florians enticed them into the renowned café.

'I needed that,' Rupert exhaled, as he signalled the waiter for another brandy.

'I meant to ask you about Lady Arabella Pembrook,' Alex suddenly remembered. 'You said you knew her husband, Sir Charles, and I vaguely know the name, but there is something else niggling at me to do with his death.'

'I only remember that he died about a year ago, but we were up at Cambridge at the time.' Rupert took a sip of brandy.

'Yes, we were,' Alex recalled. 'Did your family know the Pembrooks well?'

'Oh, yes. I never met Sir Charles myself though, but my parents were very upset at the news,' Rupert reflected. 'Attractive woman, Lady Arabella,' he added with a wink, clearly nothing getting by him.

'Yes, she is indeed,' Alex agreed, before quickly changing the subject to avoid any further questioning along that line. 'My mother wrote to me today. My father refuses to write until I at least agree to an engagement with Lady Helen, but I still find I can't do it. Even though I know it would please them so much and get me back into their good graces.'

'You know I have often wondered why you seem so different from the rest of your family,' mused Rupert. 'They are so traditional, set in their ways, and happy to hunt all day and not upset the established order. Whereas you have a best friend who is a merchant's son, you advocate for social reform, and abhor hunting!'

'You're quite right about that, although I am surprised I have never told you this story before.' Alex chuckled. 'I fell off a horse at an early age and much to my father's disgust, I could never overcome my fear after that. That's where the discord between us started. Then Cambridge changed me more than anything. Obviously meeting you,' Alex said, smiling as Rupert raised his glass to him, equally as grateful for their friendship, 'and then attending the debates, etc. In particular, I remember in my first term stumbling across a meeting of the Students Social Reform Party – I was supposed to be elsewhere, but something made me stop and listen. The speaker was so eloquent and mesmerising, and it was like a veil had been lifted from my eyes. I suddenly had a purpose to my life.'

'I did wonder if it was a fad or if you were doing it to annoy your father,' Rupert admitted.

'Probably that did come into it,' Alex reasoned. 'I rallied against everything my father stood for. I'm afraid we've never seen eye to eye, and I never felt I lived up to his expectations, unlike my younger brother, who would have made a better heir.'

'Do you want to talk about her?' Rupert asked tentatively, and they both knew he didn't mean Lady Arabella Pembrook. They had spent the last few days since he arrived ignoring the reason for Alex's disgrace which had brought him here. Rupert wondered if his friend wanted to unburden himself but had not yet found the opportunity to offer.

'Not tonight. It's too painful and I want to forget,' Alex admitted, gulping back his brandy.

'In that case, let's forego the ball. I know a very seedy gentleman's club where we can definitely forget our woes,' Rupert declared with a mischievous twinkle.

Alex smiled weakly, happy to skip the ball but not convinced the club would make him feel any happier. For his friend's sake he agreed to go, not wanting to dampen Rupert's enthusiasm. At least perhaps it would allow him to forget her for a while.

Chapter Four

The invitations had piled up in Alex's suite at the Danieli and as much as he would have liked to have hidden away these past few days, he had no idea what else he could do in Venice except step onto the social merry-go-round. He had toyed with the idea of leaving Venice, but he knew Rupert would be upset and the classical sites such as Rome held no appeal to him.

Tonight, he hoped the ball, one of the largest and famed Carnival balls held in Palazzo Pisani Moretta, might cheer him up. Now, as he stood amongst the crowd of revellers all dressed in their finest, their jewels reflecting off the sparkling mirrored walls, their shoes tapping lightly on marbled floors, Alex was beginning to regret his decision. Rupert had disappeared into the nearest card room almost as soon as they had arrived. Alex felt he could not complain, as his friend had been showing him around the city these past few days, eager as always to entertain, and he must have been missing his cards as it was clear they were a much-needed divertissement for him.

A hand gripped his arm.

'Lady Lyborn,' Alex said with a bow, his heart sinking at the thought of being paraded like a prized horse.

'Now, Viscount, there is to be no hiding away tonight. You have been neglectful in your social duties,' she trilled in her high-pitched voice, which had a note of steel to it that showed she would not be deterred in her task. 'Now, where is your dance card?' He reluctantly handed it to her. 'Not one name! That simply won't do. Come with me.' She pushed her way through the crowds, determined in her pursuit of finding ladies for him. He knew he would look churlish and rude if he refused, so he resigned himself to his fate, silently cursing himself for not joining Rupert at the card tables. Although perhaps even there he would still have been hunted down by this determined Society hostess.

By midnight, he was exhausted. His feet ached from the relentless dancing after she had ensured he had a full dance card, and his face felt like it was stuck permanently in a rictus of a smile. His brain was befuddled from the vacuous conversations he had conducted with girls whose names and faces all blurred into one, for they were not remarkable in any way. Alex glanced around him hoping to slip away unnoticed when he caught a glimpse of dark hair and pale luminous skin. Lady Arabella was sitting amongst a sea of carrion crows – older women also draped in the black of widowhood. He could see the ladies meant well, talking earnestly to her, yet he recognised the sadness and boredom in her eyes which he too had felt since arriving in the city.

'Ladies,' he said, bowing to the group. He observed a few frowns that a young man should interrupt the widows in their shared mourning, but equally a trill of excitement from those who missed male attention, especially from one so young and handsome. 'Would you take pity on this poor Viscount worn out from dancing, and allow me to accompany Lady Arabella to take some refreshment?' She rose to accompany him and rewarded him with a dazzling smile.

'My Lord, you are quite the gallant,' she whispered, as they walked into the large dining chamber where the refreshments had been set up, now serving ices and drinks at the late hour. A footman obligingly found them a table secluded from the loudness of the room, for it too was still packed with late night revellers.

'I hope you didn't mind me interrupting your soiree with the good widows of Venice?'

'They are kind, but widowhood can be so tedious in these situations. I agreed to come because my seventeen-year-old stepdaughter Sophia was desperate to come to the Carnival ball,' Arabella explained.

'I did wonder why you were alone.'

'My companion Mary is chaperoning her somewhere in that packed room, and I was somehow sequestered with the rest of the widows. The gown does not help.' She plucked at the black silk of the dress, which even in its simplicity was magnificent on her and made her stand out from the rest of the bright peacocks in the room. 'I have yet to dare to wear lilac,' she whispered.

'Well, I have been doing my social duties as directed by Lady Lyborn and have danced with pretty much every single maid in Venice worthy of my status,' Alex said with a laugh.

'So, we have rescued each other.' She smiled conspiratorially, her face transformed, dazzling in its natural beauty.

'We have indeed.'

They sat in silence for a moment, enjoying the ease of each other's company.

'Are you enjoying Venice?' Arabella asked him after a few moments.

'To be honest, I find it tedious. All these balls and dinner parties where I constantly have to play a part. But I don't know what else I can do. I cannot go home so soon after arriving, and I have no real desire to go to Florence or Rome,' Alex confessed.

'Yes, I agree,' Arabella said earnestly, 'I myself find it too much.'

'Of course, you are in mourning too! Forgive me for sounding so trivial,' Alex corrected himself.

'There is no need to apologise,' she assured him. 'It's my own fault for returning here so soon, but I wanted to cheer Sophia up and I thought the Carnival would as she always wanted to see it. But I am told it's a pale imitation of what it once was. Perhaps Venice tries hard to regain its glory as do I. And now it has made neither of us happy. Too many memories and a life that can't be regained.' Sadness descended once more on her face and Alex desperately wanted to make her smile again.

He changed the subject and instead they talked about the many things it appeared they had in common. He was impressed by her interest in social reform and wanted to hear more, but they were soon interrupted.

'Here you are!' a gruff voice exclaimed, as a tall, thin woman approached the table followed by a younger girl. 'We have been looking for you everywhere and I am exhausted.'

'Alex, Viscount,' Arabella stumbled over her words. 'Please allow me to introduce my stepdaughter, Sophia, and my dearest companion, Mary Manners.'

Sophia Pembrook was pretty, with soft blonde curls and pale blue eyes. Like her stepmother, there was an air of sadness around her and Alex could see she was uncomfortable in her mourning colours given their gaudy surroundings. Mary Manners, dressed in a severe grey, was almost masculine in appearance with short, cropped hair; round, rimmed glasses covered keen brown eyes, and her narrow lips shaped into a scowl. There was no frippery to her gown, and no rings adorning large hands, one of which was gripping Sophia's delicate arm. Alex was surprised that the beautiful Arabella had such an unappealing companion, but then it showed that she did not judge people by their looks, and it warmed him further to her.

Alex rose and pulled out two chairs for the ladies to sit on, motioning also to a footman for cold ices to revive their flagging spirits.

'Good evening, Miss Manners, and Miss Sophia,' Alex said with a bow of his head, which he noticed elicited a shy smile from Sophia. 'Your stepmother has been telling me you wished to see the Carnival?'

Sophia appeared startled for a moment, and then quickly regained her composure. 'Yes, my Lord, it has long been a wish of mine,' she replied meekly, looking to Arabella for assurance.

'Have you enjoyed the ball, my dear?' Arabella asked her softly, reaching out to take her hand.

'She has,' Mary answered for her. 'But we are now ready to leave.' Her stern demeanour brooked no argument.

'I don't want to be too tired for our outing to the Academia tomorrow,' Sophia blurted out anxiously.

'Are you visiting the Academia?' Alex was envious at their planned outing.

'Yes, we thought we would take a tour tomorrow as the weather seems inclement,' Arabella replied.

'Would it be rude of me to invite myself along?' Alex asked impulsively.

'We would be delighted to have the pleasure of your company, my Lord.' Arabella's smile returned his own and Alex felt a surge of happiness.

'Please stop calling me my Lord, it is Alex, remember,' Alex reminded her, caring not for stuffy formalities. 'Shall I call for you at your hotel tomorrow, say 11 a.m.? If you desire to leave now, then let me at least accompany you to a gondolier to ensure your safe passage.'

Once he had seen them on their way, Alex slowly walked back to the Danieli, avoiding the drunken revellers who swayed their way laughing through the narrow streets, bumping into walls or people given the darkness of the hour. He kept to the well-lit streets, ignoring the darker alleys leading to small bridges and deserted squares. He was aware of the seedier side of the city with its sly pickpockets, its prostitutes, and the more violent criminal who would happily thrust a blade for a fat purse, especially when spotting the opportunity of a wealthy gentleman out on his own at this hour.

As he walked across St Mark's Square with its busy cafes, he reflected how his meeting with Arabella had lifted his mood. He sensed a kindred spirit and wondered why it had been so important for him to make her smile. He knew he needed to tread carefully – she was after all a widow, and he needed no further complications in his life given the situation he had just endured. He suddenly smiled at himself, reminded it was after all just a trip to an art gallery he had agreed to, and not a life commitment. He whistled contentedly as he strode across the square, marvelling at how the city took on a different façade at night; whereby other cities could seem dreary and dull, Venice became magnificent in her splendour. It was as if she had dressed for the occasion, ready to forget her own woes, her misfortunes, and her sad past.

Chapter Five

The next morning, Rupert found Alex in the dining room finishing his breakfast. He had hoped to catch him and to hear what had transpired the previous evening, given he had spent his time losing money at the card table, and also to find out his plans for the day so that he could perhaps join him.

'I can't stay long, Ru. I've arranged to accompany Lady Arabella and Miss Sophia on a tour of the Academia.' He could see Rupert was surprised, so explained further to avoid him jumping to conclusions. 'I find her good company. We talked of many things last night at the ball. She has such a keen, enquiring mind. Did you know she is a member of the women's movement in London? She visits slums in the east of the city distributing food and helps out at the Foundling hospital not only as a patron but helping on the wards.'

'Yes, I had heard she is rather outspoken on women's rights,' Rupert concurred.

'Do you disapprove?' Alex asked him, picking up on Rupert's lack of enthusiasm.

'No, no. Not at all. I had thought we were spending the day together,' Rupert admitted, unable to conceal his disappointment.

'Oh, I am sorry, I didn't think. We hadn't arranged anything, had we?' Alex said contritely.

'No, you go and see the Academia. You know it doesn't interest me in the slightest.' Rupert grinned and Alex was relieved his friend was not too cross with him.

He drained his coffee cup and bade farewell to Rupert, who watched his friend hurry out of the hotel, keen to go meet the beautiful widow. Rupert sighed, hoping that

Alex wasn't about to fall in love again, as it hardly worked out well the last time. He buttered himself some more toast. *Things are always better after toast*, he thought to himself.

***

Alex was pleased to see it was only Arabella and Sophia waiting for him at the hotel and not their companion, Mary, whose firmness he had found disarming. In the Academia, Sophia was much brighter than the night before and attentive of Arabella's every need, eager to please her stepmother. She was shy in Alex's company and held back, allowing Arabella and him time together discussing the exhibits. Sophia drifted away to study the paintings in great detail as they wandered through the various rooms. Alex was struck once again by Arabella's impassioned views on society – she was dismissive of the artwork, believing such riches should not exist in a world where there was so much poverty.

'Wealth should be distributed equally, don't you think, Alex?'

He was pleased she had dropped the formality of his title and was impressed by her bold opinions, which mirrored his own.

'I agree,' he said. 'I want to put forward more reform bills in the House when I have the chance. I want to be effective. To use my own wealth to do good.'

'Oh, Alex, if you could see the wretched lives the women and children have to endure in the London slums. The violence, the neglect, the lack not only of food but of power over their own futures. We must educate women to allow them to have choices.'

'Yes, education is key for everyone! I would love to set up proper schools, not workhouses.' He was passionate now, enjoying the way the conversation was going. Not many women dared to offer such strong opinions, but it was a trait which he found most endearing in her.

'Workhouses are the work of the devil, if you ask me. We must do better,' she spoke earnestly.

'We must also work to ensure there is no more slavery. It is an awful blight on our society that we ever chained men and women and sold them like common animals.' Alex noticed Arabella recoil at his words and worried he had gone too far, so tried to smooth over any misstep. 'I apologise – my words are indelicate for a lady. I forget myself.'

'No,' she whispered, and motioned him away from Sophia's hearing, but she was happily engrossed in studying another Titian painting. 'My husband's cotton came from slave plantations, and it was and is abhorrent to me. I feel disgusted how my own income is based on slavery even now it is abolished.' Her eyes filled with tears at the thought.

'You cannot be blamed for your husband's wealth. You have a chance to put this right.'

'How can I? I am a woman with no rights, no votes. I am nothing in society.' She turned away from him.

'You are never nothing! Not to me or to those women you help. You are a shining star in a bleak world.' He would have said so much more, but Sophia returned to them to remind Arabella of the time. Arabella reached out and caressed the girl's cheek affectionately.

'See how she looks after me. Such a good girl. We must of course leave for my appointment, frivolous though it seems to want to see my dressmaker. I have to confess no longer having to dress like a black crow will be so lovely.' She flashed him a dazzling smile.

As they took their leave, her hand gripping Sophia's elbow to protect her against the crowds in the square, Alex realised how her words had reignited his passion. He had not expected to find someone so like-minded in among the revellers in the city, but it was a most welcome discovery.

***

Later that evening, Alex and Rupert arrived at yet another ball at the Palazzo Labia. The famous double height ballroom, with its remarkable frescoes depicting the romance of Mark Antony and Cleopatra, was already crowded when they arrived. The orchestra was in full swing and there was a gathering of dancers, a swirl of silk skirts full of colour as straight-backed men twirled their partners around in a vigorous waltz.

Rupert once again slipped away to the card room and Alex was left to press his way through the crowd, nodding briefly to acquaintances he seemed to see every evening at such gatherings. He kept his head down, desperately ignoring attempts to stop him, the dance cards dangling from female wrists eager to add his name. He kept scanning the room hopefully for a glimpse of the dark raven hair and was about to give up, when he spied Sophia standing beside Mary Manners.

'Good evening, Miss Sophia and Miss Mannners.' Alex bowed over Sophia's trembling hand. She was ill at ease still, which he hoped would soon pass once she became more used to his company.

'Good evening, my Lord,' Sophia stuttered in return.

'My Lord.' Mary's voice was deep, brusque, and unfriendly. It was clear she did not care much for him.

Alex felt a light touch on his arm and turned to behold Arabella, dressed at last in rich lilac. She positively glowed in the darker hues of the colour, not for her the pale lilac of other widows but a sumptuous shade which complemented her pale skin. Her hair was softly arranged with her dark curls framing her delicate, beautiful face.

'Viscount, I mean Alex.' She blushed at their familiarity as she put her arm through Mary's. Mary's sharp features softened, transformed in Arabella's presence. Sophia looked away, as if the scene troubled her, releasing herself from Mary's grip.

Arabella must have sensed the shift in atmosphere, as she quickly pulled away from Mary and pushed her arm through Alex's instead, quieting the jealousy he had felt at Arabella's obvious affection for her companion.

'It is so lovely to see you again. I only came because you mentioned that you would be here. Although given the hour, I was sure you weren't coming, and the evening was starting to feel so tedious.' There was a slight accusation in her light tone, as if he had kept her waiting, but as she smiled at him, he saw she harboured no ill feeling. Arabella steered him towards a quieter side room, leaving Sophia with Mary.

'Would you mind if we sat here for a while? That room was so hot, and I feel somewhat overwhelmed tonight.' There was a slight tremor to her voice as they sat down on one of the sumptuous sofas. The dark velvet drapes, green damask wallpaper, and discreet candelabra gave the room an intimate, warm feeling. An inconspicuous footman stood quietly in one corner, lending propriety but allowing them privacy too, which was rare at these lively gatherings.

'Would you like some refreshment?' Alex offered.

'No, no, please sit and talk to me a while. Tonight, it was as if a thousand eyes were upon me because I have dared to wear lilac! Surely, they do not expect me to wear black forever?' Arabella sighed.

'We are both the subject of much gossip. I fear it is my reputation as much as you daring to no longer wear widow's weeds,' he assured her softly.

'Why are you so sad?' She looked deeply into his eyes.

'You must have heard how I was quite the scandal back in London? I know Venice talks of it even though it has not deterred the mothers and Lady Lyborns of this world of trying to throw their daughters at me.'

'I try not to listen to rumours and gossip, having been the subject of such this past year or so.' She smiled weakly. 'I am not one to judge either.'

'Arabella,' began Mary, who suddenly materialised at her side, like a ghost at a wake, shrouded in her black gown. 'Miss Sophia feels unwell and has requested to return to the hotel.'

The intimacy between Alex and Arabella dissolved into the air with the smoke of all the candles.

'Oh, my poor girl! Where is she? We must of course depart immediately and get her home to bed. Alex, would you be so kind as to escort us?' She looked at him pleadingly, clearly panicked by her ward's ill turn.

'Of course.' Alex regretted the interruption but was, however, touched by her concern for Sophia. They hurried from the ballroom, cosseting Sophia in a swath of fur, and found a gondola to carefully glide them back to the Grand Hotel.

Under the cover of the darkness, with the sound of the gentle waves and the intermittent cry of the gondolier, Arabella reached for his hand underneath the soft blanket spread across their knees, and she squeezed it gently. As he handed her out of the gondola when they reached the Grand, she whispered to him to meet her the next day for

coffee in her suite. Alex felt his heart leap, and he returned
to his hotel with a gladness to his step.

Chapter Six

Alexander walked briskly in the weak morning sun to St Mark's Square, where the cafes were already seeing fine trade, pigeons swooping beneath the tablecloths ready to catch falling crumbs. He stopped in the middle of the square, admiring the magnificent architecture surrounding him, so engrossed that he nearly didn't notice the scurrying figure of Sophia emerging from one of the loggias, intent on whatever errand she was on. Her face was red and blotchy, as if she had been crying. She was startled to see him there, her whole being ready to fly away from him.

'Miss Sophia,' he said as he approached, tipping his hat at her in greeting. 'Where are you off to on this cold morning?'

'I have been to the post office for Mr Burton, and I am now going to the library to read for a while. My stepmother is expecting you, my Lord, I believe?' She seemed on edge and eager to be gone.

'Yes, she is. Are you feeling better?' He looked at her with concern.

'Oh, yes, my Lord.' She flustered, thinking back to last night. 'It was a silly headache, the heat of the room the likely cause. Thank you for escorting us back – I am sorry I interrupted your evening.'

'No need to apologise, and please call me Alex; my Lord makes me sound frightfully old.' He baulked at the notion. 'You still wear black, I see. Oh, gosh, I am sorry — that was crass of me.' He had spoken without thinking and she had noticeably recoiled at his words.

'No, my Lord, Alex, please do not apologise,' she assured him. 'Arabella would prefer me to wear lilac, but it is too soon for me. I loved my father very much.' The colour in her cheeks rose. 'Anyway, I will let you go on your way. Don't keep my stepmother waiting on my behalf. In fact, please don't say we met this morning. She would hate to think we spoke of her or about my wanting to wear black.' She pleaded with him now, fearfully searching the square in case they had been seen.

'Of course, I will say nothing if you think it will distress her, and I apologise once again for my forwardness.'

Sophia looked as if she was about to say something more, but instead she wrapped her cloak tighter around her and hurried on her way.

***

The Grand Hotel was situated on the Grand Canal, and similar to the Danieli it was a fine establishment but with the added attraction of a small garden from hence came the delicate perfume of flowers in the summer months. It was also one of the first hotels to have electric light and steam heat in all its rooms, making it particularly popular during this cold snap the city was experiencing. Arabella's suite was situated on the second floor, with long windows overlooking the canal. The water twinkled invitingly below, framed as it was by beautiful golden drapes.

Arabella herself was seated on a fine velvet couch by an elegant marble fireplace where a cosy fire crackled merrily, giving the room a warm embrace. As the maid admitted Alex, Arabella stood up to greet him. He noticed how beautiful she appeared in her flowing lilac morning gown, whose bows and ribbons gave her a softness contrasting with the darkness of her hair and eyes. She smiled nervously at him as he kissed her outstretched hand, the mourning ring heavy and innocuous on the slim narrow finger. With a slight nod of her head, she dismissed the maid and settled back down on the couch, presiding now over the coffee pot waiting on the small, gilded table in front of her. Alex took the ornate chair opposite her, looking around for Mary or her aunt to chaperone.

'Mary has gone to the shops, running some errands for me; Sophia, the dear girl, has now recovered and has gone to the library. As for my aunt and uncle, they are away at the present. They've gone to Florence to see some business acquaintance of his, so I hope you don't mind us being alone. I can call back the maid, if you prefer?' She had noticed his eyes searching the small room.

'I prefer us to talk alone at last. As a widow, there is no impropriety, is there? I don't want to besmirch your reputation.'

'I don't believe a coffee between friends should ruin my reputation, but Society is a fickle beast, is it not?' She handed him a cup of coffee, with a wry smile.

'I am already at the centre of a scandal – I would hate to drag you down with me!' He laughed weakly.

'I cannot lie to you, Alex, I have heard your story. I'm afraid it was the talk of Venice before you arrived. I expected you to be a callow, spoilt youth, arrogant and stupid, from what I'd heard,' she admitted, not meeting his eye. 'But instead, I met you and found you are so different to all the other young men here. In the short time I have known you, I feel such a bond with you. Did you love her so very much?' she asked softly.

Alex told her briefly of his meeting with Lady Margot Montagu at a dinner in Cambridge, given by one of his masters. Margot, a renowned political hostess and married to a leading member of the House of Lords, was interested in the students and liked to debate with them. She had seemed captivated, very much taken with his ideas regarding social reform, and he in turn was mesmerised by her.

'She actually listened to me, made me feel as if my views were valid, important – unlike my father, who always laughed at me. She invited me to her house, and I started spending more time there, simply talking to begin with.' He blushed now to remember when it had changed. The day when she had first kissed him on his tentative mouth, and how he had groaned with desire at her fleeting touch on his leg. Margot had smiled at his eagerness, had made him wait a few more visits before she had led him into her bedroom, where she had seduced him with an ease which he now realised was well-practised. He was not unique, not her first affair, nor would he be the last to cuckold her marriage bed.

'She was everything to me. I don't know what I expected to happen – she could never have left her husband, I see that now, and I would never have been allowed to marry her, but still it was a blow when we were discovered, and she laughed when she dismissed me.' The sound of her laughter still echoed in his ears.

'How were you discovered? She has obviously done this before, so I would have thought she was discreet?' She carried her curiosity lightly, as if her concern was for Alex's feelings above all else.

'There was another student who had had an affair with her and when she ended it, he harboured a deep resentment, hated me for replacing him, and her for moving on. It turned out he wrote to her husband and my father, knowing they were friends. They could have come to some arrangement to smooth everything over, but this student also leaked it to the press, and all hell broke loose.' He recounted the awful days that followed – his father's anger, his mother's tears, and Margot's coolness as she cut him off.

'So, here I am — the scandal of the Season.' Alex exhaled, feeling lighter in some way for being able to address the rumours head-on. 'It would have been forgiven as youthful folly if not for the press and my father's name dragged through the gossip columns. Her husband was a member of the same club – it was embarrassing for them both and that's what my father can't forgive. He sent me here so that it can all die down back in London.' For some reason, he didn't mention Lady Helen and the proposed engagement, feeling there was no need to divulge that secret as it was not widely known.

'Oh, Alex, that sounds so awful. You must try to put it behind you and move forward as I have had to do.' She placed her hand on his knee and there were tears in her eyes, a window to her own sadness. He wondered what her own story was, but he sensed she was not ready to share it and did not want to pry too soon.

'I can see in Rupert's eyes that he thinks I was a fool to fall for her, but with you it feels as if you do understand and I appreciate it so much.'

'I told you I do not judge people. We can never know what goes on in private and in one's heart. Thank you for confiding in me.' She went to say more but the door opened, and Mary entered. Alex could feel the resentment pouring out of her even though he had only spoken briefly to her, and he drew a blank as to why she disliked him so much.

He stood up to leave but as he bent forward to place his coffee cup on the table, Arabella placed her hand on his to stop him. 'Oh, Alex, before you leave, I remembered what you said about wishing to see something other than art galleries and such places. My uncle, Mr Burton, spoke to one of his contacts and he told him about an island about ten minutes by boat called San Servolo. It houses a hospital and an asylum run by a Brotherhood of monks. Apparently, they have the most interesting techniques regarding those who suffer from mental illness.'

'That sounds fascinating.' Alex was immediately buoyed by Arabella's enthusiasm. 'There are terrible reports of the asylums in our country and how much improvement is required. I would dearly love to visit it – do you know if it is possible?' Alex looked earnestly at her.

'I hope you don't mind my presumption, but my uncle went ahead and contacted Padre Domenico on our behalf, and we have been invited to see San Servolo tomorrow.' Arabella looked shyly at him. 'That is if you would be happy to accompany me?'

'Oh, that would be wonderful,' Alex exclaimed. 'Thank you, and of course to your uncle for arranging this. It is so much more important to me than all the balls and galleries.' Alex's eyes shone with fervour and Arabella blushed at his excitement.

'That is settled then,' she said, and clapped her hands in delight. 'The boat will leave outside your hotel at ten in the morning.'

All this time Mary had been watching them carefully, only relaxing into something of a smile when Alex finally got up to leave. But Alex ignored her, happy in the knowledge that tomorrow he would be spending time with Arabella in pursuit of a shared passion. As he walked across St Mark's Square, a flame of desire for something more was igniting inside him.

That night, Alex dreamed of Margot once more, of her soft, yielding body pressed against his. Her golden hair brushing his face as her cherry lips murmured desire while confident hands caressed him. He cried out and woke to his hotel room, a tangle of sweat-covered bedsheets, and a heavy feeling of loss. When he closed his eyes against the dark, and spiralled back into sleep, he dreamt again but this time a huge eagle carried his naked body over the winding streets of Venice, as he searched in vain for a dark-haired beauty with sadness in her eyes.

Chapter Seven

Padre Domenico welcomed Alex and Arabella when they arrived at San Servolo the next morning. He was a tall, handsome man who exuded calm and authority.

'I apologise, I have little English, but you are welcome to see what we have to offer here at San Servolo.' He spoke with a quiet assurance as he led the way towards the large complex of buildings. His movements were gracious in his long, dark brown habit, a simple cross around his neck with another at his waist swinging from his roped belt.

'I speak Italian, Padre.' Arabella surprised both Alex and the Padre as she answered in perfect Italian. Seeing their astonishment, she blushed. 'I have a talent for languages, it seems, and learnt Italian on my previous trip here when I met my husband.' There was a slight tremor to her voice as she mentioned Sir Charles, which Alex had noticed she rarely did. Today, she had retired to black widow attire for the benefit of the monks.

Turning to the Padre, she asked him to explain the setup on San Servolo, which she translated back to Alex.

'San Servolo is run by the Hospitallers of Saint John of God, better known as the Fatebenefratelli. The buildings we can see comprise the church rebuilt in 1759 with, of course, the monastery attached for the Brothers, the hospital complex, the apothecary, and the main building of the asylum.' She listened carefully to the Padre before continuing. 'There are currently seven hundred male patients here in the asylum – female patients are mostly attended to on San Clement, although a few are brought here. The asylum has a vast array of treatments, including therapeutic activities, hydrotherapy, and medical interventions.'

Alex was impressed with how clean and peaceful the buildings were. They were of a simple classical design, gleaming white in the weak sunshine, and were grouped around a central courtyard. He glimpsed beautiful gardens surrounding the complex, giving the island an air of serenity.

'Padre will take us into the hospital first.' Arabella nodded her understanding at the man earnestly talking. They entered a well-aired hall, where they were introduced to another monk who the Padre explained would take over the tour.

'Brother Angelo has good English.' The Padre smiled at the short, stocky man with a large, bushy beard. 'I leave you with him. God go with you.' He clasped their hands in blessing and quietly took his leave.

'Come, come and see our wards.' Brother Angelo gestured for them to follow him into a large, dormitory-style room. The ward impressed Alex with its cleanliness, its efficiency, and its freshness. Light poured through arched windows as the Brothers moved effortlessly along the pristine rows of beds. These were all patients from the mainland, Angelo explained, who needed care and rest.

'Can I speak to them?' asked Arabella tentatively.

'Of course, but they only speak Italian.' The monk smiled encouragingly.

Alex watched as Arabella gently approached the bed of an elderly man, who Brother Angelo had explained was dying and had come here because his family could no longer care for him. The man was lying against spotless, white sheets, his wrinkled face contorted in pain and sadness, his breathing laboured. Arabella took his hand and spoke softly to him. Alex watched as the man's eyes lit up and a toothless smile spread across his face. There was a bowl of water on the table beside the bed and Arabella dabbed a cloth into it and tenderly washed the man's face.

'Angel,' the man whispered as he closed his eyes, drifting into a more peaceful sleep.

'The lady is indeed an angel,' whispered Brother Angelo.

'She has a good heart,' agreed Alex, unable to take his eyes off her.

They left the man sleeping and Arabella spoke to a few more patients in her perfect Italian, distributing words of sympathy, of hope, and of kindness. Alex watched the effect her beauty of spirit was having on them.

'Padre said you were most interested in our work in the asylum?' the monk addressed Alex as they left the ward. 'Or would you prefer to see our famous apothecary first? We produce high-quality medicines, which we provide to the mainland too.'

'We are eager to see your asylum,' Alex spoke enthusiastically. 'I want to try and help reform the asylums in England, which do not have good reputations. We are told you have an enlightened approach here with up-to-date treatments.'

'We try to provide a safe, clean environment,' Brother Angelo explained, as they walked through the sunny courtyard with its pleasant, soothing fountain. 'But of course, these souls are greatly troubled. Sometimes we have to resort to more drastic treatment, but first we try activities designed to calm the spirit, such as music therapy.'

They entered another spacious hall, but the rooms off the long corridors were divided into smaller rooms and some shared dormitories depending on the levels of madness the monk advised. There was no quiet here, but rather the sounds of shouting, screaming, and the rattling and pounding of locked doors.

'I hope you are not too disturbed?' Brother Angelo checked, as Arabella turned white.

'Would you mind if I got some fresh air?' Her breathing was laboured. 'Alex, you must continue with your tour, but I cannot see these poor souls suffer.'

'Are you sure?' Alex worried at her distress. 'I could accompany you?'

'No, no, you must continue. I will be quite all right once I have air.' Brother Angelo had found another colleague to escort her to the gardens.

A little while later, Alex found her sitting in a sheltered part of the well-maintained gardens; one of the Brothers had given her a blanket to place over her knees, and fortunately there was a weak February sun with no sea breeze. He watched her as she gazed out across the lagoon, deep in thought. He remembered how taken he had been with her beauty on the night when they first met at Palazzo Grimani. Today, he had seen her inner beauty as she had tenderly cared for a dying man.

'How was your tour?' she asked as he sat beside her, turning his face to the sun.

'Fascinating, but asylums are never truly good places, are they.' He felt her shiver slightly beside him. 'They are still locked up most of the day, and whilst there are gentle therapies, they still use more extreme treatments and medical interventions. They depend on control, seclusion, and routine. There are patients physically restrained, and the cold-water treatment is basically men wrapped in cold sheets for hours on end. Brother Angelo took me to an observation room, and I watched as they strapped a young man into a chair and shocked him.' Alex faltered.

'I could not bear to be left in such a place!' Arabella cried. 'The other monk told me that there are at least twelve hundred women kept on San Clement with their children. My heart breaks for those poor innocent infants.' She placed her hand in his and gripped it tightly.

'It is too easy, in my opinion, for men to get their wives committed,' Alex lamented. 'Children should never be born or made to live in such places. The law must change. We must give women more autonomy and more independence from men.' He thought of the conversations he had had at great length on this topic with Margot – she had been the one who had opened his eyes to the constraints on women and how marriage effectively took away their rights over their own bodies and even their minds.

He noticed now that Arabella was weeping quietly, and he gently stroked her hand to comfort her.

'I am sorry,' she whispered, 'I did not realise how this place would affect me.' She dabbed her eyes, and he wanted to ask again about her marriage, as he could sense the pain and sadness that troubled her.

'Come let us leave this place behind and look towards a future we can change.' Alex helped her to her feet, and although the island had upset her, he wished that time could stand still and it could just be the two of them focusing on reform to improve conditions.

'Your boat is here,' Brother Angelo informed them, and soon they were back on the lagoon once more heading back to Venice, watching as the facades of the Palazzos, the dome of St Mark's, and the Campanile drew nearer. Alex could sense they had grown closer over the past few days, but he knew the risk he took in falling in love with her. Not least because Arabella herself was fragile, but also his family would be completely against it. He had come to Venice to get away from one emotional entanglement, yet his heart was once again captured as Arabella took his hand.

Chapter Eight

In the days that followed, Alex was drawn to Arabella, pulled like a magnet towards her. Even if they were in a crowded room at a gathering, he would seek her out. It became an unspoken agreement between them not to dwell on the past, but to move forward together. They would find themselves at Café Florian at the same time each morning, he would obtain them a secluded table, pour her a coffee, and they would plan their day together.

They had no time for the art and history that Venice had to offer; their first outing to the Academia had shown it was not a passion for either of them – a superficial pastime, they both concurred. The shops held no delights with their fripperies, and the Piazza of St Mark's tired them with its treadmill of social niceties, where people wanted to be seen and noticed. They could also feel the prying eyes following them whenever they walked in such busy places.

Instead, they would walk over the many bridges around the city, following the little canals that took them away from the main squares, talking for hours about reform, about rights for the poor and for women. They would hand coins to beggars, search out the poorer areas, and Arabella would talk to the families they found there, learning about the real Venice beyond the Palazzos. When they grew tired of walking, of endless coffees in small cafes, they would allow themselves the luxury of a gondola and quietly float in peace with their eyes closed, enjoying the familiarity they were finding in each other.

They would sometimes take the ferry to the small islands, where the glassmakers, fishermen, and lacemakers worked in tough conditions for small return. Alex would talk to Arabella of how he wanted to make a difference back home to similar tradespeople, improving their conditions and wages. Alex listened intently to Arabella's stories of the hospital in London where she volunteered, and of the women in the East End whose lives she wanted to change, as well as the occasional mention of her dead husband's workers and how she had tried to persuade him to improve their conditions.

On another day, a gondolier rowed them over to the Lido, one of the outer islands between Venice and the Adriatic, where they could see the open sea and walked over to the Jewish burial grounds with its well-sculptured tombstones inscribed in Hebrew. On the other side of the island, they ran down to the sea as the tide was coming in, laughing as the waves nearly caught them and clutching each other to prevent themselves falling. He loved to hear Arabella laugh, her eyes sparkling and the dark circles underneath them now erased as the joy came back to her. Together, they watched a fleet of Venetian fishing boats fly past them with their magnificent, orange sails spread out catching the wind, and Alex never wanted the moment to pass.

As Alex arrived back at his hotel after another such outing with Arabella, he found a note waiting for him from Lady Lyborn. Carnival had ended officially a few days ago and the streets were quieter now, as the performers appeared to have vanished into the walls. There had been little demand on his presence, as the invitations to balls had eased. However, the note from Lady Lyborn was authoritative and bore no refusal – Alex had once again been most remiss in his social duties and simply must attend her dinner party that evening. He wished he could send his apologies, but he knew she had acquaintances who knew his mother and did not want to give Lady Lyborn any cause to stir up further trouble at home, especially when familial relations were strained after his affair with Margot.

This time he attended the party alone, as there had been no sign of Rupert at the Danieli when he sought him out – George had spoken to Rupert's valet, Harry, who had said his master was out of town with Sir Roger Jobson on business for the day. He was not expected back until late, and as far as Harry knew, there had been no invitation to Rupert from Lady Lyborn anyway.

That evening, as Alex entered the lavish drawing room filled with the latest fashion craze for Chinese porcelain – he counted numerous china monkeys – he was greeted effusively by his hostess.

'You have been quite the elusive one,' Lady Lyborn chided him. 'We had begun to think you had left Venice after the Carnival, seeking new delights.' She ensured he was introduced to all the eligible young ladies before he had the honour of escorting her into dinner, finding himself seated next to her as the highest-ranking male guest.

'I hear you are keeping the company of Lady Arabella Pembrook?' she asked, having turned to him with a steely glare.

'We are indeed friends, your Ladyship. I find her company rather stimulating and much informed.' He tried not to be intimidated by her tone of voice.

'Such an unsavoury business at Ravenscourt. I was surprised to hear that she could bring herself to be in the company of men again.' She watched closely as her words had their desired effect on him.

'We have not discussed Lady Arabella's past. It would be unseemly of me as a gentleman to ask her,' Alex countered.

The course changed and manners decreed they then talk to the guest on the other side of them. Alex was relieved to meet the shy eyes of the quiet girl whom he had sat next to before. He recalled that she had asked him about Margot, but this time he drew her out to speak about mundane things.

However, when he turned once more to his hostess, she would not drop the matter of his friendship with Arabella.

'I heed you to be careful. I know the poor girl was not to blame for what happened, but your family would be most concerned by your association, and people are beginning to notice your interest in her.'

'I feel uncomfortable talking about the Lady when she is not here to defend herself,' Alex replied, deciding he could tolerate no more of this. 'If people wish to talk, that reflects on them, not myself or indeed Lady Arabella. There is nothing in our relationship to concern my family.' But he felt the prickle of alarm at the mention of them, as he knew all too well what his father would say if word were indeed to reach him.

***

Alex recounted the events later to his friend over a late-night brandy in the Danieli, buoyed by Rupert's return. 'Oh, Ru, you should have seen her face when I basically told her to mind her own business. But it was a shock because Ravenscourt was the name I was trying to remember. I am sure I read about it somewhere.'

'Yes, the name does ring a bell,' Rupert mused. 'But Lady Lyborn has a point – I'm afraid that even Sir Roger asked me about you and Lady Arabella today. He knew Sir Charles, and he hinted at unhappiness in the marriage.'

'I don't feel right asking Arabella about it because I can see the pain any mention of her marriage causes her, but did he venture as to why?'

'Well, I know someone who could tell us more,' Rupert suggested tentatively.

'I hate to talk about her behind her back.' Alex sighed. 'But it unnerved me that Lady Lyborn had the upper hand, and I was totally unprepared.'

'I suppose it depends on how you feel about Lady Arabella.'

'What do you mean?' Alex's voice sounded sharper than he intended.

'If I may be honest, I am concerned about the nature of your feelings towards her, especially after the incident with Margot. I worry for you,' Rupert dared to speak out of turn.

'Margot made her own feelings rather plain, if you must know. I did love her, well I thought I did, but my letters to her were returned unanswered and it was clear I had just been a dalliance for her.' Alex signalled for more brandy.

'I felt such a fool, which is why I couldn't speak to you about it. Shame and disappointment in myself,' Alex admitted quietly. 'You have always been such a good friend, Ru, but I couldn't begin to tell you how I felt when I came here – I felt completely broken. I was determined to put it all behind me, although I dreaded the thought of returning home to marry Lady Helen. I wanted to do my best to please my family and resigned myself to what my father wanted.'

'But then you met Lady Arabella,' Ru interjected. He had noticed the happiness returning to his friend over the past week or so, the light once more in his eyes, and it was no coincidence that this had taken effect after spending more time in her company.

'The more I have got to know her, the stronger a connection I have with her. But my feelings scare me too, and I have no idea where our relationship is heading.' Alex shook his head.

'Your family would never accept her,' Rupert warned him.

'I know they would not. So much of her past is a mystery to me, yet she ignites something inside me that I can't ignore.'

'I think we need to talk to Sir Roger's wife, Kitty,' Rupert declared. 'She has just arrived in Venice, and she too knew Sir Charles. Let's at least see what she has to say, and she will also give us a good English tea! In the meantime, it may be best to spend less time with Arabella.'

Alex was still uncomfortable with the idea of gossiping behind Arabella's back, but something about Ravenscourt niggled at him. As his feelings for her grew, he needed to know.

Chapter Nine

The next day, Alex took his leave of Arabella earlier than planned. He excused himself by saying he had urgent correspondence to deal with. He could tell she was hurt and dismayed, as they had planned to return to Scuola Grande di San Rocco, where they had been helping with the distribution of food to the local beggars. He hated to lie to her, but Arabella must know the Jobsons through her marriage. He felt guilty as he walked towards Palazzo Falier where the Jobsons resided, and part of him wanted to run back to Arabella, not caring about her past and the events at Ravenscourt, whatever they were.

The room he now entered was sumptuous in its finery. Its large arched windows looked out over the Grand Canal, but the grey sky was shut out by the fine silk blinds, giving the room a cosy warm glow. The damp of the day seeped through him as the heat from the fire found him. Rupert was already seated on the green velvet couch as Kitty, resplendent on a soft armchair by the blazing hearth, poured fine English tea from delicate china.

Rupert made the introductions as Alex accepted a cup of tea. Kitty Jobson was a fine-looking woman, dressed in colourful silk, a mass of bows and ribbons, with a kind, smiling face and easy manner. The Jobsons were renting the large apartment in the Palazzo from wealthy Americans, and Kitty still marvelled at the good fortune of her husband's business, which had given them access to such luxury as this. But she had little airs and graces and was no stilted Society lady. Her pale blue eyes twinkled, and she urged them to fill their plates with bread and butter, fluffy scones, and large slices of cake.

'My husband, Roger, does not do dainty,' she said with a laugh. 'And neither do I. So, tuck in – I hate to see waste.' She settled back in her chair, enjoying a large slice of fruit cake, and Rupert was particularly relishing the generous portions of cake after another late night at the card table.

'So, Rupert tells me you are friends with Lady Arabella Pembrook?' Kitty enquired. 'Her late husband, Charles, was once a good friend to me and Roger. He was a successful cotton producer, you know, who branched out into silk, wanting to provide luxury goods as well as the serviceable cotton. He rented a fine Palazzo near to here, although I think it's since been sold to some Americans following his death.'

'Lady Arabella is now staying at the Grand,' Alex added.

'Yes, I had heard that – she has Charles's daughter with her, I believe.'

'Sophia – a sweet young girl.'

'It's so kind of Arabella to bring her to Venice. It can't be easy being a good stepmother to his children and returning here.' Kitty sighed, putting her plate down and abandoning her second slice of cake.

'I am loathe to gossip about Lady Arabella, but I didn't like the insinuations Lady Lyborn was making the other night when I dined with her,' Alex said.

'I agree, it is not nice to talk about someone behind their backs, but I'm afraid the business at Ravenscourt is a sad tale which you should be aware of, particularly if people are already talking. I will start at the beginning and tell you what I know.' She sat forward in her chair and, satisfied they had full cups of tea, began to speak in earnest. 'Roger was good friends with Charles, part of the same business of course, and all the wives were friends too – I don't mean Arabella, but Charles's first wife Elizabeth. Sophia you have met, but Charles's heir, Matthew, is a clever boy at Oxford finishing his education. He will soon be twenty-one and able to inherit everything.' Alex smiled politely, although hearing this about Matthew made him ruminate on his own failings of being sent down. 'Anyway, poor Lizzie died a couple of years ago, at Ravenscourt, of a malingering sickness. Charles was a bit lost for a while, and the children were understandably distraught. Ravenscourt had always been such an unhappy place for the family. Charles's sister drowned in the lake there when she was barely two years old, and their mother went mad with grief.'

'There was a newspaper article about Sir Charles's death saying tragedy had once again struck at Ravenscourt, or some such dramatic headline,' Alex recalled, it all coming back to him.

Kitty grimaced, acknowledging it was the sort of story the gazettes loved. 'Anyway, a year after Lizzie's death, Charles came here to Venice, where he met Arabella. We were a bit concerned, as he was so much older than her and she was such a beautiful young girl, American of course, and so different to Lizzie. But they were happy, and we were pleased when they got married not long after they arrived in London.' Kitty stopped to take a sip of tea.

'But when we too returned to the city, we heard rumours. How he was drinking heavily, and reliant on opium, which was affecting his moods.' She paused, her voice low as she leaned forward. 'Arabella came to see me one day, extremely tearful and worried about Charles, revealing he wasn't sleeping, how he was taking opium for his back pain, which had always plagued him. But as she reached for her tea, her sleeve fell back and I glimpsed a bruise on her arm, and what also appeared like a burn of some kind. I asked her about it, but she became so upset and hurriedly attempted to cover it up, saying it was an accident.' Alex waited for Kitty to continue, shocked at how such a fragile, intelligent young woman such as Arabella must have suffered.

'Arabella also brushed aside concerns that Rupert's mother had when she'd witnessed her wincing in pain with a hand on her ribs, explaining she had tripped, how she was always so clumsy. Now, it's not my place to judge what goes on between husband and wife, but she was, is, such a delicate creature, and she loved him and those children so much.'

Alex knew men could be violent towards their wives, how in law it was not illegal to hit them, but to him it was abhorrent and one of the many things he wanted to reform. It was yet another matter that he vehemently disagreed with his father on as well. Not that his father had ever been violent towards his mother, but he was a staunch believer that what happened in a marriage was no one else's business.

'Well, we weren't happy, I can tell you.' Kitty tutted. 'It was so out of character for Charles, but we noticed her flinch often in his company and he became distant, as if he hated her even. For two people who had been so in love, it was devastating to watch what was unfolding.'

'Did anyone talk to him, try to help her?' Rupert spoke up for the first time.

'Roger eventually spoke to Charles, who denied it, became rather angry in fact at any accusation towards him. By that point, he was consumed by the drink and drug addiction which Arabella had informed us about, and he was barely in his right mind. After that, we all shunned him as much as we could and our husbands cut off business with him, which was hard as they had once been so close.' She sighed remembering those painful days. 'We even wondered about his first marriage and if Lizzie had suffered too.'

She poured more tea, refreshing their cups. 'Anyway, the next we knew, he had died in an accident there at Ravenscourt. That is all I know. Arabella went abroad soon after the funeral, taking Sophia with her. A sorry end indeed.' Kitty dabbed her eyes with her handkerchief, affected by the awful, sordid tale. Alex's own heart swelled for Arabella. She was so vibrant, so clever, and even now wanting to do good in a world where she had known such suffering. He marvelled at her strength for enduring a marriage to such a monster.

'What of her own family? Her aunt? Where were they when all this was happening?' Alex asked.

'Her aunt and uncle worshipped Charles, and I believe he gave them money, paid off some debts, so they did nothing. I know little about her own parents. She never spoke of them to me.'

'But how did he meet her if she wasn't part of Society as such?' Rupert asked, seeming puzzled.

'Do you know, I have no idea how she came to have been invited to Palazzo Grimani on the night they met.'

'How odd, that's where I met her,' Alex murmured to himself, puzzled over the coincidence.

'That is strange, why would she want to go back there of all places? But I was surprised to hear she had returned to Venice merely a year after his death. Maybe she wanted to confront the past to allow her to grieve and move on.'

'That's what she said,' Alex admitted.

The clock chimed the hour on the mantlepiece, breaking the small silence.

'Gosh, is that the time,' Alex said, leaping to his feet. 'We have kept you too long, Lady Jobson, and I have tickets for the hospital fundraising ball at Palazzo Pisani Moretta.'

Rupert reluctantly set down his tea plate and they said their goodbyes.

'Call me Kitty, Alex, and come any time for tea. But be careful – best not to get too involved.'

'But Arabella has done nothing wrong, has she? She should be allowed to be happy, to have some friends in this unkind world,' Alex reasoned, undeterred in his affection for Arabella despite what he had heard.

Kitty watched as the two men left, unable to shake an unease which she could not explain. Arabella Pembrook did deserve to be happy after what she had endured, but Kitty remembered the happiness she had seen in Sir Charles's eyes when her old friend had first met Arabella, and it pained her to think how it had ended so tragically.

Chapter Ten

Hosted by the Contessa Elizabetta Morosini, the Masquerade of Mercy Ball was a philanthropic enterprise – so loved by high society – raising money for San Servolo. When she had heard of it, Arabella had been keen to attend, having seen firsthand the work the Brothers did on the island. Alex had generously offered to purchase the much sought-after tickets, knowing full well that no one would refuse Viscount Dundarran. Aware of the gossip about them, they had agreed to meet at the party, rather than cause a stir by arriving together.

Alex knew he needed to proceed with caution when it came to Arabella and her past. He now understood her reluctance to speak to him about her marriage, which sounded like it had been a distressing period of her life. He sank back into the black velvet cushions of the gondola as he made his way to the party, not wanting to hurt her in any way but aware that they needed to discuss this barrier to a potential future together. There, he had admitted it! As the boat's oars cleaved the murky water of the canals, he was certain he wanted his future to be with her, which both excited and terrified him. He closed his eyes against his troubling thoughts as the gondola glided slowly past darkened buildings, the sound of the water lapping against closed doors as they followed other gondolas down the narrow, winding canals.

He opened his eyes as the Palazzo came into view, rising from the shimmering waters. Its rose-pink façade was punctuated by rows of pointed arches, and the tall windows, lit by flickering torches, mirrored the water below. Alex stepped from the gondola onto the private water gate and entered through to the grand central hall, with its magnificent double flight staircase already crowded with people ascending to the reception rooms above.

At the top of the stairs, a footman greeted him, handed him a dance card, an auction list, and a crystal flute of champagne. He immediately went in search of Arabella, beginning with the grand ballroom, which was lined with gold-framed mirrors hung against damask silk, and lit by ornate Murano glass chandeliers that cast a warm glow. The room was already full of richly attired couples dancing to romantic waltzes played by musicians crowded together on a raised platform at the far end of the room. He thought back to the simplicity of the Brothers at San Servolo and grimaced at the irony of the glittering jewels and sumptuous silk gliding around the opulent ballroom. She would not be in here, he decided, so he made his way to the next room.

Matrons clamoured for his attention, eager to introduce their waiting daughters. Social etiquette dictated that he should indeed be filling up his dance card with the names of the desperate candidates, but Alex continued moving forward, away from their mothers' insistent greetings, eager to find Arabella, not caring that he was being rude.

So many rooms filled with endless Rococo mirrors and luminous chandeliers, lined with faded portraits of long-dead ancestors, and still more people chattering, laughing. Alex found himself getting despondent, wishing he had escorted Arabella, as he wondered if he would ever find her amongst the silken gowns and the whispering fans. Even the sound of the orchestra began to grate on his nerves. He threaded his way through the gentlemen talking politics, horses, and gambling, not wanting to be ensnared in their discussions, which he found as tedious as being required to dance with young ladies trying to secure a match.

Finally, he spotted her in the long, narrow hallway given up as a temporary art gallery. Among the relative quiet, he saw Sophia studying one of the display easels holding art donated to the auction. Lit by candlelight, the room was a surprisingly intimate space with a bored footman languishing in the corner as Arabella and Mary, arms curved around each other, talked quietly amongst themselves. He cleared his throat, eager for Arabella to notice him and desperate to prise her away from the dour Mary and hold her in his own arms.

'Alex.' Arabella blushed as she registered his arrival. 'We thought you had abandoned us after deserting us today.'

'I was most neglectful. Please forgive me and dance with me?' Her smile lit up at the invitation, as she extracted herself from Mary's arm and came towards him.

'Do you think we should?' They both knew that what he suggested was unconventional and would definitely cause more gossip about them. *Why should she of all people be denied the pleasure of dancing?* Alex's determination to make her happy surprised him, but Kitty's sad story had only spurred him on.

'Lady Arabella Pembrook, would you do me the honour of this dance?' He bowed.

'It would give me the greatest pleasure.' She curtsied deeply, a twinkle in her eyes.

They walked boldly into the crowded ballroom, not caring what glances they drew, and he swept her into his arms. Arabella moulded to his body perfectly as they danced in glorious unison. The sheer sensation of touch infused them with a gaiety which was infectious, and she threw her head back in joyous laughter as he spun her endlessly around the gilded room. Alex only had eyes for her – the rich, vibrant colours of the ball merged into one kaleidoscopic landscape, providing the perfect backdrop to the dark beauty of Arabella. As the music came to an end and they slowed to a breathless stop, they were both aware of the fans that fluttered frantically as the ladies of the ball whispered clearly about them.

'Would you mind if we got some air.' There was a slight tremor to Arabella's voice as they left the floor, clearly uncomfortable under everyone's gaze. In one of the crowded anterooms, Alex noticed an opening in the dark velvet drapes onto a small balcony. They stepped out onto without being noticed and drank in the fresh air. Arabella smiled tremulously at him, and he pulled her towards him, holding her gently, wanting to comfort her. She rested her head on his chest, and he could feel his heart pounding now as he cautiously stroked her back. He could feel her own heart fluttering as she slowly looked at him.

There were voices on the other side of the drapes that made them freeze. Alex recognised the unmistakeable sharp tones of Lady Lyborn.

'Quite scandalous – dancing with a widow when he has not allowed any other woman to mark his dance card!' she exclaimed. 'And after that affair with Margot Montagu too. His poor father had to face Lord Montagu at his club, I am told.'

'And not just any widow,' another voice baulked, her voice dripping with disdain. 'After what happened with her husband the merchant.'

'Well, she was hardly subtle with her campaigning for abused women in the East End of London. What goes on in the home should remain in the home,' Lady Lyborn announced stoically. 'I hope none of these young girls get any of her silly ideas. Rights for women indeed, when she is obviously making a play for the richest bachelor in town.'

'I can hear the buffet gong, and I am rather desperate to sit down, Lucinda. Shall we go in?' her companion asked.

'Oh, my feet are positively aching. Let us go before it gets too crowded.' Alex heard retreating footsteps and then silence.

Arabella's face was red with shame, with tears forming in her dark eyes. She wrenched herself from his arms and turned to leave.

'Don't go!' he pleaded, grabbing her arm. She flinched, and seeing the terror in her face, he dropped his hand and they were motionless once more.

'We cannot talk here,' she whispered, 'and I fear we are already causing quite the scandal.'

He wanted to tell her he knew her story, but that would mean admitting to talking about her to another. He could see how much it had distressed her to overhear the two women talking quite blatantly about her marriage.

'Will you escort me to Mary and Sophia, so I can return back to the hotel?' she murmured weakly. 'I want you to stay here and dance with lots of young girls. Anything to stop them talking about us. Please, will you do that for me?'

'I don't want to dance with anyone but you,' he assured her, eager for her to trust him.

She smiled weakly and, reaching up, stroked his face tenderly. 'I would dance with you forever, but first you deserve to hear my story. But not here, when the vultures circle. Tomorrow, meet me outside my hotel at nine o'clock, when none of these women will have stirred from their beds and we can go to walk in the Giardino Papadopoli, where we can be alone.'

He had no choice but to escort her to her companions, but as he watched her depart in one of the gondolas, he could not bring himself to return to the ball and dance with young ladies for the sake of restoring propriety, so once more he walked alone through the dark Venetian streets.

Chapter Eleven

The next morning, there was a light rain in the air as Alex and Arabella arrived by gondola at the quiet gardens. Arabella's red eyes denoted a restless night, and even though he desperately wanted to comfort her, he had not dared reach out to touch her. The previous evening had not been kind to either of them, both now more keenly aware of the attention their friendship was gaining.

They strolled a while, taking in the sounds of the birds singing from the garden's famous aviary, and the soft rustling of the numerous trees which gave the place a feeling of seclusion. There was little colour here, as spring was still to awaken the garden, but the bleakness reflected their respective moods. They reached a small alcove housing a statue of a delicate nymph where they sought shelter from the persistent drizzle of the rain and a dry, stone bench where they could sit privately.

'When I met Charles, he was obviously older than me, yet he was everything I ever wanted – kind, intelligent, handsome, and of course wealthy,' Arabella began her story, averting her eyes from his, clearly nervous to talk of her painful past. 'I am not going to deny that his money helped me acquire a better life – my own life has not been an easy one – and he offered me security as well as love. He was such a good man – a good father too – all his friends admired him, and I thought at last I could be happy, loved, adored, safe.' Her voice quivered and her hands trembled, but she brushed away Alex's hand as he reached for her.

'You don't need to tell me any more – it changes nothing between us,' Alex insisted.

'But I need to tell you. You have to hear it from me, not those women.' As she spoke, Alex felt a pang of guilt knowing he had already heard her story from Kitty

Jobson just the day before. He could not admit to it now, knowing the anguish it would surely cause her at being the subject of gossip.

'To begin with, we were blissfully happy, but then he changed.' She exhaled heavily. 'Oh, it was the little things at first – wanting to know where I was going, who I was seeing, what I was wearing. Gradually, he hated me going anywhere without him; I could only see his friends and wear what he suggested. He started to criticise my looks, the books I read, the menus I planned, and I feared nothing I did was good enough.' She sighed at the memory, shaking her head in disbelief.

'He constantly compared me to Lizzie, his first wife, whereas before he had told me he had never loved her, that it had been an arranged marriage between his father and hers. Where he had once found me stimulating and fun, now he accused me of being too much, too loud, too brash even. He laughed at my views on politics, women's rights, telling me I knew nothing and that my place was in the home, looking after his children. Suddenly, Lizzie was perfection itself, and Ravenscourt was a shrine to her – how I grew to hate that house. He even went on about some dog she had brought him and how it was the best present he had ever received. I could not compete with such a saint.' She dabbed at her eyes, readying herself for what was to come. Alex felt a cold shiver remembering what Kitty had told him about the bruise she had seen on Arabella's arm.

'Then one day – it was such a sunny, lovely day in our house in London – we were happily sitting on the sofa in the drawing room drinking our morning coffee and discussing his son, Matthew. His teacher had caught him smoking, and I had laughed at the incident. After all, it seemed so silly; he was seventeen, practically a man in my eyes, and Charles himself smoked, had done for years.' She turned away from Alex before admitting, 'But he slapped me.' Alex gasped at hearing her husband had indeed been violent, which confirmed the suspicions Kitty had shared. 'Shouted how dare I laugh at his son. I thought this must be a joke and I laughed again – I was in shock too. He hit me again, so hard this time that I fell onto the floor, and I lay there staring at the carpet, not knowing what to do, what to say. He simply poured himself another cup of coffee and walked over to the window as if I wasn't lying on the carpet with a bruised face.' A sob escaped her, but her head remained bowed, as if she could not bear to look at Alex and see the pity in his eyes. Alex gently reached for her hand and this time she didn't reject his kindness, allowing him to stroke it softly.

'You don't need to carry on if it hurts you too much to remember,' he whispered kindly.

'I can never forget that moment.' She took a deep, trembling breath. 'I told Mary and dear sweet Sophia that I had walked into a door afterwards and Mary iced my face. That night I covered the bruise with rouge and powder, and we dined at Charles's friends' house, as if nothing had happened.' Her voice was barely above a whisper as she confided. 'But it kept happening; he would hit me over any little thing that displeased him, but now he was careful not to touch my face or show this side of him to Sophia. But once she retired to bed, he would slap my upper arms, punch me in the stomach, anywhere that didn't show.' Alex put his arm around her and pulled her towards him, no longer caring if anyone happened to be walking by and see them.

'I cannot understand why such a person would do this to you? I cannot comprehend such cruelty,' Alex said, struggling to find the words.

'By this point his dependency on opium had increased too. When we first met, he had occasionally taken it for his back pain, but the pain worsened, and he was becoming more dependent on the opium.' Alex marvelled that even after everything she had been through, she still found excuses for him. 'But the more he took, the angrier he became, and it made him so paranoid that he accused me of doing awful things. I tried so hard to reason with him and he would cry and say it wouldn't happen again. He did eventually obtain help from his doctor, and we would have periods of calm, of happiness again.' She paused, as if she was reliving those brief periods of peace. Arabella and Alex sat holding hands, listening to the patter of the rain on the leaves, as if they were just a pair of lovers enjoying the solitude of the gardens when in fact Arabella was baring her soul. Alex admired her even more for her strength and fortitude of what she had endured.

'That peace would usually coincide with when Matthew was home, and Charles would want to be good for him,' she continued softly, her voice a whisper. 'But it got to such a point even his friends noticed. I knew I had to do something to protect his children. Matthew was back at university, so I sent Sophia away with my aunt and uncle. The doctor agreed we needed to get him off that drug, but the only place Charles would agree to go to was Ravenscourt, with its rooms full of his dead wife's things. I could no longer reason with him – I hoped he would get cured there, but we were so isolated from everyone, and I only had Mary to help me.'

'What about your aunt and uncle – why did they abandon you at such a time?' Alex struggled to understand why Arabella's own family had left her to such a brute.

'Charles had paid off my uncle's debts, helped him with his business, so he could do no wrong in their eyes. Anyway, Charles sent them away, declaring we needed time alone; and I wanted Sophia to be safe, not to see what her father had truly become, but I insisted Mary came and he did allow that at least. But she simply inflamed him further – he accused her of being my lover, can you believe? That's how mad he was, and Ravenscourt became a prison with its whispering walls.'

The rain was heavier now, seeming to emphasise the misery of her words.

'You could have divorced him,' he spoke softly, trying to understand.

'You actually think I could?' she exclaimed angrily. 'Even though our marriage was never able to be fully consummated due to his addiction, he viewed me as his property. He threatened to send me to an asylum, accusing me of being crazy; and with his wealth and friends, he warned he could easily arrange it. I was scared, Alex, scared for my life.' She trembled again. 'Do you know Charles's own mother died in an asylum? He told me once how his father had sent her there when Charles was about five years old. He knew exactly what he could do.' Alex suddenly realised why the trip to San Servolo had distressed her so much.

'It's why I campaign, why I want change and why I use his money – not because I want something from him, I want nothing from that man – but so I can give other women a voice.' Her voice became firmer, defiant in its passion of championing a cause even closer to her heart than Alex had first realised. 'I was lucky, you know, the night he died. It was supposed to be me at the bottom of those stairs. We had argued; I had told him I was leaving, how we couldn't go on, and he was hitting me.' She was sobbing now as she recounted that awful night, and Alex scooped her up into his arms and held her until she had nothing left.

'I am so scared still,' she admitted. 'Matthew hates me, thinks I lie, and soon he will come of age, inherit his father's money, and I don't know what will become of me.'

They sat there silently, his arms around her as Alex contemplated the future. He wished he could be brave and declare his love for her, defy his father, and marry her. It would take all his courage to risk all he had ever known for the woman in his arms. He wanted to give her everything she had ever wanted and to protect her from the women who had whispered against her, helping her rebuild her life. He was certain that together they could achieve so much – they were kindred spirits and shared a common cause in the reform they championed.

The rain persisted as they huddled together under the umbrella, making their way back to the gondola station. Alex revelled in their newfound intimacy and was emboldened to ask Arabella further questions about her family.

'What happened to your parents? You never mention them.' Her body immediately stiffened. 'I am sorry, forgive me if I pry too much.' He wished he could retract his words seeing the misery that clouded her expression again.

'I find it too painful to talk about them,' she explained, her eyes glistening with tears. 'They both died when I was so young, and it was as if the world lost its sun and its moon.'

She stopped to watch a lone bird fly off from a nearby bridge, her gaze following its ascent towards the dull sky.

'I lost so much when they passed,' she whispered. 'From that point, I had to depend on my aunt and uncle, who are of course kind in their way, but I always had this feeling of being a burden.'

'They had no children of their own?' Alex enquired.

'They had a son and a daughter. It is not my place to talk about what happened, because it would upset my aunt too much if she knew I had spoken of them to you.' Arabella was firm and Alex nodded his head in agreement that he would pursue it no further.

'And Mary,' Alex ventured, 'where does she fit into your family?' It had been puzzling him since he had first met the dour, disapproving woman with no family resemblance to the Burtons.

'Oh, Mary has always been there,' Arabella spoke brightly. 'I could not be without her'.

Alex was about to ask another question, but a gondola had arrived to take them back and Arabella had already turned from him.

As they settled in the gondola, Arabella reached for his hand.

'Venice has such mixed memories for me – my uncle was struggling financially when we first came here, then I met Charles and thought my worries were over for a time. Now, in the midst of my grief, I returned not expecting to meet someone who truly understands me.' She blushed in her admission.

He gazed at her delicate face and wanted more than anything to make her happy again. He knew then that he loved her and that she consumed his very being.

Chapter Twelve

The growing friendship between Alex and Arabella continued to be noticed and much gossiped about in the gilded drawing rooms over china teapots, from the matronly soirees to the men's clubs and even at the gaming tables. Arabella Pembrook was too outspoken, and the thought of her presence horrified many a matron with a young girl to marry off – her stance on domestic violence as highlighted by the women's movement was seen as vulgar and best kept behind closed doors. After all, wasn't the wife the husband's property, and why put off a young girl from the sanctity of marriage?

Venetian Society, however, was more tolerant, as rich merchants such as Rupert's father and Arabella's dead husband had brought much-needed money to a city not long ravaged by war. The soldiers who remained at the Armoury bore testimony to a more troubled time. Venetians shrugged their shoulders at the petty snobbery found in their English and American counterparts, and welcomed anyone with money who would rent out their crumbling Palazzos and boost their economy. In particular, they enjoyed a scandal and were eager to see it played out under their fading frescoes.

It would appear that Alex had forgotten both Lady Helen sitting patiently in a draughty English drawing room eagerly waiting for his return, and his father, who wanted a traditional, favourable match for his son – one who would build their estate, cement their future and their family honour. Besotted as he was, Alex had made his biggest misstep by overlooking how news could spread even across the snow-clad Alps and the grey, stormy Channel. Rupert was the one who first dared to broach the subject with his friend. A newly arrived merchant acquaintance of his family had informed him about how London was once more agog with news of the Viscount and his new scandalous relationship with Pembrook's widow, and he had asked Rupert if it was indeed true. Rupert had brushed it off as tittle-tattle, but he knew with a sinking heart that if London was already talking about it then it would not be long before Alex's father, tucked away in the Devon countryside, would soon be made aware of it.

Rupert managed to find Alexander in the dining room early one morning, before it filled up with too many guests.

'Alex, good morning. Can you believe it's March already? May I join you?'

'Of course, Ru. Haven't seen you since we went to Kitty Jobson's, which feels a long time ago. Have you been busy working or playing cards?' Alex was pleased to see his old friend, the time having lapsed without his realising.

'Working, would you believe? Off to Florence soon. And you, my friend, have been fairly elusive.' Rupert raised an eyebrow as he shook out his crisp, white napkin and accepted coffee from the waiter. Alex blushed and stared down at his plate as Rupert ordered his breakfast.

'Why so coy?' Rupert asked with a chuckle, once the waiter had left them. 'All of Venice is talking about you, so don't pretend you don't know. If you are forever in the company of Lady Arabella, people will talk. Did you actually dance a waltz with her the other night at the Morosini ball?'

'Why shouldn't we dance?' Alex sulked, knowing he was being petulant.

'Because she is recently out of mourning, and because you refused to dance with anyone else. You of all people must know how it looks!' Rupert was aghast that his friend could be so ignorant.

'It's ridiculous how she isn't supposed to dance because of a dead man who made her life hell, and why should I have to dance with a load of simpering maids who have nothing to say of any interest?' He slammed down his knife and fork, the sound reverberating around the quiet room.

'Alex, my dear fellow, calm down,' Rupert urged him, surprised to see him lose his temper, which never happened. 'I agree, Society's conventions are somewhat mad, but you must realise you are on dangerous ground. The more you flaunt to Society, the more they will talk, and I'm afraid word has reached London.'

Alex halted in his anger.

'What do you mean?' Alex's expression clouded over.

'Oh, Alex, what did you expect? Another inappropriate liaison for the Viscount Dundarran, of course it's going to reach home; and how long before it reaches your father? You need to stop now before it's too late, and if you have committed yourself in any way, it is best you leave for England without delay. After all, the Season will be starting soon,' Rupert advised him.

The two men stared at each other as the waiter placed Rupert's breakfast before him and, sensing the tense atmosphere, swiftly departed.

'I can't leave her, Rupert.' Alex was distraught. 'I thought you of all people would understand, but now you sit here telling me to leave the woman I love because I am causing a scandal which my father won't approve of.'

'I am your friend and will always support you, but in this case I am worried. You fall too easily, and is it fair on her after all she has been through?' Rupert countered.

'I think I loved her from the moment I met her,' Alex declared passionately, 'and she could be a gondolier's daughter for all I care. She is kind, generous, principled, and shares all my ideals, all my values, all my dreams for a better society. The more time I spend with her, the more certain I am that I want her to be my wife.'

Rupert was stunned at such a declaration, his breakfast forgotten, congealing on his plate.

'But your father will never allow it.'

'I know, and I have no idea what to do. I can't marry her without his permission, and I know he will never give it.' Alex shrank back into his seat, deflated as he knew Rupert was right.

'You must give her up, Alex. Can't you see it's the best thing all round? Parliament will be sitting soon and you said you wanted to get involved with all that. Go home before it's too late,' Rupert tried again, hoping Alex's desire for politics would convince him.

'I don't think I can.' Alex stood up and left his friend sitting there in the vast dining room, the chatter of the room surrounding him and his appetite long gone as he now worried even more about what Alex had gotten himself into.

Chapter Thirteen

After his argument with Rupert, Alex spent the day walking alone along the canals trying to make sense of what he should do, but he knew not how to resolve it. He had agreed to escort Arabella and Sophia to a musical recital at the Palazzo Bernardo that evening, and he could tell when they met that Arabella had been hurt by his absence. After all, they had planned another outing that day which he had excused himself from, and he could not bear the concern he saw in her eyes. He was extra attentive to her all evening, revelling in her smile and the light, secret touches of their hands. He could see the relief in her eyes that she had not lost him. He did not mention his conversation with Rupert, not wishing to break the enchanted spell currently spun around them, and he pushed to the back of his mind what might lay ahead.

But after leaving Arabella and Sophia at their hotel, as he walked back to the Danieli, he could see a storm gathering across the Adriatic, a flash of lightning out at sea. His weariness swept over him as he watched the dark clouds scurrying towards him, and he hurried to reach the warmth of the hotel.

As he entered the reception, he noticed the charged atmosphere of the guests sitting around drinking coffee and brandy. The storm was predicted to be a bad one and there was a slight fear in the room. He was called over to the desk, where two letters awaited him – one from Rupert informing him of his early departure for Florence on business to avoid any disruptions the storm might bring. The other was a letter from his father. He hurried up to his room to open it away from prying eyes. With a feeling of dread, he read it.

Wisteston Abbey

Alexander,

Word has reached me of yet another one of your inappropriate liaisons with a woman. Not content to sticking with your own class, you now take it upon yourself to cavort with the widow of a merchant and an American too. Good grief, boy, if you need sexual gratification, why can't you use a prostitute like any other man?

Your mother is beside herself to hear this woman is also part of the so-called women's movement, as you know well our views on that. Women have no role in the politics of this country. I insist you return home immediately so we can announce your engagement to Lady Helen. You must see the damage you are causing to yourself and the family name with your childish behaviour. I should not need to inform you that Lady Helen is quite frankly appalled and distraught at reports of your behaviour.

If you do not return henceforth, I will have no choice but to instruct my lawyers to disinherit you – do not think this is an empty threat, as I am well within my rights to do so. I am extremely close to cutting your allowance and will not hesitate to do so if you disobey me.

I will not let you destroy this family and all we have built over the generations.

Your Father,

Peregrine

Duke of Ushington

Before he could stop himself, and to the astonishment of George, his valet, who had been waiting to undress him, he rushed out of the room, back down the stairs, and into the night, desperate to see Arabella. He struggled against the rising wind as he crossed the Piazza once again. It was deserted now, the cafes closed, the tables and chairs stacked away inside, and even the pigeons had disappeared, gone to seek shelter from the troublesome night.

The lobby of the Grand Hotel was eerily quiet, and the guests had retired to their rooms to try to sleep. The electric lights were already flickering, and the oil lamps were being readied in case of blackouts. Alex bounded up the stairs, oblivious to the staff surprised at seeing him visiting at such a late hour, but he did not care as he made his way to Arabella's suite. He knocked impatiently on her door, until he could finally hear movement within.

Mary opened the door with a fury closely matching his own. He pushed past her into the darkened room, lit only by the oil lamp in Mary's hand. He would not be prevented from seeing Arabella, who now appeared at her bedroom door. Both women were frantically tying their dressing gowns around them, hair tousled from sleep, clearly having been roused from their slumber. The fire was smouldering its leftover ashes as the two women stared in astonishment at Alex.

'What on earth is the matter?' Arabella asked, moving towards him.

Mary switched on the lights, which although still flickering held out.

'I must speak to you alone,' Alex commanded. He had no patience for the reproachful looks of Mary, who silently left the room, shutting the bedroom door behind her.

'Oh, god, Arabella,' he groaned. 'I had to see you. My father sent me this.' He handed over the now-crumpled letter which he longed to tear into pieces.

Arabella scanned the contents as Alex paced the room.

'Who is this Lady Helen he writes of?' Arabella enquired with a frown, a quiver to her voice. 'You did not tell me you were betrothed. I thought we only spoke truth to each other.'

'She's the girl my father wants me to marry. I don't love her. I love you,' he tried to explain, moving to hold her in his arms, but she recoiled at his touch. 'Oh, god. I am sorry, Arabella. Please hear me out, as I've only ever been truthful with you. I love you and I want us to marry. We could achieve so much together.'

'Marry? But your father says he will cut you off, disinherit you. How would we live, Alex? If I remarry, I lose my income from Charles's estate. We would have nothing.' Her voice was rising in anger now, disbelieving that he would suggest such a notion.

'But does it matter? Surely your uncle could help us. I could find a job, and Rupert's family would help too. We could do all the things we talked about.' He was earnest, pleading with her because he could not bear the thought of living without her.

'How can you be so stupid?' She stared at him, horrified. 'We couldn't survive in the real world. My uncle barely makes enough to support him and my aunt as it is. Where would we live? In a slum? Is that what you mean by relating to these people? By living with them?'

'But I love you and I thought you loved me.' Alex was taken aback by her refusal.

'You're a fool, Alexander. No one can survive on love alone, and I am not willing to give all this up for poverty. I know what it's like to go hungry, to be cold, on the edge of society. I can't go back to that.' He could see the bitterness in her eyes as she spoke.

He had expected more of her, having believed they were similar and that their love was all that mattered. He hoped that they would fight together for the life they wanted.

'Do I mean so little to you? Am I not enough?' he shouted, his own anger rising again.

'You are a naïve boy. Of course you are not enough for me. Now go, get out of my room and leave me alone,' she hissed. 'Go home to your father, marry this Lady Helen, and live your sheltered, pampered life. You must forget we ever met.' She tossed the letter back at him as the bedroom door opened and Mary came into the room. Arabella threw herself into her friend's arms, sobbing hysterically, and Mary indicated towards the door, making it clear she would brook no further argument. Alex snatched up the letter. He went to speak but no words would come, and it was evident he was no longer welcome. As he opened the door to leave, the lights flickered one last time and finally went out, plunging the room into darkness. He could no longer see Arabella's face, the face he loved. He rushed headlong down the stairs, through the lobby, and out into the night.

The rain lashed down in torrents of needles, drenching him as he ran through the narrow lanes. He sheltered briefly in the Piazza's colonnades, watching as lightning lit up San Marco's bronze horses poised, it seemed, to dash into the storm's glorious fury and chase it away. Water was already rising through the stone tiles of the square, and if Alex didn't return to his hotel soon, he risked getting stuck. He attempted to pull his evening jacket over his head; ridiculous, he knew, as it would make no difference with the ferocity of the rain unleashed over him. He ran, splashing his way across the square, chased by the thunder and lightning above his head.

Turning towards the Doge's Palace, he was shocked to see the fierceness of the wind battering the gondolas moored just ahead of him. Already a couple had torn loose and were being tossed and turned in the turbulent sea. The boats still tied crashed against their creaking posts as the water continued to rise. He needed to reach the safety of the hotel and return to his suite on the upper floors before Venice itself was under water or, worse still, he himself was pulled under to a watery grave. George leapt up from his seat – where he had been waiting for his young master – as Alex stumbled through the Danieli's doors; and together with the manager, he carried his sodden charge up to his room. Alex was soon cocooned in a warm bed, but his dreams were restless. He was forever running through the storm searching for Arabella, hoping he had not lost her forever.

Chapter Fourteen

Morning brought relief from the storm, and although the sky was still grey, there was relative calm over the city. Water within the Piazza had flooded ancient basements and prevented any electric lights from working. The wreckage of gondolas revealed the strength of the storm, and one such boat which had been ripped from its tethers was now bobbing forlornly and broken on the Adriatic. There would be no cafes or shops open today, no languid gondola trips, only those on the streets attempting to clean up, and soldiers protecting properties whose doors or windows had been damaged as workmen strove to make the necessary repairs.

Alex carried the weight of his misery on his shoulders as he went down to breakfast. He felt embarrassment at the scene he had caused in Arabella's suite, and despair at the realisation he had lost her. He had not been completely honest with her, he could see that now and should have told her about his family arranging his engagement to Helen. No wonder she had been so angry. And if his father did carry out his threat to disinherit him, of course he couldn't expect her to marry him if he had no prospects. He saw now how stupid he had been.

'Viscount Dundarran,' the manager called for his attention when Alex went down to the lobby. 'I have an urgent telegram for you.'

'What's happening here?' he asked, weaving his way through the luggage piled up and the clamour of guests shouting.

'Several trees have fallen overnight, blocking the train line and some of the roads over the Alps. It means guests are unable to leave at the moment if they wish to go north, and it may be several days before anything is fixed.

Anyway, my Lord, I hope this has not been delayed.' He handed over the telegram to Alex, who opened it quickly, hoping Arabella had sent word to him.

As Alex read the telegram, his optimism immediately soured. He hurried back to the desk. 'My father has had a stroke, the doctor fears for his life,' he spoke as if in a trance. 'I am wanted back home. No time to lose, my mother says.'

'But sir, it is impossible! The trains they cannot run, and to go south would mean a boat home, which would surely take too long if you are required urgently. I fear you will have to wait,' the manager warned.

'Yes, I suppose I will. Thank you.' He was dazed as he turned from the manager, colliding with a short, stout man he recognised as Arabella's uncle, John Burton. They had met briefly at one of the balls, although Arabella had explained he was tied up with his businesses so rarely ventured out socially.

'I apologise, Mr Burton, for my clumsiness.' He bowed to the man.

'My Lord, are you well? You seem most dazed,' Mr Burton observed.

'My father has been taken seriously ill, he may not survive; and the storm means I cannot return to England for the time being,' Alex replied. 'What brings you here to the Danieli?'

'I am sorry to hear of your father's ill health. I came to see if there was the chance of a carriage to Rome – I have urgent business there.'

The manager interjected, 'Yes, Mr Burton, I was correct. One of our guests has indeed hired a carriage to Rome and would be happy to share with you.'

'You are most fortunate,' Alex said flatly. He briefly contemplated whether he could send a message to Arabella via her uncle but did not have the heart for it. 'I wish you safe travels.' Alex made his way slowly up the stairs, leaving Mr Burton to finalise his arrangements.

Alex spent the rest of the day sitting in his rooms, not quite knowing what to do with himself. He sent George back down to reception to send the telegram back to his mother to explain his delay. He was overcome by immense guilt at being trapped in the city. He had been furious with his father last night, and Alex remembered the last angry words they had exchanged before he had left, and now he couldn't even go to him in his hour of need. He knew immediately the news was serious, for his mother would never have telegrammed otherwise. She was not one for emotion and his father did not play tricks – he had not the imagination or patience for it. He would not have tried to lure Alex home with a falsehood by claiming to be ill. He would have believed that his own letter with its stern warnings would be enough to bring his son home.

Dusk was now setting on the damaged city, although the water was receding at least. The hotel was silent around him, as the guests were all back in the rooms they had earlier looked to vacate. Alex was sitting by the window in his room watching the sun set when there was a light tap on the door. He hurried to answer it, his heart racing, hoping the trains were now running.

'There's a note for you, sir, from the Grand Hotel.'

The young bellhop presented a slender, cream envelope addressed to him.

Please come I cannot live without you. Yours always Arabella.

'Will there be a reply, sir?' the bellhop asked, having waited patiently while Alex read the note.

'No. I will go myself.' He tipped the boy, eager for him to be gone, and already preoccupied looking for his own hat and coat.

Once again, he found himself sloshing through water-filled streets, and once again, he cared not for the water seeping through his shoes; but this time, even though he was worried about his father, he was no longer in despair at having lost the woman he loved. She was still his after all and had wanted to see him. This time he tapped quietly on her suite door, respectful, gentle, but she was there waiting and pulled him in.

'Will you ever forgive my words?' she said between sobs, clutching him tightly to her. 'I love you. You are all that matters.'

'Always I will forgive you.' He held her dear face in his hands, looking into her tear-filled eyes. He forgot everything as he kissed her, tentatively at first but then as she responded he gave into the feelings that had been building up inside him and kissed her with a fierce passion.

'I could not sleep after you left,' she admitted, breaking apart. 'I turned you away because I was scared and, I am loathe to admit, I was jealous. I was angry that you hadn't told me about Lady Helen, yet I also wanted you to do the right thing by her and your family. I did not want to cause friction between you and them – to be the cause of you losing your title. It was because of my love for you that I had to turn you away, do you see? Then my uncle told me your father had been taken ill, and I did not know what to do. After I had sent you away, could I be so bold as to ask you back when you had such matters on your mind? But I wanted desperately to hold you, to take your pain away as you have taken mine from me these past few weeks.'

'You are too good, too kind, my love.' He kissed her lightly on her forehead, not knowing what he'd done to deserve such an angel. 'I did not tell you about Lady Helen because she means nothing to me and I was trying to forget she even existed. It is my father who wants me to marry her, but I share no such desire. Today, when the news came about my father's ill health, I felt such hopelessness and more than anything I wanted to be with you.'

'I cannot bear to be without you. I want us to be together, and we deserve our happiness. We can do so much, you and me. We can do this with our strength and our love, so that's all that matters.' Her eyes were bright with shared desire.

He kissed her again and she pressed herself closer to him as he felt his desire grow and he let out a small groan.

'We are alone,' she whispered. 'Mr Burton somehow secured a carriage to Rome, and they have all accompanied him, even Mary. I wanted to stay, to be with you. Let me take away your pain for a little while.'

She led him through to the bedroom, where dozens of candles flickered and the blinds were drawn against the approaching evening. A merry fire danced in the small marble fireplace, warming the room. They kissed again – her tongue darting inside his mouth and her hands already pulling at his clothes. The bed before them was plump and inviting. He tentatively touched her taut breasts and she moaned, her nipples hardening under his touch.

'Don't stop,' she begged, as she helped him untie the bows on her gown, which slid to the floor. She was naked before him. Her skin luminous in the candlelight, her breasts perfect orbs as if her body was sculpted from marble, and he trembled as she placed his hand between her legs.

'I want you so much,' she gasped.

Removing his hand, he quickly undressed as she lay back on the bed. He lay down beside her and caressed her body, which responded to his touch. She surprised him by pushing him back and climbing on top of him, pushing him into her as she began to ride him with such intensity, such rigour, and he could feel himself ready to explode. They both came together in a loud, exultant cry, collapsing in a tangle of limbs and sweat as he eased his way out of her and they kissed gently now, laughing at how their passion had overtaken them both.

Margot had been a lazy lover, but Arabella was energetic and without abandon. That night, she showed him how to please and be pleased, and he could not get enough of her. He did not want to leave her bed but as the clock chimed past midnight, he knew he must leave soon. They had already risked much to their reputations by him visiting her rooms.

'I love you,' he whispered into her dark hair, and she kissed his chest.

'I love you too.' She looked deeply into his eyes as she spoke the words he had longed to hear.

'However, I should return to England as soon as I can. To at least be there for my mother.' He stood up to retrieve his clothes. 'I am waiting on news, but it seems I won't be able to depart yet.' She ran a finger down his back.

'We have a few days at least,' she said, trying to defuse his anguish, his sorrow.

'I must return to the Danieli now in case there is further news regarding my father or onward travel.'

'Come to me tomorrow, promise me that.' She reached for him.

'Try stopping me, my love.' He kissed her nose and squeezed her hand.

'My love, I like that.' She fell back gently and contentedly against the pillows, watching him dress. He leant over to kiss her goodbye, and she murmured, 'You are mine now.'

'Yes, I am yours, always yours.' He loved how that sounded, that nothing should part them now.

As Alex crept down the main staircase, cautiously ensuring no guests remained to witness the hour he had left Arabella's room, he failed to notice the figure of Mary hidden behind a large potted fern, watching as he left.

Chapter Fifteen

'Telegram for the Viscount marked urgent. Shall I wait for a reply?' asked the bellhop at the door.

'George, who is it?' Alex called from his bedroom, where he was getting dressed for the day.

'Urgent telegram, sir. Should the boy wait?'

Alex pulled on his jacket and went through into the sitting room.

'The boy can go. You can go down, George, if I need to reply.' Alex feared what the telegram would convey. The boy departed as Alex slid open the small envelope. His face turned ashen as he read the words and collapsed into the nearest chair.

'My Lord, shall I fetch a glass of water?' his valet offered.

'No, George. I think something stronger, much stronger. It's my father,' he stuttered, 'he's dead.'

George hurried over to the decanter and poured a large glass of brandy, which Alex threw back in one gulp.

'Is the train line open yet?' He looked at George, but it was as if his eyes couldn't focus.

'No, your Grace, I asked again this morning.' Alex flinched at the formal use of his new title. How quickly George had adapted to his master's elevation to the Dukedom, before Alex himself had had chance to process his new status.

'For god's sake. What is taking them so long? I need to return home. Mother will be distraught. Run down and send a telegram back saying I will return as soon as possible. I will write a letter later. I need to leave. I must see Lady Arabella; she's the only one who can bring me comfort.'

His mother's telegram had addressed him as the Duke, and so he knew his father had not forsaken him. Though this pleased him, it frightened him too. The Dukedom brought much responsibility and expectation. He was now in charge of his own destiny, his own future; and although he wanted Arabella to be part of it, he wanted to do things properly as befit his position in Society. He had much to mull over, the enormity of his father's death beginning to hit him, as he made his way over to the Grand.

'Oh, my darling, I am so sorry for your loss.' Arabella pulled Alex into her embrace, and he collapsed into her, clinging to her as he wept after breaking the news. 'Come, my love, you need air and a good walk. Dry your tears and let us take a stroll to the Piazza to take some coffee. You need time to process such news.' She called to the maid to bring her coat.

'Your family and Mary have not yet returned?' Alex glanced around him.

'No, my love, I expect them soon.'

'But can we not stay here? I long to simply lie in your arms.' He pulled her back into his embrace. He could barely believe his father was gone, and although they had their differences, Alex had always wanted to please him – however impossible that had seemed at times. There were guilt and sadness as he sat beside the woman he loved.

'I would prefer some air. This room is stifling me,' Arabella said, fanning herself.

'Of course. I am being selfish. You are right, we should walk,' Alex agreed, being easily persuaded fresh air may be best.

St Mark's Square was busy, and they were forced to take a table at Florian's in full view of those passing through. Arabella was attentive as she poured their coffee, stroking his arm and at one point caressing his face when she noticed the sorrow in his eyes. *How kind and loving she is*, Alex thought as he touched her face in return. He was oblivious in his grief to the other customers, who stared in shock at such improper conduct in public. Word had already spread that the old Duke was dead, while his son openly cavorted with the widow of a merchant!

When they returned to the Grand, they ate a quiet supper in Arabella's suite. They made love urgently as Alex let go of all the emotions that had built up within him, eager to no longer feel numb, and be with the woman he loved. He slipped out into the night to return to the Danieli, where he sat down and wrote his letter to his mother. He omitted to mention Arabella and his own intentions. There would be time enough for that, and he would have to broach it carefully as she was not the match his family would want for him. He would need to handle the situation with care and thought at a suitable time once his family had mourned his father's passing. The lovers had not yet discussed marriage since their disagreement on the night of the storm. Alex believed it understood and that when the time was right, he would request Arabella's hand formally. They would marry in the family church in Ushington, with all the traditions of the Dukedom. He dreamed of showing off Arabella as his bride, but he wanted to honour his father's memory first. Despite their fraught relationship, Alex wanted to do the right thing.

Chapter Sixteen

The next day, as Alex strolled across the Piazza on his way to meet Arabella, he encountered Kitty Jobson.

'Oh, my dear boy, I heard the news yesterday. Your poor father.' She placed a comforting hand on his arm; her soft eyes filled with tears and Alex's own sorrow welled up at her kindness. Kitty, noticing his knees buckling under the weight of his grief, steered him gently towards Florian's. 'Come and sit with me for a while,' she offered, and called for coffee.

'I'm sorry, Kitty,' he responded, shaking his head apologetically. 'I just can't believe I won't see him again. I'm ashamed to admit I fell out with him again before he died.' His body slumped in his chair as he remembered the last letters from his father, knowing Kitty was a trusted confidante.

'Oh, I thought that business with Lady Montagu would have been forgotten by now,' she spoke kindly.

'No, not over her, but over my relationship with Lady Arabella Pembrook. He wanted me to give her up or threatened to disinherit me.' Alex poured out the whole sorry story of his father's anger and of his own argument with Arabella. It was a relief to finally share with someone what was going on. He longed for Rupert to return so that he would have his friend's unfailing support again at the time he needed it most.

'The poor girl didn't want me to give it all up for her you see, but now we realise we love each other and that is all that matters.' He was careful not to mention how they had made up.

'When did you two make up?' Kitty enquired.

'Just after I received the news about my father's accident. I bumped into her uncle at the Danieli, and he informed Arabella so she sent me a note. She was so supportive, so loving. I could not have gone through these past days without her,' he spoke earnestly to the kindly woman, who patted his arm reassuringly.

'I am glad she has been there for you, but don't act in haste, will you? You are in a state of shock, and we cannot always be trusted to make the right decisions at such times. Wait for Rupert to return and he can be there for you too.'

'He thinks I fall in love too easily.' Alex realised that perhaps Rupert's support wouldn't be as unfailing as it once had been. 'We quarrelled before he left for Florence,' Alex groaned.

'Well, that is a shame, because you are good friends and I know he thinks the world of you. I would advise you to return to your family now and see how you feel then.'

'I thought you at least would be happy for us, Kitty, after everything Arabella has been through too, which you know well enough. I want to make her happy.'

'Of course, my dear, I am happy if the two of you are in love, but be careful – it's all so sudden.' Kitty now seemed flustered and uncertain what to say next. Arabella certainly deserved happiness but it was clear that Alex had a lot to come to terms with, so it would be prudent to let the dust settle. The clock struck the hour. 'Oh, good heavens, is that the time? I am supposed to be at the dressmakers. I see you have your mourning band already which is good.'

'Kitty, before you go, I just remembered something I meant to ask which has puzzled me since our last meeting. You said that Sir Charles hated Ravenscourt.'

'Yes, he certainly did. I was always surprised that he went there at the end.' She sighed. 'I always thought he would sell the place, especially after Lizzie died. Why do you ask?'

'It was something that Arabella said.' Alex was puzzled, as she had implied her husband had loved the place with its reminders of his first wife. At the time, he had been intent on listening to Arabella's story, and it was only later that he recalled Kitty's words regarding Ravenscourt holding such unhappy memories for Charles's family over the years.

Alex rose with Kitty and thanked her for her sympathy and kindness before she bustled along to the dressmaker. He remained at the table, wanting to linger a while longer. The grief of his father's death and the sudden intensity of his and Arabella's shared passion had happened in such a brief, tumultuous time that he had barely had time to process it all. Perhaps Kitty was right – it would be wise to slow down and give himself time to grieve, to return to his family. Arabella would understand that and surely welcome some time apart too. They both needed to be certain that their future was together – he owed it to Arabella not to pressurise her into another marriage, especially after her unhappy marriage to Charles. Throwing down some coins for the coffee, he hurried off to the Grand to speak with her.

***

'Where have you been? I have been going out of my mind.' Arabella was pacing up and down the room when he arrived.

'What on earth is wrong? Why are you crying, my love?' He noticed the crumpled handkerchief in her clenched hand and her flushed pallor. He rushed to take her in his arms, to calm her, but she shook him off.

'I had a rather unpleasant visit this morning from Lady Lyborn. I was pleased to see her, believing I was being accepted by Society as I've long hoped. But no! She was here to ask me exactly what I was doing with the Duke of Ushington. Apparently, I have ruined not just my reputation but yours too. We are the talk of Venice.' Arabella's frustration became more evident. 'We were noticed making a public display of vulgarity on the day the news of your father's death was announced. She has also found out that you have been here late at night, alone with me.' She was distraught now, breathing fast and wringing her hands. 'Who could have told her? We should have been more careful. She looked down at me like I was a common whore, and I was mortified. Then she informed me you would not marry me as she had it on good authority you were betrothed to Lady Helen. I felt such a fool. She kindly advised I leave Venice and leave you to marry your own kind to avoid further scandal.'

'Arabella, please come and sit down.' Gently, he guided her to the couch and pulled her trembling body close to his. 'That woman is poison, and you know there is no official betrothal between me and Lady Helen. My heart is yours completely. I want to marry you, but I need you to be sure that is what you want too.' He paused, hesitant to share his plan but confident it was the right course of action. 'I must return to England, sort out my father's affairs, and of course attend the funeral. Then, if you still want to become my wife, I want to show you off like a precious jewel and for us to have a magnificent wedding in the family church. To make you my Duchess.'

'Do you mean that, Alex?' She looked at him, her face stained with tears.

'Of course, my darling girl. I thought you knew once we slept together that I would marry you. That I love you more than anyone in the world. I would have given up the Dukedom for you. But I don't want to rush you into another marriage – I want you to be sure.'

'I was so worried you were using me and when that nasty woman came, I thought it was all true. I couldn't bear for my life to be destroyed again. Not after it has taken all my strength to fall in love again, to trust a man once more.' He kissed her, glad to learn that she did trust him and could open her heart to him. 'But do we have to wait? I don't need a big wedding as long as I have you.'

'My love, given the circumstances I think it is best to be patient, to allow the required time to pass and for affairs to be handled in the proper way.'

'But what if your family hate me and try to separate us? I could not bear it.' Her lip quivered.

'Trust me, my feelings will remain unchanged. Once a suitable time passes after the funeral, we can announce our engagement. I know my mother will want us to wait awhile due to the mourning period, but I'm sure we can convince her to minimise any delays.' His mother was ever the stickler for convention, so he was not convinced she would be persuaded to a shortened wait.

'If that is what you want, then we had better stop laying together until we marry, as we cannot risk me being with child. Have you thought of that? My reputation is already in tatters, so I can take no further risks.'

'Hold firm for me and I will wait, my love. As my Duchess, you will outrank that woman and have the status you deserve, will you not?' he soothed.

She stood up abruptly. 'My family return today, so I need to ready myself. Please would you dine with us? We will need to talk to them and share our intentions to marry; after all, it's only fair on Sophia. This will be a lot for her, and I would prefer she heard it from us than through gossip circulating through the city.'

'Yes, we owe her that,' he agreed, rising to kiss her, but Arabella moved her head slightly, so his lips fell on her cheek. He felt the absence of her desire and questioned if he truly could abstain from the pleasure of her body, of her touch, during the mourning period.

Chapter Seventeen

When Alex returned to the Grand later that evening, Arabella, Sophia, and the Burtons were waiting for him in the private dining room on the ground floor of the hotel. They were seated around a large table laden with glistening silver vases filled with aromatic lilies and luscious fruits. The room was sparkling with mirrors, candlelight, and the crystal glassware on the table. The luxury of the occasion jarred with Alex, who still felt the loss of his father, and looking at Arabella – dazzling in a low-cut gown of sumptuous red velvet which emphasised her dark black hair, creamy white skin, and pouting red lips – a sliver of doubt once more crept over him as to whether he should be here. He had not expected such a show of celebration whilst he mourned his father, and it did not quite sit right with him.

However, as Alex took his seat, he noticed a tension to the room which hummed with the traces of angry words. Arabella tried to manage a welcoming smile, but it faltered on her lips, her eyes held unshed tears, and Mary – forbidding and simmering with anger – went and stood behind her as if to protect her friend. Sophia kept her head lowered and did not attempt to acknowledge him, whereas usually she made polite conversation despite her nervousness around him. Mrs Burton dabbed a delicate lace handkerchief to her eyes as she sat deflated in her chair. Mr Burton's face was red with anger as he slowly raised his bulk from his chair.

'Uncle, please no, leave it for now. Let us at least eat,' Arabella pleaded with him.

'I will not be quiet. You, sir, have ruined my niece's reputation, and you expect us all to sit here and be happy. Mrs Burton is beside herself for leaving Arabella alone to be taken advantage of once again,' he blustered furiously.

'But hasn't Arabella explained? I have promised we will be wed, but I have family matters to attend to following my father's death and want everything to be handled in the proper manner,' Alex spoke wearily, the grief of the past few days weighing down on him, and in that instance, he wanted to be gone from the situation. Away from the angry, tearful faces and the accusatory words.

'Oh, yes, I know your type. With your big title and your money, taking what you want and making false promises. You'll leave for London and then there will be no word.' He turned to Arabella. 'He will leave you with nothing but regret. His class do not marry your type.'

'Uncle, please stop being so melodramatic. Alex has explained the situation, and we must respect that. He has recently lost his father after all,' Arabella pleaded, trying to defuse the tension.

'Arabella knows my intentions are true, Mr Burton,' Alex tried once again to explain. 'Tonight, we wanted to share the happy news, but as this is a sad time for my own family who are grieving, I must hold off for now. It would give them time to come to terms with our engagement, and we can have a grand wedding befitting my new Duchess, Arabella.'

'You must think me stupid, your Grace. My niece here has already had Lady Lyborn visiting, insulting her, telling her to leave Venice, yet you think your family will welcome Arabella with open arms? I don't trust any of your kind. I trusted Sir Charles, accepted him as a son, and look what he did to my niece.' He scoffed.

Sophia pushed her chair back and rushed from the room sobbing.

'Uncle! Now look what you have done. Mary, please go after her, check she is all right. This was exactly what I feared would happen. I didn't want the poor girl upset. This will unsettle her even more,' Arabella admonished her uncle, as Mary silently left the room, glaring at Alex as she passed him, her disapproval evident in her stern face for the upset caused within the family.

'It needed to be spoken,' harrumphed Mr Burton, who sat heavily back down on his chair. 'You have been through so much, and now you risk it all for another rich and powerful man. Mark my words, he will return home and marry the lady he is betrothed to. You will be laughed at for even thinking you could become a Duchess. You are a fool for love once again, but I've stated my piece.' He took a large gulp of wine.

'I cannot bear this.' Arabella tearfully shook her head, then fled from the room.

Alex went to follow her, but she slammed the door in his face. He looked at the remaining two guests – Mr Burton stared ahead, slowly drinking his wine, while Mrs Burton looked pleadingly at him.

'If you leave Venice without her, you will destroy her.' The sadness in her voice was much evident. 'I don't think she will be so strong this time; you have no idea how much she has already suffered. She won't be able to live without you.'

'But I mean what I say.' Alex was adamant and growing impatient now. He was being presented as the villain when he was trying to do the right thing, for both their sakes.

'You would leave her here amongst these she-wolves with their gossip and their slander and think she will be able to rise above it?' she countered with a rueful laugh. 'Oh, you will be fine, back home with your family. Men such as you never get the blame, do you? Your friends will pat you on the back for a jolly jape well done, while she is denounced as a whore. She went through so much with that man, tried so hard, went out in Society with bruises, hiding her tears, and did her best for those poor children while he was drugged up to the eyebrows on opium. She was shunned when she spoke out, tried to help others. You are no different to him – cruel and heartless.'

'I am not that man!' Alex exclaimed, horrified.

'Prove it then.' She turned away from him, and Alex had no choice but to leave.

Chapter Eighteen

The next morning Alex left the jewellers with a ring in his pocket and hurried once again along the familiar route to the Grand Hotel from San Marco. The ring would surely prove his love for Arabella and his honourable intentions. Angelo Missiaglia, Venice's upmost jeweller, had assured him that the exquisite single diamond set in antique gold was not only unique but of timeless elegance befitting a Duchess.

Alex needed to persuade Arabella to see him to set things right. Last night, she had refused to admit him to her presence after he had left her aunt and uncle sitting amongst the ghost of the dinner party that had not transpired. He wanted to assure her of his love, and if she would not see him, he was not sure what he would do. He was running out of time. News had come that the train line was finally reopening within a matter of days, and he wanted to be gone as soon as possible. His mother was expecting him. She had telegrammed last night to say they had held up the funeral as long as possible and if he wanted to be there, he had to make haste as soon as he could travel. He longed to be gone from Venice now, away from all the intrigue and drama it represented, to move on with his life and to settle down with Arabella.

'Good morning, Miss Mary, I wish to see Arabella if I may?' He spoke calmly and respectfully when Mary opened the door, even though she could not hide her disapproval.

She paused and at first, he thought she would deny him entry, but then she slowly pulled back the door, reluctantly allowing him to enter. Arabella stood by one of the long windows gazing down onto the Grand Canal lost deep in thought. She was dressed in a sombre dove-grey morning dress which gave her a fragile air. Her dark hair was tightly coiled around the perfection of her face, and as she turned to greet him, he could see the return of the dark shadows under her eyes which were red from crying. He strode across the room and gently touched her arms.

'My darling, please no more tears, no more sadness. I love you and that is all that matters. Come and sit with me so I can give you my gift.' He slowly guided her to the couch as Mary silently left the room, but he knew she would not stray far from her friend. He produced the small jewellery box from his pocket and placed it in her trembling hands. Arabella opened it and gazed upon the sparkling diamond ring, knowing what it signified. She started to sob as he tenderly placed it on her ring finger.

'I give you this ring as a symbol of my love. As soon as I can tell my family, you can wear it publicly and we will announce it to the world. Will you marry me, my darling girl?'

'Oh, Alex.' She kissed him passionately as her hand pressed upon his upper thigh. He felt himself stir and harden. He moaned as she found the buttons of his trousers and expertly undid them, freeing his manhood, surprising him with her amorousness. She slid down between his knees, caressing him as he groaned softly, and she took him in her mouth, sucking and stroking him until he came in ecstasy, shuddering to a climax.

'Marry me, here in Venice, prove you truly love me,' she whispered in his ear. 'We can be together and would not have to be apart for any length of time. Every night I can give myself to you, make you mine. Come, Alex, do you want to wait for me? Can you truly bear to be apart? If you love me as you say you do, you would not be able to leave me behind.'

He gazed down at her, still kneeling between his legs as she continued to stroke his manhood with her beautiful, delicate hands. The primness of her grey gown against such a tableau made him laugh as he threw back his head shouting, 'Yes, yes, I'll marry you whenever you choose.'

She laughed with him as they both tumbled onto the floor, pulling his head by his dark curls to kiss her deeply, and he could taste his own saltiness in her mouth.

***

Mr Burton went to the English church to speak with the vicar there and managed to secure a special licence which meant the wedding could take place in two days. Money and title spoke volumes to the Church, and Alex had both. There was much excitement between Arabella and her aunt, who were frantically planning what to wear. Alex had been to the train station to enquire about first-class tickets home to England. Sophia, however, was quiet, lacking in appetite as they dined that evening, appearing to sit in abject misery. Mary also did not make an appearance.

Alex was relieved that everyone appeared to have forgiven him, and the previous evening's ill-fated dinner had been forgotten, but he felt a numbness to the occasion. It felt as if events were galloping away from him while all the time he was still coming to terms with his father's death. He regretted agreeing to the hasty marriage, but he wanted Arabella to be happy and soon they would be on their way home at least, so he could be there for his mother.

'Alex, sweetheart,' Arabella whispered to him, and he turned to see a troubled expression on her beautiful face. 'I did not say anything before, but I have since realised where my ring came from.'

'Yes, it came from Missiaglia's. I am told it is the best jewellers in Venice.'

'Actually, dearest, I was hoping we could return this and buy one in Paris at Mellerio's. After all, if they are good enough for queens of France, surely they are good enough for the Duchess of Ushington!' She caressed his thigh under the table.

'Of course, if you don't like the ring we can change it here.' He couldn't help but feel disappointed, as he'd taken great care to choose something he hoped she would like. 'I can't think when we will have time to travel to Paris in the next few months with all the things we have to do.'

'My first ring came from Missiaglia's, and I just wouldn't want it to feel like a bad omen,' she worried.

'Oh, my darling, I never thought! Of course, we can change it, but I can't see how we can do that in Paris. I really must travel home when the train line reopens.'

'I thought we could stop off in Paris on the way back to England, so I could acquire some new clothes too. I can hardly meet your family in my cheap gowns.' She smiled sadly as her hand gripped his thigh tighter.

'But I need to return, my love. I will already miss my father's funeral because of our wedding. I can't delay any further,' he pleaded with her.

Her hand caressed him, and he felt his resolve weaken as her hand stole further up his thigh. 'Surely one more day or two cannot hurt. I have always so wished to go to Paris – a place we could call our own and a ring with purely happy memories, not to be clouded with the past. As you say, you will miss the funeral given the delays caused by the storm and now our wedding, so what's the rush?'

Alex stuttered, trying to gain control. 'I think my family needs me though, and it does not feel right to be parted from them for so long after our loss.'

'Don't you want me to look my best?' Her eyes widened. 'I am terrified of meeting your mother, and now you want me to look positively dowdy in front of her. She will already think I am unworthy and merely a shabby merchant's widow.' Her voice rose in distress at the differences in their class. 'I don't want to let you down.'

The rest of the diners watched on quietly, as if willing him to agree. Mr Burton glowered, and Mrs Burton dabbed her eyes. The mood had changed once again, and Alex was keen to avoid another evening being soured.

'Of course, of course we will stop in Paris. You deserve the best, my love,' he relented once again, and Arabella's grip loosened on his thigh, her face once again relaxed, her happiness returned, and they all breathed a sigh of relief that the matter was settled.

'And you can have a new ring, my darling,' he whispered, thinking to himself, *How stupid I was not to realise her first ring would come from Venice too. She deserves Paris after all she has been through.*

Mr and Mrs Burton were smiling proudly at him and Arabella, but he felt Sophia's eyes on him. They seemed to be filled with such pity that the hair lifted on the back of his neck. Arabella's searching hand soon brought his focus back to her and he wanted to do anything to ensure her happiness.

***

The next morning, as he was returning from the train station where he had finally sorted out tickets for their return to England the next evening, he came across Sophia staring across the water at a small, narrow Palazzo. He was surprised to see her out alone. There was a chill in the air and a drizzling rain, but she stood resolute looking at the peculiar building, as if in a trance.

'Miss Sophia, are you all right?' he enquired gently, trying not to scare her as she was so deep in thought.

'Oh, your Grace, I did not see you there.' Once again, she was fearful in his presence and her eyes darted around as if she was checking to see if they were noticed standing there together. There was no one else there but she did not appear to relax.

'You look rather taken with that building,' Alex said, pointing across the canal.

'It is called Palazzo Contarini Fasan, but it's known as the House of Desdemona,' she whispered.

'Desdemona? Wasn't she the wife of Othello?' he asked, recalling the Shakespeare tragedy he had read at school.

'Yes, local legend has it that the Palazzo was home to Nicola Contarini, known as "the Moor" because of his dark skin. His wife Palma Querini left him due to his brutality and jealousy. I think there are other versions the story, but over time the Palazzo became known as Desdemona's House.'

A chill came over Alex as he remembered the play and the senseless murder of Othello's innocent wife. Sophia's next words cast a colder shadow.

'My father once thought about renting it as he admired its strange design and the neatness of the rooms, but once he was told its history and nickname, he couldn't bear to live in it. He always found *Othello* one of Shakespeare's saddest tales. He could never understand Othello's jealousy and his utter belief in Iago's lies. He told me no man should treat his wife so badly. He was a gentle man, you see.' Sophia stared at him defiantly; he became uneasy and looked away. How could this sweet girl still defend her father after all he had put Arabella through? A sudden squall of rain had whipped across the canal, and they had both run for cover, rushing towards the Grand.

When they arrived at the hotel, Sophia had placed her small hand on his wet sleeve and, lowering her voice, whispered to him, 'Take care not to ever listen to an Iago;

false tales can change a life.' She hurried to her room, leaving him astonished at her words.

Chapter Nineteen

The church was plain, austere, and cold. Alex couldn't help but feel a little saddened that he wasn't in the pretty Norman church in Ushington, where his family had worshipped for generations, where countless Dukes had married their wives, and where now his father would be buried without him in attendance.

When he had entered the church earlier, he had been surprised to see a packed congregation, and it appeared Venetian Society were eager to witness the much talked of union between the new Duke of Ushington and the Lady Arabella Pembrook. He even noticed Lady Lyborn amongst them. He could see the women talking behind their fans as he tried to walk confidently up the aisle to take his place beside Rupert in front of the Anglican altar to await his bride. Sophia sat in the front pew wearing a lilac gown, but he could feel her sadness permeating the joy of the day, and he smiled weakly at Rupert hoping for some encouragement at least from his friend.

Rupert, arriving late the night before, had agreed to be his supporter, but Alex had sensed his reluctance and the worry behind his friend's congratulations. But Rupert said nothing against the marriage and for that Alex was grateful, pleased to have his old friend by his side on this momentous day, especially after what he had endured in the past week. Now Rupert smiled back at him, and he felt himself starting to breathe slowly again.

Arabella walked towards him a vision in ivory silk holding her head high, ignoring the stares, the whispers, and the looks of disdain even now. He knew it took all her courage, all her determination and strength to walk past those Society vipers. He shivered as he turned to Arabella to say his marriage vows. But her radiant smile soon chased away his doubts or disappointments that the day hadn't been how he had originally envisaged it. She was all he needed; all he wanted.

Now, as they declared their vows to each other, she would finally be his Duchess and would no longer be ignored by these women who, in most cases, would have to give precedence to her title. The thought made him smile, and Arabella had been right to insist on the marriage taking place sooner rather than later. She deserved her place in the sun of Society, and together they would dazzle and be able to shine a light on the causes closest to them.

The bells rang out from the church, and he walked out with Arabella by his side as man and wife into the spring sunshine. The rain of the previous day had been scattered away across the Adriatic, the sky was a welcome blue, the canals were tranquil and languid once more, and the gondoliers, upon seeing the bridal couple, called out their blessings.

As the Burtons, then other well-wishers, added their congratulations to the couple, Alex scanned the congregation but could not see Kitty Jobson amongst them. It saddened him as she had been so kind to him, but perhaps it would have provoked unhappy memories of Charles's sorry end.

Rupert joined them at the private, intimate reception at the Danieli, but made his excuses as the couple got ready to make their own departure. A card table called him, where he would forget for a while his concern over his friend and the widow. He had a rare run of luck, winning a small fortune, and he thought maybe the wedding was fortuitous after all.

As Rupert toasted his winnings, the wedding party arrived at the train station. Catching the night train would be Alex, Arabella, and of course Mary – whom Arabella insisted she could not part from – along with Alex's steadfast valet George, who would be providing all the servants' duties. The Burtons and Sophia were there to wave them off, to make an occasion of it, a flurry of hugs, kisses, and a small tear from Mrs Burton, who was all happiness now her niece was not ruined but made a Duchess! They planned to depart for London the next day.

Alexander would say goodbye to Venice, full of happiness, his misery when he had first arrived dissipated into the depths of the murky canals, and he would look fondly on the faded grandeur of the city as he departed on the rattling steam train with his beautiful bride beside him. He closed his eyes as he held Arabella's hand in his, and a sense of peace finally came over him, all doubts gone – even the loss of his father diminished and forgotten for now. Venice had given him such a blessed jewel, and he would be ever grateful as he bid farewell to the city. What a future lay ahead of them, and he wanted to shout with joy.

The train rocked slowly across the snow-topped Alps, and that night as he lay asleep in their compartment, he dreamed once again of the giant eagle bearing him through the Venetian streets he had grown to know, but the streets were dirty, full of decay and scurrying rats. As he looked down, trying to search for the dark-haired woman, shrouded figures in black cloaks and the sinister masks of Carnival gazed up at him, mocking him, and no one would save him from the eagle's talons. He rose higher and higher away from the city and he cried out, waking now with a start to an empty sleeping compartment. He was so exhausted he drifted back into a deeper sleep without dreams. Arabella would laugh at him in the morning and tell him he must have still been dreaming, for where could she have gone in the middle of the night? She had been right there in the bed across from his, listening to his gentle snores. She had been too happy to sleep and had wanted to spend the night watching his dear face, her beloved husband. He had smiled at her happiness and his night fears vanished across the snowcapped mountains.

Part Two

Chapter Twenty

Paris – April 1880

Paris had been a whirl of dressmakers, shops, and more shops as Arabella was eager to ensure her wardrobe was befitting that of a new Duchess. They also visited Mellerio, the famous Paris jewellers Arabella so admired, where she chose a large, square-cut diamond surrounded by a small cluster of sparkling rubies. Arabella adored it and happily gazed at it on her long, slender finger, although Alex thought it too large, too ostentatious, and he struggled to cope with the cost of it, as it would have wiped out several months of his old allowance as the son of a Duke. But Alex revelled in his new wife's happiness and would do anything to see that radiant smile of hers.

Arabella insisted Mary dine with them too at the best restaurants in the city. She explained to an incredulous Alex, desiring to be alone with his wife, that they couldn't expect her to sit in the hotel's servants' hall with George for company, and she was reluctant to have her dear friend eat alone. He therefore endured three nights of Mary's obvious disdain for him as Arabella happily prattled on to both of them about the gowns, cloaks, shoes, and jewellery she had purchased each day. Their bedroom was the only sanctuary from the grim-faced Mary, and he was glad to have his wife to himself for a while.

On their last night, when Alex and Arabella lay in bed, he broached the subject of the sullen companion.

'My darling, when we go to Wisteston Abbey, you do realise Mary will be treated as a senior servant and unable to have the freedom she has now.' He gently stroked Arabella's arm but sensed a storm gathering.

She sat up, eyes blazing. 'I cannot treat my dearest friend as a servant!'

'My love, it will be hard enough with my mother,' Alex admitted, thinking briefly of the constant stream of letters which followed his travels, Lady Caroline's disdain dripping with every word, and he shuddered inwardly. 'It would not be good form, and you don't want Mama to think you gauche.' He knew how first impressions would count with his mother and was eager to smooth things over on his return.

Arabella started to kiss him, her hands stroking his body, and he began to feel himself respond. He knew that she wanted him to allow Mary to continue as she was, but he could not give in to her as much as he wanted to. He needed to appease his mother as much as possible and asking her to accept Mary as a companion and to dine with them would be seen as a step too far. She murmured 'please' again, but he shook his head firm in his position. Abruptly, she stopped what she was doing and grabbed her robe, leaving the room in a fury of displeasure. Alex lay there groaning with frustration, but he let her go as she would not be able to make him change his mind on this matter. He hoped that she would understand his position and see sense.

He somehow managed to fall into a deep sleep, waking when George opened the thick drapes, letting in the morning sunshine.

'Her Grace is waiting for you in the dining room. Shall you dress before breakfast? There is plenty of time before the train leaves.'

Alex weighed up his options, not knowing what mood his wife would be in, but his stomach got the better of him, so he pulled on his robe and made his way to the suite's private dining room.

Arabella sat alone at the small table, her robe tied loosely, and her dark, luscious hair falling around her shoulders. As she noticed him, she smiled happily, and, rising, pulled him to her for a prolonged kiss as she trailed a finger down his chest where his own robe gaped open. Alex's breath quickened with sudden desire.

'Oh, Alex,' she whispered, her breath warm against his neck, 'I hate it when we quarrel. I do ask for your forgiveness on the matter. I'm afraid I find it so hard to understand your Society ways. After all, I am merely a merchant's widow from America.'

'You are no longer a merchant's widow but my wife, the Duchess of Ushington, and worthy of a thousand of my family. But I want you to make a good impression on them.' He drew back from her, looking into her eyes which brimmed with tears. He hated to have hurt her, so sat down and gently guided her onto his lap, enfolding her in his arms.

'You see, my love, all of my life I have tried to be the perfect son – I studied, I was dutiful to old aunts, and I was kind to small children. I have always adored my mother, who was loving and kind, whereas my father was cold and distant, sending me to boarding school at a young age, believing I was mollycoddled by her. I enjoyed school and I came out unscathed and fairly intelligent. But as I grew older, my parents pushed me into a friendship with Lady Helen, as you know.' Arabella pouted at the name and, laughing, Alex kissed her jealousy away.

'She was in their eyes the perfect match and it was their hope to see us married, whereas I felt nothing for her. To me, Helen was simply a friend, and I had no other feelings for her. For the first time in my gilded life, I was uneasy and had a need to rebel. But of course, I did not have the guts to speak out through fear of upsetting my father and displeasing my mother – she loves Helen, and it was her dream to have her dearest son married to her. I had a reprieve as it was decided I would go to Cambridge, but I knew they hoped for a marriage when I graduated. You know the sordid story of my affair with Margot – you know there are no feelings towards her now, don't you?' Arabella nestled in closer and this time she was the one to kiss him, encouraging him to continue.

'My first act of rebellion and it was huge! My father's friend's wife and a scandal in Society news. I had never let them down before, but subconsciously I wanted to sabotage my match with Helen – well, I certainly failed at that, as it made them more determined. I managed to buy myself some time by coming to Venice; I wanted desperately to do the right thing, and I wish I could have loved her, but in loving her I would never have found you!' He kissed her again to reassure her of his unfailing devotion to her. 'You complete me in a way I never could have imagined, and I would not change that, but it has come at a cost. I now need to try and put it right with my mother, whom I love so much. You must see how it makes me feel and how much I want us to be forgiven, to be accepted, and them to love you as I do.'

She wrapped her arms tightly around him and he drank in her softness and her sweet scent. She stared deep into his eyes. 'Oh, Alex, I love you so much and I want you to be happy. I promise I will spend my life making you happy, and I will do everything to make your family love me. We will show them how suited we are together, and perhaps when I bear your son your mother will forgive me!' She laughed now, tossing back her hair, and as she kissed him deeply, her hands pulling his dressing gown apart, his joy returned.

Chapter Twenty-One

Wisteston Abbey

It had been a long journey from Paris to Alex's family home, Wisteston Abbey. Arabella made it clear that her preference was to spend a few days in London before catching the slow train to the West Country. Alex, however, was mindful he had delayed long enough, so insisted they board the night train at Paddington as soon as they had arrived in England. Arabella had dressed appropriately in a black travelling coat with a black satin mourning gown beneath it. She had taken much care to comply with tradition, and Alex knew how hard it had been for her to put on mourning clothes once again, feeling she had only just been able to cast them aside.

The morning mist was beginning to lift as they mounted the carriage sent to collect them, and soon the honey-coloured walls of the old house appeared in the distance. Alex always loved his first glimpse of his ancestral home – the beautiful sweeping drive, the ornate lawn with its magnificent fountain at its centre, and the display of colour just starting to bloom as spring began. At the sight of the approaching carriage, the doors of the house creaked open, and all the servants streamed out to greet their new Duke and his Duchess. He turned to give Arabella an encouraging smile after feeling her hand tremble. As they descended, his mother appeared on the threshold, and he could immediately see the disdain etched on her face. Lady Caroline, the now dowager Duchess, was dressed in black crepe, her widow's peak attached to greying hair, and Alex noticed she had aged considerably since he had left. Her face was hard and bitter as she looked at them. Arabella smiled effusively and acted as if she were a much-welcomed guest. He squeezed her hand and was thankful that she seemed to be turning a blind eye to his mother's hostility – she had not yet moved to greet them, and the servants shuffled awkwardly.

'Mama, allow me to introduce my wife, Arabella,' Alex said, affecting a cheerfulness he did not feel as he guided Arabella forward.

'Welcome to Wisteston Abbey.' Her tone was icy as she barely touched Arabella's hand.

'Thank you, Lady Caroline. It is a pleasure to be here at last,' Arabella spoke softly and curtsied.

'Well, you certainly took your time getting here – you were expected a week ago.' Lady Caroline dropped her hand as if she were scalded, then turned to the butler. 'Emmerson, introduce the new Duchess to her household. Tea is served in the small drawing room, Alexander. Mrs Muffet will see to your servant. I am afraid I have a headache.' With that, she retreated back inside the Abbey.

The dour Mary reluctantly allowed herself to be escorted away by the housekeeper as Emmerson, the butler, made the introductions. A tedious, drawn-out process that did little to settle his wife's discomfort. Alex noticed the tightly drawn smile as Arabella tried to show interest in the sea of faces. He was sure his mother had set it up to intimidate his wife, as he had expressly written to tell her not to stand on formality on their arrival as they would be tired from travelling and ready just to meet the family. He had clearly been ignored, perhaps as punishment, and there was no other family to greet them – simply his disapproving mother, who had decided to keep tight reins on proceedings.

'Emmerson, we will take tea in our room. We both need to freshen up after our journey,' Alex said, deciding to take control; after all, he was the Duke now. Emmerson dithered briefly but then remembered himself and nodded his acquiescence.

'Lady Caroline has put you in the Scarlet Bedchamber, your Grace.'

Alex frowned. He had not, of course, expected the master suite – it was too soon for that transition – but the Scarlet Bedchamber was small and cramped, looking over the side of the house with no view over the beautiful Abbey gardens and with no separate sitting room. He could hardly make a scene in front of the household, but he would be sure to make it plain that he recognised the snub and he would have to act on it.

Unfortunately, Arabella noticed the slight as soon as they entered the room and before Alex could make amends. It was smaller than their Parisian suite and the deep red wall coverings which gave it its name enclosed the walls around them, while the old four-poster bed that dominated the room had seen better days. She walked over to the heavily draped windows and glanced down at the kitchen gardens. When they had entered, George and one of the housemaids had been busy unpacking their luggage in the small dressing room, and Emmerson had followed soon after with a footman bearing the tea tray. The room had become unbearably crowded and Alex could see his wife's struggling with all the commotion. He signalled to George and the maid to leave, ushering both butler and footman out too.

'I am sorry. This is not what you deserve, my love.' He swept Arabella into his arms once they were alone.

'We knew this would be difficult, my darling. But I am astonished that your mother would be so clear in her hatred of me.' Arabella sniffed. 'Well, we must make the best of it and try to win her round.'

'I know she has recently lost her husband; and I did miss the funeral, but this is unforgiveable, and I will speak to her about it. Let's hope this is her way of punishing me and now she has, relations will surely improve.' He was trying to convince himself as much as he was attempting to soothe Arabella's own anxiety. 'I will arrange for us to be moved into a more suitable room though.'

'Oh, Alex, let's just leave it. Let her think she has won.' Arabella sighed. 'I am just too exhausted to move now anyway.'

'As long as you are sure, my darling.' He kissed her, grateful that she was being so understanding and resolving to make it up to her.

***

The small dining room where luncheon was served was also devoid of family when they entered. Alex looked to Emmerson when he noted only two places were set.

'Her Grace, the dowager Duchess, has taken to her room; and the rest of the family are out visiting, I believe,' the butler confirmed.

Alex was astounded to think his sister and his brother would choose today to go visiting when he and Arabella had just arrived, but perhaps his mother had seen to it. Alex's ire rose further when he found out that the estate manager had been told by his mother not to attend on him today. He immediately sent a note to the man telling him he would meet him at the estate office at two o'clock. He would brook no excuses. He needed to assert himself now.

After lunch, he accompanied Arabella on a stroll around the magnificent gardens, hoping it would lift their spirits.

'You must be strong, Alex. You are the Duke now. Show them who is in charge,' Arabella spoke firmly, and he drew on her remarkable strength.

'How dare they make a fool of me,' he spoke angrily. 'I cannot believe my mother could be so cold and unforgiving. She must still see me as a child she can punish.'

'Show her you are a man now. You have a wife, and we will have heirs – we are the future, my love,' she urged him. 'I was so proud of you when you insisted on seeing your estate manager. He cannot take orders from your mother anymore and will soon realise he is to do your bidding.'

'It will mean I have to spend time with him before we can return to London, making sure he knows I mean to take charge.'

'I am sure it won't take too long – state your intentions and how he must conduct all business through you. This place already stifles me, and I have to admit I long to be gone from here.'

'But you have barely seen it,' he said with a laugh.

'It's old, poky, and dark. It reminds me too much of Ravenscourt.' She shuddered at the mention of its name.

'I thought Ravenscourt to be a fairly new house?'

'New pretending to be old. No, this place is stuffy and old-fashioned – can you not see it?'

Alex had always held a special affection for his old childhood home – the history the house had, the quirkiness of all the different centuries mingling and living with each other. Yet he recognised its limitations – it was a rabbit warren of small dark rooms which were cosy enough in winter but gloomy in the light of summer. It was spring now and the gardens were starting to bloom, which he had hoped would delight Arabella. She had barely noticed them, perhaps wounded by his mother's earlier behaviour, and he sensed her distaste for the old house.

***

Dinner did not lighten either of their moods. The family were already assembled in the large drawing room as Alex and Arabella entered, and the silence that descended on the party was telling. As befitting the mourning period, it was a small gathering of his mother, his sister and brother, the vicar Reverend Nicholls and his wife Esme, and much to Alex's surprise, their close neighbours Lord and Lady St Caur and their daughter Helen.

As she was introduced to the ensemble, he could see Arabella's own frisson of shock, but she recovered quickly and complimented Lady Helen on her gown, which even Alex could see was old-fashioned in comparison to his wife's expensive, stylish confection of silk and taffeta. The room in full mourning resembled a flock of carrion crows ready to pick over them, but Arabella rose to the occasion and ignored their cold snubs with a display of politeness and contentment which subdued the company further. She made a point of being extremely tender and loving towards her husband, lightly touching his arm constantly, which he observed made his mother visibly recoil.

His sister, Charlotte, seated next to Lady Helen, gripped her friend's hand as both ladies struggled to keep their disapproval from their eyes. His brother, Henry, however, looked bemused by Arabella, whose beauty could not be denied. Reverend Nicholls did his best to make polite conversation but found himself on the receiving end of fierce looks from his wife for his efforts. He was not the only one to be relieved when dinner was announced. Lady Caroline led the way on her youngest son's arm and Alex let the slip-on social manners pass – he and Arabella as Duke and Duchess should have led the company on the arms of the next senior guests, but instead they trailed in his mother's imperious wake. But even Alex did not expect the next snub – his mother had seated herself at one end of the table in the place that should now be his wife's.

Arabella merely raised an eyebrow and followed her husband to the other end of the table, where he at least took his rightful place. She sat herself next to him while the other guests settled themselves accordingly, but dinner was now a stilted affair with false propriety and nervous chatter. The vicar found himself next to Arabella, with his wife next to Alex as if no one else had wanted to get too close. Whenever Arabella spoke to him, Reverend Nicholls' hands shook slightly, and his cutlery clattered against his plate as he stuttered his answers while his wife fixed her beady eyes on him. Lady Caroline glared at the poor man too, and Alex was tempted to remind the man who the Duke and Duchess of the Ushington estate and church were now, but he would bide his time and let the initial froideur settle. He attempted to converse with his dining partner, but Esme Nicholls was frugal in her responses. Eventually, the table descended into an uncomfortable silence. When the meal was finally over, Alex quickly rose to his feet and announced how he and his wife were tired from their journey so would retire.

'I could not stay in that room another second,' he exclaimed when they were back in the safety of their bedroom, 'and let you be left with those rude, cold women while I smoked a cigar with men who could barely look at me.' He tore off his bow tie and wrenched his jacket off as George and Mary arrived hastily to help them after word had reached them that Alex and Arabella had returned to their room. Both noticed the charged atmosphere, the tears starting to form in Arabella's eyes, and the fury on Alex's face. Mary raised her fierce eyebrows at her friend, who shook her head and motioned her to leave with George.

'I promise you, my darling, I will let them know who is in charge now and they will in future pay due deference to you as my wife.' Alex stroked her hair as they lay in bed.

'We have each other, my love, which is all we need. We can create our own family now,' and she soothed his anger away with her lips caressing him, her hands stroking him as her legs wrapped around his eager body. Alex knew then that with her by his side, he could be the man he wanted to be, and to hell with his family and anyone else who snubbed his beloved.

Chapter Twenty-Two

The next morning, Alex braved entering his father's study as he wanted to prepare for his appointment with the family lawyer. The lingering smell of his father's cigars brought back childhood memories of when he used to be summoned to his father's presence either to be lectured about duty, responsibility, etc., or to be punished for some minor misdemeanour. His last conversation with his father had in fact taken place in here about Alex's affair with Margot. He could still remember the anger, the revulsion in his father's voice as he accused Alex of besmirching the family's reputation. The old Duke's fury had known no bounds, and it was as if the hurtful words still hung in the air like tiny daggers piercing his heart, as he now regretted the pain he had caused. He had resented his father so much, and now there would be no grand rapprochement, no forgiveness and pride restored.

He had barely sat down in the large leather chair in front of the old oak desk, when his mother entered. Alex stood up to greet her, hoping to start afresh after the coldness of their treatment yesterday. But it would appear Lady Caroline was in no mood to relent as she abruptly sat down in one of the chairs in front of the desk, gesturing him to sit opposite her.

'I loved you so much,' Lady Caroline spoke softly, her voice practically a whisper. 'You were my firstborn, my pride and joy. When I first held you, it was as if I finally knew my purpose in life and I wanted to give you the world. Your father thought me soft, of course, but though he was an old-fashioned man who found showing emotion hard, he allowed me to look after my children, not merely foisting you off on nannies, and you rewarded me with such love.' Alex smiled optimistically that she did understand after all the depth of true love.

'But you betrayed my love – first with that woman in Cambridge, and now by marrying a merchant's widow and an American at that!' Her voice trembled as she fought to compose herself. She raised her hand to stop Alex from responding, making it clear she was not done. 'So much promise and you throw it all away. I can never forgive you for making the last year of your father's life unbearable. His doctor warned him it did him no good to work himself up, but the news of your actions made his anger worse. He thought you would see sense, and after his last letter to you I hoped so too. He told me you would never disobey him; he was convinced you knew your duty to the Dukedom, to the family. Before he died,' a sob now escaped her, 'he was going to look into her background as he was so worried for you. He told me you were too soft, too kind-hearted, and a fool when it came to women. He wanted you to be happy, but he also wanted to protect you.'

'He threatened to cut me off! He never ever listened to me,' Alex interjected angrily. 'He treated me as a child, a mere idiot incapable of making my own decisions. He ridiculed my ideas, my beliefs, my opinions. I was always wrong.'

'He was trying to make you see sense,' his mother tried to placate him. 'He could see you were vulnerable after Margot Montagu, and he blamed himself for letting you go to Venice while you were still upset. I admit now, I should have been kinder and more understanding, and you should have stayed here.'

'But you weren't!' Alex reminded her. 'You were the one person I thought loved me and understood me. You couldn't even look at me, let alone talk to me. You both wanted me to marry Helen – a woman I did not love.'

'You would have loved her in time! Surely you could see what a good match it was,' she insisted.

'That shows me that even now you aren't listening to me. I love Arabella,' Alex declared, trying to get her to understand his own point of view. 'I could never have loved Helen – she's nice and sweet but there is no passion, no conviction in her. I need someone who will work alongside me to change things, to make life better for those in society who have so little.'

'Oh, grow up, Alexander!' his mother spoke disdainfully, forgetting her son was now the Duke. 'You are a boy playing at things you do not understand. Women of our status do not work alongside their husbands – a Duchess runs a home, has a family. How can women possibly understand social reform and this so-called women's movement which is an effrontery to me and women like me.'

'It is you who needs to open your eyes, Mama. The world is changing – women are not mere chattels but intelligent, independent people who deserve the vote and so much more.'

His mother stared at him and announced coolly, 'I no longer know you and I can never accept her. She is common, vulgar, and base, and your father was driven to his death by your relationship with her. But now you must make the best of it – there can be no divorce, as I do not want a further scandal attached to this house and this family.'

There was a knock on the door before Alex could respond, and the butler announced the arrival of the lawyer, Sir Michael Ward. Lady Caroline stood, and as she left she uttered with a quiet strength as if wanting her son to promise: 'No divorce.'

Sir Michael and his firm had represented the family for many years, so there was nothing they did not know about the legalities of the Dukedom and the estate. The lawyer was a similar age to Alex's father, a thin reed of a man with a nasally voice.

'The will is pretty much as expected – the Dukedom obviously passes to you as the eldest son, as do the various properties and estates. Usual bequests to the family and a few of the older servants. Your father's valet has been pensioned off. We will need to pay succession duties, which will be high I am afraid, but we have several options to explore and once I have the exact figure, we can decide the best course of action. Fortunately, the Ushington estates and various businesses are still strong compared to other families, as I am sure you are aware.'

Alex agreed, 'Yes, I know Deepdene House and its estates are still being sold off after Henry Hope's death. But father was a good businessman, and getting rid of the Irish estates when he did was a clever move. There is a lot of unrest there now.'

The lawyer cleared his throat before continuing, aware this next matter was more sensitive in light of recent events. 'There was an amendment made shortly before you went to Venice regarding any future marriage – it stipulates that there is to be no divorce within the first five years of said marriage otherwise there will be financial consequences. I have the paperwork here for you to look at.' Alex scanned the papers as the lawyer explained, 'Your father was most concerned regarding the current trend in the courts; in particular, he spoke to me at great length about the case of Henry Fitzroy, grandson of the 5th Duke of Grafton, who married a young courtesan, I believe. Your father abhorred the scandal surrounding the court case as much as he despised Fitzroy's choice of wife, and he wanted such an exposure of private family life avoided at all costs.' Alex could hear his mother's warning in his head and was inwardly furious that his family seemed to have expected him to make the wrong choice in his marriage. He was determined to prove them wrong as the lawyer continued with what Alex thought were further insults to his own integrity.

'He had hoped you would marry Lady Helen, and the land agreements had already been drawn up, but of course these are now null and void. He wanted to be prepared for every eventuality, and he did believe you were easily distracted. Divorce, he believed, would also damage any political aspirations you have, as I am sure you are aware.' Sir Michael looked at him sharply.

'I assure you, Sir Michael, I have no intention of divorcing my wife, and I find it most abhorrent that we are even discussing it so soon after my marriage. My father wrote to me whilst I was away saying he intended to disinherit me if I married Arabella, who is definitely not a courtesan,' Alex spoke in a tight voice, trying to calm down his rising anger.

'He did talk to me about it but to disinherit a Viscount is difficult legally as the Dukedom is entailed to the oldest son. He would have had to prove insanity on your part. I advised him against such an action as I believed this would also cause scandal.'

'And scandal seems to scare this family!' Alex was exasperated now.

There was another light knock on the door, which opened to reveal Arabella.

'Ah, Sir Michael, speaking of marriage, allow me to introduce my wife, Lady Arabella, Duchess of Ushington. I have asked her to join us while we discuss our future plans regarding the estate.' The lawyer appeared momentarily confused at such an unusual request for a woman to be present during such conversations, but he quickly gathered his composure and greeted Arabella with suitable deference.

'We desire Lady Caroline to make her home in the dower house as soon as can be suitably arranged,' Alex began, buoyed by his wife's presence to make the demands they had planned the previous evening. 'We will allow a generous sum of money to be allocated to make it habitable and comfortable, but have plans to modernise the Abbey, which will be instigated as soon as Lady Caroline leaves. In the meantime, we intend to make Ushington House in London our main residence whilst the modernisation takes place and expect all senior staff to move with us. Emmerson has already been instructed to leave for London this morning to ensure the London house is prepared for our arrival.' Despite sensing Sir Michael's disapproval, Alex continued unperturbed. 'I have instructed the estate manager to work with you on an inventory of the house, and any requests from the Dowager Duchess for any items within the Abbey must be made formally. My brother and sister have financial provision made for them and can stay in the dower house with my mother.' Arabella indicated her approval, and Alex was delighted to see the satisfied smile which lit up her beautiful face.

'This is most sudden, your Grace, at such a time,' Sir Michael remarked.

'We have plans of our own,' Arabella announced. 'When we have children, we will need the room of course, and we feel it would be much better if the Abbey was our own. It certainly does need modernisation – a proper functioning bathroom would be a start! I feel his Grace has been most generous allowing sufficient time to make any changes and providing an allowance to do so. Don't you, Sir Michael?' There was a sudden sharpness to her voice which took Sir Michael aback. 'After all, he now owns the estate, does he not?'

'Of course, of course, your Grace. I will inform all parties of your wishes, unless you would prefer to do so yourself, your Grace?' He turned to Alex, eager to continue to be in his favour lest this talk of modernisation would mean finding a new lawyer to handle such affairs.

'No, my husband and I are leaving today,' Arabella answered for them, clearly not intimidated to be in such counsel. 'We yearn for London Society. The countryside has proved dreary and there is nothing for us here.'

'You leave so soon? I would have thought you would have much to do,' Sir Michael replied, startled by the haste.

'As my wife says, we leave today. I spoke at length to Roberts yesterday in the estate office and he is currently collating all the relevant documents I need and will ensure all matters are conducted via my new London secretary. I will be in touch with you also regarding the succession duties, of course. My mother has made herself fairly clear regarding her own position, so we will be gone in the next hour having not been extended any real welcome.'

The strength emanating from Arabella pushed Alex onwards, and he would be more than happy to leave his family home where he no longer felt wanted or loved. He also wanted to be gone from the unhappy memories it held, particularly feeling the lingering presence of his father, which overwhelmed him. His mother's words had intensified the guilt he already felt over his father's death as well, and he could currently see no way back with his family for relations to become more cordial in the immediate future.

Alex and Arabella did not relay their plans themselves to the family, who were shocked to be informed they were to leave their home so soon after the old Duke's death. Alex did not have to face his mother's tears when she was told nothing was to leave the house without her son's permission except for her own clothes and personal jewels, but even these must be approved to ensure none of the ducal pieces were removed. They missed the awkwardness as the lawyer told Lady Caroline the paltry sum allowed to make her new home comfortable – Arabella's revenge now evident for surely her son, her boy, would never be so cruel despite the harshness of her words to him in their earlier conversation.

As the carriage made its way down the driveway, a smile formed on Arabella's lips as she gently caressed her husband's hand. 'Us two against the world, my darling,' he whispered to her, kissing her on the cheek.

'Always,' she murmured, surprised it had been this easy to get her way and return to London so quickly.

Chapter Twenty-Three

'Aunt Harriet, dear Sophia, I am so pleased to see you,' exclaimed Arabella, as she swept into the large entrance hall of Ushington House in St James's Place, where her aunt and stepdaughter awaited their arrival back from Wisteston. 'Look, Alex, they are here!'

Alex entered his London residence, which always surprised him with its lofty grandeur, its brilliant white lines, and sweeping staircase with its deep red carpet giving an air of luxury. In comparison with Wisteston Abbey, the cluttered, jumbled manor house built around the ruins of the old fourteenth-century monastery, Ushington was modern and fresh. It was a fairly new building, finished just under fifty years ago by his grandfather in the classical design that was still so popular, and he was certain it would be more to his wife's tastes.

'Oh, Alex, the house is simply wonderful,' Arabella marvelled, as she turned back to her aunt. 'Have you settled in, Aunt? Where is dear Uncle John?'

'Yes, my dear. We arrived a few days ago and have been well taken care of. You will be delighted with your new home, won't she, Sophia?' The young girl nodded meekly. 'As for your uncle, he's out on some business or other, but he will be back in time for dinner, of course. How was the Abbey?'

Alex grimaced and waited nervously for Arabella's reaction. Mary stiffened behind him, and he immediately tensed.

'Let us change from the awful train journey and then we will take tea and tell you all.' Arabella glanced around her, unsure now of her new role as lady of the house, and then she appeared to freeze when she noticed the line of servants on one side of the vast hall. Alex should have thought to warn his butler, knowing how the display of servants at the Abbey had threatened to overwhelm her.

'Oh, heavens, how rude you must think us. Alex, you should have warned me.' Her smile was brittle, as she took in the faces staring back at her.

'Don't worry, dearest. Everyone could see how pleased you were to be reunited with your family,' he assured her, not wanting her to dwell on the faux pas. 'Now, come and meet your household. Emmerson, our steadfast butler, you have already met at the Abbey before he left to come here and ensure the house was ready for us.'

The old butler came forward and bowed his head over his mistress' hand before the rest of the servants were introduced in turn.

***

'I tried so hard,' Arabella complained later, as they took tea with her aunt and Sophia in the sumptuous drawing room overlooking Green Park. 'Didn't I, Alex? But everything I did was wrong. I was so terribly out of place and utterly inadequate.' She sighed dejectedly.

'You were wonderful, darling,' Alex soothed her. 'My mother is very old-fashioned, and of course still grieving my father,' he said tactfully, trying to downplay how badly the visit had gone, it feeling a little gauche to be so open about it.

'She made pointed comments about my being American and a merchant's widow. There was this dreadful dinner party with your neighbours where that insipid Lady Helen positively snivelled in your direction as if I had stolen you. It was so uncomfortable, and your mother knew it. She wouldn't even let me sit in my rightful place at the head of the table opposite you.' Arabella pouted, turning to her aunt to fuss over her after enduring such an ordeal.

'I know, it was terribly awkward, but I have spoken with her firmly to ensure it won't happen again. I'm afraid it is hard for my mother to adjust to no longer being the Duchess. You were wonderfully gracious, and I was so proud of you that night,' he said, placing his hand on her arm, but his wife flinched at his touch, which surprised him and the rest of the tea party. There was a studied silence as tea was sipped, and cake was crumbled on delicate plates.

Alex stood up, feeling unwelcome. 'Well, I must retire to my study until dinner to go through my correspondence. You ladies must have much to catch up on.'

'Arabella, your ring is stunning, I have never seen such a large diamond,' exclaimed Aunt Harriet as he left the room, not acknowledging his departure.

***

He entered his father's old study and smoothed his hands over the large mahogany desk. Everything was as his father had left it – his pen, his blotter, his seal, all ready for a return which never came. He was once again overcome by the absence of his father. There was a large pile of letters his secretary had left him in order of importance to attend to. There was a stack of condolence cards edged with black, and another smaller pile of crisp, white invitations which he hoped would please Arabella who looked forward to being welcomed into Society. Now aged twenty-two, he was a Duke and a husband, and the weight of responsibility bore down on him. Life had been so much simpler as a Viscount, or rather back in Venice. He wished it was just the two of them tonight, although that would be impossible as her family seemed to always be around. He knew he was being churlish, especially after his own family had behaved so badly.

***

When he went to dress for dinner, Alex was relieved to see that the master suite – with its connecting suite for the mistress of the house – had been made ready for their arrival, and his mother had been unable to interfere in the running of the London house. These suites of rooms had little personal value to either of his parents as they had rarely come to London – his father preferring to stay in his club if his mother had not accompanied him, which she seldom did, preferring the countryside. Alex was worried now at the cost of keeping two large households and determined to look into savings to be prudent and not too extravagant with their finances. He hoped Arabella would have no immediate plans to refurbish this home as the rooms were spacious and elegant, more modern than the Abbey, whereas the thought of the cost of renovations there made Alex wince.

As George held out his dinner jacket, Arabella entered through the connecting door. She shimmered in a green, silk dress cut low, giving a glimpse of pale breasts. Around her neck she wore the diamond necklace which he had purchased for her in Paris – Arabella hinting it would be a handsome pair matching her ring. It sparkled in its magnificence, and he had to admire the way it enhanced her beauty.

'You look absolutely wonderful.' Alex gazed adoringly at his wife, who looked radiantly back at him.

'It is so lovely to be home at last.' She seemed to glide towards him as she stretched her hands towards him and George discreetly left the room.

'Are you happy, my love?' Alex enquired, as he took her hands.

'More than happy,' she replied, kissing him passionately, pushing her tongue into his willing mouth. It was all he could do not to undress her and pull her onto the bed, but he was aware they were expected at dinner.

'I have a request, my love.' She pulled away slightly, gazing into his eyes. 'Would you mind if my aunt and uncle stayed on here? Just while I establish myself? This house is so daunting, and I am terrified of all that I am expected to do, so it would bring me great comfort.'

'Of course, my darling. This is your home now, and you need never ask permission for your family to stay.' He could not deny her, although his heart sank and he wondered if they would ever be alone.

'And Sophia too?' she asked tentatively. 'I know she is another man's child, but I look on her as my own beloved daughter.'

'You, my love, are too kind, but of course she can stay. We must make her feel welcome.' Alex felt selfish beside her kind, loving nature – she just wanted to ensure the happiness of the people she cared about, whereas he just wanted his wife to himself.

The dinner gong sounded and so they joined the rest of the family in the small drawing room for drinks.

As they settled into their chairs for a small family dinner, Alex couldn't help but notice how the elegant green dining room emphasised Arabella's beauty, and he smiled at how easily she fitted into the London house, how at home she appeared, and he once again knew a surge of happiness - the previous days at the Abbey with all their tensions melted into the back of his memories.

'Why do you smile?' Arabella asked with a laugh from the other end of the table, correctly seated this time as his Duchess.

'I was thinking how perfect you look in this house and how lucky I am,' he declared, and with that he raised his glass to her.

'Dear Aunt and Uncle,' Arabella said, pressing her hand onto her uncle's, who sat to her right. 'Alex and I want you to stay here indefinitely, as I need all the help I can get to come to terms with all this grandeur!' she trilled gaily.

'As if we would say no,' exclaimed Aunt Harriet. 'We have always tried to support you ever since your dear parents died, and we are so pleased to see you make such a grand marriage, a Duchess no less, and we could not be prouder, could we, John?'

'No, we could not, and as long as his Grace is happy for us to stay, then stay we will.' John looked at Alex.

'You are family now,' Alex declared, although he was a little annoyed that Arabella had said they could stay indefinitely when their earlier conversation had made it sound like it would be for a short time. But he knew he could not raise that here, so instead he assured them, 'You will always be welcome here. You too, Sophia.' He turned to the quiet, subdued girl on his left, whose wine and food were untouched.

'Thank you, your Grace,' she murmured, not meeting his eye.

'Alex, everyone must call me Alex, I cannot stand all these titles,' he spoke softly to Sophia, hoping the girl would come to accept him at some stage and not feel like she had to stand on ceremony, for that must be what was clearly making her so uncomfortable.

'Of course, my Mary is going nowhere,' Arabella said, looking happily to the dour woman on her left – who had steadfastly been eating her food, no emotions crossing the plain face. For a reason Alex couldn't quite put his finger on, her presence was the most troubling of all, but perhaps it was because he sensed her dislike of him.

'Well, isn't this just dandy,' Aunt Harriet said with a smile. 'One happy family at last.'

'It will be fortunate for Arabella to have you around her, as I fear I will be busy the next few weeks,' Alex announced as dinner was finishing, and the ladies were getting ready to retire.

'Why so, my love?' Arabella's eyes narrowed, surprised by the first mention of him having much to attend to.

'The Prime Minister has called an election, and I need to talk with various political friends. Lord Hartington has invited me to attend a meeting at my club tomorrow. Obviously, I intend to take up my seat in the House of Lords, but I need to define my role and acquire some allies.'

'How exciting, my love.' He was a little surprised that his wife didn't seem to share his enthusiasm, particularly after they had talked at length about reform. 'But I was hoping you would be around to help me establish my own place within Society with the Season about to begin. You know it won't easy for me, and now it looks as if you are deserting me.'

'I will be on hand to accompany you to such events as require it,' he assured her. 'But you know how much this means to me; we spoke of it on numerous occasions and now is the perfect time for me to become involved.' He watched in confusion as her face changed, with anger burning in her eyes.

'Do you truly think they will take much notice of you though?' Her words were pointed and deliberate. 'Why, you are a mere boy of twenty-two, hardly experienced except with other people's wives.' She laughed cruelly as he blushed at the accusation. The room was silent – even the footmen were frozen in their tasks, eyes darting towards Emmerson to see what they should do, but the butler waited too, unsure of himself.

Alex felt for the first time that he seemed to be in a room of strangers. He was shocked at his wife's rebuke, puzzled as to what had brought it on and why she felt compelled to behave this way in company.

Arabella rose from her seat before he had the chance to reply. 'Ladies, shall we take our coffee in the drawing room and leave the men to talk politics, seeing as though it interests my husband so.' She laughed again and swept from the room, leaving Alex with John, the older man embarrassed by his niece's outburst.

'She does not mean it. She has always had a bit of a temper,' John assured Alex while puffing on a fat cigar. 'She is also a bit worried about Society. You know what women are like, and she wasn't particularly well received in Venice by the English, if you remember. She simply needs to find her way.'

Alex, as humiliated as he was, could not be rude in his own house, and signalled for the port and brandy to be brought to the table.

'She knows how much I want to take my place in politics, although you are right – it won't be easy for Arabella, so perhaps I have neglected that.' Alex sighed as he remembered Lady Lyborn and his own mother and how they had treated his wife. He now understood how him sharing his plans may leave her feeling that she was being thrown to the wolves. They finished their drinks in silence before going to join the ladies, only to find the drawing room was already empty. Alex was informed his wife had retired to bed with a headache and was not to be disturbed. He spent a restless night feeling not just her absence but the sting of her earlier words.

Chapter Twenty-Four

Those first few weeks were difficult and put further strain on relations between the newlyweds. It appeared that London Society was not ready to accept Arabella into its midst even though she was married to one of the premier Dukes of the realm. She waited in morning after morning for visits from the Society ladies who never came, took carriage rides in Hyde Park where she was never acknowledged, and there was a discerning lack of invitations to social gatherings.

Alex dreaded coming home from his meetings at the House of Lords, where he was slowly launching his own political career, to see his wife's disappointment.

'Why don't you reach out to your friends in the women's movement?' Alex suggested one May evening when he had arrived home late. Arabella had burst into his bedroom as he was getting ready for bed, distraught at the continuing lack of interest from her peers. 'In Venice, you were so keen to return to your causes, and I am sure Millicent Fawcett would be glad of your help and support. I could speak to her husband Henry if you wished?' He hoped this would give her a purpose or at least something to keep her occupied, although he had been surprised she hadn't acted on this herself. Perhaps she feared that now she was responsible for the household, he would not approve of her attending such meetings, so he wanted to reassure her he supported her endeavours.

'Of course, I want to do that eventually, but don't you see what good I could do if I had a place in Society – the influence I could bring.' Her eyes were shining with tears as she sank down onto the bed and pulled him towards her. 'I want to play a part in social reform as much as you, but I can't achieve that if I hide myself away in back streets, workhouses, and hospitals. If I am to bring my patronage and attention to the causes I want to champion, I need contacts, don't you see?'

Alex agreed she had a point, and after all she deserved to be recognised as his Duchess. The first major event of the Season at the Queen's Drawing Room was not long off, and etiquette demanded they had been invited. The new Duchess of Ushington was required to be presented to Queen Victoria or another senior royal. It did not necessarily mean that his wife would be accepted into Society afterwards, and Alex was concerned that Arabella would still feel snubbed.

'Let me speak with Lord Hartington – to see what can be done,' he cajoled, trying to take her into his arms, but she twisted away from him.

'Do what you can, as I cannot continue like this, Alex. I will return to Europe with or without you. There, at least I would be recognised and received as a Duchess.' Arabella swept from the room, slamming the interconnecting door, and as the key turned in the lock it felt as if it was not only locking him out of his wife's bedroom but out of her life. She had seemed so happy when they had arrived in London, and he was unsure of how to handle her change in mood and low spirits. He sighed and climbed into the large, empty bed facing another night alone, an all too often occurrence of late, the intimacy of both Venice and Paris swiftly disappearing. He hoped that once Society accepted her, they could get back to their previous happiness. If his wife's own spirits were restored, perhaps she would feel more amorous.

***

The next day at his club, he sought out Spencer Cavendish, Lord Hartington. He hated disturbing such an important man with his own domestic business, but if he wanted to advance his political career, he needed Arabella to be happy. He worried that her threat of returning to Europe was not an empty one, which would draw unwanted attention to his marriage and overshadow any endeavours he'd been making within politics.

Hartington was alone in the club's drawing room, drinking coffee as Alex approached him.

'Ushington, come and join me,' the older man called to him. 'I wanted to talk to you about Gladstone's campaign.'

'Thank you,' Alex said, sitting down as Hartington poured him a coffee. 'I have a somewhat delicate matter I wish to talk over with you first, if you don't mind?'

'Of course. I noticed you have been distracted recently. I put it down to newly wedded bliss!' he said with a chuckle, but then noticed the strain on Alex's face.

'I wish it was so.' Alex sighed, and he proceeded to confide in him what had been happening, how Society was snubbing his wife and how she was threatening to leave for Europe if the situation continued. 'I don't know what to do,' he conceded, running his hand through his hair.

'Women can be terribly snobbish creatures, I'm afraid, and sticklers for tradition. Unfortunately, your wife is not only an American, not even a rich one at that, but the widow of a merchant. I believe that the Dowager Duchess, your mother, is also not best pleased with your marriage, and she still has some influence with the older generation who don't take well to change.' He signalled for more coffee as Alex slumped dishearteningly in his chair at Lord Hartington's warning. 'However, the Liberal Party needs you, and we want to ensure your happiness. Society needs to change all this nonsense, if you ask me. I will speak to my dear friend, the Duchess of Manchester, and ask her to take your wife under her wing. Between you and me, the Duke of Manchester keeps her in financial penury, so if you pay her handsomely, she will smooth the way for you both.

She will be most sympathetic to your wife's predicament, as she herself knows all too well what Society can be like.'

Alex knew of course about the rumours regarding Louisa, Duchess of Manchester. A German by birth, she had married the Duke in 1852 and bore him five children, but the marriage for all its fecundity had not been successful. With her husband becoming more and more unstable, it was said that she had turned to Hartington for comfort and their closeness had been much speculated over. However, she was an influential woman in her own right – a friend of both the Prince and Princess of Wales – and therefore would be well-placed to help Arabella, whose spirits would hopefully be lifted by a powerful ally.

True to his word, Hartington dispatched the formidable Duchess to Ushington House, and within days Arabella found doors to salons, soirees, and other such events opening slowly to her. She was a good match with Lady Louisa, who was as forthright and imperious as Arabella was, and they found they understood each other well. Both were outsiders and with disastrous marriages in common, although Arabella chose not to speak of her first marriage to Sir Charles. Lady Louisa admired Arabella's resilience, whose story resonated with her own unhappy marriage. She was therefore determined to make Arabella a success.

Alex was relieved to see Arabella's spirits much restored, although now she was rarely home as she and the Duchess embarked on a social offensive to ingratiate her into London Society. In no time at all, Arabella had been introduced to Edward, Prince of Wales – a man who appreciated beauty and had a fondness for Americans. The Prince also relied on his confidante, the Lady Louisa, and her judgement in bringing anyone into his inner circle, so Arabella soon charmed him. He enjoyed her sharp wit and her flirtatious ways. Arabella was finally finding her place in Society, just as Alex was finding his way in politics. Alex hoped that soon Arabella would use her newfound

influence and become the political hostess they had
envisioned in Venice to complement his own work striving
for new legislation.

Chapter Twenty-Five

August and the Season were both drawing to an end, but Alex had barely seen his wife, as her diary was always full. He too had been busy with his political endeavours, so he was pleasantly surprised to find Arabella alone at the breakfast table, whereas usually she would take it in her bedroom.

'Good morning, my love,' Arabella spoke brightly, smiling at him.

'Good morning to you too. How lovely to see you.' Alex had moved around the table to kiss her before taking his own seat opposite her.

'Well, I thought we hadn't seen each other so much lately apart from last night, of course.' She laughed softly. The previous night, she had actually come to his room sometime after 2 a.m. and aroused him to such an extent he had no time to resist her even if he had wanted to. It had been a long time since they had been together sexually, and he had been overcome in the ecstasy of the moment. However, he had fallen asleep quickly afterwards and by the time he had awoken she had gone.

'Yes, you do appear rather busy and popular,' he grimaced, accepting the coffee from the butler.

'And what is that face for?' Arabella spoke sharply.

'Simply that it would be nice to dine with you occasionally, and why pray is your Aunt Harriet seemingly still running this house instead of you?' He had resented waking alone after the intimacy of the night and had felt her absence even more.

'You know such things bore me, and why should I spend my time on dreary household matters such as menus and the servants' minor problems? As for my so-called neglect of you – you would seem to prefer to go to meetings at your club rather than come to such frivolous things as balls and soirees – your words, by the way!' she intercepted the protestation that formed on his lips.

The atmosphere had quickly turned, and they glared at each other across the table. The butler discreetly motioned to the other serving staff to leave the room as he stepped back out of sight.

'I thought you believed they were frivolous too. When will you be interested in my work? In fact, everything we discussed in Venice, you no longer want to be involved in. All I hear is of you gallivanting around with the Prince of Wales and his set, but of course he has always had a thing for Americans,' he spoke bitterly.

'Perhaps I cultivate such people as His Royal Highness for your good, and I have my own causes which I do in fact actively promote. In fact, tonight I am attending the Society for Women's Welfare fundraiser, and I was hoping you would accompany me and support the cause.' She spoke softly now, and he felt stupid – childish even – at his outburst.

'Well, that's the first time you have spoken about your causes since Venice, so forgive me for doubting your motives,' he spoke petulantly, still not ready to concede to her. 'Unfortunately, I have a meeting tonight at Parliament to discuss my political future, which I will succeed at with or without the Prince's influence, and if you had been around, you would have known how advanced I have come with realising my ambitions.'

'My life does not revolve around you and your career. I foolishly thought you would be pleased I had been accepted by Society, that at last I was having some fun.' Tears welled up in her dark eyes, her pale skin now flushed. 'You know how hard my life has been, and for once I wanted to laugh, to dance, and be happy. I would have hoped you of all people would not begrudge me this.'

Alex wanted her to understand how much he missed being with her, but he stubbornly continued, his resentment lingering. 'Of course, I want you to be happy, but every night you come in later and later. You are never home; even at weekends I am told you have gone to stay at some such estate for a house party, or you are at Ascot, Henley, any event going,' he could hear himself whining, 'I look a fool, Arabella, for you never tell me where you are – I have to ask your aunt or Mrs Moffet, the housekeeper! Only yesterday, I was asked by one of the members at my club why I never accompany my beautiful wife. The joke is that the Prince of Wales sees more of you than I do, and we both know what that infers.' *Do you even love me*, he thought, as he watched disgust flit across his wife's face. He could not bring himself to ask her, scared as he was of her answer.

Arabella flinched. 'Listen to yourself, Alex, you sound pathetic. And how dare you suggest I am the Prince's mistress. I do try to tell you where I am, but I can never find you! You are either closeted with your secretary; at the House of Lords; or at one of your wretched gentleman's clubs, which I can hardly enter to tell you all my movements. You never said you wanted to keep me a prisoner here. You were all for women having an independent life, and now you want a stay-at-home wife with no friends, having no fun.' And with those words she rose from her chair and swept from the room.

***

Alex left the Houses of Parliament as the clock chimed nine, stepping into a light evening shower – as summer was coming to an end, the nights were slowly getting darker. His meeting had finished earlier than expected and he was buoyed by the news he had finally been given a place in Gladstone's cabinet working with Henry Fawcett – a man who believed in social reform and women's rights as much as he did. Alex felt like he was making progress at last and was excited to tell Arabella of his new role. As the evening was yet young, he decided to surprise his wife at the ball.

As Alex walked the short distance to the fundraiser at Grosvenor House, he hoped his appearance would show Arabella his unwavering support and try to mend the disagreement from that morning. Alex was relieved he had walked when he noticed the long line of carriages waiting outside the house as guests kept arriving. The powdered footmen stood to attention as Alex joined bejewelled guests entering the porticoed front doors, and he was ushered into a vast decorated hall with a soaring marble staircase. Flowers overflowed in large Grecian urns – their perfume making the air heady – and he could hear applause from the rooms above, the ball already a lively affair.

After dropping off his hat, he had made his way through the throng of people, climbing the staircase to the reception rooms above. There was to be an auction later to gain funds for the women's hospital in the East End, and Alex knew that some of the most powerful aristocracy had already pledged to help. The women's movement had moved apace in recent years, and working with Henry Fawcett now meant he could fully align himself with it and make the positive strides he had long sought.

He entered the large salon, where one of the guest speakers had just finished. He scanned the room for Arabella and spotted her talking earnestly to a group of friends. As he was about to make his way to her, he was waylaid by two older ladies whom he vaguely recognised.

'Your Grace, how delightful that you have come to support us. We have been told such admirable things about you from our dear husbands. I am Lady Constance Lytton, and this is Lady Dorothy Stafford.' Both ladies had the bearings of importance and of wealth. Alex knew them to be major contributors to that night's events and that they were in fact patrons of the hospital that the fundraiser was in aid of.

'Ladies – a pleasure and honour to make your acquaintance. Your husbands are indeed good friends. You must of course know my wife, Arabella,' he said, gesturing towards her, still conversing and not yet noticing his arrival amongst the crowded room.

'Only vaguely,' Lady Dorothy demurred, with little enthusiasm.

'Oh, I thought as a longtime supporter of your cause, especially after the end of her previous marriage, you must have met by now,' Alex explained, surprised by their muted responses.

'Ah, yes, well, she did attend one of our rallies not long after Sir Charles's death. You must remember, Dorothy,' Lady Constance said, raising her eyebrows to her friend, 'that occasion when she spoke of her own experience to those poor women in the East End?'

'I do indeed remember, Constance, it was held at the hospital, and the women had all experienced violence in the home. Most of them had significant physical injuries that had brought them into the hospital, they were battered and bruised, if memory serves me well,' she said with an abject look in her eye. 'Lady Arabella was the picture of health and wealth, and forgive me if I speak out of turn, your Grace, but she was not a popular speaker. It appeared as if she revelled in her so-called misfortune, and she showed little empathy to those poor women, which was strange given the circumstances.' Dorothy's lips were pursed, and Alex sensed yet more animosity towards his wife.

'But I thought she had helped out at the hospital?' Alex enquired, uncomfortable to hear their account.

'You must be mistaking her with Sophia Pembrook, Sir Charles's daughter. She was a regular volunteer with us at one time. A dear, sweet girl similar to her mother, Elizabeth, but of course you put a stop to her time with us, I believe?' Lady Constance confronted him. Alex was confused by her words, and as he was about to question her further, there was a tight grip on his arm, and his wife appeared.

'Alex, darling, what a lovely surprise,' she said with a smile, but she seemed tense at his appearance. 'And I see you have met some of our lovely patrons. My husband is enamoured with women's rights and hopes to do some good in his own small way, don't you, darling?' It was not lost on him that her tone was disparaging, belittling his endeavours in politics. The ladies quickly made their excuses, leaving them to each other.

'I did not expect to see you,' she said, her words dripping with disdain.

'My meeting finished early and I thought I would surprise you, showing an interest and supporting you as you wanted.' He had thought she would have been more welcoming to his presence at the prestigious event.

'You did indeed surprise me, by gossiping with those old fools who know nothing about me and dislike me because they were once friends with Charles's first wife!' she hissed. 'This place is tedious and my head aches. Can you at least escort me home?'

Alex held his tongue, not deeming it appropriate to ask her about what the ladies had told him, and instead demurred to her wishes. In the carriage she studiously ignored him, and when they arrived home, she swept up the stairs to her bedroom. Alex followed her, determined to speak and clear up what must be a misunderstanding. Apart from the previous night, he had hardly been in her rooms or she in his over these past few weeks. Even when she had been home, the interconnecting door between their suites had been firmly locked on her side. He had not desired to be a husband who demanded his rights, especially after hearing how she had suffered during her previous marriage, but tonight he needed to talk to her before the rift went too far.

'How dare you follow me!' She spun around, her face white with fury.

'You're my wife and we need to talk,' he pleaded, hoping she would see sense.

'So, I am your possession, your chattel who has no privacy, is that it? You are just like all the other men. You barge in here without my permission because you know you can!' she spat the words at him, and he flinched at the ferocity of his anger.

'Please calm down and let's put this right, whatever is troubling you.' He moved towards her, trying to remonstrate with her calmly but, before he knew what had happened, her fist hit his head in a sharp blow. He turned away, clutching his head, but as he did so, she screamed, dropping to the floor theatrically, and shouted, 'Please, Alex, don't hit me again!'

Her dressing room door and the interconnecting door simultaneously burst open at her cry. Mary and George both hurried into the room, with Mary practically throwing herself at her stricken mistress and cradling Arabella in her arms as she sobbed. George appeared bemused as he surveyed the scene, while Alex stood frozen in shock. *Had she actually said that?* George, sensing his confusion, ushered him from the room and into his own bedroom suite, quietly shutting the door and locking it behind them.

Chapter Twenty-Six

'I did not hit her,' Alex whispered to himself, as George poured him a glass of brandy.

'I hope you'll forgive my intrusion, your Grace, but as soon as I heard raised voices, I came to the door to check all was well. I opened it quickly as she screamed and saw her drop to the floor with my own eyes. I could see you were turned away from her holding your head, so could not have struck her.'

'She hit me.' Alex was incredulous, it all happening in such a blur.

'Sleep on it, your Grace, and talk it over with her in the morning. I am sure it was all a misunderstanding,' he soothed.

'Wait, George.' His valet had been with him for many years, so he could sense there was something he was not saying. 'I need you to answer me truthfully. Do you have concerns over my wife?' George flushed and seemed wary to respond. 'I promise I won't be cross with you if you speak the truth, however bad it might be. You witnessed what happened just now and I have recently discovered something that has concerned me about my wife. Right now, I would appreciate honesty from someone I trust.'

George gulped. 'I don't like to speak out of turn but yes, I have my worries about both the mistress and her companion.' He took a deep breath as he took the decision to reveal all he knew to his master whatever the consequences, being in an impossible position whichever way he looked at it.

'I have to admit, my Lord, I have had my concerns since you first made the Lady's acquaintance. Of course, I could see you were smitten, but you see I recognised her type. Growing up in the streets of the East End, you learn a lot about women such as her, and I recognised the hardness in her eyes which, at first, I thought had come from her first marriage. It's her companion that scares me though – she is a piece of work.'

'What do you mean?' Alex listened intently to his valet's words, hoping it would explain what he hadn't been able to put his finger on about Mary.

George recounted a time in Venice when he had been waiting for a maid, Lucia, whom Rupert's valet had introduced him to. George was outside the servants' entrance of the Grand as Mary returned from some errand. Lucia had come out at the same time and almost collided with her.

'Stupid girl. Watch where you are going.' Mary had been brusque, and Lucia had cowered in her presence. 'Pathetic creature like all the Italian girls who work here,' she muttered to herself. She had not noticed George but pushed Lucia out of the way with such force she had stumbled, and George had to quickly catch her.

'I didn't know what to say at the time,' George explained to his master. 'You were so happy with Lady Arabella, and I suppose I thought it would all be all right. But now here in this house I'm afraid to report that Mary Manners controls the household through fear. Yes, Emmerson is in charge, but that woman is subtle; she whispers threats in the young maids' ears, and they know she has the mistress' full support. I watch her and I know what she does.'

'Good grief, George, you should have come to me sooner!' Alex gasped, ashamed to hear this bullying had been going on in his household.

'Would you have believed me?' George asked earnestly.

'I don't suppose I would have done,' he reluctantly admitted, but only because it was difficult to believe this had been allowed to happen. 'But I do now, and I need you to be my ears and eyes, to talk to no one about our conversation, and above all to be careful.'

Alex watched George leave but felt even worse, his mind in turmoil. The night had brought so many unwelcome revelations and events. He needed to speak to Arabella in the morning, to understand what was behind her sudden change of demeanour and clear up the misunderstanding about her work in the East End, as well as regaining control of his household. He would not stand by to see his servants, some of whom had been with his family for years, treated in such a manner.

***

When he awoke the next morning, Alex was determined to speak to Arabella sooner rather than later. He had expected the interconnecting door to her bedroom to be locked on Arabella's side, but it opened easily. The room was quiet, the morning sun peeping through the curtains which were slightly drawn. Her bed was empty, the sheets tousled and flung back, and he noticed indents on both pillows which momentarily puzzled him, but then he heard voices coming from the adjoining bathroom, the door was a little ajar, and he crept further into the room.

'You went too far last night – you could have blown it all.' Mary's voice was full of contempt.

'I couldn't help myself last night. I am bored with this endless charade.' Arabella sighed. 'And you need to keep an eye on his valet; I don't like the way he hovers. He was very quick to appear last night.'

'Well, if we want to be set for life, you need to get an heir by your so-called husband.' Alex's heart started to pound at what he was hearing.

'Why do you think I went to him the other night? Do you think I wanted to?' She was incredulous. 'At least I have the Prince as a friend, which makes life much easier now.' Alex could hear the smugness in her voice and he blanched.

'A stroke of luck, I admit, but you still need to sleep with your husband a bit more though,' Mary admonished her.

'Once a week is all I can stomach, but I suppose it will keep him happy at least if I give him more. I could go to him tonight, pretending to be all contrite over what happened. One suck of his little cock and he will be hard between my legs.' They both laughed and there was a large splash of water. Alex was chilled by the arrogance of her words and how easily she thought him to manipulate.

'And no preventative measures now,' Mary said, sounding stern. 'You need a son.'

'This water is getting cold – get out and ring for more before we freeze to death,' Arabella said, ignoring her, giggling again.

Alex quickly rushed back to his own bedroom before he could be discovered. His heart was racing, sweat trickled down his back, and bile rose in his throat as he tried to process what he had just heard. There was so much to take in. It appeared that his wife was not only sharing a bath with her companion, but all she wanted was his status and an heir by him – which would effectively tie her to him for life. *She does not love me*, he realised, *my marriage has been a charade! How stupid I have been.*

He rang the bell to summon George – he needed to confide in someone, and he trusted George with his life.

'What will you do, your Grace?' George was concerned as Alex paced up and down, pondering the right course of action.

'I need time to discover exactly what is going on, and we need to act as if all is well for the time being. Can I count on you to help me?' He met George's eye.

'Of course, your Grace.'

Alex was relieved to have at least one ally in this house of vipers. He knew he must now be on his guard and not succumb to Arabella's seductive ways, all while trying to maintain the façade that his feelings had not changed and he did not suspect her plans. *How quickly*, he mused, *that love can turn to repulsion*. He didn't want to believe what he had discovered but surely the signs had been there since they had returned to London, even if he had been desperate not to admit it? Arabella had barely been in his company, had shown no interest in his work, and only seemed interested in what she could gain from Society. He was sickened that he had facilitated that, even pitying her to the point he had arranged the acquaintance of Lady Louisa to make powerful allies for her. His mother's words came back to haunt him, and he dreaded what she would say if there was a scandal or a divorce, so he had to handle this with great care, and it was imperative that Arabella suspected nothing.

Chapter Twenty-Seven

Later, as they all sat down to luncheon, the green of the dining room seemed to close in on him, the sounds of children playing in the park outside making a mockery of his prior happiness and Alex could barely eat. Arabella entered the room full of gaiety and sparkle, laughing with her aunt and teasing her uncle. It was as if the events of last night had not happened and she had never uttered those ghastly words that morning to Mary.

Sophia had slipped in quietly behind them, taking her seat, and now she sat picking at her food. She was pale and tired – a mirror of Alex's own despair. At least Mary had not made an appearance, as Alex could not have borne her presence. Now all he could hear was the loud ticking of the clock on the marble fireplace as time stretched ahead of him – a future married to a woman he now knew had never loved him.

'Alex, my love, are you well?' Arabella's words cut through his misery like a blunt knife.

'Yes, of course.' He attempted a smile, but he could not manage an endearment despite his best efforts to carry on as normal.

'I was asking you what plans you have today?' she continued gaily.

'I'm afraid I have work to do,' he replied, hoping that if he did indeed seem distracted, she would put it down to business affairs and ask no further questions.

'So, Mary and I can use the carriage?' He nodded his head listlessly as she continued to arrange her day. 'I have an appointment at the dressmakers. Aunt Harriet, do you wish to come too? It will be such fun.'

'Your uncle and I have an appointment today.' She looked tellingly at her niece and gave no further information, and Arabella nodded slightly as if she understood their secret meaning.

'Sophia, perhaps you would like to come instead of staying cooped up in the library again?' She fixed her gaze on the poor girl, who looked up startled at the mention of her name.

'Oh, I have such a headache and feel so tired. I would much prefer to stay here.' Her voice trembled as she made her request.

'If you must. You are becoming so dreary. You need another one of Mary's tonics for your head,' Arabella advised. 'I will ask her to make sure you take one before we leave.'

They were soon dispersed in a flurry of energy after luncheon, and Alex retired to his study where he sank into the chair, listening to the quiet of the house until a light tap at the door disturbed his troubled thoughts.

Alex was surprised to see Sophia timidly standing there and was once again struck by the paleness of her skin; how thin she had become and the tiredness showed in her eyes of late.

'May I speak with you privately?' she whispered.

'Of course. I wish to speak with you too.' He gestured towards the two chairs by the window and closed the door behind her. They could see across the park, where the trees were just starting to turn into their autumn colours. Alex briefly wondered where this disjointed family would all go once the London Season officially ended in a matter of weeks from now. Society would be moving to their own country homes, and it was unlikely that the Abbey would be habitable.

'Before you speak, Sophia, I have a matter I wish to clear up. I met Lady Constance Lytton last night and she mentioned that I had stopped you volunteering at the hospital. What did she mean by that?' Alex spoke gently, as he could sense a nervousness about the girl when he broached the subject.

'Arabella told me you had forbidden it and claimed it was unseemly given my name and my father's reputation. I sent a note to Lady Lytton apologising. I am sorry if I did wrong, but I didn't want Lady Lytton to think I had let them down, as I had so enjoyed my work there.'

'No, no, I am not annoyed in the slightest. I couldn't be, because you see I never said that. I would never forbid you to do anything. I am not your guardian after all, although I want you to be happy with us and well-cared for.'

'Oh, that is most odd, but then again maybe not. I have wanted to speak to you but have been hesitant to raise it. You see, I think Arabella is preventing me from communicating with my father's lawyer. I have tried to write to him, but my letters go unanswered. I thought I would speak directly to you to see if you had forbidden this also, as I couldn't understand why you would.' She could see from Alex's response that he hadn't, and he nodded at her to carry on. 'I wish to return home in a few months when I am eighteen, when my trust fund and shares become mine.'

'When you are eighteen?' Alex seemed perplexed. 'Surely you mean when you are of age?'

'My father believed I should have my independence at eighteen – he felt women had the right to their freedom and have more than just marriage to look forward to. In the event of my father's death, Matthew was to inherit the business and estates but only when he reached twenty-one, after he had finished university. My father thought that it would allow him that time without the pressures his inheritance would bring,' she explained. 'So, you see I want to go back to Manchester, to continue my parents' work in social reform. I have nothing here, I feel so alone, and I have had no word from my brother Matthew either.'

'Your father supported social reform?' Alex asked, leaning forward.

'Yes, of course. He was well known for it, especially when my mother was alive.'

'But Arabella insisted he was against it, that he was still involved with slavery,' Alex recalled their conversation in Venice months prior.

'Arabella says a lot of things which are untrue! Especially about my father, who was a good man. He would never have been involved with slavery.' Sophia was horrified by the accusation.

Alex thought back to the previous night, to the words he had overheard that morning, and once again he began to doubt everything his wife had ever told him.

'I came to speak to you about helping me get away.' Sophia looked at him beseechingly. 'I believe Arabella is hiding my letters and I am worried what she will do next. I sensed today something had happened between you and decided to seize my chance in case it is my only one. Am I wrong?' Her voice was stronger now and more determined.

'No, you are not wrong,' his voice stuttered. 'Last night, I started to question my own sanity, and now I don't know what the truth is, what lies I have been told, and what I should do next.' He sank back in his chair and briefly closed his eyes, as if to help clear everything that troubled him.

'I wanted to warn you in Venice, but they kept me from you when they could. I was too scared to speak out, knowing Mary followed me everywhere,' Sophia spoke in earnest. 'Arabella practically dragged me away from you that day at the Academia just in case I got too familiar with you and prevented the opportunity of us speaking alone. Every meeting, everything she did in Venice, was aimed at ensnaring you and I was helpless to stop her. I knew you were falling for her, and when you spoke about my father, I knew you believed her lies and that she had got her wish.'

'Did your father speak to you about her? Kitty Jobson thought you were close to Arabella.'

'My biggest regret is believing her lies and ever doubting my father. He spoke of his sanity too, of being fooled, and I didn't want to believe him, for Arabella seemed so nice at first and initially restored his happiness. But he wrote to me just before they left for Ravenscourt that final time. He was so unwell, and the note was strange.' She paused, as if remembering what had troubled her about it. 'He told me he was afraid to go there for he hated that house, and he worried he would not see me again. It was then I started to have my own doubts for I knew he would never have chosen to go there. But he also stated he would write down everything that was happening and send it to Sir David Norton, our lawyer, so we would know the truth in time.'

'And did he?' Alex pressed.

'Sir David never heard from him after he left for Ravenscourt, and of course, Arabella could have destroyed any papers that awful night – especially anything which discredited her.'

'But there's a chance it exists?' Alex persisted hopefully.

'Yes, and knowing my father, he would have made sure it was hidden somewhere in the house, most likely his study for safekeeping, if he was afraid of her,' Sophia ventured.

'We need to find it.' Alex was sure it would give him the answers they both needed and may even help him get out of the marriage. It was a long shot but had to be worth a try. He wanted desperately to avoid any scandal which would devastate his mother further than he already had.

'She watches me like a hawk, her and that awful woman, so I don't see her allowing me to leave. It has to be you, but you would need to lie. She must not know you are going to Ravenscourt, and you must not allow her to accompany you,' Sophia urged, and he understood now how scared she was of his wife, and he recognised the same fear within himself. Ravenscourt was where Sir Charles had died, and it could hold the truth.

'You are right, Sophia, we need to be careful. Listen, I can write to your lawyer via my club and arrange to get access to Ravenscourt on your behalf. If you could write to him giving me your permission, I can send it. I agree that your mail is most likely being intercepted, so we need to send and receive any communication outside of this house,' he advised as they came up with their plan.

'Mary sees everything, and I have long suspected her influence within this house. The younger servants are scared of her and of Arabella – after all, she is the mistress. I am sure the maid who cleans my room spies on me but what can I do?' Sophia turned to him for help. 'I cannot challenge Arabella, and to be honest I feel so tired these days; my head aches, and I have no appetite, so I keep to my room whenever I can.' He could see the shadows under her eyes and the strain this was having on her health. He was no longer surprised – all this time she had lived with Arabella knowing her own father had been afraid of her, so it was bound to take its toll.

'Never fear, Sophia,' he said, squeezing her hand to reassure her. 'We will find out what is going on and I will ask your lawyer – you say it's Sir David Norton in Manchester – about the correspondence,' she nodded her confirmation, 'and why don't you write to Matthew so he can hear from you too. He must be worried about his sister.' At the mention of her brother, Sophia brightened. 'I'll go and speak to Emmerson to ask him to alert me if the carriage returns. Hurry, Sophia, I want to leave for my club before they come home but must have your letter. They must not suspect anything. I believe we can trust Emmerson as he is my family's man through and through.' Alex hoped that he was, as he remembered George's account about the fear in his own household which Alex had allowed to happen without even knowing it. If he was to be able to successfully execute his plan, he needed those he trusted around him.

Chapter Twenty-Eight

Alex kept to his club as much as possible, trying to immerse himself in his work as he waited to hear back from Sir David Norton after writing to him. But he found it hard to concentrate on social reform whilst trying to work through the mess of his own marriage. He tried to keep up the pretence that all was well, although at times he wondered if he had dreamed the conservation he had overheard. Whenever he began to doubt it, he thought of Sophia's pale face that day she came to speak with him in his study, and it reminded him that it was all too true.

'There you are, my darling,' Arabella said, coming into the dining room, surprising him once more at breakfast on an early September morning, resplendent in her dark pink, silk dressing gown which emphasised her curves, her glorious dark hair cascading down her back. 'Oh, did I startle you?' She smiled as his coffee cup shook.

'Well, it is rather early for you, and you were out late last night, so I thought you would sleep in.' He swallowed back the bile that had risen in his mouth and tried his best to sound pleased at her appearance.

'We never see each other, my love,' she purred as she walked behind him, her hands gently massaging his shoulders. 'You are so tense, preoccupied with work making you quite the dull husband.' He let out an involuntary shudder as she wrapped her arms around him, pressing her face against his, her breasts against his back. 'Don't you miss me in your bed? Always locking your door because you are so tired,' she mocked.

'We need to talk about your spending.' He stood up abruptly, and Arabella stumbled backwards in amazement, for when she used her femininely wiles, he normally could not resist. 'Your debts are out of control beyond your monthly allowance, and it seems I am funding your aunt and uncle too.' He knew he was being too combative, but he needed to force an argument in order to get away from her and not succumb to her advances. His secretary had informed him yesterday that the household bills were getting high and various debts were mounting up. There were piles of dressmaking bills for Arabella and Harriet, plus the gambling chits of John Burton, as well as restaurant bills the man seemed to have accumulated over the past few months.

'Is this because of that silly misunderstanding the other night?' She began to put some food on her plate, serving herself from one of the breakfast tureens. 'You are punishing me for my little temper? I am so sorry, my love – I was most distraught over those awful women gossiping about me to my own husband. You know I didn't mean it, don't you?' She sat down at the table, watching him as he stood completely still.

'Oh, do sit down, Alex, you are making me nervous.' She laughed, no real remorse in her face as he stood, unsure of what to do. 'What is wrong with you? Can we not forget that night and move on, or are you determined to make me beg? Is that why you lock your door – are you scared of little me? Ah, Emmerson, there you are.' Arabella briefly turned her attention to the butler, who had appeared in the doorway. 'Could you bring us some fresh coffee; this pot is positively lukewarm and tastes awful. In future, please ensure it is fresh and hot when I come down.'

She watched as the butler retreated obediently.

'No, my love, of course I am not scared of you.' His words felt like glass in his throat, but he forced himself to utter them. 'I am just concerned regarding your bills. I was told you have engaged an interior designer for this residence when we had not discussed it.' He sat back down, hoping it would look like he was making an effort.

'Yes, I have! Although if you had been around, I would have told you myself.' She was animated now as she relayed her vision. 'I want to emulate Marlborough House – Princess Alexander has such wonderful taste, don't you think? This house is too stark, uncluttered, and so I have been shopping for more antiques to furnish it with. I can't do it alone, of course, so Her Highness kindly gave me the name of their own designer. Imagine how excited I was when he had availability. I know you won't mind, as you did say I needed to treat this as my home to reflect my tastes.'

'I wish we had discussed this,' Alex protested. 'I like the uncluttered look, and you despised Wisteston Abbey for that reason – you insisted it was too cluttered, and we are already spending much money on modernising it.'

'The Abbey is not the same, darling, it's old and boring. Marlborough House is so modern and if we want to entertain the Prince, we need him to feel comfortable,' she reasoned.

'At what cost?' he countered. 'We need to talk about this later, Arabella, before you go too far.'

'We could talk about it tonight – just you and me like it used to be,' she said, smiling suggestively. Alex recoiled, knowing exactly what she meant. Once more he stood up hastily, with a strong compulsion to flee from her, the room, and from what his life had become.

'We will discuss it with my secretary when my diary allows. In the meantime, no further expenditure will be signed off,' he warned, eager to put his foot down to protect his finances. 'Now, I must be gone. Enjoy your day.' Alex could not look at her as he left, not wanting to see what would be in her eyes this time – anger or tears.

She had acted so calmly and played the part of the injured party, yet she could make his body desire her with just one touch. He wanted more than anything to be able to believe she loved him, but her words haunted him. There had never been love, he knew that now. His own family and Rupert would laugh if they could see him now. How right they had been. He had heard that Rupert was still abroad, and he missed his friend's company, which he needed more than ever.

Alex hoped to hear from Sophia's lawyer soon with the answers he sought. He had to know what had happened at Ravenscourt and if Sir Charles had known anything about his wife's past which could help his cause to end his marriage while avoiding the scandal of divorce. At night he made sure he locked the door to his bedroom again, ignoring the rattling of the handle, feigning sleep which when it did come came with dreams and nightmares that pursued him in his waking hours. Hours he spent in all-consuming business meetings to keep him from the house as he waited for word from Manchester, which could not come quickly enough.

Chapter Twenty-Nine

The letter he hoped for finally arrived after five long days. It confirmed Alex's and Sophia's fears that neither Sir David Norton nor Matthew Pembrook had received Sophia's letters. There was also growing concern over letters they had also sent to Sophia, which had gone unanswered. Alex knew she had never received them. He could not understand why Arabella would have intercepted such correspondence. Sophia would soon be eighteen and Matthew was due to inherit his father's business as he was entering his final year at Oxford. He was also puzzled as to why Sir David, as Sophia's guardian, had not intervened when he had not heard from her?

The lawyer had consented to meet Alex, agreeing that there was too much to discuss by letter, while Matthew had also approved Alex's visit to Ravenscourt. The letter burned in his pocket when Alex had returned to Ushington House that evening. He wanted to leave immediately but he would need to explain his prolonged absence to his wife without arousing suspicion.

As he entered the hall, Emmerson approached him enquiring whether he was dining with the rest of the family that evening. Alex was dismayed to find that they were home, but perhaps it was after all fortuitous as he could inform them of his fictitious trip in person – there would be no misunderstanding and it would appear that he did not have anything to hide.

He hurried up the stairs to get changed and to inform George of his plans.

'I need to be gone early tomorrow,' he informed his valet in a hushed tone. 'There must be no chance of anyone following me.'

'Am I to accompany you, your Grace?'

'No, I think it is better if I go alone and you remain here to keep an eye on Miss Sophia.' George nodded in agreement. 'Pack a light bag for me – enough for a week. I will send word via my club, so try to get there each day if you can. They already know to expect you.'

'Will you travel by train or by the carriage?' George asked.

'Carriage would take far too long, and she will find out when I plan to go. I trust few people in this house not to inform her. I have my train ticket – one of the club servants procured it for me. The train leaves tomorrow at dawn before the house stirs. Now I need to go down to dinner.' The gong sounded. 'Remember, not a word to anyone, even Emmerson.' He still trusted no one apart from George, even though the butler had been with his family a long time.

Alex's palms were already sweating as all eyes turned to him upon entering the drawing room. He wondered what they actually thought of him despite their smiles. Arabella's words replayed in his mind. He knew now that he had been too easily entranced by her, his body was weak and his heart too willing. He dared not recall his mother's words or think about the disappointment his father would now be feeling, so it was a blessing in some guise that he had not lived to see this.

'Alex, my love, how wonderful that you are able to join us.' He marvelled at Arabella's duplicity, as she rushed to embrace him, almost making him believe she was happy to see him. He greeted her aunt and uncle, trying to hide his disgust at this greedy, conniving pair – only today he had once again been looking at the household accounts and realised how much they were costing him.

Mary Manners met his eyes defiantly as always – he steeled himself against her gaze. He could not falter in his own pretence but fortunately she hated him so much that she barely acknowledged his own response to her. Was she truly his wife's lover? He could not forget that morning when he had discovered they were sharing a bath, and he had also realised they had been sharing a bed – the two indented pillows had belied the fact. George had confirmed they shared Arabella's bedroom and that the servants thought the relationship unnatural, but they dare not speak out. The thought turned his stomach as he sought out Sophia's gentle eyes to steady him. He could not risk speaking to her with the family in the house, so hoped she would guess the true reason for his soon-to-be-announced absence.

Dinner was called immediately; Alex had been slow coming down, not desiring to prolong his proximity to this nest of vipers. As they began the first course, Alex informed them of his upcoming absence, hoping they would be distracted by their meal.

'Just to let you know, I shall be leaving tomorrow on a business trip to Dorset. I will be taking the carriage after lunch,' he lied smoothly, and looked to Arabella for her reaction.

'Why, Dorset is said to be lovely this time of year, why don't I accompany you, my darling. You have been so busy of late, I have hardly seen my dear husband,' Arabella suggested flirtatiously. 'I am sure I can rearrange my diary. It would be so good to spend time with you – a second honeymoon, if you will! You have been so tired of late; I am sure the fresh air will do you good.' She was quick to play the part of the doting wife.

'I would not want you to be bored, my dear. After all, it is a business trip, so I'm afraid I have matters to attend to and not enough time to devote to you. It is better that I go alone.' Alex replied firmly. He knew she was alluding to him locking his bedroom door and pleading tiredness each morning when she berated him for ignoring her pleas to be admitted. He could only hope she wouldn't be as bold as to discuss their private affairs in front of the family.

'Uncle John, I am sure you have acquaintances there? We could all go, so I won't be bored in the day!' She was relentless in her pursuit.

'Oh, yes, several in fact,' Mr Burton blustered, and Alex knew he lied.

'I am sure you have plenty to occupy yourselves here in London. Balls, dinners, etc. Indeed, now you are such firm friends with the Princess, I am sure your presence would be greatly missed, and you do not want to fall out of favour. It will be exceedingly boring for you, so really, I insist you all stay here.' Alex was once again adamant, which silenced them all, and he knew he raised a good point about Arabella's new connections which she was keen to nurture. He noticed a slight nod being exchanged between Harriet and Arabella. Sophia's hands trembled as she kept her eyes averted from his. Mary slowly looked at him and then at Sophia, her eyes narrowing at the young girl's determined concentration on her food. She glared back at him, and he flinched. The spell was broken as the footmen began to remove plates, and Alex quickly changed the subject.

'What are your plans tonight, my dearest?' He put emphasis on his term of endearment, hoping his words sounded sincere. 'I am sure you must be attending some soiree.' He truly hoped she was otherwise engaged, as the thought of an entire evening spent in her company, playing the part of the loving husband, filled him with dread.

'I have been invited to Marlborough House,' she preened, 'for what the Prince thinks will be an amusing musical interlude.' He could see she loved to mention the Prince, believing it gave her power, and he was concerned it did. Because whatever he might discover, he wondered how much he would be able to use against her without causing a scandal which could impact the royal family through his wife's friendship with the Prince and Princess of Wales. The Prince had been embroiled in too many scandals of late, and Alex wondered if he dared embroil him in another. His whole political career could be at risk, but first he had to find out what exactly he was dealing with so he was better prepared.

'How wonderful,' he said, matching her lightness of tone.

'The Prince says he likes to have me around him, doesn't he, Aunt?' She was deliberate in her implication.

'Oh, yes, you are quite the favourite!' her aunt said with a smirk, sensing Alex's discomfort. 'He was only saying the other day what an asset Arabella must be to you, your Grace.'

'Did he indeed?' Alex almost broke into hysterical laughter at the idea that his wife was an asset when it appeared she was determined to ruin him and not just financially. 'Well, my love, you have most certainly had a huge impact on my life.' Arabella looked at him sharply, but he returned her look, smiling as he held up his wine glass to toast her. 'To you, my love.' It could almost have been a challenge.

A glass smashed and everyone jumped.

'I am so sorry,' Sophia whispered, her pale face now flushed a bright scarlet at the scene she had caused. 'The glass slipped as if it had a mind of its own. I could no longer keep hold of it.'

One of the footmen crossed himself, and the feigned joy dissipated into the misery it really was. There was silence as the diners finished their meal, ignoring the footman carefully collecting the shattered glass at Sophia's feet. She ate nothing more as she stared into space, a cold, vacant look on her face, a gentle rocking to her body that everyone studiously ignored. Alex wished he could comfort her, but he knew it was impossible, and he watched in hidden despair as Mary soon led the poor girl from the table.

Arabella, along with her aunt and uncle, soon left in the carriage for their evening's divertissement, and the house settled into silence with a malevolence in the air. Alex was glad to escape once more to his club.

Chapter Thirty

Manchester

Alex closed his eyes as the train rocked its way out of London bound for Manchester. He had left the house at the crack of dawn, George ensuring that everyone else was still asleep and did not hear him leave. They had planned it meticulously, as he could not trust Arabella not to ambush him as he left and be ready to accompany him, which would have been difficult to refuse. George had acted as if his master were to depart in the carriage after luncheon, as Alex had announced at dinner the previous evening. He told Alex that Mary had been present when he made the arrangements and he had seen her pack a small valise ready in her mistress' room. Alex had felt a jolt of fear at this – so, his wife had planned to force herself into his presence. Arabella had finally arrived home at midnight; he had listened as she had tried his locked door as she had done the last few nights, but once again was thwarted. She had called his name, and he had held his breath, pulling the covers over his head to shut out her insistent beguiling voice that called to him like a mermaid trying to bewitch him. He let silent tears fall down his face and the door remained locked.

As morning began to dawn, George had lightly tapped on Alex's door and whispered it was time to leave. Quietly, they had gone down the servants' staircase, Alex carrying his own valise as George lit the way with a single candle. They had startled the night porter, but he was easily satisfied when he spotted his master, although confused over the hour and style of his departure from his own house. Alex no longer cared; he needed to be gone. The street had been fairly empty, with a few carts starting to make deliveries, but George had managed to hail a hansom cab to take Alex to the railway station. He would have preferred to have taken George with him, for company more than anything, but he wanted him to keep an eye on Sophia – he couldn't shake off the disquiet he had experienced since he had learnt her letters were being intercepted. He hoped Manchester and Ravenscourt would provide some answers.

Alex jolted awake a few hours later as the train steamed its way slowly up north. He was briefly disorientated, dreaming perhaps that he was still on the Venice train coming home, but thankfully Arabella was not opposite him, just an elderly man reading his newspaper. Wearily, Alex watched as the countryside changed from lush, vibrant green to drab grey as the mills of Manchester spewed out their smoke into bleak, dust-ridden skies. When he arrived at the station, he was relieved to see Sir David's man waiting to accompany him.

'Your Grace, please come into my office. Would you care for some refreshment after your tiring journey?' Sir David Norton was a small, rotund man of middling years, his remaining wisps of hair greying. He wore wire-rimmed spectacles perched on a bulbous red nose, but his blue eyes twinkled, and his smile was generous and kind. His office was at first sight disorganised, with precarious piles of paper and files filling every spare space on his large oak desk, while bookshelves were crammed with all nature of legal texts.

'Please call me Alex, I hate such formality; and a small glass would be most welcome,' Alex said, nodding politely, taking an armchair next to the fire which Sir David had gestured to.

'Then please call me David,' the other man countered, pouring two glasses of a fine wine and settling in the opposite chair.

'It was good of you to see me.' The wine was reviving after the tedium of the train.

'I must confess, I was surprised to receive your letter. Of course, I had learnt about Lady Arabella's new marriage, as being Sir Charles's lawyer I am informed of any such change. However, when I also read Miss Sophia's letter, I understood matters were most concerning.' He shook his head ruefully. 'You see, as I indicated in my letter, this was the first time myself and her brother, Matthew, had gotten word from her in such a long time. We had written several times, and in my capacity as the family's lawyer it was strange not to have any response. However, Lady Arabella herself wrote to me recently to inform me that Miss Sophia was unwell, that it was best not to trouble her too much and as she is her legal guardian, I'm afraid I could not force the issue.'

'Arabella is Sophia's legal guardian? I thought you were.' Alex was startled at that revelation.

'No, Miss Sophia is not with Lady Arabella through choice, but perhaps I should start at the beginning?' Alex nodded his assent and Sir David continued. 'I had known Sir Charles since we were young boys, as my father was his father's lawyer. On my father's death I took over his clients, including Sir Charles by that time. Contrary to what you may have been told, he was a good man and a good friend to me and my family,' he spoke affectionately of the man.

'He was also handsome and charming.' Sir David smiled. 'He had a charisma about him few men have. The death of Lizzie, his first wife, hit him hard, and I don't believe he was ever the same. But he continued their charitable foundations in her memory, and he truly wanted the best for their children. I was therefore surprised when he returned from Venice a year after her death engaged to marry Lady Arabella. I was concerned, of course, about how much money he settled not only on her but on her aunt and uncle too. They all had considerable debts which Sir Charles covered, and he invested in John Burton's business. He also bought them a house in London.'

'A house in London? Do they still own it?' Alex was surprised at this news, as well as disturbed by some parallels to his own situation.

'I believe so, as I still hold the deeds in this office – however, if they sell it the property reverts back to Sir Charles's estate anyway. But he provided generously for them under his will, which felt odd to me. Now, normally I wouldn't be disclosing such information, but I have a letter from Matthew to give to you once I have explained the state of affairs.' He tapped the document beside him with his long-tapered fingers.

'Sir Charles set up a new will which would appear fairly standard when he remarried, entitling Lady Arabella and any issue to a generous settlement, a property to live in, etc., but here's where it becomes unusual – he stipulated Lady Arabella would be sole guardian of Miss Sophia until she reached the age of eighteen or married, though while she remains a minor she is not permitted to do so without her stepmother's permission.' Alex frowned, the clause indeed sounding peculiar.

'Miss Sophia would live with Lady Arabella, who would control not only her allowance but the income from Sophia's shares in her father's business. In the event of Miss Sophia's death before she reached eighteen or was married, Arabella would inherit all of Sophia's money and shares – a considerable amount, as you can imagine. Sir Charles was a wealthy man. I see from your face you are shocked, and I agree it is most unusual.'

'Arabella told me she had lost all income from Sir Charles's estate when we married. She was adamant she relied solely on the allowance I gave her. Is that not correct?' Alex sought clarification.

'Good lord, no. No such stipulation was made. In fact, when I tried to put one in, Sir Charles was steadfast and insisted he wanted Arabella to have independence. He was incredibly agitated, if I remember correctly.'

'This makes no sense. And Matthew, what of his share?' Alex enquired.

'Matthew being the heir and his son would indeed inherit the business, the main properties, etc., but this was because Sir Charles's own father had entailed them all on the male line, and Sir Charles could not change this even if he wanted to. Matthew was also nearly an adult when Charles remarried and already at university. He remains under my guardianship and has spent some holidays with my own family or abroad learning the family business.' Sir David took a sip of his wine. 'The sad part of the tale is that Matthew would love to see his sister, but he fell out with Lady Arabella shortly after his father's death, so she forbids his presence. As Miss Sophia's guardian she has full control, I'm afraid.'

'Did Sir Charles ever contact you after his marriage, attempting to change his will?' Alex questioned.

'Sir Charles became quite a sick man by the end, however I did receive a note that he wanted to see me to make changes to his legal affairs, but I was away on business at the time. A day later, he collapsed at his warehouse here in Manchester and his doctor and Lady Arabella took him off to Ravenscourt to convalesce. I never saw him again. When I returned from my trip, I had instructions to send some American correspondence to him, and I feared then that something was amiss, but although the packet was sent on and I had arranged to go out to Ravenscourt, it was too late. I do remember being surprised that he had gone to that house, knowing he hated it, and I felt a sense of urgency to get there. But he had already died. A sad tale. Those poor children – losing both parents in such a small space of time.'

The room was quiet now as both men reflected on the past, and Alex digested the lawyer's words. He had no reason to doubt his account.

'Sophia didn't go to Ravenscourt with them,' Alex recalled.

'She was taken abroad by John and Harriet Burton, although I can't believe Sir Charles would have been happy with that, as he doted on his children.' Sir David sighed and, taking off his glasses, he rubbed his eyes. 'Of course, neither Matthew nor I have ever believed Lady Arabella's stories about Sir Charles. As I said before, he was a good man. His friends should have known better and stuck by him when he needed them.' He replaced his glasses and stood up, walking over to his desk, where he picked up a letter from one of the tottering piles.

'I will leave you to read Matthew's letter. Then we'll have some luncheon before you leave for Ravenscourt. I am not sure what you will find – when I got there after his death, it was obvious his desk had been searched.' He sighed at the memory of the dishevelled drawers. Sir David had booked a carriage to take Alex to Ravenscourt, a journey of roughly two hours dependent on road conditions. It had been a wet summer in Lancashire and there was further rain forecast.

'I hope the river holds while you are there,' Sir David fussed. 'You should arrive there before dusk. The house has been shut up since Sir Charles's death, and only Mr Parsons and his wife take care of it now. They live in the gatehouse, but they will have made the house ready for you and will ensure you have some comfort. I have allowed a few days for you to search the house, and the carriage should return to pick you up once you send word – Parsons will arrange that. I trust that is amicable to you.' He left the room, and Alex could see the man had been affected by his retelling of the story. Alex himself was glad of the respite, the time alone with Matthew's letter. It was brief and to the point.

Dear Sir,

My dear sister trusts you and is in fact afraid for you too. We have long held doubts regarding our father's widow – I cannot bring myself to write her name. My father's will stipulated Sophia must remain with her until she is of age, but it was against my own wishes. I truly wish I had been of age myself so I could have taken on full responsibility for both my father's business and my sweet sister. I count the days until we are free of that woman. You, sir, should do the same. I will say no more, as I want to get this letter to you before you go to Ravenscourt.

My father never felt happy in his family home, but his study was the one room he found comfort as he had made it his own – no memories of his own father within it. Sophia writes of a document which may be hidden there. If such a thing exists, he would have made sure it was not in an obvious place like his desk or business safe, especially if he felt his life was in danger.

Good luck, sir, I hope you find it and that we discover the truth for all our sakes.

Matthew Pembrook.

Part Three

Chapter Thirty-One

Ravenscourt – September 1880

Alex had eaten little of the fine lunch Sir David had provided for him, his mind troubled by what he had heard. He wished now he had listened to Rupert in Venice instead of being such a lovesick fool, and he felt the absence of his friend keenly. He hadn't heard from him since the wedding, guessing that Rupert was keeping his distance instead of having to watch him fall under Arabella's spell. Before he left for Ravenscourt, he arranged for Sir David to send a letter straightaway for him to Rupert, knowing he would have need of his good friend when he came back. Sir David would be waiting for Alex on his return, so he could update Matthew of course, and also provide any further assistance.

And so, Alex made for Ravenscourt with a heavy heart and trepidation at what lay ahead. The coachman was eager to return back to Manchester before it got too late, so the carriage travelled at a fair pace. The countryside once again rattled past Alex's window, although it was decidedly more uncomfortable than the train and he longed to rest, for a bath, to sleep. The carriage was stuffy and smelt of human sweat. It slowed as it began to drive over the narrow bridge which crossed the tumultuous river, the water high up the banks from the heavy rainfall Sir David had mentioned. The horses whinnied in protest, heads tossing as the coachman urged them forward. They jolted onwards and Alex could sense the relief as they cleared the turbulent waters below.

'Not long now, sir. You can just see the house through yonder woods,' shouted the coachman.

Alex leant out of the window, savouring the fresh September breeze, the smell of rain in the air as he noticed the grey clouds brooding in the distance. The road curved slightly as it began its descent; he could now see the woods below and then peeping through the secluded valley he could see glimpses of a large honey-coloured stone building. Tiny Gothic turrets poked through the trees and then they were gone. Alex ducked his head back from the window as the carriage now plunged into a dark avenue of lime and golden yew. The horses slowed their pace as the entwined branches swung low over them, catching on the sides of the carriage as if the trees themselves were trying to reach within and pull Alex out. Apart from the sound of the horses and the wheels creaking, the avenue was quiet, nothing stirred in the gloom, and even though dusk was not yet upon them, the day's light barely penetrated the trees' tight embrace. Alex was chilled by the stillness as the horses' clip-clopped reluctantly along the rutted road.

'Ravenscourt, sir,' the coachman announced, and the carriage came to a sudden halt. 'I can go no further. I need to turn here and go back. Should be a man here to meet you.'

Alex stepped down from the coach, clutching his valise. Scarcely had his feet touched the ground and he had closed the carriage door then the coachman had swung his team of horses swiftly around and was already making his way back down the dark avenue.

Alex stood in front of large iron gates, elaborately decorated, which were now slowly opening to reveal the tree-lined drive ahead and the gatehouse to his left. It was a small Gothic building with gabled windows, its front door closed as the chimney smoke signalled some life within at least. There was a man standing in the porch pulling on the winch, which was now closing the gates behind him. Alex breathed a sigh of relief and nearly laughed at his fear of being alone here. The man doffed his cap in greeting as he walked towards Alex.

'You must be Sir David's man. I am Parsons, the steward here at Ravenscourt.'

'Yes, I am here on business for Sir David. Brown's the name,' Alex said, shaking the rough, calloused hand of Parsons, keeping up the story that he had agreed with Sir David, both believing it was best he pretended to be a clerk from the firm who needed to go through some papers of Sir Charles's. Parsons was a tall, rangy man with a weathered face which sported a fine set of whiskers topped by unruly red hair.

'House has been opened up for you. Mrs Parsons and I have prepared the study and one of the guest bedrooms for you as per Sir David's instructions. My wife has also left you some supper in the study, but I am afraid the rest of your meals will have to be taken at our cottage. We can only manage so much between us, and you will find the main house sadly in a state of neglect. We best be walking up there, get you settled while it's still light. Storm a brewing too.'

They walked slowly up the long leaf-strewn drive, weeds now trespassing where once fine carriages had driven. In the silence their steps crackled on the dead leaves, punctuating the air as if they were being mocked by crackling crones watching from the surrounding trees. Alex fought the urge to turn back, but then the house came into view. Even the trees appeared to stand back from it, as if declaring a disassociation from this place of sorrow, which was stark against the glowering sky. With its elaborate windows, silver turrets, gables and spires, and richly patterned roof, it should have been magical; but as they advanced, Alex could feel the house's reproach. The windows were all shuttered, so there was no welcoming light or sparkle from the small diamond panes of glass as they approached, nor any comforting smoke coming from the vast array of chimney pots, and the large oak entrance door was firmly shut against the world. Looking up at the clock tower which formed part of the impressive entrance, Alex noticed even the clock had stopped. It seemed to be a place frozen in time.

Parsons had not spoken on the walk to the house. His geniality at the gatehouse dissipated as they drew closer. There was such utter stillness that when a bird started cawing in the tree above them, both men jumped.

'Bloody birds,' muttered Parsons. 'Of course, they gave this place its name. Ravens.' He threw a stone at the large black bird, but in doing so he disturbed the woodland around the house, and a thick menace of ravens screeched up into the bleak sky, their large black wings carrying them up to perch on the house itself, the red clay roof turning virtually black. A small piece of masonry fell from one of the carved cervices which adorned the façade. The ravens shrieked with delight.

'An unkindness of ravens,' murmured Alex, as he flinched at the unholy sound.

'A murder more like, and I would murder the bloody lot of them.' As Parsons produced a large set of keys, the clouds, moving swiftly, cloaked the sky in darkness, making a misery of the day. Alex once again questioned if he should have come, but Parsons had opened the door – which was surprisingly smooth, with no ominous creak – and Alex shook off his fanciful thoughts.

They stepped into a small Gothic cloister with a low vaulted ceiling supported by finely carved stone pillars. Parsons lit a lantern which stood on a table in the style of a stone altar, and in the gloom Alex could see a plain tiled floor. He followed Parsons into the central hall, where the remains of the daylight streamed through the lantern roof which looked down on the cantilevered stairs rising up into the galleries. It was a vast, imposing room which would once have impressed any visitor, but the short burst of sunlight peeping through the clouds exposed the thick lingering dust and the cobwebs between the finely carved oak stair posts. Coverings shrouded the furniture, and the chill of the room was emphasised by the huge, empty stone fireplace which would have once provided warmth. The red patterned stair carpet had been discovered by moths, and probably even mice, and was riddled with fine holes, threadbare in places, and also covered in a thin layer of dust which betrayed the footprints leading up and down the stairs where Parsons and his wife had been so recently.

'Used to have a staff of one hundred and fifty in its heyday. Now there's only me and my wife, and we are simply here to keep an eye on things until the young master decides what to do with it when he inherits. I inspect the roofs and attics – make sure the house is dry at least, but it's a lot for one man.' Parsons was embarrassed at its state of disrepair.

'Of course it is,' Alex concurred, wanting to make clear he was not here to judge the poor man. 'How quickly a house such as this can fall into such neglect.'

'Well, even when Sir Charles was alive it had begun to change. Her Ladyship got rid of a lot of the servants in the last month of the master's life, so it was uncared for even back then. Anyway, we tidied up the study and a bedroom for you, so hopefully you will be comfortable. I'll show you to the bedroom first.'

Parsons led Alex up the stairs, turning right at the first landing. As they walked towards the next set of stairs, Alex paused to look down into the cavernous hall with its large stone archway leading back to the front door, and smaller arches leading further into the house. He noted the numerous portraits on the green patterned wallpaper, and it was as if the eyes of Ravenscourt were mocking him. Parsons paused at the door on the left and opened it slowly to reveal a charming bedroom with a comfortable-looking four-poster bed, which Alex longed to climb into after his tiring journey. The room had obviously been thoroughly cleaned and aired, as it had none of the neglect of the hall below. Fresh water had been left in a jug on the nightstand, and a fire had been laid, ready for lighting, in the decorative fireplace. A pretty golden armchair was set beside the fire, inviting one to linger in comfort. The wallpaper and drapes were decorated with charming songbirds perched on winding branches.

'This is one of the turret bedrooms.' Parsons signalled to an alcove in the corner of the room. As Alex stepped into the octagonal turret, Parsons pulled up one of the blinds and they could see down the leaf-strewn drive.

'Best show you the study so I can get back before the rain starts,' Parsons muttered, noting the gathering storm clouds.

They made their way back down the stairs and Alex could see more dark, shadowy corridors leading off the galleried landings, where doors were shut against forgotten rooms. Alex paused by a fine, full-sized portrait of a man on one of the walls. He was dressed in modern attire, but it was the face that Alex noticed – there was a certain charisma to it. Framed by dark brown hair, the face was handsome; with fine cheekbones, a secretive smile played on the full lips, but it was the dark brown eyes that pulled the viewer in. There was a hint of sadness in them, as if the man longed to step away from the view of the house behind him. There was a large gap next to the portrait where another picture must have hung.

Parsons noticed Alex studying it. 'That is Sir Charles,' he explained. 'Lady Elizabeth's picture used to hang next to it until the last mistress came and ordered it to be taken down.' They returned to the entrance hall, where Parsons opened a large, arched double oak door. 'This is the library. The study is through this door. We have made you comfortable in there rather than opening this room up, I'm afraid.'

Alex could understand why, as the library was a huge space with its double height ceiling rising up into a timber framed roof. It had a church-like quality to the room but in the shuttered gloom, with its shrouded furniture, it appeared sinister and unwelcoming.

The study however was a small, cosy room with a comfortable set of chairs in front of a carved fireplace and another fire laid ready to be lit. There was a sturdy oak desk, behind which stood large bookcases and red velvet drapes matching the red silk wallpaper. A small portrait of a beautiful, dark-haired lady hung over the fireplace. Holding a small child in her arms, she had such a sweet face that Alex felt comforted by her. It belied the absence that haunted the rest of the house.

'It will be dark soon. I'll get the fire lit and Mrs Parsons has left provisions over here for you.' After making sure their visitor was comfortable, Parsons departed, clearly eager to return to his wife in their snug cottage.

Alex was left alone rattling around the large, quiet house – all clocks stopped, no other living soul. He examined the room. The dust covers had obviously been removed, and an attempt made to clean and air it. The window shutters however remained shut, making the room feel like a red tomb. He could already hear the rain that had threatened beginning to fall outside. But the fire was welcoming, as were the wine, bread, and cheese he had been left. He was glad to sate his hunger at least, and he readily did so before he began his search. Even now he was eager to be gone from the place, and the sooner he found the journal or any revealing papers Sir Charles had left the better.

The desk was clear, as if all traces of Sir Charles had been swept away, and he remembered Sir David's account of it being like this in the aftermath of his friend's death. Alex opened the drawers to find some papers, old invoices, some plain stationery, and an old appointment book. He wondered what had become of it all – his father's desk in both London and the Abbey had been full of his father's life, but this desk was bereft of any trace of its owner. He slumped down in the chair by the fire, worrying his trip would be futile, and closed his eyes. But of course, Sir Charles would have left nothing secret in so obvious a place.

The storm outside had intensified, and Alex was jolted awake by a clap of thunder overhead as the rain lashed at the shuttered windows. The fire was dying slowly in the grate, and the room was growing colder. There was a stillness to the room and his heart pounded as beads of sweat prickled on his back even though his body began to shiver from the cold.

A loud crash, followed by the sound of shattering glass within the house, made him jump and he gripped the chair. Alex's breath came in short, shallow gasps as his eyes fixed on the study door, watching to see if the handle would turn. He sat there, waiting, but there was nothing. The house was quiet once again, with just the rain tormenting him, pushing as if to be let in the windows, rattling the shutters in denied fury. His heart rate slowed as he convinced his trembling body it was simply the storm which continued to crash around the house. There was no one there.

His pocket watch showed the hour to be two in the morning. He rose slowly from the chair, his body stiff and his nerves frayed. He left the study, ignoring the shadowy library with its vaulted ceiling, and gripping the lantern, he retraced his steps back to the hall to find the prepared bedroom.

His oil lamp afforded minimal light, and the hall was darker now as the night's black mantle dulled the lantern window. Alex shivered as he gazed up at it, high above him, a sickly reminder of another ceiling from which had shone stars from a Venetian sky. As suddenly as it had come the storm had now passed so there was an eerie silence, and the shrouded furniture within the hall played tricks on the imagination. Alex grasped the first newel post of the stairs, glancing upwards once again at the shadows as if he expected to see the figures of Arabella and Mary waiting for him. He slowly climbed the stairs.

Once inside his own chilly room, he removed only his shoes, and pulling back the heavy damask cover, he climbed into the bed fully clothed as the coldness gripped him. Wrapped tightly in the cover, at first he thought sleep would evade him, his mind still full of turmoil, and his senses acutely on edge. But soon his eyes grew too heavy, and he could no longer fight his exhaustion even though he was not yet ready to sacrifice himself to the house.

Chapter Thirty-Two

Alex awoke with a start as the door opened, and a woman of middling age entered with a jug of water.

'Good morning, sir,' the woman spoke, not a ghost after all. 'I am Mrs Parsons.' She bustled around the room, setting down the jug and pulling back the curtains, then unclipping one of the shutters to allow some daylight into the dark room. She sparked up the ready laid fire and, as the flames caught, it lent a cheerful air.

'Thank you, Mrs Parsons.' He struggled against the heavy coverlet to sit up. 'I was so exhausted I did not undress,' he attempted to explain, his voice cracking with the dryness of his mouth.

'Breakfast will be in the cottage when you are ready. Mr Parsons is out looking at the storm damage. He explained about meals being in the cottage, I take it?' she asked, glancing anxiously at him.

'Yes, he did. I wouldn't want to be a burden.' He wanted a respite from the house already; even the Parsons' company would be better than the silence of the study which he needed to return to.

The cottage kitchen was cheerful and warm as Alex entered. Mrs Parsons was cooking eggs on a sturdy range, and the table was laid with a freshly baked loaf of bread, lightly churned butter, and jugs of fresh milk with a large pot of tea.

'Mr Parsons should be back shortly.' She bade him sit at the empty table. She was a short, plump woman with grey curls escaping from a clean white cap, ruddy cheeks, and a ready smile. Her lively eyes keenly watched her guest as he helped himself to the good wholesome food which revived his spirits after a disturbed night.

'Did you know Sir Charles?' Alex attempted to converse.

'Oh, yes. I came here as a girl in his father's time. Sir Thomas were old by then and Sir Charles was newly wed to the first Lady Pembrook. She was such a gentle woman, and he doted on her and the children.'

'What job did you do?'

'I came as a laundry maid and later helped in the nursey when Mr Matthew were born. After I married Mr Parsons, I moved here to keep house for him. They were happy days, though we weren't blessed with children ourselves.' She sat down at the table, her demeanour saddened.

The door opened and Parsons came into the kitchen. 'News is not good, Mr Brown.' The man was soaking wet and his clothes muddy. 'The river has burst its banks submerging the bridge which also looks like it could be damaged. I doubt you will be able to leave for a good few days.'

Alex's heart sank as he faced being trapped in that house. He could hardly believe he was once again delayed by a storm after his experience in Venice.

'The farm manager is one of Ravenscourt's tenants, so he will fix it as soon as he can,' Parsons explained, taking off his coat and hanging it by the kitchen fire. Mrs Parsons handed him a towel to dry his wet, unruly hair.

'Where is the farm?' Alex had not seen sight of a farm – or village, for that matter – on his way here.

'Over vale – can't see it from the road but we are separated by the river. Crops will be damaged too.' He frowned.

'I thought I heard glass shattering in the house last night,' Alex confided.

'I will just get a dry shirt and then I will come up to the house with you to take a look.'

As they walked back up the drive, the day was slightly brighter than the previous one, the black, sentient birds were quiet, and the trees rustled softly. Autumn was nearly upon them, and the leaf-strewn drive would soon be covered even more. The house still wore its neglected air but was benevolent in the lightness of the day.

Alex followed Parsons through the myriad of rooms, each shrouded, shuttered, and shimmering with dust. They checked behind each shutter and Alex began to doubt his own memory as each window appeared intact. Then Parsons opened two large doors which led off the Billiard Room into a huge Glass Room. Its glass dome had collapsed, and the room was a shatter of glass, wood, and chaos. They took in the destruction of what must have once been a beautiful room.

'Best not.' Parsons stopped Alex from moving forwards and pointed upwards. Jagged pieces of glass roof not yet fallen still dangled, its large shards ready to impale them. 'Well, that's that then.' Parsons sighed sadly. 'Can't do much until the bridge is accessible again.'

'Was it built with the original house?' Alex asked.

'Aye, it was,' he spoke softly, his devastation clear at the house falling apart under his stewardship. 'It was Lady Catherine's favourite room. She was Sir Charles's mother. She grew all sorts of exotic plants here and she loved the view over there, where the lake used to be.' He pointed to where a large body of water should have stood but all that was left was a mound of earth with a fountain marooned in the middle, weeds sprouting in its empty basin, ivy curling around what must be entwined sculptures where once water cascaded.

'Who drained the lake?' Alex questioned.

'Sir Charles's father drained it after his daughter drowned in it and Lady Catherine could no longer bear to see it. This room was closed up until Lady Elizabeth, Sir Charles's first wife, came to live here but even then, Sir Charles refused to enter it. He would be glad it was gone, I reckon.'

Parsons closed the doors on the unhappy memories of the Glass Room. As they walked back through the hushed house, Alex remembered once more the newspaper article concerning the tragedies at Ravenscourt.

'I best be getting on,' Parsons announced when they reached the hall. 'If there is anything you need, I am always around at mealtimes.'

Chapter Thirty-Three

Alex felt the house settle around him, and the stillness intensified with each step now he was alone. Back in the study he could smell the staleness of last night's wine, even though it had been cleared away, and a fresh fire laid in the hearth. He pulled open the wooden shutters that creaked loudly in protest as he let in a flood of natural light. The room appeared ordinary in the day, a gentleman's study as per any house in the country, and Alex breathed a sigh of relief – there were no ghosts after all. Even the loud crash from the previous night had been explained. There was no one else in the house.

He sat back at the desk, searching the drawers in case he had missed something in his tiredness last night, feeling for secret compartments. Nothing yielded itself up. He pulled out books on the shelves surrounding the desk, flicking through random pages in case Sir Charles had hidden anything within them.

This is useless, I can't go through every book. He sighed. *There must be something I am missing.*

He glanced at his pocket watch and realised it was almost luncheon. The morning had already passed without discovery. The fresh air revived him on his walk to the cottage, and he was happy to see the friendly face of Mrs Parsons.

'Sit yourself down. Mr Parsons is checking on the trees in the wood, so you get started with your lunch,' she urged him.

'You getting on all right?' Mrs Parsons asked, as she joined him at the table.

'Not really. I am looking for something for Sir David, and so far it is proving elusive.'

'I doubt you will find much left in that house. Mistress and her companion made a thorough job of it.' Her mouth formed a tight, disapproving line.

'Is that so?' Alex proceeded carefully. 'What was she like? His second wife?'

'The American?' She tutted. 'Pure evil, both of them.' She crossed herself.

Alex was taken aback by the vehemence of her words.

'Now Betsy, that's enough.' Alex and Mrs Parsons started, as Mr Parsons appeared at the door. 'Mr Brown doesn't need to hear all of that.' He began to wash his hands at the sink as his wife bristled with indignation.

'You know full well what she was like. Sir Charles would still be alive if he hadn't married her!'

'You don't know that.' Mr Parsons sat down at the table, helping himself to bread and cheese.

'He were a good man,' Mrs Parsons continued, not letting it drop. 'You of all people know that, and she made him out to be such a brute. His father – now he were a brute – but not Sir Charles. A true gentleman, he were, and the kindest soul that ever were.'

'Enough!' Mr Parsons glared at her, and she abruptly left the room.

Alex quietly took his leave, sensing Mr Parsons would not be drawn on the subject and returned slowly to the house. He couldn't face the study with its reproachful air and his own sense of failure at not finding anything so far. Instead, he climbed the moth-eaten stairs to explore the bedrooms. There was a smell of damp when he entered the master suite, and when he pulled open the shutters to afford the room more light, he could see water trickling slowly down one of the walls, the dark blue wallpaper already starting to peel. He turned to look out of the window, saddened by the neglect of the room, but he was further dismayed at the sight of the now-neglected landscaped gardens, with the forlorn fountain, and then on to the moors beyond. It was a desolate outlook which enhanced the isolation of the house. Looking around the shrouded room, he briefly wondered if Sir Charles had shared it with Arabella, but no, he knew she would have had her own rooms as she would surely have wanted that privacy with Mary.

He lifted the white ghosts from the furniture, looking for any hint of a journal, but he couldn't believe that it would be hidden in this room. He opened the wardrobe, releasing a mixed smell of mothballs, cigars, and a faint smell of what he discerned to be citrus fruits. An odd smell to find here amongst Sir Charles's clothes, which still hung there as if awaiting his return. Alex was surprised to find that his things had not been packed away – the chest of drawers held ties, undergarments, socks, and a man's dressing set. The cabinet by the bed revealed a book, a comb, and a pair of glasses. But the bed had been stripped bare, only a sumptuous coverlet underneath its pale ghost. He could almost imagine Sir Charles returning to the room and finding little amiss, but this was the room in which he spent his last days, and there would be no returning for the master of Ravenscourt. There was also no trace of Arabella in the room, and he wondered where she had slept.

He made a mental note to tell Parsons about the leak in the master bedroom, although the man might wonder why he had been snooping around.

Returning to his own room, he found it had been tidied and the bed remade. He realised now that it was an extremely feminine room with its large but delicate four-poster bed and the dainty bedroom furniture accompanied by the soft chair by the fireplace, a strange choice of room by the Parsons.

He opened a side door and was astonished to find a bathroom. The house was more modern than he realised. He turned the tap on over the bath and there was a horrendous clanking sound and then a gush of cold brown water.

'Boiler doesn't work these days.' He started at the voice behind him. It was Mrs Parsons bringing him a jug of fresh water to wash with. 'If you are wanting a bath, I will get Mr Parsons to fetch a tub, and we can boil you some water down in the kitchen. The range still works down there.'

Alex hated to be the cause of further work, but he could feel the grime and dust from the house seeming to encase him in its own layer of dirt.

'I would appreciate it if it's not too much trouble.' He nodded gratefully.

'We can do it for you in the morning as I have dinner to prepare now and Mr Parsons is still busy securing the storm damage.' Without further ado she was gone, shutting the door behind her before he had the chance to ask her whose room this had been. But the thought fluttered from his mind as he washed his face despondently. It had been a waste of time coming here, he mused; there was no journal, and he was now trapped by a broken bridge and proving a nuisance to two elderly staff.

***

Dinner was another quiet affair but there was beer for Mr Parsons and a decent wine for Alex in the good parlour afterwards. Mrs Parsons made her excuses and left the two men to it. There was a warm, cosy feel to the room and Alex knew he would be loath to leave. As they sat drinking, Alex remembered to tell Parsons about the leak in what he presumed was the master suite.

'I heard water when I was on the landing and thought I would just check where it was coming from – I hope you don't mind?' Alex lied.

'It does sound like the master's room. I imagine there has been damage to the roof.' He sighed, another job to be added to an ever-growing list trying to maintain the place.

'Would you like me to inform Sir David of the numerous issues with the house? Perhaps he can provide further help?' Alex offered.

'That would be kind of you, sir.'

Having got in the man's good books, and with the wine having loosened his own tongue, Alex boldly broached the subject of Sir Charles. 'Did you know the master well?'

'Aye, I came here as a boy when he were a lad. I worked in the kitchen as a pot boy, then the stables, and later I took over the grounds. Mrs Parsons were a nursery maid under Sir Charles's first wife, Lady Elizabeth. Lovely lady she were. Happy house back then too. Not that Sir Charles ever loved this place, but with Mistress he were happy here.'

'Not with Lady Arabella, his second wife?'

'This house were never happy thereafter and she had that woman with her.' He crossed himself as if to ward away evil spirits. 'You stayed out of their way if you could help it. We were lucky to keep our jobs when they came here that last time,' he muttered. 'He were so ill he could hardly argue with her, so she dismissed most of the staff. Just ten remained in the house and us in the gatehouse with a couple of lads in the stables. She didn't trust us and warned he needed seclusion, that she would nurse him herself. Pah, she were one making him ill if you want my opinion.'

'What was wrong with him?'

'Addicted she reckoned to opium, and she said there was of course madness in the family. She declared he needed complete rest and no one else but her and that woman were allowed to attend to him.'

'Madness?' Alex hesitated.

'She was alluding to Sir Charles's mother, of course. I had just arrived at Ravenscourt when Lady Catherine was taken off to the asylum. Poor woman never got over the death of her daughter. It were an odd business, as Sir Charles always insisted his mother had not been at the lake with them that day.' Parsons stood up, signalling the end to their conversation. 'Well, we best get you back to the house, it's getting late.'

As they walked back, the darkness of the countryside was all-enclosing; there must have been clouds as no stars twinkled in the sky, and the only sound was the crunching of their feet on the gravel of the drive. Once again, Alex found himself alone in Ravenscourt. The house was no closer to yielding up its secrets.

Chapter Thirty-Four

Mrs Parsons had been as good as her word, and when Alex awoke to bright sunshine the next morning, she bustled in telling him his bath was almost ready. He wrapped his dressing gown tightly around him and followed her down the servants' back stairs into the house's cavernous kitchen corridors. The servants' hall, the storerooms, anterooms, were numerous and deserted. Their feet echoed in the silence as they made their way to the large kitchen where the range had been prodded into life, large pots of water boiling on its top, and its warmth encased the room. A large tin bath stood beside the range and Parsons was busy pouring hot steaming water into it. Mrs Parsons sprinkled some lavender salts in and pointed out the fresh towels warming on the rack. Once all was ready, they left Alex in peace to enjoy the water's warmth as it seeped into his skin, lifting the dirt of the past few days from his tired, aching body.

He must have fallen asleep in the soothing caress of the water and slid slowly into the bath, as suddenly he was struggling to breathe as if a force was holding him under. His hands gripped the sides of the cold tin as he pushed against the soapy water, surfacing while gasping for air. The kitchen was cold and empty. He froze as he heard the faint sound of laughter in the corridor. A door slammed and he scrambled out of the bath, grabbing at the towels. His heart pounded and he shivered in the cold. All was silent. He padded across the kitchen, his feet leaving a trail of prints on the dust of the floor and intermingling with the ones left by the Parsons. He peered in trepidation down the long corridor. It was empty – no scurrying maids, busy footmen, harassed kitchen maids. Only an emptiness of past lives.

***

In the cosiness of the Parsons' kitchen, he could shake off his fear from the house, and he convinced himself he must have been dreaming and that the wind must have caught a door. Mrs Parsons laid a hearty breakfast in front of him as Mr Parsons departed to dispose of the bath.

'Any luck in your searching?' she enquired, as she sat at the table, pouring herself a cup of tea.

'Not so far,' he admitted. 'Would you be able to tell me more about Sir Charles?' he asked, intrigued to hear more about the man whose life was becoming more and more entwined with his.

'He were a good master.' She smiled at the memory. 'Such a happy family when he married Lady Elizabeth, and I loved those children as if they were my own. I remember when the mistress brought Sir Charles a dog – he was like a child at Christmas.' She chuckled. 'He had always wanted one, but his father had never let him. There were the gun dogs of course, but they were kept in the stables and Sir Thomas wasn't one for pets.' Alex recalled a conversation with Arabella regarding a dog as Mrs Parsons continued. 'He called her Rosie. She was a black spaniel, and we used to laugh and say he loved that dog more than his own children, but it weren't true as he loved them all. That's why I don't believe a word that woman said.' Her lips pursed together in a grim line.

Mr Parsons returned, and Alex knew his wife would say no more in his presence.

'Reckon the river be subsiding now. Think I will take a look,' he stated gruffly.

Alex offered to accompany Parsons on his walk to the river, not wanting to face the house. But this just depressed him further – the river was still a teeming torrent, and the bridge was still submerged. He was no closer to getting home, yet no nearer to finding out the truth either.

***

That afternoon, he sat by the fire in Sir Charles's study – the weather had turned again; the clouds had chased away the morning sun and had blanketed the sky in dark grey. Alex feared more rain was to come. His nose had started to run, his head felt fuzzy and ached, his limbs were heavy, and he realised he had picked up a chill from being in the draughty old house. Things, he decided, could not get any worse. Rupert would be laughing at him if he could see him now, but his friend would definitely be appreciative of Mrs Parsons' food. He chuckled at that thought but wished once more that he had listened to his good friend's sage advice back in Venice. Rupert had been right that Alex had been too young, too foolish, and easily charmed. Alex sighed as his own self-pity washed over him. He glanced around Sir Charles's study in hopelessness.

There at the side of one of the heavy red damask drapes, almost hidden from view, he could see a small portrait of what appeared to be a black dog. Alex slowly rose from his chair and walked over to it. The dog was painted in this very room, languishing by the fire, a pink bow around its neck with a disc attached inscribed with a name. Alex carefully lifted the portrait from the wall to get a closer look at the name, the dust making him cough as he read the word *Rosie*, but as he went to put the picture back, he gasped. There was a small wall safe. He eagerly tried to open it but found it was locked. His heart sank, wondering where on earth Sir Charles would have hidden the key. He was still holding the portrait when his hand felt a small bump in the frame. He turned the picture over and he could see a little indent in the bottom left-hand corner. Pulling back the taping gently, he found the key nestled in a tiny cubby hole within the frame. He laughed in relief. The noise echoed in the empty house.

The safe opened and to his excitement he found a small journal, a pack of letters, and a gold locket. He took them over to the desk and placed them carefully down to examine them further. He put the pack of letters and the journal to one side, as he opened the locket. Within it was a portrait of a young woman on one side and a lock of golden hair on the other. The name *Lizzie* was engraved on it. Alex felt as if he was intruding on Sir Charles's first marriage – the fact he had hidden it away made Alex sadder and fearful of what he was yet to discover. But of course, Sophia would be glad of her mother's locket, and he placed it down carefully on top of the letters. He took the journal to his seat by the fire. The house stilled as he turned the first page.

Chapter Thirty-Five

Ravenscourt – January 1879

Sir David,

It has been a few days since we arrived at Ravenscourt – Arabella, Mary, me, Doctor Ward, and his nurse. I wish I had been able to see you, but the doctor insisted we came here straightaway. I am starting to feel more lucid and awake than I have done in a long time but tomorrow the doctor and nurse leave and will not return for a week or so. I am afraid, so very afraid, and wish they would stay. While I have the energy and the wherewithal, I will write down my own account of what my life has sadly become. I want you and my children to know the truth and only hope I can send this to you before it is too late – if the doctor comes back before I die, I can entrust it to him surely – but if time runs out as I fear it must, then I hope my dear children will find my hiding place behind my beloved Rosie. I must never leave this journal unattended, for I do not trust that it will not be destroyed otherwise.

My wife watches me like a hawk, so I must write this at night in my study whilst she takes her pleasure elsewhere. I have until my candle runs out as I dare not light the lamp or the fire as her spies will notice and I will be discovered. She thinks I sleep, and when the doctor leaves I will have to use all my wits to be able to finish this. I watch her as the doctor explains the correct dosage of my medicine which I need to ease me of this vile addiction, but I know she will be merciless and feed it as much as she can, so I become pliant, listless, a shadow of the man I once was to do her bidding. You, my dear friend, must forgive my ramblings – I have to be quick, I have no time to edit, to rewrite. It has to be as it is – the clock ticks and the candle melts slowly away.

Alex recoiled as he read Sir Charles's words – all Alex's fears and misgivings had been right. There was also a mix of guilt and disbelief – guilt that he had believed Sir Charles had been the brute that Arabella had described, but a sliver of disbelief – after all, these could just be the ramblings of an addict. But Alex knew what he read was true – why would Sir Charles go to such lengths to hide his words, scared over what his wife would do if she found them, and of course Alex himself had heard Arabella's conniving plans.

But I will start at the beginning, so you will know the extent of my wife's perfidy, the lies she has spun, and her malignant intentions towards me and my family. You will of course wonder at my actions, at my own foolishness. There is much I need to write down so I can explain to you and my children why I have let you all down in my weakness.

I see now how much of it goes back to my past and my own childhood. I hate this house. Even when my sweet Lizzie was alive, this house held dark memories. I was born here, and I will probably die here – a cruel end for someone who has always hated this place. I feel the misery of my childhood weigh down on me. Every room holds an unhappy memory. My father was a nasty, violent man – he believed only in his own happiness and happiness equalled money and status. He made his fortune on the misery of others – the mill workers, the cotton slaves, any expendable life. After my sister's death, he barely tolerated me as his one surviving child and heir, but my mother he banished to an asylum as soon as he could. Did you know this, David? Your father, his lawyer, knew so I wonder if you knew too. But my children never knew this sad tale, so I will record it here. It seems fitting to tell her story in this house before I begin mine, as the two are entwined and I warned you this story would not always be as organised as it should ...

My mother was Catherine Corbeau. I smile now at her name – the French for raven – I wonder if my father named the house for her. A cruel irony, for she truly was a raven caught in his trap rather than courted by him. She was the daughter of a wealthy plantation owner who brought considerable riches to my father – so much so that he was able to build this wretched house. I know little of my grandfather or how my father met him. He died not long after the marriage, having settled large sums of money on my mother. I do remember my mother – a dainty woman with long black hair which shone blue/black when she brushed it; her skin was dark too, which gave her a healthy glow belying her delicate constitution, but it was her startling green eyes I most recall for they were kind and loving. She was my dearest mama who would sweep me and my sister, Lily, up for cuddles and kisses – attentive to our every need. She would argue with my father, who thought we were too spoilt, but even at the age of five I noticed the bruises on her arms and the traces of her tears on her beautiful face. I hated my father as much as I loved her.

But when she miscarried for the third time after a particularly nasty fall down the stairs, my father grew intolerant. The doctor had told him there would be no more children and I believe from what I discovered when I was much older – servants talk – that he had also advised there could be no more marital visits. Divorce, however, was out of the question as my father relied too heavily on the income from her father's investments which he had left in her name.

The doctor had prescribed sedatives for my mother's nerves, not realising the real reason she was a shadow self – barely functioning in my father's world. My father used this to his advantage and one fateful day he made sure she was drugged so deeply that she slept whilst he decided to pleasure himself with our nanny. I vaguely remember that day – she was a pretty girl with blonde hair and blue eyes who giggled a lot and took us down to the lake to play. And then she was no longer there. The lake dappled in the heat of the sun and it appeared enticing. I was absorbed in my toy train and Lily was playing with her hoop. Lily – if I close my eyes, I can just recall her sweet face sticky with jam, always smiling, but it is such an incomplete memory. She must have chased the hoop down to the lake's edge because I heard a splash, I think. I must have gone searching for her because I was screaming at the lifeless shape in the water, the hoop floating beside her.

Afterwards, my father blamed my mother, but I tried to tell the doctor that it wasn't true, that she had been sleeping. My father claimed I must have been in shock from seeing my dead sister to discredit my account. Some of the servants knew of course, but dared not speak out – it was years later that my elderly housekeeper told me the truth after my father died, as it had long been on her conscience. She told me that the nanny left not long after with money and good references. My poor mother was beside herself at my sister's death and believed my father's lies. She wouldn't eat, she barely slept unless she was drugged, and she cried until there were no more tears. She even tried to drown herself in the lake but was recovered by our servants before it was too late. I watched them bring her dripping body into the house one day when father was out. If my father had been home, he probably would have let her drown. Instead, he and the doctor decided to have her committed to an asylum not far from here. I can still remember that day even now so many years later. It was the day I began to hate Ravenscourt as my mother was taken away from me. I can still hear her screams as they dragged her down the stairs. She begged them, she fought them, but they pulled her kicking and screaming down the stairs to the waiting carriage. I never saw her again.

When my father died, I asked your father to tell me where she had gone so I could see her, but she was already dead. She had died a few months prior to him – I had been too late. I did visit the asylum. She is buried there on that wretched moorland. A miserable place, and I vowed I would never commit anyone to a place such as that. I truly believe such places are hell on earth. I think Arabella would have committed me if it had suited her needs; she knows my views on such places and she would delight in the cruelty. She has hinted to Doctor Ward that madness afflicts my family, and I worry he concurs. After all, he is the son of our old family doctor who had my mother committed. But it is my death Arabella most desires, for my living will not bring her wealth and independence, will it?

But my mother was not mad. I grow tired now and my writing is slow and painful. I feel such sadness at my mother's life. I too know what it feels to be resented, unwanted in your own home. A cuckoo in your own nest surrounded by vultures who want you gone. I wonder if she loved him as I loved Arabella and what she went through when she realised he no longer needed or wanted her? It is a cruel realisation when your life falls apart.

I must hide this journal now as my candle flickers as it burns low, I need some light to return to my bedroom, and the night will soon be done.

Alex sank back in his chair digesting what he had read. He had been fascinated by Sir Charles's story as it explained his vulnerability and the very valid reasons for the man's hatred of the house with all its tragedies. Alex stared out of the study windows, and he could just make out the spectre of the outline of the lake's mound in the encroaching darkness where poor Lily had drowned as her father had taken his pleasure with the unfortunate nanny – Alex wondered if the girl had been willing. He doubted it. He was saddened over Sir Charles's memories of his poor mother and how this must have affected the young boy that he had been. As he tried to process Sir Charles's words, he glanced once again at the portrait over the fireplace – the dark-haired beauty holding the small child – and he guessed that it must be Lady Catherine and her son.

Most of all, Alex was afraid of what else the journal would reveal about his wife, and part of him wanted to throw it into the fire – to deny the truth of the man's words – but he knew he could not, for Sophia's sake as much as for his own. There was a couple of hours left before dinner. He turned the page.

The doctor has left. I feel his absence immediately. There are less servants too. She has banished or dismissed most of them, especially those of the indoor staff she feels are too loyal to me. All that remain are the cook, two housemaids whom she hired in Manchester, a young footman, and a couple of kitchen girls. I know little of what is happening outside, but Parsons and his wife are confined to the gatehouse, and he can only tend the grounds. I am left at her mercy.

Alex flicked through the next few pages, which detailed Sir Charles's marriage to Elizabeth, desperate now to find out what had happened with Arabella, but he stopped when he read the following words.

Lizzie and I shared the same passion for social reform, both of us abhorring the slave trade, and when our fathers died we began to improve our mills, educating not just the children but their parents too, making sure everyone had a decent wage and a clean workplace with better homes. We cut all ties with slavery and sourced our cotton responsibly. We didn't simply leave it to others to check – I myself went to America to ensure no slaves provided supplies to us. In my absence, Lizzie ran our businesses and she, as you are more than aware, was more than capable.

Arabella's description of her dead husband painted a very different story regarding social reform and slavery. Alex began to wonder what his dear wife said about him and how soon he too would be cast in a villainess light. As he continued the journal, the words only showed Sir Charles as a good, honest man who loved his family and whose upbringing made him crave kindness.

I miss her even now as I sit in the study she had redecorated when we finally took Ravenscourt over. I wanted to sell it but Lizzie for some strange reason fell in love with the house, even knowing I hated it, and I could not deny her. She tried to make it a home, and this room is a reflection of her love for me – the care and attention to making it my own space, trying to banish the unhappy memories. It pains me in some ways to sit here, feeling her loss, and knowing how I have destroyed my life since she died. All she had tried to achieve is crumbled to dust. Now I worry what I have done to our children too, and I wish more than ever that I could have seen you before I left, David, so I could have remade my will. I could have put right all the mistakes I have made and ended this cruel charade of a marriage. I hope my children will forgive me.

Mine and Lizzie's children were ever our blessing – Matthew and Sophia. We lost a couple of much-loved babies along the way as all families do, and each one we mourned but we were fortunate with our two. Lizzie was wonderful with them and, even though she helped me so much, the children were always her priority. We were a happy family. It was just in the bedroom we lacked compatibility. I apologise, David, for being so crude, but it will help you to understand my passion for Arabella. Lizzie, to be most blunt, did not enjoy marital relations in the bedroom and I never once saw her naked. She would insist on darkness and her nightgown pulled up. She endured it so we could have children – it was her duty, she said – but once Sophia had been born, I could tell she found it more and more distasteful, and I could not bring myself to cause her such discomfort. We had separate bedrooms from then onwards. I could not take a mistress – I could not betray the woman I loved. I would not become my father.

When Lizzie died last year, my world fell apart. The children were distraught. She had not been ill long and the doctor, the same man who has just left this house, did all he could but she declined swiftly. This house, where she died, became once again a mausoleum of grief and pain. I couldn't bear to be here; I needed to get away. Matthew went back to university, and you and your dear wife offered to have my gentle Sophia to stay. Your family we knew so well – we were all such friends – and your own daughters loved Sophia. You gave her such comfort and love whilst I, her father, was drowning in my own misery.

I had long been suffering with a bad back – a weakness I inherited from my father, whose rages of pain the whole household would hear and suffer from. With Lizzie's death, the pain in my back had intensified, so I started to take a little laudanum, which gave me some relief from the nagging aches and the grief I held in my heart. With the pain subsiding, I could at last plan my departure, and I had long wished to see Italy – I had a love for the arts which I had learnt at school and developed at university.

In particular, the Romans fascinated me, and the great Renaissance painters such as Titian, Tintoretto, Michelangelo, and da Vinci called to me. So, with everyone's blessing, I decided to go to Italy, to visit places I had merely read about. I could combine it with business too, as Venice had long been a gateway to the east, the finest silks and glass too came from that fine city, and I had friends who often stayed there – Roger and Kitty Jobson,

*who had known Lizzie and I for years. Most of all, it held
no memories of sweet Lizzie. A place to restart, to renew
myself. I should have stayed at home, but hindsight is a
wondrous thing ... Each word exhausts me ...*

    *I thought I heard a sound just then in this silent
sleeping house, so I will hide this now. The hour is late; I
do not want to be caught out of bed, for if she suspects
anything I am sure she will lock me up. At present she
cannot lock my bedroom door – I hid the only key. I am in
the master suite which once belonged to my father, and he
would allow no spare key – one of the few good things he
has inadvertently done for me. She cannot lock me in, but I
also cannot keep her out. My nights are long and fearful
when I am not in here writing. I have such dreams but
enough, I must stop.*

The back of Alex's neck prickled as he sat alone in the
same house. He was glad of the last vestiges of daylight
coming through the windows. The silence of the house
settled uneasily on his shoulders, but he was determined to
read on – keen to know what had happened in Venice when
Sir Charles met Arabella.

Chapter Thirty-Six

The house had been asleep; there had been no sign of her or her spies. I am safe for now in my nighttime scribbling, but I can feel myself getting slower. She knows how much my body craves the opium, so she leaves extra doses within my reach – I struggle not to succumb, but I grow more tired. I sleep when I can in the day, but it is never enough. I must continue with what little strength I have left.

Venice was the most beautiful of cities. I would describe its wonders, but I have no time. I must solely write how I came to be ensnared by Arabella and the opium. I fear I have rambled enough.

I had been in Venice a few days when I had managed to acquire an invitation to the Palazzo Grimani for one of their Carnival balls. I had long desired to see inside the Palazzo, as the family had been huge collectors of Roman antiquities and I had been told of their incredible Tribune room. I can close my eyes and remember the night when I stood inside the Tribune and observed the awe-inspiring Ganymede sculpture suspended from the vaulted ceiling. I thought my heart would stop. There was such a feeling of stillness, of grace, and of beauty, as I gazed upon it. I was already emotionally weak as I stood studying the eagle flying off with poor Ganymede, gazing upon its beauty.

Then in the stillness, I heard a voice.

'Forgive me for disturbing you.'

And there she was – Arabella. God, she was a beautiful creature, and once again I could barely breathe. I had loved Lizzie, but Arabella was a dream, a goddess returned to earth. She bedazzled me in an instant. I don't have to describe her to you – you have of course met her – but I must tell of the impact she had on me. The total need

I had for her. Stupid how one can be caught in a snare so quickly, and shallowly of course, it was her face – her perfect face – that made me fall. Many might say I was an old fool to fall so hard for a young woman such as her. She could have been my daughter, but Society does not wonder at such a difference, do they? What they did wonder at was her lack of money, her lack of name, of her place within my own social circle – even rich merchants have their conformities, as do all layers of Society. But it never mattered to me because I fell in love – not straightaway, but not long after our first meeting, yet I digress. In that room there was only the two of us, with the moonlight illuminating the magical space with the magnificent sculpture hanging over us.

'It's so striking,' she whispered, and there were tears in those wonderful, beguiling eyes. I still had not spoken; I was simply drinking her in as if she was a love potion. 'Poor Ganymede, I wish I could pull at his feet and free him!'

Both her words and American accent charmed me.

'I don't think we should try,' were my first words to her, and she looked at me and laughed. It is easier for me to write our words as they occurred as if I were writing a fiction book and perhaps you may well believe this is a fiction, but I assure you my tale is all too real.

'No, I guess we shouldn't. Arabella Burton.' She held out her small pale hand. Her touch was gentle, cool, and pleasurable. I let myself breathe again.

'Sir Charles Pembrook. So, you know poor Ganymede's story?' I asked.

'Oh, yes, I made sure of an invitation simply so I could slip in here and see this room, this sculpture, and these magnificent treasures.' Her eyes sparkled as she gazed around the Tribune.

Alex froze as he read the account of that first meeting – another chill ran through his body. That same room but a different reaction – Arabella had played her part to perfection in each separate encounter, and he could only feel sick as he sat in another shared room. Would she achieve the same ending for him? He could only hope not, as his resolve to be rid of her intensified with each word.

Was it the difference between lovely, decent Lizzie, with her sensible buttoned-up clothes; and this golden, luscious young woman which made me crazy, mad even in my actions which followed? I was certainly vulnerable – I missed Lizzie but there was so much more to it than grief and loss. My repressed sexual desire was ignited by her single touch, though I did not realise then.

The next few days passed in a blur as we spent more and more time in each other's company visiting every art collection, every museum in Venice. We studied every painting and sculpture. We talked for hours about art, the classics, and history, and our shared interest in it all.

His wife had claimed she had no interest in art, yet in Sir Charles's account she seemed to be so knowledgeable and interested. Alex could only feel dismayed by the parallels of their courtships as Arabella played on their common interests, making it seem like she was each man's kindred spirit. Who was the real Arabella?

She had told me she was a widow, so we had little need of a chaperone – although now I think on it, she always went by her uncle's name. Her aunt did sometimes accompany us, but she soon grew bored. We dined with them often and John impressed me with his business acumen, and wanting to impress Arabella I was happy to invest in his schemes. Looking back, I wonder why I never questioned his past, what he had done in America, and why they were effectively exiles in Europe. But now I believe slavery was involved, even though it was outlawed. It was the one thing Arabella and I disagreed on during those first halcyon days. She believed slaves were a necessity, which was a touch of darkness in our golden world. But love is indeed blind, so I glossed over it, but I should have been more cautious and more questioning.

We had returned one afternoon from a visit to one of the small private galleries, and I had escorted Arabella back to her hotel – they were staying at the Grand. We were laughing as we entered her suite and that was when I met her companion Mary. She was a stiff, glowering creature standing by the unlit fire waiting for Arabella. Her presence sapped the joy from the day, making the room even colder than it already was with a grey pinched face clouded with anger. Mary was formally introduced to me a day or two later and she was cordial, but her eyes betrayed her hatred for me. But I ignored her hostility – she was surely merely concerned for her friend – and Arabella was sweetness itself.

The candle stutters and I realise the hour has trickled by again. My eyes are heavy once more and I begin to feel my pain acutely. My hands are beginning to tremble; I hope my writing is clear, but I crave the opium that I know is by my bed. I dare not bring it with me to this room, for once I drink it, I feel its ecstasy for a brief time, but oblivion soon takes me and I cannot be caught in this room. I must finish my tale.

Chapter Thirty-Seven

Alex's watch struck six and he knew he needed to leave for dinner. He quickly returned the journal to the safe, putting the picture back in place. He could not reveal its whereabouts as yet. His mind was in turmoil as he walked through the silent house. He glanced into the hall, looking up at the galleried staircase as if he expected to see Sir Charles climbing furtively up the stairs desperate not to be discovered. Alex didn't linger and quickly left the house, but as he walked along the now-familiar drive, he thought about all that he had just read.

There was both a similarity and a dissimilarity to the woman they had each married – he recognised Arabella, yet she was also a stranger to him in this account. She had thrived on Charles's grief as much as she had on his own heartbreak over Margot, and Alex pitied the man Charles had become. He empathised with both Sir Charles's despair and fear – a fear he was beginning to know all too well.

Alex could barely eat the good dinner Mrs Parsons had laid out for them, and as the meal progressed a fever built within him. The sweat was pouring from him, and his body began to tremble.

'Are you quite all right, Mr Brown?' Mrs Parsons asked, concerned.

'I fear I have taken a chill, and I feel rather unwell,' Alex stuttered.

'You need to get to your bed,' she said, fussing over him. 'Mr Parsons will take you back now. Should you be on your own? I wish we had room here but there's only the one bed.'

'I will be fine, Mrs Parsons. I just need to sleep,' Alex assured her, not wanting to inconvenience the poor woman any further than he already feared he had.

On returning to the house, Alex went straight to his bedroom, unable to face the journal or the wretched study. His body was exhausted and he craved respite, but once in bed he sank into a feverish sleep full of dreams. Once more he was in Venice running through the streets, an eagle flying above him waiting to pounce. Faces flashed before him as he ran down alleyways – Arabella taunting him, Mary laughing, and poor Sir Charles urging him to run. And then he was at Ravenscourt watching a child run towards the lake with a hoop; as he dashed into the house to call for help, Arabella and Mary appeared on the stairs calling him softly to take his medicine, to return to bed where all would be well.

***

Alex woke in a tangle of sheets yelling, 'No!' There was just darkness and the howling of the wind, which must have intensified in the night. He fumbled for a match and lit the candle on the nightstand. His body was soaked, and he stumbled from the bed, tearing off his nightgown and splashing water from the jug over himself. The fire had burnt out, and he trembled in the chill of the room. His fever had abated at least, and he pulled his dressing gown around him. His watch showed one in the morning, but he knew he would not sleep again; he could not risk those awful nightmares. The study was now drawing him to it, and he knew he wanted to read on as much as he was loathe to creep through the house at this hour.

He lit the oil lamp on the dresser – at least this would not flicker out as easily as the candle – and he carefully opened his bedroom door. His dreams still haunted him as he slowly walked down the stairs, gripping the lamp tightly. The light bounced around the walls creating shadows, which heightened his unease, and his heart leapt in his mouth as one of the stairs creaked loudly, reverberating noisily through the house. He scurried as fast as his weak legs could carry him to the relative peace and calm of the study, chiding himself for his foolishness. *I am alone in the house; the Parsons are close by in the gate house, and I am perfectly safe* he murmured to himself as he entered the study.

The fire had been laid for the next day, and the shutters were closed against the outside world. Alex set the oil lamp on the table by the fire which he now lit, and he noticed with gratitude a fresh carafe of wine on the desk. He poured a glass and took a gulp to steady his nerves. The wine flowed through his body like a balm and he felt temporarily soothed. Then he carefully removed the journal from the safe.

I have started to vomit regularly now, my stomach contracting constantly in sharp spasms, and I have to force myself out of bed. I can only allow myself my opium after I have finished here in the study, otherwise I will never make it to this room. I have long suspected arsenic poisoning. It is an easy poison to obtain even now with the new act; we use it for the rats here. My wife has free access to all my victuals, and she watches me as I eat, ensuring I finish every meal even when it gags me to do so. She mocks me, telling me I will feel better if I eat it all; the doctor, she says, was most specific, but instead she knows it will kill me. She wants my death, my friend, I am sure of that. I hear her whisper to her friend that it will not be long now. She grows complacent and has started to leave me alone with her potions, which I pour away into the chamber pot to give myself more time unless the opium gets me first – it's a fine battle between those two evils – opium and arsenic.

But when we first met, she was loving, kind, and my most beloved friend, so the creature before me now is night and day from the one I fell in love with. The first kiss we shared was an instant of passion from which I would not be able to return. We had found ourselves back at Grimani, another ball, and we stole back into the Tribune room and under that glorious sculpture our eyes met, her lips parted, and I gently pulled her towards me. I met no resistance as my lips tentatively kissed hers. But as I went to pull away, she grasped my head towards hers again and her mouth pushed against mine so my lips parted, and then her tongue was unexpectedly in my mouth, probing me as my own tongue responded. I had never experienced such a kiss. It was as if we were devouring each other's souls. My hands gripped her waist and I was drowning, surprised by the fervour of her passion.

I dream these days of Ganymede and the eagle and in my delirium, I am borne away by a harpy, naked for all to see and ridicule. I wake drenched in sweat, my heart racing, but I am still within the nightmare. My veins pulse as the opium and arsenic battle to consume me, but still I must write.

That night when we kissed, my fate was sealed. I wanted nothing more than to possess her, but I still had some propriety. I did not want to cheapen her, to sullen her name, and I tried to show some decorum to Society at least. I may be a merchant, but I am wealthy, have influential friends, and she was beautiful and young, so we were spoken about in social circles. Our pleasure in each other's company was evident to see, but Society in their cruelty turned on her of course and began to snigger, to say that I was using her – at least, that is what she told me. Was she all too keen to hold my arm, to caress my face, and touch my hand when she thought she was being watched? I doubt the very memories that I have.

We had been at a recital one evening at the Doge's Palace in the magnificent room where Tintoretto's masterpiece was all around us. Kitty and Roger Jobson

228

Once again, each word he read struck Alex forcibly. He could hardly believe what he was reading about his own wife but there on the pages he could see her unfurl in all her wickedness, and once again he was staggered by the resemblances in his and Sir Charles's own stories. The Tribune room would forever haunt him too, his memories tied up with the man whose words terrified him; and he could hardly bring himself to continue. The fire crackled making him jump, and he poured himself some more wine to try once again to steady his frayed nerves. The house was still, daring him, as he sat in a dead man's house, to read a dead man's words.

Chapter Thirty-Eight

I woke this morning with Mary standing over me sneering as she pulled a syringe out of my arm; the sweet citrus smell of the opium briefly teased my nostrils, and oblivion soon took me again. I am sure they are increasing the opium too, although I cannot be sure how often they inject me without my knowledge. I woke an hour ago – midnight I could hear the clock chime. I practically dragged myself from my wretched bed, filthy with my sweat, and other such excretions. Have I lain in my filth for just one day? I lose track of the actual days – the clock may chime the hours but not the days. I know only when it is night and day by the light from the windows.

I caught sight of myself in the mirror as I struggled to put on my dressing gown – my hair is dirty and wild, my face unshaven and gaunt as if my own skull was looking back at me. My thin arms are now full of needle marks, with vivid bruises where they grip me. My eyes are bloodshot, and I could see the terror within them as I stared at this creature I have become. I searched for some water to attempt to clean myself but the bowl I found was full of cold, grimy water. This is what I am. They have been clever in sending the servants away, so they do not notice the sorry state I have fallen into. The house at least is quiet – mocking me with its darkness and shadows as I steal through its corridors to this room. Every step pains me.

Their constant presence looming over me is a stark change from Venice, when after my talk with Kitty, I deliberately avoided Arabella for the rest of the day. I excused myself from that evening's soiree so that I could clear my head. I decided that I could not merely send her a letter calling off our friendship; I would not be that coward, I told myself. I would go to her in person – I owed her that.

The next morning, I sent a note to her hotel and received an instant reply urging me to attend her at once. With heavy heart, I made my way to her suite. I was astonished to see her still dressed as if she had recently risen from her bed – her magnificent black hair was loose and hung down her back like a silken robe, and she wore a dressing gown of luxurious cream silk trimmed with soft white fur which accentuated the curve of her young body. I shivered with desire for her, but I needed to stay resolute. She could see my agitation and bade me to sit beside her. I stuttered over my words as her soft fingers lightly stroked my trembling hands. I explained I did not want to damage her reputation; that I was too old and could not expect her to want to be with me – a man with two teenage children. She had youth, beauty, and a remarkable intelligence that deserved so much more. I told her I could see she had been hurt by the gossip and believed I should leave Venice to protect her name.

Her eyes brimmed with tears at the suggestion.

I remember now how I told her I loved her too much and could not expect such love in return. I hoped I had not taken advantage of her. At these words, she did a surprising thing. Standing in front of me, she untied her robe and let it fall to the floor. She was naked – her smooth alabaster skin shone in the morning light. I had never seen a naked woman before – Lizzie would never permit such audacity, and I had never visited a prostitute even at university when my fellow students had tried to tempt me to visit the local brothels with them.

Arabella gently sat back down next to me and placed my hand on her breast as her lips sought mine. I was taken aback but assumed that Americans were perhaps less prudent than us, and I groaned with longing. I was already lost even before her hands sought my trouser buttons. My hand explored the wonder of her breast, the curve of softness, the hardness of the nipple. She pulled herself away and I felt the sudden loss, but she knelt down before

231

me freeing my manhood, which was now hard with lust. I write this not to shock but to demonstrate how gullible I was, how ready I was to be ensnared, and how much I wanted her. I was a lost man when she took me in her mouth, and I experienced feelings I had not had before. It was as if my world exploded into a world of colour, of excitement, and I could see a future I could only have dreamed of. At that moment, I would have given her all she desired. I did not know then how malignant and horrifying her desires would be. In her room in Venice, she sat back on her heels, her naked form tantalising me, and she licked her ruby red lips.

She stroked her breasts, her stomach, and then the dark hair that nestled between her legs – promising me all this would be mine if we were to marry, and fool that I was, I begged her to become my wife there and then.

Alex squirmed as he read how his wife had seduced Sir Charles – he remembered his own sexual encounters with her in that same hotel, and how special he had felt, how it was as if they were soulmates and how no one else had made them feel that way before. He knew now that sex to Arabella was a weapon with which she wrought destruction on her victims. He too had been led by sexual desire, and he could deny her nothing in those moments. Her confidence and experience as a widow had not surprised Alex. Alex after all had been seduced by Margot Montagu, herself a married woman; who had initiated Alex in the sexual act, and he had not thought to question it. Besides, he thought guiltily, he had enjoyed it. It was also clear to Alex that Arabella had lied about Sir Charles and the non-consummation of the marriage. Alex doubted every word she had ever spoken – the truth seemed to be foreign to her.

Arabella quickly dressed and squealed with delight, calling for her aunt with her happy news before I knew what was happening. I registered Kitty's shock at the ball that evening when Arabella proudly showed off the large ruby ring I had procured that day at Missiaglia's, but it soon turned to congratulations when she perceived how joyful we were. Those were halcyon days as we arranged to return to London where we would be married – all thoughts of continuing my travels gone. I would never see Florence, Rome, Naples, never gaze upon David, stand in St Peter's, and walk in Pompeii.

But even before we left, the bills started to come in, as Arabella began assembling her marriage trousseau, and I could hardly deny her as my intended wife. Her uncle confessed to a cash flow problem, so of course I settled that and lent him further funds. Every time I questioned such a request, she knew how to bring me round. For example, after her hotel bill had been presented to me to settle, she took me to her bed and performed such acts upon me that once again I could deny her nothing. The trap was sprung and how I was falling into it.

She insisted we stop in Paris on the way back to London. She wanted new clothes for her new life and once again I could not resist her tears, which she readily shed when I tried to deny her. In Paris, she insisted we visit Mellerio's to see where the French royal family had purchased its jewellery. I had of course pandered to her whim, but once there she had fallen in love with an expensive diamond engagement ring and I – wanting only to make her happy – had bought it for her. I now wonder what became of the other ring.

Alex could only feel angry now at the way Arabella had lied to him yet again. She had insisted they stop in Paris when he had been desperate to return home to his family – his father had just died and she had spun a sorry tale of how she had never been to the city, how her ring held unwanted memories, and he had fallen for her tears just as Sir Charles had done. How easily beauty and lies ensnared them.

Arabella wanted to spend the Season in London, she had never been to England, and it would have been churlish to disagree, so for decorum Arabella and her family stayed at Claridge's Hotel, paid for of course by me, whilst we arranged the wedding. At that time Sophia came down and stayed with me in the house I began renting for the start of my married life with Arabella. Sophia was in awe of the young and fashionable Arabella, who was kind and loving towards her. They soon became fast friends and were often shopping together for new clothes, visiting acquaintances for tea and suchlike, and deciding on how to furnish the London house, all the things Sophia had missed out on since her mother had died. Arabella was like an older sister, which suited Sophia who was now at an age when she needed friendship.

They were so close that when I drew up my legal papers after the wedding, it felt appropriate to place Sophia under my new wife's guardianship in the event of my death. I recount how you tried to persuade me otherwise, advising me to wait awhile, but I would not listen, believing I was ensuring my daughter's future happiness in case further tragedy was to befall our family. How I wish now I could live long enough to change it so she would have you as a guardian, my dear friend, instead, and if I had been able to see you before we returned to this house I would have done. I worry I have failed my beloved daughter and placed her in the hands of a monster.

As I sit here and write, my stomach contracts and I know the drugs are fighting a deadly battle. I can only hope I can live until the doctor's next visit, but the snow is falling heavily outside, and he may well be delayed. Ravenscourt being in a valley tends to become cut off when the weather turns white and the river freezes. I watch the snow from my bed, losing track of the days and what is real and what is a gruesome nightmare. Even as I write, I wonder if I dream, but then the candle flickers and I am reminded I must return to my bed where at least I will be warm after the cold of this room. I cannot be discovered. Not yet.

It grieved Alex to read of sweet, innocent Sophia also taken in by Arabella. It clearly had been part of Arabella's scheme to act the part of loving stepmother, to gain the trust of both father and daughter, so that for Sir Charles it was an easy decision to make Arabella Sophia's guardian, with the financial reward that came with it. Alex felt guilt too at believing the poor girl had been deluded over her father, when she had in fact been trying so hard to warn Alex in Venice. A memory of Arabella gripping Sophia's arm and dragging her across St Mark's Square came to him, and with sudden alacrity Alex knew that Arabella was indeed slowly poisoning Sophia – the tiredness, the headaches, all pointed towards the symptoms Sir Charles had described in his journal. As soon as the bridge could be repaired, he must return to Manchester then London to ensure her safety.

Chapter Thirty-Nine

Alex skimmed the details of the wedding, which by all accounts was a happy day with Sir Charles's children in attendance – Matthew was even his best man. Alex's eyes paused on the details of the financial arrangements, shocked once more at the audacious schemes of Arabella's family to elicit money from those around them.

As part of the marriage settlement, I had also bought a house for the Burtons in London. I had settled another large sum of money on John and invested in his new business – all to please Arabella. I was looking forward to being alone with my wife in our own house, which was now furnished to her requirements – at considerable cost, I might add – but still her aunt and uncle moved in with us. I no longer remember the reason as to why they came but we were hardly ever alone apart from in our bedchamber.

However, not long after our marriage the pain in my back intensified, and Arabella suggested I increase my laudanum intake. Mary knew of a stronger form of the drug which could be injected straight into you, thus causing instant relief in managing pain, and she had been able to procure it for me. Arabella appeared concerned and loving. I could only be touched and eager to please her, so of course I was happy to take whatever she recommended. She had declared she was so loathe to aggravate my suffering that she withdrew from our marital bed. She had insisted it was for my own sake, how she wanted me to get better, but her absence from my bedroom after such a short period of marriage, only highlighted my advancing age and my own infirmity. I was already letting her down as a husband and my old insecurities played on my mind. One morning, as I came down to breakfast, I overheard her crying as she told her aunt I was already underperforming in the bedroom, that she would never have children of her own, and what was she to do? I believe now she knew I was listening, and it was part of her scheme to get me to increase my opium dependency. I felt such guilt, I would have agreed to anything in that instant.

Opium is a false friend. When I first took it in its most powerful form, I experienced such euphoria and much-needed relief from pain. Arabella came to my bedchamber when I injected that first dose and that night my senses were heightened to a new level. She, already so beautiful, became magnificent in my eyes. I was invigorated as the pain no longer hindered me; touching her skin felt as if she were made of silk, the taste of her was the nectar of the gods, and I truly believed I had discovered heaven. I was once again the man I wanted to be for my beloved wife.

But of course, this feeling cannot and does not last, and the pain returns, and with it a feeling of such worthlessness that the body and mind crave the drug once again. Arabella encouraged it as she whispered how much of a man I had been that night. So, I took more of the opium and over the next few weeks became more dependent. Now my head constantly ached, and tiredness consumed me, and I also became impotent from the drugs. Arabella started to shun my bedchamber again. She had little patience for my flaccid manhood, which lay limply mocking me in my misery.

As I became weaker, she and her fiendish companion became stronger, asserting their control over my household, my family, and my life. Servants were gradually replaced, my business began to suffer, and Sophia grew to hate me as her bond with Arabella grew stronger.

At the start of our marriage, we had enjoyed the Society afforded to the wealthy merchant class of London. Kitty and Roger had also returned from Venice, and we often joined them and their friends at various engagements, including lavish dinner parties at their London home which they had long owned. Arabella was soon embraced by all the wives, who loved her American style and her sharp wit. Her beauty was much admired, and I could see the envious glances of the men who thought me a lucky man.

But as the opium gripped me, I could see them subtly change towards me. I began to slur my words, knock over wine glasses at dinner as the room grew fuzzy, and my appetite diminished to such a degree I barely ate. I knew my appearance was beginning to alarm my friends, but of course my wife used my unkempt appearance to tell them how I would not be helped, and they began to slowly turn against me.

By now, she had made herself into an object of pity, turning it to her advantage as I was soon to learn, as her plan to alienate me from friends and family began to slot into place. One such evening, I was tired; my eyes could barely focus on the port being passed amongst the men, and I wanted to sleep, to slump onto the table in blessed oblivion. As we stood up to leave the table and join the women, Roger took me to one side and requested a private word in his study. There, he told me how disappointed he was in me and how I needed to get some help. I recall his next words clearly even now, as they cut so deep.

'I know a man should not interfere in another man's marriage,' he began nervously, 'but Kitty insisted and well, it isn't what I expected of you to be honest. Arabella is a lovely young woman who deserves better.' I tried to interrupt; to explain the back pain, and the desire to get better, but he raised his hand to silence me. 'Kitty was most distressed the other day when Arabella came to call on her. She observed cigar burns and bruises on her arms. You need to stop this, Charles, before it goes too far.'

Even in my befuddled state, I was shocked at his words. I had no idea what he could possibly mean, and I replied as much.

'Good grief, you can't actually be denying you are hurting your wife? I expected some remorse having known you all this time and thinking you a decent man. This shocks me very much.' With that he left the room, and I stood there a wreck of the man I once was, unable to leave even though my legs had begun to shake and my heart raced with fear – from what I could not even comprehend. Arabella made a fuss of taking me home as Kitty looked on in abject pity and disgust. When we arrived home, I pulled Arabella into the drawing room and confronted her with what Roger had accused me of.

'What a pathetic man you are,' she mocked. 'Look at you, Charles. You can barely stand up, let alone get your tiny cock up.' She poured herself a brandy and tossed it back as I slumped down onto a chair.

'But he said you told Kitty I beat you!' My mind was desperately trying to focus.

'How would you know if you didn't? You hardly know what day it is. Look at my arms, Charles, this is what dear Kitty noticed.' The bruises were livid against her lily-white skin. 'Where did these come from? It must have been my nasty brute of a husband who can't get his cock up for his young beautiful wife, who most of the men in that room want to fuck. Perhaps I should let them.' The words were coarse and shocking from her beautiful mouth.

'But I wouldn't, I couldn't have done that. I will come off the opium. I'll be a better man, but don't say I beat you. It cannot be true.' I sank to my knees in front of her and she laughed.

'Look at you begging. What a man you are,' she spat out the words.

As Alex closed his eyes, trying to block out the pain of the
man's words which seemed to echo his own living
nightmare, there was a loud groaning sound followed by a
crash of glass shattering. Alex jumped up as the journal slid
to the floor, its pages fanning out on the faded carpet – the
words leaping out in reproach.

He swiftly gathered up the fallen journal and hid it
back in the safe. His watch showed it was now four in the
morning, and dawn had not yet arrived. *It must be the Glass
House*, he reasoned, but then there was another loud thud
within the house, and he could no longer ignore it and stay
within the safety of the study. Seizing the lamp, he crept
into the corridor, through to the dark hall with its watching
gallery of portraits. Sir Charles looked down on him, and
he experienced a new closeness to the handsome man with
sadness in his eyes. He was shaken out of his thoughts by
further banging coming from the direction of the Billiard
Room. Alex, with his heart still pounding, made his way
towards it, his hand trembling as he grasped the lantern
with grim determination.

He slowly opened the door to a scene of
devastation. The double doors which opened onto the Glass
House had blown open, the wind carrying glass and debris
across the tartan carpet. Stag heads had fallen from the wall
as if the wind had chased something around the room,

pulling the stags down in a futile attempt to catch whatever it was. The doors kept banging and, after placing the lamp on the billiard table, Alex struggled against the wind's violence to grab one of the doors. In the darkness, he could just make out the further destruction of the Glass House, where the remaining glass had fallen down, with the last pieces of the frame snapped and hanging precariously above him. He quickly battled to close the doors and turn the lock once more. He was sure Parsons had locked the doors the other day and taken the key with him, so he was puzzled as to how they had opened. Alex hoped the locked doors would now hold out and stop the wind from releasing them once more. The lamp flickered, casting shadows around the room, the forlorn stag heads which remained on the walls looking reproachfully at their fallen comrades as Alex picked his way through the scattered glass.

He was once again drenched in sweat and weariness overcame him. He took the lamp and shut the door on all the chaos – more issues for poor Parsons to deal with – and crept back up the stairs to his bed, trying to reassure himself that there was no one else in the house – only the memories of a dead man haunting him.

Chapter Forty

Alex was woken the next morning by Mrs Parsons, who was aghast at his paleness and the dampness of his bedclothes. She soaked a cloth in cool water and gently mopped his brow to ease the fever. In his semi-conscious state, he struggled against her, thinking it was Arabella or Mary attempting to drug him.

'It's only me, Mr Brown.' The soothing voice of Mrs Parsons broke the illusion, and he sank back gratefully into the pillows in the knowledge he was safe and being cared for. 'You still look unwell. How did you sleep?'

'I had such dreams in the night, and you have to tell Mr Parsons about the Billiard Room. The doors blew open from the Glass House. I don't know how.' Mrs Parsons became worried as Alex rambled incoherently.

'Don't you fret about that. You take your time, and I've left you fresh towels and a nice clean shirt. Mr Parsons will fetch your breakfast to the study, and I can get your bedding changed. Do you think you can manage getting dressed?' she enquired kindly.

As she left the bedroom, he wished Sir Charles had been left in the care of this good faithful couple, and then his untimely death may not have befallen him.

Alex suddenly remembered seeing a large cabinet in the corner of the bathroom the previous day, and he pulled himself out of bed, stumbling in haste into the adjacent room. On opening the cabinet, he found it was full of medicines, and he rifled through the bottles. The labels revealed laudanum and opium as he suspected. He opened a bottle and inhaled the sweet citrus smell that Sir Charles had described. Alex quickly replaced the stopper and put it back on the shelf. As he rummaged further through the innocuous bottles of harmless tinctures, he discovered at the back of one of the shelves a half empty one labelled *Poison*. He turned it over and there on the back of the bottle were the words *Prescribed to Mary Manners for the disposal of rodents*. He was surprised they had left the bottles there. The discovery of the medicine cabinet, obviously used by Mary, gave him an uneasy feeling that they were, it seemed, extremely overconfident their scheme would not be discovered.

He closed the cabinet firmly, shutting away its skeletons, and he quickly dressed and went down to the study, eager to speak once more to Parsons, who would soon be arriving with his breakfast.

'Parsons, whose bedroom am I in?' he asked the man as he walked through the door, already suspecting the answer.

'It was Lady Elizabeth's room when she became ill, and then the last mistress took it because it had the one working bathroom – it were added, you see, by Sir Charles when he started to modernise the house some years ago.'

Alex felt nauseous knowing now whose bed he slept in, but of course Parsons wasn't to know, because to him Alex was Sir David's clerk. Instead, he forced a smile and changed the subject to the issue of the Billiard Room.

'That is strange, as I definitely locked it and I have my key here on my chain. There was a key in the lock, you say?' Parsons was puzzled.

'Yes, there was,' Alex insisted.

'I checked the room before I brought your breakfast and there is no key in the door, but the room is certainly a mess.' Parsons sighed.

'How strange. I am sure I left it there. I must bring the house bad luck,' Alex spoke softly to himself, confused as to what was happening.

'There's always been bad luck here.' With those words, Parsons was gone before Alex could question him further.

Alex hungrily devoured his breakfast, and sure that he was once again alone in the house, he removed the journal from its hiding place. But he could not bear to be in that sad, stuffy room any longer. The wind from the night before had scurried away and in its wake the day was sunny at last, and he decided to pull on his coat and sit outside on the terrace. Fresh air would do him good, and hopefully lessen the darkness of the words he needed to finish.

I tried so hard to come off the drugs but each time I attempted it, she would taunt me, slap me, and on occasion she would even burn one of my own cigars into my arm until I cried with pain. She would delight in my misery.

I could no longer go out for I was shunned by my friends, who thought me a drug-addled brute. I could no longer focus on my business. Sophia would not even see me. My heart breaks as I remember how my own daughter, sweet Sophia, believed I was hurting her beloved stepmother and how I had become addicted to a drug that was destroying all she held dear as my business suffered and friends shunned me. My wife, however, was not afraid of me, as I never once hurt her. But I was afraid of her. I still am.

One day, when Arabella had gone out with the family, one of the servants heard me vomit violently and sent for my London doctor – Dr James, a young and upcoming man – who taking one look at me declared I needed to go to a sanatorium for a while to try to recover from my addiction. Arabella was furious when she returned to find me being taken away. She tried to persuade Dr James she could nurse me herself, but I had already consented to his planned treatment. In law, at least, I had the upper hand on that occasion. How I wish he was here in Manchester too ...

That blessed stay saved me for a while and my health improved despite the initial struggles of withdrawal from the opium which my body had become accustomed to.

When I returned for Christmas – only a few weeks ago, but already it seems like a lifetime – I was determined to regain my family and my life. But of course, it was not to be, otherwise I would not be writing this journal. It was an uneasy time. However, at least my appetite had returned, and I was eating once more. I was more lucid than I had been, the drug's grip had loosened enough that I could have a clear conversation, and my mind was functioning again. There were a lot of outstanding business matters and I resolved to go to Manchester after Christmas. I was eager to see you, my friend, and wanted to find out what you had discovered in response to my request to dig into the Burtons' background – a request I had sent from the sanitorium, having been unable to write before for fear her spies would intercept any mail.

Having Matthew home from Oxford helped immensely, as Arabella played the adoring wife once more, considerate of my care and making sure I ate. I had no reason at that point to know she was already starting to poison me. My stay in the sanatorium had worried her, no doubt, and she needed to speed up her plan. I should have spoken to Matthew then, but I wanted us to have a happy Christmas as the year before had been so sad after Lizzie's death. Sophia, I could see, was bewildered, and I think she too was starting to have her own doubts, but she is a child still and what could she know or do? I will not blame her for turning against me, but my heart did break at her coldness.

I tried to ignore the opium Arabella had left by my bedside, but I am ashamed to confess my spirit was weak. The opium was a blessed relief once more as I watched

245

Arabella at Christmas and knew behind her glittering smile lay my enemy, and she was not done with me. She is still not done.

My hand gets ever heavier as the nights go by, as I reach the end of my story, but still the doctor does not come. Dr Ward is also easily influenced by Arabella's beauty and her act of the compassionate wife too; and clouded by his own father's treatment of my mother, who was believed to be mad. I would feel more optimistic if Dr James was still overseeing my care, but I am left to hope Dr Ward will return so I can get a letter to you begging you to come. I do not think I can entrust this document to anyone but you. My wife is cunning and would do anything to destroy this if she knew of its existence. She has already been manipulative enough to ensure we have returned to Ravenscourt despite her knowing how I despise the place, and it feels like its walls close in on me.

It does not help that I am trapped here with Mary, who lives at Ravenscourt with us and who is in fact my wife's lover. I hope that doesn't shock you too much, my friend, but it's the stark truth, and this is an honest account (how much of this you show my children is up to you – possibly Sophia should be shielded, but Matthew should know the truth so he can at least not make the same mistakes as me).

Mary hates me and I should have known from that day in Venice when we first met; I excused it as I did anything in those days to avoid spoiling my idyl. She is a plain, tall woman with a masculine manner about her. I never see her in any colour but dark grey. Her clothes are plain and practical, as if she wants to blend in with the background. Her thick eyebrows meet in the middle, making her look as if she is permanently scowling, and her eyes are fierce in their jealousy. She rarely smiles or speaks in company. She is a silent sentinel, watching her mistress and bestowing hatred on anyone else. I don't believe I have even seen her interact with the Burtons either – they merely

246

ignore the fact she is there. She is a heavy presence in all our lives, but my wife loves her. They give nothing away in public and I did not realise myself until I witnessed them with my own eyes.

It was Christmas night. The London house was quiet as everyone slept, or so I thought. I was suffering from withdrawal symptoms from the opium, and I thought to get a glass of port wine from my study as Dr James had recommended it as an aide to the process. As I left my room and quietly stole down the corridor, there was a sound from Arabella's room – her suite was a little way down from mine. We had no adjoining rooms in this house, which we were both glad of. I had stopped at the sound as it was as if someone cried out in pain. The door was slightly ajar, so I crept towards it. I could hear Arabella moaning quite clearly now and I was immediately concerned, but then I recognised the type of moan she was making. It was the same ecstasy I had heard when I had pleasured her in the past, when she had allowed me to touch her intimately. I was shocked, as I could not believe she had managed to smuggle a man into the house and that she had the audacity to do so.

I pushed the door slightly, bracing myself – uncertain what I would do. Arabella was indeed naked on her bed, knees drawn up to her chest, but there was no man between her legs – but Mary, who was the giver of such joy now showing on my wife's blissful face, eyes closed in rapture. Mary too was naked, as her white plump bottom bobbed up and down with the rhythm of her tongue. For a brief second, I grew hard as the scene turned me on, and I wanted to be part of that debauched scene so starved I had been of pleasure those past months. But my lustfulness disgusted me as much as the two women on the bed, and I turned away quickly and silently hurried down the stairs to the sanctuary of my study and the port wine.

So, Alex had not misinterpreted the scene back in London when he had heard his wife and her companion sharing a bath. The confirmation of Sir Charles's words sickened him, and he could only shudder in the warmth of the sun. He pulled his coat tighter, as if to shut out the monstrosities on the pages before him.

I watched them after that night and things began to make more sense – Mary's hatred, Arabella's need for her, and the closeness they held for each other. As we travelled to Manchester, my unease at being left with these two intensified and Mary's grey eyes bore into mine, Arabella lightly touching her lover's arm whilst mocking me with her smile. I wonder if she knew I had glimpsed them on that night. Here in Ravenscourt, they do not care who hears them, and they cavort long into the night. I am afraid that at the hands of these two witches, my fate is sealed.

Tonight, I wish Ganymede's eagle would take me away, but I am already caught in Arabella's talons. Talons that have dropped me here in Ravenscourt, the house which mocks me in silence. I did not want to come back here. She knew I hated this place. We had talked of it during those enchanted days in Venice and I had confided in her my mother's tragic tale, Lizzie's sad death, and how the house haunted me even more. Arabella had sought to soothe me of my fears with her talk of love. But in fact, I had handed her my biggest fears.

When we arrived in Manchester, we had been met at the station by my mill manager, Arthur Dodds, and he offered to take me straight to my office. I could see Arabella struggle – she could hardly refuse me, but she insisted on accompanying us. Once there, my dear secretary, Miss Smith, bustled Arabella away to refresh herself after the train journey. I knew I had to be quick.

I asked Dodds to send for you as soon as possible to come to the house, but if for some reason I could not speak to you he must ask you to ensure any correspondence from America must be delivered into my own hands or via two people I trusted most in my households. He knew the names. I also took the trouble to write a quick note to Sophia, and I know she will tell you what I wrote. It was all the time I had before Arabella returned and sat listening to Dodds and I talking business. She never once wavered from her desire to hear every single word.

Even with my newfound optimism, I had my doubts over my safety. I knew my wife would be waiting to strike. I did not believe she intended our marriage to continue. Once I had written my will, I had effectively written my death warrant. She aimed for my fortune. Too late I had realised this, and I knew I needed to change it as soon as I got to Manchester and could see you. But of course, word came to the house how you were away on business for a week or two – such a bad stroke of luck – so I could not see you that one last free day. How Arabella must have crowed with delight with the news you were away, but then she also knew that I had tried to contact you. She had to act.

That night at dinner I ate heartily, although I was in the company of vultures, and though none of us uttered a word to each other there was an unspoken menace in the air as Arabella and Mary watched my every move. I knew I needed to eat to improve my strength, but I had misjudged them and now I realise the food must have been poisoned. During the night, my stomach spasmed in acute pain and I could barely leave the chamber pot, which soon ran over with my foul mess. But I was determined the next morning to go to my warehouse, accompanied of course by those two harpies, so when I collapsed on the warehouse floor, my body convulsing in agony, she immediately took over and called Dr Ward. She played on his knowledge of my family past, spinning her web with her beautiful lies, and persuaded him to let her look after me – my adoring, loving wife; and what better place to go than to my beloved family home. My fate was sealed.

Tonight, when I entered this room, I noticed a change in the air and found a dark black raven's feather on my chair, and I recognised at once what the earthy smell lingering in the room meant – Parsons. When I was a child and my father was home, he often withheld food from me as a punishment, but Parsons would smuggle food into the old schoolroom. He would always leave a raven's feather on my chair to signify he had been, and the food would be hidden behind the curtain.

Behind one of the heavy drapes, tucked away out of sight in the corner of the window seat, was a small packet of letters with an American stamp addressed to you. I have no idea how you all managed to ensure their safe passage to me, but I have hope you will come soon.

Such horrors these letters contain. I cannot believe the news they bring. The wicked story chills my very soul and breaks my wretched heart even more. If I can only live until the doctor returns, I will insist you come immediately. Dr Ward must allow me to speak with you, my lawyer. But now I must be careful, as one of her spies may tell her Parsons has entered the house – it was a risk he had to take, but I fear it may yet cost me. I cannot come back to this room again until the doctor comes, as she may well discover me and this journal, and I cannot allow her to destroy it. I will try to resist the opium, the food she brings. I will rest and secrete all these things in my hiding place until I see you.

I hope, David, I do see you again, but I do not believe she will let me live. I pray God my children find this, and my truth be told. I hope she will be uncovered for the fiend she is before she kills my daughter or finds another unfortunate soul to seduce and ruin.

I know I must go now but I am afraid to leave this room. I am so scared, David.

Pray for me, my friend, and for my children who I love with all my heart.

Your dear friend

Charles Pembrook

Chapter Forty-One

The day had cooled now in the weak September sun and Alex was chilled mentally and physically. As he digested those final words, he looked once more towards the outline of the covered lake, and he could sense the house looming oppressively behind him. Tears pricked his eyes as sorrow filled his soul. He walked back into the empty house, not daring to look towards the stairs that Sir Charles had climbed after those last words had been written. He could only imagine what had happened to Sir Charles when he had left the room Alex now returned to. Sir Charles had said he would not risk returning to the study – therefore, she must have been waiting for him that very night. Alex was convinced there had been no tragic accident on those stairs, and it was in fact her fists that had struck the poor sick man. There was no way Sir Charles would have been capable of confronting Arabella and her lover given his weakened state.

Was everything she ever told me a lie? Alex asked himself again, as he sat in the dead man's study, his words ever imprinted in his mind. Alex would never be able to forget Sir Charles's despair, his fear, and the wickedness of the woman who was now his wife and who seemed to have filled his head with lies too. He would have to act, and he owed it to Sir Charles to protect his daughter whose life was, he believed, in great danger. He placed the journal back in the safe, taking no risks until he left and could deliver the journal to Sir David. He must speak to Parsons to find out the state of the bridge and when the roads would open up.

He picked up the American mail and once again there was a prickling unease as a slight shiver overcame him. Charles's words haunted him as he debated what to do with them. He was of course curious, but he was nervous that he was not actually ready to face what they would reveal. Would it be better to hand it all over to Sir David, a man of the law, who would know what best to do with it? But he remembered his own family and what this could do to them, their own reputation and place in Society. He owed them after the mistake of his marriage to Arabella. Sir David might be honour bound to act and then the consequences would have to be faced. Alex had to know what they contained before he decided whether to give them to the lawyer. He slowly opened the packet and with shaking hands pulled out the contents. He sank heavily down in the chair; the colour slowly drained from his face as he unfolded each document. The final horror revealed.

Alex wanted to be gone from the dark enclosing room with its mocking misery, to be gone from this house of nightmares, of shattered dreams and discovered secrets which could not be put back in their box. But he needed to be strong. Mrs Parsons startled him as she bustled in with his lunch.

'Oh, Mr Brown, you look as if you have seen a ghost. You are even paler than you were this morning,' she fussed, as she set down the lunch tray. She touched his forehead. 'No fever at least.'

'Mrs Parsons, could you stay a moment? I have some questions I would like to ask you, if you don't mind?' He gathered his strength as she nervously sat down. 'Can you tell me more about the last time Sir Charles was here? I know you didn't like his second wife.'

'His wife was evil, and I for one don't believe his death were an accident. He could barely walk by the end, let alone tussle with her on the stairs,' Mrs Parsons confided in Alex. 'Oh, yes, we know what she told that fool of a doctor who was infatuated with her. That woman made sure he were alone in the house; she got rid of all the house staff, and we were lucky to keep our jobs after Sir Charles died. She accused Mr Parsons of being in the house that day, wanted to know what he were doing there.'

'Why did she think he was in the house?' Alex pressed.

'We never did know who or when one of her spies told her, but it was odd that Sir Charles died that very night. After his death, the household were in uproar, and everyone was hysterical by the time the doctor came. They were trying to accuse my husband of doing something, but it didn't stick. Besides, provision had been made in Sir Charles's will to keep us on until Mr Matthew came of age, so she can't get rid of us if she tried. It is his house now, of course.'

'And was your husband in the house that day?' Alex sought clarity.

'My husband never told me but all I know is I have eyes, and I saw him that morning meeting a man secretly in the wood – how he got there in the snow I don't know.' She leaned forward. 'I had gone outside to check on the hens, and I spotted the stranger hand over a large packet. Later, my husband disappeared for a while, and I think that's when he sneaked into the house. Mr Parsons was loyal to the master and would do anything for him.'

'You mentioned the doctor – when did he arrive?'

'That were the sad thing.' She wiped away a tear that had fallen. 'He arrived that morning and Sir Charles were barely cold. If he were so ill and should have been resting in bed, what was he doing on those stairs? It made no sense.' She sighed and got up, her distress evident. Alex watched her leave as he sat back in his chair.

***

He slept that afternoon in his wife's old bedroom – a deep, untroubled sleep at last. The truth of the journal appeared to have broken the spell of his nightmares for the time being, as he shut out the worst of the horrors the letters had revealed. He woke to a dazzling sunset filling the pretty room with glorious light. He stood in the turret room and watched as the golden rays made the trees glow, and the leaves gently blew across the drive, even the desolate moors shone in the sun's setting. A cawing sound jolted him from his reverie, and he realised it was almost dinner time. He was hungry and there was now a need to get stronger for what lay ahead. His desire to leave intensified as he wanted to get back to Sir David to share Sir Charles's truth, which the good lawyer had never doubted, and he just hoped the weather would continue to improve so he wasn't further delayed here.

Alex wished he had news from London too – he hoped George was watching out for Sophia and would be able to prevent Arabella from carrying out her murderous intentions. Sir Charles had been correct – he had signed his daughter's death warrant, and it was up to Alex now to stop his wife.

Chapter Forty-Two

The sunset had signalled the start of a blessed spell of warm, calm weather. The river slowly retreated back to reasonable levels, and Alex and Parsons watched the farm men and villagers slowly repair the stone bridge. Mrs Parsons was delighted to see the colour return to Alex's face as she plied him with wholesome food and made him drink full, creamy milk to make him stronger. He would be ever grateful to the kind couple for helping him in the depths of his own despair.

Whilst they waited for word on the returning carriage and when it would be possible to journey back to Manchester, the two men took an inventory of all the damage incurred at Ravenscourt for Alex to share with Sir David. They opened doors, and inspected ceilings and walls of countless guest bedrooms, the old nursery, and finally the servants' rooms themselves high up in the attic space.

As Alex opened one of the servant's doors up in the attic space, he gasped as a woman appeared to stand before him. Parsons placed a steady hand upon his arm.

'It's the portrait of Lady Elizabeth!' Parsons exclaimed. 'So, this is where they banished it to. Well, I never.'

It was a beautiful portrait. Alex was puzzled as to why Sir Charles had said she did not compare with the beauty of Arabella, for the blonde woman in the picture had such kindness, such softness in her delicate face, that you could not help but warm to her. She was dressed in a long, gold dress with a delicate, blue gauzed wrap entwined around her arms that enhanced her femininity. Her smile was gracious but with a hint of mischief. There was such joy in her that Alex could only compare her favourably to the artifice and sharpness of Arabella. It was as if the scales had been removed from his eyes. The portrait he realised was also the perfect companion to that of Sir Charles, who had the same kindness and joy in his face. But his eyes held a hint of sadness, whereas Lady Elizabeth's had a look of love that Arabella had never shown either man.

The two men removed the painting from the damp attic space and carefully lifted it down the stairs. They grunted, as it took all their combined strength to manhandle it to the next landing where they rested it against a wall, pausing to catch their breath as they decided what to do with it.

'Well, we can't hang it up.' Alex laughed, tired by their efforts. 'But it is better here out of that damp room. I suggest we leave it propped up on this wall opposite Sir Charles's portrait until proper arrangement can be made to get it rehung.'

Parsons agreed happily, and for Alex it brought a form of closure to see Sir Charles reunited with his first wife.

***

The next day, the farmer and his men arrived to take a look at the Glass House and brought with them the welcome news that the carriage from Sir David would be arriving that afternoon to return Alex to Manchester.

Alex slowly walked around the silent house, listening for ghosts, but all he could hear was the farm men clearing the glass, shouting and laughing in the early autumn sun. He made one final visit to the study – where he removed the contents of the safe, the portrait of the little black dog put firmly back in place – and had one last look around the sad room where Sir Charles had spent his final moments. A black feather lay on the desk. A door slammed on the floor above.

Alex walked out into the hall.

'Hello? Parsons, Mrs Parsons, is that you?'

His voice echoed in the silence. He glanced up at the staircase, but it was empty, only the dust dancing in the sun's rays, which poured through the lantern roof.

The front door opened, and Parsons appeared.

'Carriage is here, Mr Brown,' he called, picking up Alex's valise. Alex quickly checked the study once more, clutching the document case to him to ensure he had all the papers he needed. The feather had gone. He must have imagined it.

The carriage was waiting once more by the sturdy gates. Mrs Parsons came out of the cottage to bid Alex farewell and pressed a package of food into his hands. On impulse, Alex hugged the woman to him. She hugged him back, beaming with delight, and a tear formed in her eye. He shook Mr Parsons' hand and thanked them both for their kindness.

The carriage trundled back down the drive of twisted trees as the ravens silently watched from the house's roof. Alex did not look back at Ravenscourt.

Chapter Forty-Three

Manchester

The carriage arrived at Sir David's house in a leafy suburb of Manchester; it having been arranged that Alex would come straight there and spend the night. Sir David, he knew, would be a great ally – discreet, capable, and knowledgeable of the law, which is what Alex needed to work out his next course of action.

Sir David anxiously searched Alex's face and he nodded briefly to signify he had the journal in his possession. The older man gently steered him up the steps into the welcoming house, which was in sharp contrast to the one he had left behind – here there was the sound of laughter coming from one of the rooms; the oil lamps lit up the cosy hall, dispelling the drabness of the grey afternoon as a tall, angular woman came towards him. At first, her sharp-featured face gave an impression of severity enhanced by her black hair pulled back tightly into a plain bun without the softness of any corkscrew curls, but her gown was a cheerful green and, when she smiled, her eyes danced in welcome.

'My wife, Abigail,' Sir David introduced them.

'Welcome, your Grace.' She bobbed a curtesy, knowing his true identity.

'Please call me Alex, Lady Abigail, I have no pretensions,' he said, taking hold of her warm, soft hands.

'Come, you look worn out,' she observed. 'There's a fire in the small drawing room and a tea tray. I'll ask the maid to draw you a bath in your room, and after you have spoken to David, you can freshen up before dinner.' He gratefully accepted her kind hospitality.

He sank into the chair by the fire, still clasping his bag containing the journal and the documents, closely guarding the only proof they had of Arabella's heinous deeds. He faced Sir David as Abigail swiftly poured tea and then quietly departed. For a moment, there was just the sound of the clock ticking and the crackle of the fire as Sir David waited for Alex to begin.

'You were of course right to be worried about the river, and I can't believe I was trapped there for nearly a week. It was like Venice all over again.' Alex shuddered, glad now to be free of Ravenscourt.

'It was most concerning when we were given the news, and such bad luck for you. But I trust the Parsons looked after you?' Sir David enquired, as he sipped his tea.

'I was made most comfortable.' He smiled fondly when he thought of the kind couple who had been most accommodating. 'I can understand why Sir Charles trusted Parsons, and of course he was your trusted source at Ravenscourt, wasn't he?'

Sir David seemed surprised at the breach of confidence from Parsons.

'Parsons is true to his master even now and did not speak a word of it. But I found the journal,' Alex assured him, removing it from his valise. 'It's addressed to you, but I took the liberty of reading, and I am afraid it is far worse than we ever could have imagined.' He was relieved to hand the journal over.

'I'll read it while you bathe and dress for dinner, then together we can decide what to do next,' Sir David promised him, realising from his words that Alex would indeed need his wise counsel.

'I am worried about Sophia. I believe she may well be in danger, but I don't know how to warn her without alerting Arabella.' Alex winced as he spoke the name he once held so dear. 'I dare not even risk trying to contact my valet, George, in case she suspects something.'

Sir David was concerned but also recommended caution. 'If Arabella is dangerous, we must proceed with care, and after all you are to return tomorrow, I presume. You will need to be strong now.'

Alex reluctantly followed Abigail up the stairs when she returned to tell him his bath was drawn.

'We will make this right,' Sir David called after him.

Alex tried to scrub away the memories of Ravenscourt; to get them out of his skin, but they would forever be part of him, they would never leave him, and, just as Sir Charles never got to escape, he would always carry the memory of the house, the journal, and his own life with Arabella. He just hoped he could find a way out.

He felt refreshed as he left the bedroom and made his way down the stairs to where a maid waited to show him into a large drawing room at the rear of the house from whence came the sound of happy voices.

Sir David rose to greet him, but Alex, spotting a familiar face that was so dear to him, could only exclaim 'Rupert!' as he advanced towards his good friend. 'I cannot believe you are here.' Tears sprung in his eyes as he hugged his friend close, a display of affection which he could tell surprised Rupert. 'I am so sorry I ever doubted you,' Alex whispered as they pulled apart.

'I sent a telegram straight to Sir David after receiving your message. Once we knew when you would be returning from Ravenscourt, he kindly invited me to stay. Knew you would need a friendly face, and to be honest, no one could have kept me away.' Rupert smiled at his friend, assuring him there was no ill feeling on his part.

'Oh, where are my manners? Please forgive me, ladies. It was a shock to see my dear friend. I haven't seen him in such a long time.' Alex turned to greet the two young girls sitting smiling at him. They looked to be a similar age as Sophia.

'My twin daughters, Phoebe and Anna. My son, Andrew, is at university with Matthew Pembrook.' Alex felt his heart sink as Sir David mentioned Charles's son.

'Your Grace, how is Sophia? We have not heard from her for so long and we miss her so much,' Phoebe enquired, daring to speak out of turn.

'I know she would love to hear from you both, and please be comforted that she has not been deliberately ignoring you all this time. One day she will explain it to you, but for now I ask you to believe me when I say she never forgot you. If you write to her before I leave tomorrow, I will ensure she receives your letters.'

'Oh, thank you, sir, we will gladly do that.' Both girls smiled happily at him, and that matter at least was settled.

'Come, girls, we must get ready to leave. We are dining at my sister's tonight, so that you three men can have time alone.' The girls curtsied to Alex, kissed their father farewell, and blushed as they said goodbye to Rupert, who had obviously amused them in his charming way.

As they dined, Rupert regaled them with stories of his latest escapades and his gambling successes and failures, having left Venice not long after Alex. He had travelled around Italy for a while, still learning his father's business under Sir Roger, and later journeyed on to France, where he had spent the summer on the Riviera. Fortunately for Alex, he had arrived back in London the previous week and had been meaning to look him up.

'Had to spend time with my father, who reckons I now need to actually do some work.' He chuckled as he chewed on another lamb cutlet. Alex smiled, as his friend's moustache appeared to carry as much food within its whiskers as his plate, until Rupert wiped it vigorously with one of Lady Abigail's white linen napkins.

The journal and its contents hung over them for all of Rupert's diversionary tactics, and they readily agreed to skip dessert, taking the port decanter into Sir David's study where he offered fine cigars.

Fortified by the port, Sir David broached the subject of the journal.

'I have never read anything more unsettling and disturbing in my life. I just wish I could have saved him. I should have gone there and got him out. Wretched snow – I thought it best to simply send my man with the documents Charles had requested and later go myself when the weather was better. I will never forgive myself.' Sir David wiped his eyes. 'I have briefly filled Rupert in on its contents – I knew you wouldn't mind. I think, like you, I needed to share the burden of it too. But I can imagine the horror you experienced as you read it alone in that house.'

'I cannot believe the poor man was being poisoned and abused by that woman. How his friends would feel if they ever knew!' Rupert was incredulous at what he had heard. 'I know Kitty will be distraught.'

'We will all carry guilt,' Sir David admitted. 'We should have had more faith in him, but she was so clever, and it seems she still is.'

'Well, she certainly fooled me,' Alex spoke with resignation. 'Now I fear Sophia is being poisoned too.'

'Good grief! We need to save her from that woman and her so-called companion.' Rupert remembered fondly the pretty, shy girl who trailed in Arabella's wake.

'I urge caution,' Sir David calmly interjected. 'Now we have the journal, we have the upper hand, but we need to think our actions through.'

'I also found the American papers in the safe,' Alex admitted, taking a deep breath. 'I wanted you to digest the journal first.' He removed just the items which he had carefully selected from his jacket pocket. 'It contains documents and correspondence pertaining to Arabella's previous marriages. It would appear she was first married to a James MacDonald in South Carolina when she was merely seventeen years of age. There are two further marriage certificates regarding men she married when she was twenty and then twenty-four. MacDonald is listed as a timber merchant on this certificate. The other two men were wealthier – a banker and next a lawyer. Both these men are dead – their death certificates are enclosed, along with copies of their wills which leave all their money to Arabella. Not long after the death of her last known husband, she and the Burtons leave America for places unknown – the trail goes cold according to the letters. But James MacDonald was deemed very much alive, as there was no record of his death when the letter was sent to Sir Charles and there had been no divorce as far as they could ascertain. They were continuing with their enquiries and hoping to have tracked him down soon.'

'That does significantly change things,' Sir David said, taking the packet from Alex to peruse.

'If he is still alive, you can't be married and can acquire an annulment. Surely, she must also be tried for murder?' Rupert became more animated.

'I am afraid the evidence for Charles's murder is too flimsy, as much as I would like his good name restored. A court of law would find it difficult to try the Duchess of Ushington on the word of a drug addict – I speak plainly and as a lawyer, although I am certain she killed him,' Sir David calmed down Rupert, who wished to protest further.

'I agree with you, David, it is a difficult one regarding Charles's death and she has witnesses in Mary and the Burtons who would protect her,' Alex surmised, having had plenty of time to think this through. 'No one ever witnessed her administer the poison, and I think the doctor who attended him in those last few weeks would not want to appear negligent, for it would only harm his reputation.'

'But you can at least go for an annulment?' Rupert insisted, wanting his friend to be free from his marriage but to avoid the scandal of a divorce.

'If I go down that course, Society will laugh at me, and my mother will be mortified. Especially if it came out Arabella was a bigamist and was sent to jail.' He wanted to do the right thing by the family he had already hurt so much, and felt ashamed when he thought of what he had put his mother through.

'There is a further issue which I am sure you have considered.' Sir David cleared his throat. 'If you annul the marriage amicably without suing her for bigamy, she would be free to go, and who knows what she would do next. You know what she is capable of, having read the journal, and I presume from your own experiences which led you here to discover the truth for yourself.'

'Of course, the opium and the poison were bad enough, but it was the way she moulded herself to become the woman he wanted her to be which horrified me. With Charles she loved art, visiting museums, etc., but she told me she found art frivolous and boring. She wanted to do good, to be by my side on social reform. It was as if she was a different woman, apart from the way she manipulated us both.' He shook his head sadly and the two men waited for him to continue.

'I'm afraid she also used her wiles to exert control over us, although she had claimed her marriage to Sir

Charles was never consummated. It was difficult reading it, as I slowly realised what a fool I had been. She presented herself as my perfect woman who adored me. Charles and I simply wanted to be loved, and neither of us listened to the warnings of our friends. I truly thought I had found someone who believed in me and all my ideas which my family had always dismissed.' He slumped in his chair, running his fingers through his hair, clearly agitated.

'You are right regarding the manipulation,' Sir David said, pouring more port. 'It makes me wonder how those two men died and if James MacDonald is still alive. She is a dangerous woman.'

'And what of Mary? She always unnerved me,' Rupert admitted.

'Was there anything in the packet to explain who she is?' Sir David asked, rifling through the documents once more.

'No, there was nothing.' Alex sighed. 'Maybe Sir Charles destroyed some of the papers as he mentioned he wanted to,' Alex suggested. Rupert watched his friend's face and wondered why he lied. He had known him a long time, so he knew when he was lying, but he would not push him at this time – he had enough to bear.

'When did her behaviour change towards you?' Sir David asked gently, keen to ascertain the facts.

'She slowly changed as time went by, as if she can only keep the act going so long – supportive, loving wife. She has slapped me on occasion, and she uses sex to obtain her own way.' He blushed at the admission, as the men looked shocked. 'I also overheard her and Mary saying she needed to gain an heir by me.'

'I believe she finally thinks she has hit the pinnacle of her marriages,' warned Sir David. 'You are a Duke, and she will want to keep her status. She needs a son who would inherit the Dukedom, thereby allowing her to hold on to her newly claimed position in Society. She also thinks Alex is unlikely to divorce her if she has his son, knowing reputation means a lot to him and his family. I presume you have spoken about children?' he asked, turning to Alex.

'Yes, of course. It was my dearest wish to continue the Dukedom and leave a legacy.'

'So, once she is with child, she has her grip firmly on you and your money. The demands will increase as she uses your child against you – even in the law, she will have some rights over the child, and you don't seem the type of man to deprive a child of its mother.' Sir David sipped his port and then continued. 'Sir Charles and the other men were mere stepping stones to you, as she aimed higher each time – trading on her beauty, her youth, and her desirability. But if you cast her out, she will want money to go quietly, and you have already said you wish to avoid scandal.'

'I truly believe she would make life difficult even with the scandal it would cause, her having become a particular favourite of the Prince of Wales.' Alex hesitated. 'Knowing her, she is likely to make up some sad story about believing MacDonald was dead and how I would be a brute to desert her.'

'We do need to check if he is still alive,' Sir David advised.

'I agree, but where does that leave us in the meantime?'

'You can't remain married to that harpy!' Rupert cried, concerned for his friend.

'I do have a suggestion to make of which you may not approve. As her husband, you have certain rights, and with the help of two amenable doctors you could have her declared insane – possibly citing her enhanced sexuality –

and have her committed to an asylum. Still scandalous, I agree, but inside she can cause little trouble, yet of course you would still in the eyes of Society be married to her,' Sir David conceded.

'An asylum! Good grief, I could not do that to her.' Alex's face reddened in horror at the suggestion.

'But she is insane,' declared Rupert, not afraid to speak plainly, 'and your mother would prefer it – far more fashionable to have a mad daughter-in-law silenced forever than a bigamist on the loose besmirching the family name. And your mother would certainly not want any child of hers to inherit the Dukedom.'

Alex knew Rupert made a good point, although it was one that did not sit easy on him. He remembered Sir Charles's mother and how he had been distraught over such an action. Alex too had strong views on the rights of husbands over their wives, especially concerning asylum laws, adultery, and domestic violence. Could he, without conscience, go against all that he stood for? But Rupert was right in his convictions that Arabella was insane and a murderer who would escape justice whatever they did. Was this the only solution?

'There is a lot to think on,' the practical voice of Sir David spoke, 'and I suggest the following steps. I will reach out to Sir Charles's American agents and see if they have ascertained if MacDonald is still alive and found out any further information. Alex, you must return home and see if you can remove Sophia from the house. Perhaps you could call in your own doctor, and he could at least see if she is seriously ill as we fear?' Alex nodded at this suggestion.

'I could look into asylums, have a quiet word with a few people which wouldn't arouse suspicion on your part, Alex,' Rupert offered, eager to help in any way he could. 'I am sure I can find two doctors who would help even if your family one won't. I appreciate you aren't keen, old chap, but we need a backup plan, as we don't have a lot of options at our disposal.'

Alex wearily ran a hand through his hair, wishing there was a better idea. 'It's all we have, I know. All correspondence must go through my club from now on and, Rupert, I will aim to be there each morning by ten, as Arabella rarely rises before eleven, so I can safely leave the house without causing concern. If I am delayed, I will try and send George with a note. Surprisingly, I have heard nothing from him today, and I was expecting a message regarding Sophia.' He sighed, his concern rising for them both. 'What will you tell Matthew, Sir David?'

'I will write and tell him we have papers belonging to his father, which I am acting on and will share with him at Christmas when he returns from university. After all, it is only a few months away, so hopefully he will be happy to wait. I don't think I can say much more than that without firing the young chap up, but a letter from his sister would reassure him for the time being.'

The three men sat in silence as they absorbed all that the night and Ravenscourt had revealed. The clock ticked, the fire crackled, and the candles flickered, but no more words could be found until at last the clock chimed midnight and they rose wearily for their beds, where a restless night awaited them.

Part Four

Chapter Forty-Four

The leaves were slowly falling in the square as Alex returned to Ushington House the next day. He shivered as the carriage came to a halt at his London home, lights glowing in the early evening light, apprehensive as to what to expect.

When he and Rupert had finally boarded the train this morning, he had willed it to go faster, particularly as it had been discovered that Arabella had spent much of Sophia's trust fund taking her on a grand tour of Europe after Sir Charles's death. Fortunately, Sophia's shares could not be touched, and Sir David was seeing to it that his clerks would inform him of any further withdrawals of Sophia's funds. He had hoped for a message from George, but none was forthcoming, so he had a sense of something being amiss – his valet was usually dependable, and it only worsened his anxiety about returning.

'Your Grace, we did not expect you.' Emmerson held the door open, the porter having signalled his master's return, as Alex bounded up the steps.

'I was unfortunately detained much longer on business than I had anticipated and forgot to message ahead that I was returning. I was of course keen to get home. Is my wife in?' He had deliberately not sent word, wanting to surprise the household, but went to great lengths to hide that now.

'Your Grace, I thought you would be aware that her Grace has also left town.'

Alex's heart sank as he tried to comprehend what this might mean and where on earth she could have gone.

'No, I had no idea. Has everyone gone?' He glanced around the hall hoping for answers, surprised that George had not sent word to warn him, knowing his true whereabouts.

'Yes, your Grace, they all left the day after you departed. Her Grace advised us that Miss Sophia was feeling unwell, and she thought a change of air would suit her. She neither mentioned where they were going nor when they would be back. I assumed they were joining you in Dorset.' Emmerson was concerned now at the lack of communication regarding his mistress.

'I am sure she has left me a note explaining all, although I am sorry to hear Miss Sophia is unwell.' Alex's heart began to race as he worried that he had been gone too long and he was now too late to save Sophia,.

'She did not look at all well when she left. Miss Manners had to support her, and Mrs Moffet has been most concerned. As housekeeper and the most senior staff, she did suggest we call the doctor, but her Grace was convinced all Miss Sophia needed was rest.' Emmerson was concerned he and Mrs Moffet would be seen as careless in their duties in some way upon noticing Alex's agitation.

Alex, of course, knew exactly why Arabella had not called a doctor and it only served to confirm her intentions. He needed to speak to Rupert and send word to Sir David in case there was a request for funds from the trust – at least that way, they could discover where they were. But his wife had an allowance from him which would easily tide her over in the meantime. He hoped George could shed some light on the whole matter, as surely he had kept a close eye on them even if he had good reason for not sending word sooner.

'Thank you, Emmerson. Please send some tea into my study; I will eat at my club tonight. And could you send George to attend me.' He began to walk towards his study.

'Your Grace, I thought you knew.' The colour drained from Emmerson's face. 'George had an accident.'

'An accident? Of course I didn't know! It seems like I know nothing about the goings on in my own house.' His pulse quickened, the sense of dread forming like a pit in his stomach. 'What happened?' he demanded to know.

'One of the maids found him at the foot of the back stairs the night you left. He was unconscious, barely breathing. I, of course, called the doctor straightaway, as her Grace was asleep and she had been adamant we were not to disturb her. It was lucky the maid had got up when she did – she had gone to retrieve some sewing – as the doctor believed it could have been a lot worse if he had lain there too long.' He could not meet his master's eye, feeling awful for having to relay the news of the incident to him. 'He was removed to the hospital. I believe he has broken his leg and is severely concussed. Her Grace was most fretful when I informed her of his condition.'

'Was it afterwards that my wife told you they were leaving?'

'Yes, your Grace,' Emmerson confirmed.

'Don't bother with my tea. I will simply fetch some papers from my study and then I have business to attend to at my club. Send word there if my wife should return.' He had been about to ask the butler to send a message to Rupert, but he didn't want anyone to know of his contact with his friend because he could not risk it getting back to his wife. He remembered Sir Charles's words – which of Alex's own servants were spies for his wife? He felt he could trust no one, not even Emmerson, although his sadness at George's accident seemed genuine.

There was no note in his study from Arabella. He had expected that, but he searched his drawers to check for any disturbance in case she had been rooting around in his absence. Most of his papers were with his secretary, who had already left for the day. There was a memo from him detailing some business which involved the Abbey and a note regarding his new will, which had been drafted up earlier in the summer with its provisions for his new Duchess. Alex had delayed signing it at the time because Arabella had been insistent that it was not generous enough to her status if she had an heir. It had been another of their heated disagreements where he had tried to reason with her and she had wept, fleeing the room, and then later making a contrite apology which ended with them in bed together.

***

'Well, thank god you didn't sign it,' exclaimed Rupert later over a large whisky in their club. 'So, she has been berating your man over it?'

'Poor old Simmonds has been getting it in the neck over why an amended will hasn't been made yet. But that's the least of our worries, Ru. I need your valet to visit George to find out what happened. I'm afraid it would arouse too much attention if either of us went.'

'Yes, that makes sense. I'll send Harry first thing in the morning. But where has she gone?' Rupert could not bring himself to say Arabella's name, knowing she had only brought misery into his friend's life.

'I have no idea. I am so worried about Sophia,' Alex confided.

'Would she have gone to Dorset to find you?'

'It's possible, as the Burtons claimed to have friends there. Would she dare though?'

'You must have worried her by leaving early that day.'

'Yes, I realise that now, but at the time I had no idea of what she was capable of. I know I had my concerns, but murder is something else!' Alex whispered now even though they were encased in the panelled room.

'Look, one of my friends knows a private detective – used him once for some shady business concerning a prostitute and his father – anyway, I could see if he could trace where they have gone. My friend said he was exceedingly discreet,' Rupert promised.

'It is worth a shot at least. But somehow, I don't believe she has bolted. My fear is over Sophia and how desperate Arabella is to claim her money.'

'But if Sophia should die, surely she would be suspected this time?' Rupert didn't want to think of the poor sweet girl dead, even though they were in no doubt that Arabella was quite capable of killing her.

'As my Duchess, she probably thinks she is invincible; she knows I would not want a scandal, and she has no idea what I have uncovered.' Alex too did not want to think the worst, but the words in Charles's journals were forever planted in his mind.

'Do you think your absence has made her reckless though?'

'Yes, I think she wants Sophia's money as backup and she could use it to flee the country, make a new life,' Alex determined. 'I don't know what she has in mind. All I know is that it scares me.' He knew he needed to act for Sophia's sake as much as anything, and he feared time was running out.

***

Alex and Rupert met again the next day at the club; Arabella and the others still having not returned.

'Harry says George is in a bad way,' Rupert reported glumly. 'He was lucky to survive the fall it seems, according to the nurse – told her he was his brother so he could see him. George was woozy but knew well enough who Harry was and managed to say, "Tell master I was pushed".' Alex went pale at Rupert's whispered words.

'Good god, Ru. We need to get George out of London at the earliest opportunity. Can you arrange somewhere for him to go to recuperate? Nowhere that can be traced back to me.' Alex was eager to ensure George could convalesce without further interference.

'You think he is still in danger?'

'I don't know, but I don't want to take the risk – I want George safe and well.' He thought fondly of the man who had been a loyal servant to him and his family.

'I've contacted the detective,' Rupert said, breaking the silence that fell between them, 'and he's checking out the stations and ports. I have also been in touch with a Harley Street doctor who specialises in asylum referrals. He was most accommodating – advised how he and a colleague would happily sign off on a committal, for a nice fee of course, and he recommended a place called Ticehurst in Surrey, which has become fashionable with Society.' He recognised his friend's hesitation but knew it was the only way. 'Showed me a brochure, and it has various suites and therapies – looked like one of those spa hotels that are all the rage.'

Alex was still struggling with the idea of incarcerating a woman in such a place.

'It does look nice and, Alex, what's the alternative if she is a danger to Sophia, if she did murder Charles, and tried to kill poor George? We aren't lying! She obviously needs help, as she is clearly a mad woman – along with her creepy companion.' Rupert grimaced as he thought of the intimidating Mary.

'I should have listened to you in Venice, Rupert, so I will listen to you now.' Alex looked apologetically at his friend. 'I cannot dither any longer and have to put this right. Get the doctors to draw up the paperwork and as soon as she returns, I will get her committed to Ticehurst. I trust you and only wish I had done so before!'

Rupert waved his hand dismissively, not wanting his friend to feel worse than he already did, and after all they could not change the past. 'What will you do about Mary, by the way?' Rupert enquired.

'I don't care what becomes of her as long as she leaves and disappears along with the Burtons – it's Arabella who is tied to me by marriage.' Alex was adamant, although he was uneasy at the thought of Mary Manners still being at large after she had been the one to acquire the rat poison at Ravenscourt.

'Let's hope they all leave,' Rupert concurred.

'I have no legal rights over them, but I can order them to leave my house. I wish I could do it on their return, but I don't want her to bolt until we have everything in place to put her away in the asylum and prevent her pulling these tricks again. That is my priority now – to stop her before she causes any more harm.'

Chapter Forty-Five

The week dragged by as Alex waited for further news of his errant wife. The detective Rupert had found had drawn blanks so far, but it was hoped she had not left the country. He had checked for sightings at the fashionable seaside resorts of Brighton, Margate, Eastbourne, and Broadstairs, but no one had seen Arabella's party. Dorset, in particular Bournemouth and Poole, had also been ruled out, and there was no record of any business acquaintances of Mr Burton either. It was, the detective advised, a painstaking and long process, and not necessarily foolproof, for Arabella had the means to disappear for a while at least.

Alex hoped she had gone on a house visit with one of her Society friends; after all, September was the time for shooting parties and other such country pursuits. But his wife was not a fan of the country, as she had demonstrated so well at the Abbey, so he was not convinced that was what had happened. He also could not imagine her taking Sophia and the Burtons with her unless of course they had split into two separate parties. He and Rupert had attempted discreet enquiries, but London was quiet, and he could not risk the embarrassment of asking anyone outright if they knew where his wife was for the gossip it would elicit about his marriage.

On Saturday morning, as he was about to leave for his club for another futile meeting with Rupert, where no doubt they would have no further news, there was a loud commotion in the entrance hall.

'Alex, darling, you look as if you have seen a ghost.' Arabella strode towards him, smiling as if nothing were amiss.

'Where have you been?' was all he could manage, his throat constricted as he quelled his shock.

'Did you not receive my message? Oh, silly me, did I actually forget to leave one in my haste, and of course I had no idea where you had sneaked off to, you naughty boy. Have you acquired a mistress?' She laughed gaily, and he was too stunned by her accusation to respond. 'Well, my love, we had to leave as Sophia was most unwell, and we were all very worried. Harriet and I thought it best we retired to the seaside for some fresh air and lots of rest. I wanted her to have complete relaxation with no distractions, so we went to Llandudno in Wales. One of the ladies at the women's movement recommended it and look what wonders it has done for our darling girl.'

Sophia emerged from the small crowd of people within the hall – the Burtons of course, Mary glowering, various footmen, and a perturbed-looking Emmerson trying to organise the unexpected arrival, which had caused much chaos. Alex was astonished at how well Sophia appeared. There was colour in her face, and she walked calmly towards him with her shy, tentative smile that he knew so well.

'It is good to see you, my Lord. I hope all is well with you?' She gripped his hand, and her smile did not falter but her eyes signalled a warning as Arabella watched intently.

'I am glad to see you so well, Sophia.' Alex looked enquiringly at her, hoping for a sign from the young girl, as he was puzzled by Sophia's seemingly quick recovery. None of it made any sense and he had a foreboding that all was not as it seemed.

'Now come, Sophia, you must still rest. Mary will take you to your room, and see you are settled. Such a long journey we have had, and I insist you stay there for a few days. I want no relapses, and Mary will take good care of you, my dear.' Arabella practically pushed Sophia away from her husband, but all in the name of being a caring stepmother. Mary grabbed the girl's arm, and hurried her up the stairs, and Sophia turned around once, a quick telling look. All was indeed not well, but Alex felt powerless to act in case it raise Arabella's suspicions and cause her to hasten her schemes.

The Burtons came over and fussed over him and, before he knew it, they were all settled in the drawing room drinking tea as Arabella continued her relentless gaiety, recounting what a time they had enjoyed. Alex sat quietly, smiling gallantly as if he were enchanted by her as she clung to him, her dark eyes searching for any change in him, but he remained steadfast.

'Are you pleased to see me, my love? You know I was only teasing about a mistress.' Her hand was now stroking his thigh, and his body quivered in remembrance at how easily it gave in to her touch.

'Of course, my dear.' He swallowed. 'I was worried about you. You should have sent me a message.'

'But, darling boy, I had no idea if you were home. After all, you had crept out of the house that day without a word. I was distraught when I found you gone! I was convinced you had left me.' She sobbed now, tears her choice of weapon again to try and manipulate him. 'Dear Aunt Harriet had to calm me down, and Uncle explained a man needed to do his business. Then Sophia became ill. I panicked and wanted some time to think, to get Sophia well of course – I would never forgive myself if something happened to her.' He did not believe a word she uttered, but forced himself to nod along, feigning understanding. 'Oh, Alex, I missed you so much but, well, I have some happy news to share!' She regained her composure, brushed away the tears, and smiled ecstatically at him as the Burtons looked on delighted. Arabella watched him now with greedy, lascivious eyes. His blood ran cold as he saw her triumphant face.

'Can you not guess?' She smirked and preened.

'No, I cannot,' he stammered, as the room seemed to press in on him, trapping him in its crimson web.

'I am pregnant with your heir!' Alex's world fell apart as she delivered her blow. 'Are you not happy, my love? It is all we ever wanted.' She gripped his hand tightly. The spider had caught the fly.

'Oh, how wonderful, my darling.' He had to keep up the pretence of happiness, but he knew she had detected a change far greater than the one he had gone through before he had left for Ravenscourt. Her news changed everything – if she carried his child, his heir, he could barely see a way out and could not send her to an asylum.

'Such marvellous news, is it not?' Aunt Harriet broke into his despair. 'Arabella has been so excited to tell you. As soon as we knew, we agreed we must return, but she wanted Sophia to be healthy before we attempted any further journeys.'

'Such an angel she is to a child who isn't even hers!' John Burton blustered, but he too wore a satisfied look that their future would be assured.

Alex's mind raced and he tried to stop himself from screaming, knowing the importance of playing happy families for now. His face ached from smiling as he finally left for the club after Arabella had agreed to rest without his presence in her bedroom. He hoped Rupert had waited for him whilst also relieved his friend had not taken it upon himself to send a note. Now more than ever, his wife must not know Rupert was around.

***

Rupert was dozing by the fire in one of the club's small drawing rooms, a glass of whisky by his side, when Alex finally arrived hours later than planned.

'Good grief, Alex. I was getting worried. Are you all right, old chap? You look frightfully pale!' Rupert observed.

'Arabella has returned,' he announced, as he sat down wearily. After ordering further whisky, he proceeded to tell Rupert the story of where they had been, and Sophia's miraculous recovery, but he could barely bring himself to tell Rupert the final piece of news. 'She's pregnant. It's over and I'm trapped. We have to halt our plans regarding the asylum.' He drained the glass in one gulp.

'Oh, god. This is the worst possible news. But, Alex, what if she is lying?' Rupert had never believed much of what Arabella had said, and he was loathe to believe this.

'Would she lie over something that could soon be proved incorrect?' Alex knew his wife was a practised liar, but this seemed a long stretch even for her. 'It would be a huge gamble.'

'I don't know. But it seems too convenient. Maybe she is buying herself time while she works out exactly what you know,' he theorised, as he called for more whisky.

'But Sophia is well again – what does it mean?'

'Perhaps Arabella realises something is up and is panicking. Look at what happened to poor George. Another incident on the stairs. That wasn't very clever actually and reeks of desperation to me.'

'True enough, but I am still confused over her plans.'

'She can't know the full extent of what you know – remember, she doesn't know the journal even exists, but she has worked out you are on to her. Perhaps Sophia being ill was too obvious, so she had to get her better – divert attention and then, of course, having your heir is her trump card,' Rupert continued. 'However, if it turns out she is still married to her first husband – MacDonald – your heir will be illegitimate.' Rupert was trying to make sense of it all, but neither man was convinced that they could work out what she was up to.

'You may well be right, but the baby changes everything. I can hardly send the mother of my unborn child to an asylum, and for the same reason I certainly can't divorce her.' Alex sighed.

'Look how many times she has been married, yet not one child. I may not be a medical man, but it strikes me as odd,' Rupert mused, always being of sharp intellect. 'From what you've shared, we know she uses sex to control her men, and while there are ways to prevent such things, they aren't exactly foolproof. My father gave me the big lecture on that matter before I went up to Cambridge.'

'Oh, yes, my father too. Seemed proud to be telling me how to bed a prostitute and not contract some sort of disease or unwanted child! But, Ru, I am trying to think about the last time I slept with her – I am sure she must be at least a few months gone, so we would surely know by Christmas if she is lying. Therefore, she would have to be planning something soon. Until I know for certain though, I can't risk it.'

'I still think she lies.' Rupert shook his head, eager to see his friend freed from the vulture. Alex's announcement had caught him off guard, so he nearly forgot the news he had meant to update him on. 'Oh, by the way, George has been discharged to the rest home we agreed on. All the paperwork in his new name of James Collins. Nothing should lead back to you or I.'

'Thank Harry for me,' Alex said, grateful for some good news at least. 'She asked about George, but I informed her all I knew was that he was still unconscious in hospital. I pretended to be shocked that she would think a Duke would turn up at his valet's bedside. She seemed to believe it, but I'm glad he's out of there as she mentioned someone should go and see him, which sounded ominous.' He signalled for more whisky.

'Good work saying he's still unconscious, as we don't want her to suspect that you know he was pushed.' Rupert nodded his thanks to the waiter who refreshed their drinks. 'George confided in Harry that he was too scared to return to the house, but worried for you. I must say I am worried too. What if her plan is to kill you? You have no one in the house you can trust now.'

'It may well have been her plan in getting rid of George. I will have to be more careful, but I can't see her killing me until the baby is born alive and well.' Alex tossed back his whisky. 'After all, she will not receive much if there is no heir, and if it's a girl I am not sure what that would mean for her. She must realise the title and estate are entailed on male heirs.' It had indeed been a gamble for her to play this card, as it did not necessarily assure her future as she hoped. 'I need to speak to Sophia to find out what happened in Wales. God, I feel sick at the thought of going home, but I must be back in time for dinner. I am not sure I can eat, let alone pretend to celebrate.' Alex sighed as he stood up.

'Be careful and try to act with some normality. I will be here each day, and if I don't see you within a two-day period, I'll send that detective around in disguise to make sure you are fine.' Rupert grasped his friend's hand as he walked him to the door of the room.

'I hope Emmerson will look out for me too. He's been in our family long enough and I am not sure he cares much for Arabella or Mary, but I am loathe to involve him – for his own safety more than anything after what they did to George.'

They parted then and Alex, with heavy heart, returned to Ushington House to celebrate his apparent future heir.

Chapter Forty-Six

Emmerson had temporarily promoted one of the footmen to assist Alex in dressing for dinner that evening but the man had a sly, inquisitive air, asking Alex questions about his day, so he greatly felt George's absence. He had noticed the way the younger staff fawned over Arabella and how careful she was to give them a kind word or two, though he could now see the insincerity in her smile and her cold, dark eyes, so he did not want to divulge anything to the footman, unable to trust his own household in case they were spying on him.

He reluctantly joined the party in the blue drawing room for pre-dinner drinks, where he stood detached from the inane chatter of Arabella, Harriet, and Mary. John Burton sat, self-satisfied, by the fire happily consuming his sherry. With some relief, Alex realised, although they dined as a family, his wife was clearly dressed for a night out, and he could hear from her animated talk about the evening's ball at Marlborough House, a fundraiser of sorts. He knew the invitation would have been much coveted, coming as it did from the Princess of Wales herself thanks to the friendship Arabella had managed to cultivate. Alex rarely accompanied his wife to such events; she had attached herself to the Duchess of Manchester's set and they tended to go together without their husbands to have more fun.

Sophia quietly slipped into the room as the gong sounded for dinner. Alex noted the shock and displeasure on Arabella's face, so he quickly greeted the young girl and gave her his arm to escort her through to the small dining room.

'Are you well, Miss Sophia?' he asked.

'As well as I can be,' she replied softly, and her delicate fingers pressed his arm gently. 'Was your trip successful?'

'Yes, I obtained my objectives, and it was as expected.' Sophia's eyes widened at his words, and she returned his smile.

'What are you two talking about?' Arabella appeared behind them, making them jump, clearly not allowing them even the briefest of moments alone. Her voice was gay but there was a brittleness to it, and he noticed Sophia tremble. 'Come, my love, finally we are all together again as a family and we have much to celebrate.' Arabella pulled him away from Sophia as they took their places at the table.

There was a false gaiety to the intimate dinner party, with Arabella resplendent in the Ushington diamonds and red, low-cut gown, which offset her pale complexion and her black curling hair. *She has never appeared so beautiful*, Alex thought, *but beneath such beauty lies such cruelty, such evil.*

'Alex, darling,' Arabella addressed him, 'I think we should give a ball. The Duchess of Manchester, dear Lousia, thinks it is the right time even though it is almost October. She believes we have all mourned enough in this house and we can call it a belated wedding celebration. I have also been entertained by so many gracious hostesses that I believe we should at least return the favour so as not to appear to lack manners.'

'But we are still officially in mourning for my father, and surely you should also be taking it easy?' Alex was aghast at the prospect of having to endure the charade of a ball.

'Darling, I am with child, I am not ill.' She laughed, daring him to refuse her again.

Sophia's knife clattered onto her plate as she stared at Arabella, her mouth agape.

'Oh, Sophia, did I not tell you?' Her voice had a dangerous undercurrent as she stared at the girl. Sophia seemed confused and went to speak, but Arabella spoke quickly, not giving her chance. 'You look tired, my dear. I told you to rest, did I not? Mary, I think you should take Sophia up to her room and give her one of your tonics. All that travelling has obviously exhausted our poor, weak Sophia.'

Mary rose from the table, obediently moving towards Sophia.

'I am fine, Arabella. Your news took me by surprise, but how wonderful for you both,' Sophia feigned excitement and glanced towards Alex, who could see she wanted to say something to him. Of course, she must realise what this meant for them and how bound up they were with the woman they feared.

'No, I insist. You must go with Mary and rest. I do so hope you haven't relapsed.' There was no arguing with Arabella, and Mary was already taking Sophia's arm, practically lifting her out of her seat, so Sophia had no choice but to leave. Alex watched powerlessly.

The meal continued in silence as the footmen cleared the plates and served the next course, while Alex longed for the ordeal to be over and his wife to depart for the evening.

'Alex,' Arabella regarded him across the table, eyes narrowed in suspicion, 'something has been niggling me about your trip. Why did you sneak off in the middle of the night without taking George. It seemed so odd, and I was so upset – wasn't I, Aunt Harriet? – that you had gone without saying goodbye.' Mrs Burton nodded but kept silent, as they all stared at him awaiting his answer,

Arabella carefully choosing her moment to confront him about it during dinner with her family.

'I apologise. I should never have lied to you.' Alex cleared his throat, taking a large gulp of wine to steady himself. 'I actually went home to Wisteston Abbey to speak to my mother. Our estate manager had written saying how she had refused to leave the Abbey, and I know how keen we both are to start the renovations, so I decided the best thing to do would be to see her face-to-face and demand she leave. George was due some leave, and I knew I would be entirely sufficient without him at the Abbey with a full household of servants.' Alex noticed the slight frown on Emmerson's face, but his own butler could hardly question his master.

'You visited your family and kept it from me?' Anger flashed in Arabella's eyes, and she gripped her wine glass; *ready*, he thought, *to hurl it towards me*.

'I knew you would be upset but I wanted to sort this out for you, my love,' he attempted to appease her. 'I want the Abbey to be our home. I know how much you want to host weekend parties there next Season, so we need to move quickly to get the Abbey up to scratch so we can proudly show it off to our guests.'

'Has your mother agreed not to interfere further?' she asked, gripping her wine glass tighter.

'Yes. It took a lot of negotiation, but she understands she has no choice. I was exceedingly firm,' he lied to his wife. 'I also spent time with my steward going through the renovations we discussed.'

'Did you tell your mother she would receive no further money from us?' Her smile was dazzling, as she believed his words and the perceived victory she had achieved over his mother.

'Of course, dearest. She understands her position now.' Alex could feel the bile rising in his throat as he spoke the treacherous words, realising how shabbily he had treated his own family simply to please this creature before him. Of course, he had not seen his mother recently, but his letters to her sent via his secretary had been cold and firm before he had discovered the truth about his own wife. He questioned how he could ever make any of this right again but hoped that once Arabella was dealt with – one way or another – he could turn his attentions to just that.

'Well, as I could not have any weekend parties at the Abbey, at least we can have a ball here!' Arabella was triumphant, knowing she had him and he could not raise further objections. He had walked into her web again, but he needed something to distract her, and her throwing herself into preparations would give him more time to continue to slip out to the club and meet Rupert.

'Of course, my darling, you are right, you deserve a ball.' He watched as her face lit up, her grip loosened on her wine glass, and she clapped her hands in glee at his agreement.

'I shall speak to dear Louisa tonight and begin to plan. Oh, Aunt Harriet, how exciting – my first ball in my home.' She turned to her aunt, who smiled back at her, and Alex caught the look between them – which conveyed not only victory over the ball but victory over Alex, who they believed to be pliable to her every whim. He shivered as the web seemed to tighten, and he struggled to believe how he would get out of her clutches. At that moment, his wife held all the cards as she and her aunt left the dining room in a whirl of excitement – how swiftly her anger melted once she got what she wanted. He could not bear to sit there with John Burton, who smugly reached a podgy, grasping hand for the port decanter, belching as he did so, clearly having made himself at home here.

'Please excuse me, sir, but I too have an appointment to go to,' Alex said, hurrying away, making for the safety and comfort of his club.

Later, in the small hours of the morning, Alex woke to the sound of his bedroom door being rattled.

'Alex,' Arabella implored, 'unlock the door. I crave your body, my love.'

He pulled the bedcovers over his head to shut out her false words, even as his own treacherous body still desired hers, glad he had the foresight to lock the door. Even after all he had learnt about her, he still worried he would be powerless once her caressing hands were on him, her black magic having its desired effect. Tomorrow, he would have to lie to her, as the locked door would anger her once more, but he would say he did not want to hurt the baby, when truthfully he could not face sleeping with the woman he now knew her to be.

Chapter Forty-Seven

The Duchess of Manchester had been fully committed to a ball at Ushington House, and had decreed the date one month hence, plunging the household into a whirlwind of preparations and organisation. The large ballroom and accompanying rooms were all unwrapped after years of disuse by the old Duke and his wife. Alex could not remember a ball in his own lifetime being held here; his sister had not yet reached the age of bringing out, and his parents had disliked much of the London scene, especially after the death of Prince Albert, so had retreated to their countryside abode. Now, the carpets were being rolled up, the floors beeswaxed, the walls draped with fabric decorated with plants and flowers on a pale-yellow background, suggested as the perfect hue by the Duchess of Manchester – who it seemed was the font of all knowledge.

Arabella was determined to make the ball the talk of London Society, and no one seemed to baulk at such an event during the mourning period for Alex's father, or the fact that it was during October, when the Season was officially ended – in fact, it gave it extra kudos, as Society had to return from their country estates expressly for the occasion. Alex was relieved the preparations took up most of his wife's spare time, so she was distracted as she procrastinated over the invitations (of which there were at least four hundred sent out), the menu choices for the banquet for the chosen few beforehand and for the supper to be given later, and of course her own magnificent ball gown. She continued to socialise, attending various balls, charity events, and weekend parties. She declared she would not be announcing her pregnancy as yet, decreeing it was too soon, and Alex was more than happy to go along with her wishes. He also wondered if this was another sign that she was lying, and the fact that she still attempted his bedroom door each night heightened this belief. But it still took all his excuses to keep his bedroom door locked, and of course this had angered her.

'You no longer love me,' she wept a few mornings later when she found him alone in his study, determined to see him before he left for the day after his bedroom door had yet again been locked the previous night.

'Of course, I do, but you know I worry about the baby. We should not risk anything happening to it.' He rose quickly from his chair as she tried to sit on his lap, but she clung to him like a limpet. He had to hold her instead, trying to soothe her. But it just encouraged her, as her hand plunged down his trousers, surprising him and his weak, foolish, body – which betrayed his own desire as much as he tried to suppress it.

'You know you want me, Alex,' she purred into his ear, nibbling his lobe, her tears dried up as her hand caressed him. He groaned and could so easily have succumbed if he hadn't seen the glint of triumph in her eyes, and his desire quickly fell away with his repulsion that he was like a puppet to her. He jerked as nausea rose up inside of him, and he desperately tried to keep his face passive.

'For god's sake, are you not a man? You are pathetic,' she denounced, letting go of his flaccid penis and pulling her hand out of his trousers. In her frustration, she slapped his face. It shocked them both in its sudden violence. 'You make me do this; you make me angry by leaving me frustrated. I am your wife, and I deserve to be loved, but you fail me all the time.' She was so close to him, her spittle flicking onto his face in disgust. He had no words in response. He tried to gently push her away, but she gripped his arms tighter.

'I sent gifts to the hospital yesterday for your valet, George.' The change of subject floored him, and he was instantly wary. 'But it appears he has long gone. Where is he, Alex? Your little pet?' she hissed as he gulped.

'I made arrangements for him to be taken to the Abbey to recuperate. He is still very confused and unlikely to recover soon.' Alex hoped the lie was convincing and that she could not argue further on the subject.

'Of course, only the best for him. Well, I hope he recovers soon.' Her cheeks were still flushed, her anger remained, and she dug her nails into his arms. 'I think you hate me, Alex. Do you?'

'No, my darling, I don't, but you are hurting me.' He tried to loosen her grip on him. 'Come, my love, let us stay calm for the baby's sake,' Alex cajoled her, knowing as soon as he reminded her of the child, she would have to be careful.

'Hurting you? Oh, but I love you, my dearest. You are my world. You belong to me forever and always. Are we not perfect together?' There was a madness to her as her dark eyes locked with his.

There was a knock at the door, and she released her grip on him at last as he called, 'Come,' and the housekeeper entered the room.

'Excuse the interruption, your Grace, but Miss Manners has just popped out, and Miss Sophia appears to be in some discomfort. Mr Emmerson and I were wondering if we should call the doctor,' Mrs Moffet spoke up nervously.

'No!' Mrs Moffet flinched at the sharpness of Arabella's dismissal. 'I mean, no, not yet.' Her voice was softer, more controlled. 'We will discuss it with Miss Manners when she returns. I am sure all she needs is a tonic.'

'Maybe we should call the doctor. Sophia has not been well again these past few weeks and surely it cannot hurt to obtain a medical opinion?' Alex interjected, realising this was his best opportunity.

'You are such a good man, my darling, but I know best in the circumstances. Sophia has long been a sickly child, and to be honest she does somewhat play on it. I fear since her father died she craves my attention, and what with the ball, etc., this is usual behaviour for her. So please be assured all will be well.' Arabella was both reassuring and convincing, at least to the housekeeper. 'After all, Sophia is under my care, not yours,' she reminded him that he had no legal right over the poor girl.

Sophia had not been out of her bedroom since the night of the dinner a few days previously, so he had not been able to see her. Arabella had told him Sophia had become ill again, and Mary was nursing her. He watched as his wife hurried out of the room with Mrs Moffet and knew time was running out. The ball was now a week away. Arabella would not want to get rid of Sophia before then, as her death would once again throw the house into mourning and the ball was to be Arabella's big triumph, so she could not jeopardise that. Alex had to stop Arabella, although he had no idea how he could do it without risking his unborn child, even if he did have severe doubts as to the legitimacy of her pregnancy.

Chapter Forty-Eight

Desperate to leave the house, Alex rushed off to his club, hoping to find Rupert and to talk it through with him. However, his friend was absent, but he found a letter from Sir David waiting for him. He had finally heard back from Sir Charles's American lawyers, forwarding the correspondence to Alex, who sank down into a chair in a secluded nook and nervously began to read what they had discovered.

Dear Sir David,

Your enquiry was most interesting. As you are aware, Sir Charles had previously asked us to look into his second wife's background and at that time, we had just managed to find some information regarding her still-existing marriage to James MacDonald. We have since indeed managed to track the man down and talk to him at length.

Mr MacDonald now resides in Newport, which is why it took so long to find him. He claims to have met Arabella Burton in South Carolina when she was sixteen. Her parents are John and Harriot Burton, and she also had a brother and a sister according to Mr MacDonald. John Burton owned four slave ships, which delivered slaves to plantation owners locally and to Alabama. He was assisted by his son, John Junior, who was married to a somewhat plain-looking woman. Mr MacDonald did not meet the sister as she was unwell and he believes she was in a hospital of some kind, possibly an asylum.

Mr MacDonald was a friend of Arabella's brother, coming from a family of timber merchants who had business connections with the Burtons. The Burtons had made considerable money but as slavery became less and less profitable, with laws declaring it piracy, the family were soon in financial and legal trouble. Mr MacDonald had recently inherited the timber business from his deceased father, and he agreed to give the Burtons a sizeable dowry in exchange for marrying Arabella. However, once the money was paid after the wedding, things between the two families soon soured.

John Burton had run an illegal slave ship whereby many slaves had died, and his son – who was in charge of the ship – had been arrested by the state authorities. Mr MacDonald was not willing to be caught up in such activities, fearing for his own reputation, and was adamant his new wife should not be involved. Arabella, however, was not willing to forsake her family. Mr MacDonald describes her, even as a young girl, as manipulative and wilful with an enthusiastic, immoral nature. He returned from a timber trip one day to find his wife gone, along with a substantial sum of money taken from his business safe. Her entire family had also absconded, leaving a pile of debt behind them. He later learnt that her brother had died in prison, and the authorities had been closing in on John Burton. He was unsure of the whereabouts of John Jnr's wife. He did attempt to trace them, more for the money they had stolen and owed him than anything else, but it was half-hearted. He knew the money was lost and he was glad to be rid of them. He is adamant, however, no divorce had ever taken part between them and subsequently he has been unable to remarry himself.

Mr MacDonald had long given up hope of finding the Burtons and is reluctant to become involved even though he now has a family of his own and a divorce would be most welcome. We have negotiated a fee, as requested by yourself, for his silence for the time being. We had, of course, already informed Sir Charles of the relationship between his wife and the Burtons, whom he had believed were her aunt and uncle, and already supplied the necessary legal documentation. We can reconfirm James

MacDonald is alive, therefore still legally married to Arabella Burton.

We were deeply saddened by the news of Sir Charles's death – he was a truly good man, and we await his son's control over the business. We had learnt of his wife's new marriage to the Duke of Ushington and were most perturbed. We are more than happy to assist in any way we can.

The letter, signed by Sir Charles's American lawyer, confirmed much of what Alex already knew about Arabella and her family; and of course, some of the information he had withheld from Sir David would now be known to the lawyer, but her background made for an uncomfortable read and was at odds with the way she had portrayed herself regarding slavery. He was sickened at the news of the deaths and wreckage of so many innocent lives by the Burton family.

Sir David had written his own thoughts, advising that Alex could easily dissolve the marriage and the law could see Arabella arrested for bigamy. This in turn could dissolve her own guardianship over Sophia, as Arabella had never legally been Sir Charles's wife either. But of course, Arabella claimed to carry Alex's child – a child who was innocent in all this – and Alex's mother would never forgive a bastard. The family's reputation would not survive the scandal of both bigamy and illegitimacy – Alex was convinced of this. It might also affect his own burgeoning political career, especially if her background was revealed. He would be seen as a hypocrite denouncing slavery whilst married into a notorious slave-trading family, so he found himself in an impossible position.

Sir David had suggested that the best option would be for Alex to await the birth of his child and afterwards commit Arabella to an asylum, which would at least mean the child was safe. They could affect a quiet divorce between James MacDonald and Arabella on the grounds of desertion or adultery, which Alex winced at. Alex and Arabella could then get married again, hopefully making the child his legitimate heir. He could buy her family's silence whilst keeping her detained within the asylum but, as Sir David said, it was complicated and a risk, so he felt no closer to a solution. These things were rarely kept secret, and he may yet have to ride out the ensuing scandal.

Alex could not see how he could manage another year of 'marriage' to her, but he knew Sir David was right and it might be the only course of action available. His thoughts quickly turned to Sophia. Arabella wanted her money, and the course of action Sir David suggested meant they still had to pretend Sir Charles's marriage to her was legal. To challenge it in any way broke down the ties that held Arabella and Alex and the unborn child. Alex sighed deeply.

Rupert touched his shoulder and Alex jumped.

'Are you all right?' his friend asked, as he sat down beside him.

Alex handed him the letter and called for large brandies as Rupert read it.

'We know she will keep Sophia alive until after the ball at least. Can you get to speak to her before then?' Rupert asked.

'It's impossible. Either Mary or Harriet are with her at all times. Believe me, I have tried. I also wanted to give her the letters from Sir David's daughters and reassure her regarding Matthew, let alone tell her about her father's journal.'

'You have to get a doctor to her at least,' Rupert insisted.

'My housekeeper was most concerned today, but Arabella reminded me that I had no legal rights over Sophia.' Alex had a thought. 'However, I reckon we could trick her into calling the doctor at some point, so I don't get suspected.'

'That's a good idea. A fait accompli. But then if he suspects poisoning, he might create a fuss.'

'But then what? If Arabella thinks we are on to her, she may flee and take my unborn child with her. Especially if Sophia is out of her clutches.' Alex was concerned again – whichever way he turned, it seemed she had the upper hand.

'Would she genuinely give up her place in Society?' Rupert asked doubtfully.

'If she thinks we know something, flight will seem her only option.'

'Then you have to see Sophia without alerting Arabella. I know – what about the night of the ball?' Rupert exclaimed, the idea coming to him. 'Arabella will be somewhat engaged, as will Mary and Harriet surely?'

'Yes, that's a good point. I will try then; it could be my one chance.'

'If you get to see Sophia and think her life is in danger, we need to be prepared.' A plan was formulating in Rupert's mind. 'I suggest we get those two doctors to sign Arabella's committal forms so we can act at short notice. We cannot dither at the slightest chance we have, even if she is carrying your child,' Rupert persisted.

'I think you are right,' Alex finally conceded, 'and can we ask the asylum to be prepared too?'

'I will send instructions later once I get the paperwork and put everything in motion. I am worried we are leaving too much to fate.' Rupert appeared restless.

'Time is not on our side, and I cannot see us being able to see out her pregnancy, if there is such a thing, without harm coming to someone.'

'You still don't believe her regarding the pregnancy, do you?' Alex watched his friend intently as they motioned for more brandy to fortify them for the work ahead.

'I don't trust a word she says, and I never have done.'

'I think you are right. I can think of no other reason why she would still want to sleep with me if she was already with child. She told Mary it was an ordeal to share my bed, and it was Mary who insisted she had to as she needed to get pregnant.' Alex had to convince himself that she did lie as it was the only way to be free from her.

Chapter Forty-Nine

The house was filled with finely attired guests, all adorned in their magnificent jewels which glittered in the candlelight, reflecting off the candelabra decorated with crystal pendants placed in front of large ornate mirrors. An illusion of light and wealth enhanced the radiance of the evening. Music drifted down the stairs into the entrance hall, where Alex and Arabella greeted the guests as they arrived, his wife in high spirits and thrilled to be hosting her first ball.

It seemed as if all of London Society was coming; not one invitation had been turned down as everyone was eager to see Ushington House and its beautiful hostess. It was even rumoured the Prince of Wales might attend due to their friendship.

The past week had been filled with frantic preparations and Alex had been relieved Arabella had been so distracted she had barely noticed him – let alone tried to seduce him – although he knew it was a temporary state of affairs.

Alex moved away from the welcoming party now as etiquette allowed. He made his way through the crowd to ensure all the young ladies were provided with partners, that their dance cards were full. He hurried, hoping Arabella would be detained at the door a while longer as the hostess was required to welcome each guest. Harriet was with her; John was ensconced in one of the smoking rooms and unlikely to move anytime soon, as he savoured his after-dinner port. It just left Mary, who must be around somewhere. She had been at the banquet earlier, dressed in her usual plain grey gown, and she would be expected to attend the ball, but would they risk leaving Sophia for that long?

He knew he must act before the Prince of Wales arrived, as he could not be seen to be absent. The Prince would most likely come late, so Alex had a window of time. He came across Emmerson directing one of the hired footmen, and he quietly asked if he had seen Arabella's companion.

'I believe she has joined the Duchess, and I have just seen Mrs Burton go into the red drawing room to speak to the Duchess of Manchester regarding the Prince of Wales's attendance.'

Alex thanked the butler and hastily left the ballroom, seizing his chance. He left the main reception rooms via the servants' staircase, making his way up to the bedroom floor and to Sophia's room.

He tapped lightly on her door, his heart racing as he listened for an answer. There was silence. He slowly opened the door to find the room dimly lit by one lamp on the chest of drawers on the opposite wall, and the diminishing fire glowed faintly in the grate, but apart from the figure in the bed, the room was empty. He shut the door behind him and approached the bed. Sophia was lying very still, her breathing laboured, and her skin feverish when he reached out to touch her. Her eyes flickered open and she gasped as he came into focus.

'Alex,' she croaked, her voice weak. 'How are you here at last?'

'The ball has finally kept them occupied, but I don't have long. I needed to see you, and I promise I will send for a doctor to attend you once this night is over.' He clasped her small, cold hand.

'Listen, Alex. You must know this.' She eased herself up to a sitting position, determined to tell him what she knew, summoning the little strength she could muster. 'She is not pregnant! She had her courses in Wales when we were away. I saw the evidence. She moaned to Mary how she still could not get pregnant, but they agreed they would pretend to keep you in her clutches. I never thought they would go through with it though.' The tension he had been carrying these past few weeks lifted from his shoulders, as Alex knew he could put into action his plans without feeling any guilt for an unborn child.

'Rupert knew she was lying.' He shook his head that he had nearly been deceived again. 'This changes everything, but we must be careful, Sophia. She is dangerous.'

'I know she is poisoning me for those wretched shares. It is in the tonic that awful woman gives me. I try!' She gasped. 'Oh, god I try, but I cannot stop them. I fear I have very little time left.'

'She poisoned your father. I found the journal,' Alex spoke rapidly, knowing he did not have much time. 'He was a good man, and he loved you so much.' He could see the joy lighten up her pallid face as tears filled her eyes. 'I also have letters for you from Matthew and Sir David's daughters, but I dare not pass them to you.'

'I am so glad you found the journal,' she whispered. 'But I have to warn you, Mary has been following you. They know you meet Rupert, and she has seen him leave your club. That's why they are trying desperately to get rid of me.' Her energy was waning and she struggled to speak.

There were voices in the corridor, and they stared at each other in fear. They could not be caught – not now. Alex dived under the bed as Sophia sank back down onto her pillows, closing her eyes. Mary and Harriet entered the bedroom.

'Is she sleeping?' Harriet asked brusquely.

'Yes, of course she is. I gave her a sleeping draught so we could attend the blasted ball,' Mary grumbled.

'You know Arabella needs us near her.' Harriet paced up and down the room.

'And what she wants, she gets, of course,' Mary sniped.

'Stop your moaning. Everything we have is because of her,' Harriet admonished, as she duly sank down on one of the chairs by the fire, stoking up the dying flames. 'Anyway, how long before the girl dies? We need that money, as his Grace will soon realise Arabella is not with child.'

'Arabella decided we needed to wait. She was hoping she could at least get pregnant when we came back from Wales. Him and his wretched friend know something, so the Duke won't touch her. We should have finished the girl off in Wales and then we could be gone by now.'

'That friend of his is an idiot. He doesn't know anything, but why she can't get pregnant is beyond me. The one time we haven't tried to prevent such a thing. We should have been set up for life, but no, she has to ruin it with that temper of hers,' Harriet whined.

'You just argued how she does it all for us and now you are moaning,' Mary chided her. 'All those awful marriages she has been through, the babies she got rid of all put a strain on her, you know. This time, she thought it would be different. He is young and would be easy to manipulate, but she grew fed up with his immaturity, the way he clung to her in his neediness, and his constant morality, wanting to do good. You know she simply wants to have fun.'

'And you, of course. Sometimes I think she just wants and loves you. Not me or her father. We are merely accessories in all this. I am getting too old for all this running away and need to live a more settled life.'

'Blame your husband, not her!' Mary retorted.

'Anyway, his Grace is not here. So, we had better find him before she gets mad at us and the Prince of Wales arrives. Shame she couldn't get her hooks in him, but that would have been far too dangerous even for us.' Harriet let out a high-pitched laugh and stood up from her chair.

Mary gave Sophia a cursory glance and the two women left the room.

'They have gone,' whispered Sophia, sitting up, and Alex scrambled up from under the bed, brushing off the dust. 'You must leave before one of them returns. Luckily, I spat the sleeping draught out when Mary was distracted, otherwise you would have found me asleep as they intended.'

'You have done so well, Sophia, and I can act now I know for certain she does not carry my child. Stay strong just for a little time longer.' Alex was resolute at last, as he lightly kissed Sophia goodbye.

The ball was in full swing as he passed the gilded rooms, the air heady with the abundance of overly perfumed flowers. He found his way to the peace of his study – where he hastily penned a note to Rupert – but as he stood up to leave, the door opened and his wife entered. Her face was rosy from the heat of the rooms, and there was triumph in her eyes as she discovered her prey.

'Alex, darling, there you are at last! You simply must dance with me, otherwise London Society will say you don't love me anymore.' She laughed, though it sounded hollow.

He managed to slip the note into his pocket before she noticed.

'How could I resist my beautiful wife?' He took her arm with a forced smile. 'Come, let us dance.'

'Such a poor little rich boy, aren't you, Alex?' she murmured as they waltzed around the vast dance floor. All the time she smiled as she gripped his arm and whispered poison into his ear. 'Such a fool, but you know you love me, desire me. Look at all those envious men who watch you dance with me. What a prize I am.'

'Indeed, you are, my darling.' He could not rise to her jibes. It was imperative she must not notice any further change in him. 'You should be happy, for you must know how proud I am of you and how much I love you. We have our child to think about too, and what a future we can give him or her.' It took all he had to stop the bile from rising in his mouth, his hand caressing her back.

'I knew you still wanted me.' She smirked, radiant in her victory as the dance ended and they were both claimed by other partners who had their names scribbled on their respective dance cards. Alex had not anticipated how fortunate one written commitment could be as he got away from Arabella. The next few dances passed in a blur as he kept up his part of gracious host, the note burning a hole in his pocket. He could feel eyes upon him as Arabella danced past him, with the ever-watchful Mary and the dutiful Burtons standing sentinel at the side of the dance floor.

He had a moment's respite after one of the waltzes and, as he left the dance floor, one of the hired footmen came up to him with a tray of drinks. Alex reached gratefully for a glass but as he went to thank the man, he recognised Harry, Rupert's valet, powdered and disguised but trying to meet his eye. With some relief, Alex nodded his acknowledgement, and discreetly passed him the note, with the melee around them ensuring it went unnoticed by the watching hawks. It was just in time, as Harriet materialised beside him and claimed him for the next waltz.

Alex slowly exhaled, relieved his link to Rupert had been at hand as he noticed Mary Manners still watching him, her gaze never wavering, but her inaction assured him she had not noticed the exchange with Harry; if she had, she would have certainly followed the man.

As the clock struck midnight, a flurry of excitement swept over the house as the Prince of Wales and his latest mistress, Lillie Langtry, appeared – sealing Arabella's triumph. Nothing else mattered to her – not her husband's suspicious behaviour or the dying girl in the bedroom above her. She, the Duchess of Ushington, had finally made it in London's high society, and for one glittering moment she could convince herself she was a success.

As Alex bowed over the Prince's hand, his chest tightened. He wondered how fond the Prince was of Arabella, and if he would intervene on her behalf.

'You have a beautiful wife, Ushington, and I am glad you did the right thing by marrying her,' the Prince whispered into Alex's ear.

Alex couldn't hide his surprise at the comment.

'She told Lousia how you seduced her and were going to leave her high and dry. A rum thing to do to such a vulnerable woman after her first marriage.' The Prince tutted, oblivious to the hypocrisy of his lecture given his history of mistresses. 'Anyway, pleased you came through in the end. She is a credit to you. Always makes me laugh, doesn't she, Lillie?' He turned to his mistress, who had been admiring Arabella's dress and the sumptuous decorations.

'Lady Arabella is a fine addition to any event, Your Highness.' Lillie smiled as she extended her hand to Alex. She was a beautiful woman with fair skin, large, expressive eyes, and abundant chestnut brown hair. She was as tall as Arabella but had a softness his wife lacked.

The orchestra struck up a popular waltz, and the Prince took Arabella's hand and led her onto the dance floor. Alex in turn partnered Lillie, but every step was an agony as if the wretched night would never end. His smile was fixed in place, and his eyes followed Arabella as if he thought she would be magicked away by the Prince himself.

'If Bertie was attracted to your wife, he would have acted by now; besides, his eyes are already elsewhere.' Lillie laughed bitterly as she mistook Alex's interest in his wife and the Prince. 'He prefers more subtle women, and your wife is not subtle, is she. She is fascinating though – she reminds me of an actress who plays many parts. Oh, she is charming of course, but I sense beneath it all there lies someone cunning, but you know all this, don't you?' She had watched his face cloud over as she talked of Arabella.

'My wife is never dull, that is for sure,' Alex remarked, careful not to say too much, learning to trust no one in Arabella's circle, but it gave him strength that Lillie recognised her type and that he had possibly nothing to fear from the Prince, despite his earlier comment.

'Oh, she could never be accused of that.' Lillie sensed he was being deliberately obtuse. 'Bertie doesn't become involved in other people's marriages if it is not in his interest.'

As the waltz came to an end, Lillie leaned forward and whispered in his ear. 'Yes, I know her type. You may not want to hear this, but she will ruin you if you are not careful.' She pulled away and glanced around the ballroom, her eyes searching for the Prince. 'Now, I must claim Bertie before he gets bored and insists on leaving, for that would definitely upset her Grace.'

Lillie swept towards the Prince and Arabella, who clung to him like a limpet, wanting to hold onto her royal prize. Bertie smiled in relief as his mistress returned to his side and agreed readily when she suggested a game of cards. Alex wished the man gone but knew there was little chance while the cards kept being dealt and the Prince kept winning.

'Your wife is a triumph,' purred the Duchess of Manchester, sidling up to him. 'She has found her place at last and will no longer be ignored.' She looked for compliments, but Alex could only shiver as Arabella smiled triumphantly across the room at him, as if daring him to do anything other than stay with her. He hoped he had the courage and strength to face the morning, and that the men from the asylum would arrive in time to take her away.

Chapter Fifty

Alex sat in his study watching as night faded into the morning light. He could still hear the servants clearing up the remains of the ball as he sat and waited, retreating to the safety of these walls after the family had retired to bed in the early hours.

The clock struck seven and Alex left the study, quietly making his way through the house. Harry had already informed him Arabella had gone to bed alone, as Mary was in Sophia's room – Alex could not help but worry at this news. No one would stir without Harry knowing. When the rest of the temporary footmen had been dismissed, he had hidden himself on the bedroom corridor. With the servants busy upstairs and the cook still resting – believing the family would not stir much before midday – the kitchen was empty as Alex crept to the servants' entrance, where Rupert was waiting as planned.

'I have the papers all ready for you to sign.' Rupert thrust the documents at Alex, not dilly-dallying.

'Keep an eye on the stairs, Ru, while I sign these. We must not let any of her spies know something is up.'

Alex's heart was racing as he signed the relevant forms, which would change Arabella's life and the course of his own. Rupert raced down the street with the signed papers, where the men from the asylum were waiting, while Alex hurried back upstairs into the house ready to admit them. Within minutes, their carriage was outside and several burly men entered the house. Rupert was positioned at the servants' door once again, ready to rouse the alarm if Arabella attempted to flee.

The men had their orders and knew the layout of the house. Harry was primed to show them the door to Arabella's bedroom. Alex waited downstairs nervously.

For a second all was silent, and then there was uproar as Arabella screamed. The servants, alerted to the disruption, rushed into the hall in both alarm and curiosity.

'Go back to your work!' Alex commanded, signalling for only Emmerson to remain, and so the others obediently scurried away.

The men appeared at the top of the staircase, forcibly dragging a distraught Arabella, who was crying and begging them to let her go. They had at least managed to get her into a large plain coat, which covered her flimsy nightgown, and Alex was grateful for their discretion. Doors were slamming above, and he waited for the Burtons to appear, but it was just Arabella who came down the stairs still struggling and attempting to wriggle free. She spotted Alex as he stood watching in the hall.

'You dare do this to the mother of your child?' she howled, still persisting in the lie.

'There is no child. You are delusional,' Alex stated calmly. 'The doctors feel you need a good rest to try to dampen your hysteria.'

'You cannot send me there, Alex! My love, I beg you. You hate such places; you can't do this. You love me,' she pleaded, sobbing.

But Alex stood firm, watching as the men carried her out of the house towards the waiting carriage with its barred windows and strong safety locks. He knew they would sedate her once inside, away from prying eyes. But as they got her to the carriage, Mary hurtled down the staircase, screaming Arabella's name. Alex dashed out into the street after her, eager to avert a scene in front of any onlookers.

'No, Arabella! My love. They can't take you.' She darted into the road, desperate to reach her lover.

'Mary! Stop them!' Arabella tried to lunge towards her.

A hansom cab had rounded the corner of the street just as Mary had left the house; the wailing of the two women had spooked the horse, who jumped forward, jolting the reins from its driver. Mary screamed as the horse bore down on her; it reared up in alarm, and its flailing hooves caught Mary in an instant and she fell to the floor trampled.

'Mary!' Arabella shouted, trying in vain to reach her as she was bundled at last into the carriage and the door was slammed shut, as pandemonium gripped the street. The house porter had caught the reins, bringing the terrified horse to a halt. The driver had managed to stay in his seat, but he jumped down to help the porter.

'I am sorry. Is the lady all right?'

Emmerson and Alex had followed the porter down the steps and rushed to the stricken woman as the asylum carriage trundled away. They had their patient and their business was finished.

Rupert ran from around the corner and stopped short at the scene greeting him. The horse, still attached to the hansom cab, snorting in terror, sweat foaming on its flanks; the fearful driver asking for forgiveness; and the fallen body on the road. The few people around at this early hour of the morning had stopped to gape, curtains twitched at windows, and porters from neighbouring houses were peering down the street.

'We need to move her off the street into the house,' Alex ordered, and the porter quickly gathered a couple of footmen to help him in the gruesome task.

'Is she dead?' Rupert softly asked his friend.

'I am afraid so.' Alex left Emmerson to sort out the hansom cab driver, who was still fearful of being blamed, but Alex knew it had been an accident, and his butler would absolve the man of any responsibility. He had seen with his own eyes how Mary had run into the road, and it had all been an awful accident. 'Someone had better fetch the Burtons and explain what has happened. And we need to get a doctor for Sophia.' Alex's voice was shaken, and his face was pallid, but there was a strength to him now as he took control of the crisis.

They entered the hall as Harry appeared at the top of the stairs.

'The Burtons have gone,' he spoke breathlessly. 'They scarpered as soon as they heard the uproar. I would have stopped them, but I was still watching Mary, and when she rushed out of Sophia's room, I didn't know what to do!'

'It's all right, Harry. It is probably for the best they have gone. There is nothing that can be done about them from a legal position, and I am glad I no longer have to live with them,' Alex assured the man.

'As soon as the men entered the Duchess' bedroom, she started to scream and shout, enough to wake the dead. I could hear the Burtons crashing around, obviously packing up what they could, and I knew then they weren't going to help her. But the Duchess screamed, "They have me, Mary, you must finish it for me." I have no idea what she meant.' Harry was perplexed.

Rupert and Alex stared at each other as they grasped what Mary had been doing in that short window of opportunity she had been presented with.

'Sophia!' Alex shouted, and they returned to the house, dashing up the stairs. 'Let's hope we are not too late!'

Chapter Fifty-One

Ticehurst – December 1880

As the carriage pulled up outside the impressive building, Alex could almost imagine he was visiting a country house for the weekend, such was the grandeur of his surroundings. He had glimpsed an ornamental lake with a Gothic summerhouse standing at its edge; and in the distance, he had spotted a pagoda which would not have appeared out of place at Chatsworth. The illusion was further enhanced by the liveried footman who came to greet the carriage, but Alex could not forget this was in fact Ticehurst, an asylum for the rich, and he was about to come face-to-face with Arabella.

It had taken a couple of months to sort out all of the legal implications of her surviving husband, and her nefarious behaviour towards both Sir Charles and Sophia. He had not needed to come to Ticehurst – he could have left it to Sir David or Sir Michael, his own family lawyer – but he had been resolved to accompany them. He had wanted to see if the woman he had loved showed any remorse and, more importantly, he sought to have closure for himself.

But now they had arrived, Alex's hands were clammy and his mouth dry, as he got nearer to seeing her again. Sir David sensed his agitation and understood what this visit was costing Alex emotionally. Alex smiled weakly and nodded to assure him he was fine to go ahead.

The doctor greeted them in his office, wishing to speak to them before they met her.

'Welcome, your Grace, Sir David, Sir Michael.' He motioned to the seats in front of his desk. The office had views across the lake, where Alex could see people strolling, wrapped against the winter chill, as if they were ordinary folk taking a stroll around any park or estate. He was glad it had an air of normality about the place, and it allayed his own fears and conceptions concerning the asylum he had committed Arabella to. But part of him knew this was the exception rather than the rule, and he fleetingly thought about Sir Charles's mother in that awful institution tucked away on those isolated northern moors.

'Lady Arabella is progressing slowly with her treatment,' the doctor informed them as Alex made himself focus on his words. 'I would suggest she does suffer from female hysteria, with a tendency to flatter and deceive as you are already aware. She took the news of Mary Manners' death exceedingly badly, and I believe her grief will take a long time to recover from. I recommend when you see her, you proceed with some caution if her name is mentioned, as she is prone to fits of extreme anger.' Alex quailed at the prospect, having already suffered at the hands of her temper.

'But she knows why we are here?' interposed Sir David, who had noticed the colour drain from Alex's face.

'Yes, she is aware she needs to be informed legally about her position in light of her bigamy, and of course her perceived role in the poisonings of both Sir Charles Pembrook and his daughter Sophia, although I am aware it is hard to prove in Sir Charles's case at least.' The doctor paused. 'Also, regarding her committal here, I am content to approve the motion to keep her here indefinitely. She is, in my professional opinion, a danger to society.'

Alex let out a sigh of relief knowing Arabella would remain enclosed here, and a small weight lifted from his tense shoulders.

'I suggest we go and see her now, and you can explain all this to her.'

They entered a small, stuffy drawing room. It could have been any drawing room Alex had ever been in, with

317

its comfortable sofas, filled bookcases, display cabinets, a writing desk, and even a piano. The French doors were bolted against the cold air but there was a cheerful fire burning in the grate, and the thick heavy drapes adorning the windows kept out the draughts.

Arabella was sitting utterly still, gazing out of the windows. She wore a loose-fitting black gown free of any adornment, her black hair was coiled into a bun with strands of hair escaping, giving an impression of disarray, and her long, ringless white fingers twisted her gown in agitation. A male attendant sat in a corner watching her intently.

'Arabella,' the doctor spoke quietly and softly, so as not to alarm her, 'here are the visitors I spoke about.'

Her face jerked towards them; her dark eyes darted as she stared at them, but her pale face showed no emotion. She did not speak as they sat down, the two lawyers directly in front of her with Alex to the side, not yet daring to meet those cold, black eyes.

The doctor took his place by the male attendant. He had explained she could not be alone with them for both their sake and her own.

'Lady Arabella,' Sir David began. 'We are here to speak with you about the crimes you have committed, and how you stand legally. I am the lawyer for Sir Charles's estate and his heirs, and Sir Michael Ward here represents the Ushington family.' She nodded, her hands still twisting and plucking at her dress distractedly.

'You are aware your first husband, James MacDonald, is still alive and no divorce was ever obtained, therefore any subsequent marriages you entered into were illegal and you are therefore declared a bigamist in the eyes of the law.' Sir David placed a piece of paper on the small table in front of them, with a copy of the marriage certificate. 'This paper is for you to sign releasing Mr

MacDonald from your marriage on the grounds of adultery on your part based on the testimony of his Grace, the Duke of Ushington. Mr MacDonald has been compensated on your behalf by his Grace. It is in your interests to sign it.' She drew it towards her and scribbled her signature on it without any protest. The scratching of the pen nib jarred the quiet of the room.

'As I said, all subsequent marriages are null and void, and therefore you no longer have claim on Sir Charles's estate or that of his heirs. Sir Matthew Pembrook has agreed to allow you to keep the money his father settled on you, in lieu of you signing here that you will make no further claim, and with all other conditions set out in his father's will null and void. We have documents which declare this, and you need to sign to signal you have understood.' Again, the scratching of the pen nib broke the tense silence.

'The same of course goes for my client, the Duke of Ushington,' interjected Sir Michael, as he produced more paperwork. The pen scratched once more. Sweat trickled down Alex's back as he listened to his own marriage being scratched out in one small flourish. It had taken mere moments legally, but he knew it would take him much longer to recover from emotionally.

'Lady Arabella,' Sir David continued, 'you have been charged with the act of bigamy in the Court for Divorce and Matrimonial Causes but, having spoken to the Lord Justice and with the doctor here, it has been decided you should be kept here at Ticehurst instead of being sentenced to prison for your crimes. As your marriage to the Duke has been declared invalid, he has no control over your committal here, but you have been signed over instead to the doctor in charge. All decisions made for your future stay here will be his. Do you understand?' She nodded once, with the trace of a smile forming on her face.

'The Duke has kindly settled a sum of money on you to pay your fees here,' Sir Michael explained firmly. 'But you of course have no further claim on his Grace or his family. In fact, Sir David calling you a lady is a courtesy you do not deserve.' Sir Michael had indeed rallied against giving Arabella any such money. Alex, however, could not be so cruel; at least here she would be comfortable, he had reasoned.

'We have also tried to locate your parents, the Burtons, but without luck,' Sir David spoke once again. There was still no reaction from Arabella, who stared into the distance as her hands continued to knead the black cloth of her gown.

'You are also suspected of the murder of Sir Charles Pembrook, and of the attempted murder of Sophia Pembrook, but the doctor informed me you continue to deny this.' Sir David paused to see if this would elicit any reaction.

Arabella laughed then, a harsh and brittle sound. Alex and the two lawyers flinched at the suddenness of her change in demeanour. She turned her gaze at last to Alex and smiled that familiar triumphant smile at him, causing a shiver down his spine. He would not drop his eyes from hers and stared defiantly back at her.

'You call me a murderer?' her words dripped with venom. 'When you killed the one person I ever loved? Sir Charles was an opium-riddled old man who fell accidentally down the stairs, and you cannot prove I killed him!' The doctor stepped forward as her voice grew louder and more hysterical, but Alex motioned him to wait.

'You and I both know what you did, and you will have to live with it. You are right, we would find it hard to prove it, but we have Sir Charles's own testimony and of course Sophia's.' Alex noticed her face change at the mention of Sir Charles's words. 'Yes, you see I went to

Ravenscourt, and I found his journal.' Her reaction was immediate.

'You lie!' she hissed. 'You are trying to trick me like the fool that you are.'

'He knew you would look for it, so he hid it in a locked safe in his study behind the portrait of his much-loved dog.' He watched her confusion, confirming she must have turned the house upside down looking for any papers from him. 'Sir Charles knew exactly what you and your family were up to and wrote every sordid detail in his journal. I am guessing one of your spies witnessed Parsons enter the house that day and told you. Unluckily for Sir Charles, you correctly believed he was getting closer to the truth, so he had to die before Sir David arrived, otherwise you would lose everything. Although, when you searched the house and found nothing, you thought you had got away with it.'

Arabella was silent, and he feared she could snap at any moment. He was glad they were not alone, and it emboldened him to continue, to finish what he had come to say.

'As for Sophia – we all know why you wanted her dead. You could only use her allowance for so long; once she was eighteen, you would lose control. As she got nearer to that age, you coveted the shares you would receive upon her death. Shares you knew would give you an independent fortune, a safety net if all else failed. We found a half-drank potion by Sophia's bed laced with a significant amount of arsenic, which Mary had tried to administer until she knew she was running out of time to come and save you.'

Arabella screamed and went to lunge at him, a black crow of fury. The male attendant was too fast for her and grabbed her, restraining her arms behind her back in one swift motion.

'You killed her! My Mary.' She crumpled into the man's arms, sobbing loudly. 'I hate you. I don't care what you think I did. Without my love, I am nothing. Life means nothing. You are nothing, just as Charles and Sophia were nothing but a means to an end. I am glad they are dead. I would kill them all again if it only meant Mary lived.'

'I think this needs to stop now,' the doctor spoke firmly, putting an end to proceedings to avoid further agitation to his patient. 'You have all you need from a legal position, I trust?' he asked the two lawyers, who both nodded in agreement as they quickly shuffled their papers ready to depart.

'Did you ever love me?' Alex asked Arabella as he stood up, knowing the answer yet needing to hear it from her.

'Of course, I never loved you. You were just a silly rich boy; you are still a silly rich boy. But you will always love me, won't you?' She started to laugh manically as the attendant took her away. He could still hear her laughter until the doctor mercifully closed the door. Alex hoped he would never see her again.

Epilogue

Alex stood at the back of the hot and stuffy meeting hall listening to the enthusiastic voices of the women speakers campaigning for the right to vote, all clamouring to be heard. They were being shouted down by working class men who refused to listen, insisting women were not capable of voting, that only men had the intelligence and right to change the world they lived in. Alex had come incognito to listen to the women's arguments he knew were gaining pace across the country. As an established Member of Parliament and an enthusiastic supporter of women's rights, he liked to keep abreast of public opinion and hear the views of the working class as much as those of his own Society.

A hand touched his arm, startling him.

'Alex, is it really you?' asked a soft voice.

'Sophia!' he exclaimed, recognising her grey eyes. 'What are you doing here?'

'I could ask you the same thing.' She was jostled against him as the crowd grew more agitated, and he briefly steadied her.

'It's been a long time,' he shouted over the increasing noise. 'Shall we get out of here and find somewhere to talk?'

She agreed and he guided her outside.

'There's a reasonable tearoom a few streets away where we can get some refreshment,' she suggested, and they walked companionably, her arm through his. It had been two years since he had seen her last and she had grown into an assured, beautiful young woman with a healthy glow to her face.

The tearoom was relatively empty, so they settled in a quiet corner with a pot of strong tea. At first, neither of them spoke as there was a feeling of awkwardness, of not knowing where to start after all they had endured.

'I apologise,' Alex broke the silence. 'I should have been in touch after that awful day but Sir David and I both thought it was better for you to recover in Manchester with his family and with your brother, of course. I met Matthew, did you know? When he came to see you in the hospital.'

'Yes, Matthew liked you, but he could see you were haunted by what had happened and that you needed to recover in your own way too. I went abroad after my health improved, to Italy.' She smiled at his astonishment. 'I know it seems an odd thing to do after what happened, but not to Venice. I journeyed to Florence, Rome, Naples, all the places my father never got to see. I wanted to do it for him after reading the journal.' There were tears in her eyes and Alex reached over and took her hand.

'I am sorry you had to read it.'

'Matthew and I both decided it was for the best after father tried so hard to save and protect us. However, you were the one who saved me, and I wanted so much to thank you, but I was worried you wouldn't want to be reminded of what happened.'

'That day, I had no idea what to do. In the aftermath of Mary's death and Arabella's committal, we thought you were dead when we found a half-drunk potion by your bed, and you were so unresponsive. We called the doctor, and he must have thought he had entered a mad house with that woman dead, and you overdosed on arsenic. It took a while to sort it all out and, by the time I came out of what I can only call a daze of emotion, Sir David had fetched you back home where you could be protected from it all.'

'I heard it caused a huge scandal, I'm sorry you were put through that,' she said, looking at him kindly.

'It was hard for a while of course, especially when the news came out that the Duchess of Ushington had been committed to an asylum the night after her ball, that her companion was dead, her so-called uncle and aunt had fled the country, and you, her charge, had been grievously ill.' He laughed bitterly. 'But Rupert was a godsend, and he helped me through it. My mother, as you can imagine, was initially mortified, but she came up to London and was marvellous in the end too.' He had braced himself for a tirade of anger and disappointment, but she had dealt firstly with the Duchess of Manchester, who had been berating Alex over the treatment of his own wife, her protégée and friend, and then after ensuring all other business in London had been cleared up, Lady Caroline had taken her son back to the Abbey for much-needed recuperation. She had even taken tea with the Princess of Wales and assured her that the Prince was not implicated in any way.

'After a while, I began to heal and reflect; I had to decide after all what to do next, especially in regard to my marriage to Arabella, and what it could cost us all.'

'I know you and Sir David set me and my brother free by declaring her existing marriage, and we are so grateful to you.' She squeezed his hand softly, knowing the pain he must be feeling to talk about Arabella.

'We set James MacDonald free too, and of course bigamy is a crime, but as you know she was kept in the asylum instead of serving a prison sentence.'

'You said was, is she not there now?' Sophia was startled.

'I don't know.' He sighed. 'It seems a new doctor treated her with some success, he believed, and he declared she was cured of her hysteria and had become a reformed character. The doctor did have the courtesy to inform me when he allowed her to be released a few months ago. He was profoundly taken with her. Described her as charming and refined.' They looked at each other, knowing neither of them believed she would have changed. 'I have no idea what has become of her or the Burtons, as I never heard from them again.'

'Sir David found out that, although they never returned to the house my father bought for them, they sold it illegally not long after. We didn't pursue it as we wanted nothing further to do with them. But, Alex, there is something I need to ask you.' Sophia paused.

Alex leaned forward.

'In the documents my father received from America,' she continued, 'I noticed there was nothing pertaining to Mary Manners. Who was she? Was she the wife of John Burton Jr?'

'No, she wasn't.' He cleared his throat. 'Mary Manners was actually Mary Burton, Arabella's sister.'

Sophia gasped. 'Oh, my goodness, but they were …' she stuttered, unable to speak the words.

'It's grotesque, isn't it?' he concurred. 'Her birth certificate was in the bundle in your father's safe. I kept it because it was so abominable and I wanted to protect us, I think, from any legal implications Sir David might have posed. According to the documents, she had been in an asylum in America for poisoning her governess.' He could barely bring himself to say the words, but it was time the truth was out, and Mary Burton was dead after all.

'The horror my father wrote about. It all makes sense.' She shook her head at the realisation of what her poor father had endured.

'When I was at Ravenscourt, I couldn't believe what I was reading, what my eyes discovered, and then having to face her again believing she carried my child. Even before she told me she was pregnant, something inside me prevented me from telling anyone the full extent of her wickedness. I suppose I was so ashamed for having fallen prey to it.'

'My dear father,' Sophia whispered, 'how fearful he must have been. I wish we could have charged her with murder, but I understand it would have been hard to prove, and what would we have gained but more misery, more horror.'

'She admitted it when we visited her in the asylum but then denied it later. Blamed her parents, anyone but her and Mary.' Alex shuddered at the memory.

'She truly loved her,' Sophia spoke quietly.

'Yes, and her death completely unhinged her. She declared she could not live without her.'

The tea had gone cold, and they ordered some more so they could remain in the warmth and talk further.

'And you, Alex, are you happy now?' Sophia looked him directly in the eyes, hopefully.

'I have my role as a Member of Parliament and I am campaigning for better workers' rights, for the poor, and for women, as much as I can, so I am certainly content. I try to be as active as possible regarding workhouses, schools, and better education. But I will let my brother, Henry, use Ushington House once he is married. I have no wish to live there anymore,' he explained, clearly still unable to live with the reminders of what had happened. 'I have an apartment near Westminster, and I am in the country a lot managing the estate. Mother is getting older, and as my sister has recently married and moved to Scotland, I keep mother company.'

'I hope you will remarry at some point. You deserve to be happy.' She gently placed her hand on his.

'I am not sure I can face it. She took everything from me – my youth, my happiness, my love. Strangely, I still love the woman she was in Venice, but I realise she was a made-up creature, a mythical being who haunts my dreams.'

Her hand remained on his and he liked the sensation of her touch. 'You have so much to give,' she encouraged him.

'I was a stupid fool who deserved what I got.' He sighed.

'No one deserved her and her wickedness. You wouldn't say my father deserved his death would you, when all he did was love her.' He nodded in agreement at her wise words and smiled.

'And what about you? How is your life?' he asked gently.

'Father's money allows me much freedom, and I am trying to continue my mother's work with the poor and needy. I too am on several committees and help Lady Constance as much as I can to raise funds.' Alex remembered the formidable woman he had met.

'What's Rupert up to these days?' She smiled in remembrance of his dear friend.

'Still gambling and enjoying life, of course.' Alex laughed, not surprised his friend had not been changed by the ordeal.

'Someone is happy at least.' Sophia smiled; a tinge of sadness crossed her face.

Dusk was falling and the tearoom was closing, so they finally took their leave.

'Let me hail you a cab.'

'Will you not share it with me?' she asked gently.

'I need to walk awhile,' he replied, and she understood.

'It was good to see you, Sophia.' Alex smiled as he helped her into the hansom cab.

'Promise me you will be happy, Alex, and live your life to the full,' she urged.

Alex watched as the cab bore her away and he wondered why he had not asked to see her again. He continued to walk towards the city away from the East End, listening to the sounds spilling out of the public houses, as he kept his wits about him knowing a sleight of hand could easily relieve him of the small amount of money he had upon him. He had learnt a lot in these past two years. He was older and definitely wiser, perhaps jaded by what had occurred.

As he walked, he recalled the sounds and marvels of Venice on that first morning, that moment on the Grand Canal as the gondola bobbed against the swelling water as the city unfurled its grandeur, its magnificence, and its glory. He remembered the first time he saw her face; how beautiful she had been. When she had looked at him in the Tribune room, Ganymede suspended above them, he had known such love for her. It had all been a false façade, and beneath the beauty of Venice and Arabella had been only decay and rottenness. Nothing, he knew now, had been what it seemed.

Manchester Evening News

January 1882

Another Tragedy at Ravenscourt

A fire has swept through Ravenscourt, the country house belonging to Sir Matthew Pembrook, set on the Lancashire Moors. The property has been completely destroyed by the fire, which started in the early hours of the morning. Sir Matthew was not in residence at the time, as repairs were being made to the house, and the alarm was raised by his steward, Mr Parsons, who lives in the gatehouse on the estate. Villagers and neighbouring farm tenants rushed to the scene, but it was already too late to save the house, which had fallen into a state of disrepair.

It is believed that new electric light cables being installed may have been the cause of the fire, but arson has not been ruled out.

The incident is the latest in a long list of tragedies to befall Ravenscourt since Sir Matthew's grandfather Sir Thomas Pembrook built it. Sir Thomas's daughter Lily drowned in the lake on the estate; his wife Lady Catherine was committed to an asylum; and Sir Thomas died there in distasteful circumstances. Sir Matthew's parents also both died in the house – Sir Charles's death had been seen as a tragic accident, although it has since been rumoured that his second wife, Lady Arabella, may have had some part in his death. Lady Arabella, a former favourite of the Prince of Wales, was herself admitted to an asylum after her marriages to both Sir Charles and the Duke of Ushington, whom she married after Sir Charles's death, were declared bigamous. However, her present whereabouts are unknown.

Villagers have long spoken of the curse of Ravenscourt, which was built on land where it was said a woman accused of witchcraft was burned in the 1600s.

Sir Matthew and his sister Sophia have made no comment on the latest tragedy to strike Ravenscourt.

Historical Notes

Two years ago, I returned to one of my favourite places, Venice, on a research trip for this book. When I had the idea for *Ravenscourt*, I knew I had to begin the book there and, of course, it gave me an excuse to go back. This time I went on the hunt for locations that could feature in the book. One of the reasons Venice is so perfect for historical fiction is the way it appears set in time: all those gorgeous Palazzos, San Marco, the gondolas, no cars, the list is endless.

So, on a gorgeous March day, I set off to find Palazzo Grimani di Santa Maria Formosa, which is now a state museum. Owned from 1521 by the Grimani family, the Palazzo was home, not only to various Doges of Venice, but to a wonderful collection of antiques all displayed in its magnificently decorated rooms. By 1865, it was no longer in the Grimani family, but for the purposes of my story they remain in situ. But I digress, as all writers do, and I can still recall my first glimpse of the glorious Tribune room, and how that stunning sculpture of Ganymede brought tears to my eyes. I knew immediately I had to use it as a plot motif in my book. I also use the Palazzo's beautiful frescoes – the owl ensnaring a smaller bird that Alex sees is indeed on one of the ceilings. If you are ever in Venice, this place is really worth a visit – follow in the footsteps of Alexander, Arabella, and Charles.

I also used various famous Palazzos which are now mainly privately owned – all the named ones in the book do exist. I dearly wish that I could have looked around Palazzo Contarini Fasan. Built in the fifteenth century, this small Gothic Palazzo is the width of one room, and known, as Sophia explains to Alexander, as the House of Desdemona, and was owned by the Contarini family. According to legend, Nicola Contarini, a famous leader in the wars against the Turks, once lived in the Palazzo, and was nicknamed the Moor due to his dark skin. His wife, Palma Querini, was so fed up with his jealousy and violent rages, she returned to her family.

If I had travelled to Venice in the nineteenth century, the Baedeker guide informs me that my best option would have been by train and, depending on the route I took, it would take me approximately fifty-five hours. A typical route would be Dover, Calais, Paris, Strasbourg, Munich, Brenner, before arriving at the Venice train terminal. I would have required a sleeping car ticket and could look forward to such food as Vermicelli broth, broiled steak, macaroni, and cake. On arrival at Venice, I would make my way to the gondola station to be taken to my hotel.

I could stay at the famous Hotel Danieli, which dates back to the end of the fourteenth century, when it was known as the Palazzo Dandolo. It was converted into a hotel in 1824 by Giuseppe Dal Niel, known as Danieli. It is still one of the most famous hotels in Venice. I drew on the letters of Effie Gray, who stayed at the hotel with her famous husband John Ruskin from 1849 to 1852, just after the city was recovering from the war with the Austrians.

Palace of Wonders Venice by Elsa Gregori describes in great detail the Grand Hotel Britannia managed by Carlo Walther in the 1880s. He was a pioneer of the first electric lights in the hotel. It was also famous for its gardens. It is now known as the St Regis Venice.

I missed the chance to visit San Servolo, an island in the Venetian Lagoon which housed the famous asylum and hospital described in the book. The asylum only closed in 1978, and the island now houses a centre for research and education. Effie Gray did visit the island in 1850, meeting the monks and describing the gardens, the inmates, etc.

I did, however, take coffee in Florian's in San Marco – the oldest coffee house in Italy, founded in 1720. It was, at that time, the only coffee house that allowed women. It is wonderful, not just for its gorgeous artwork, but for the people watching if you sit outside – which I could do on a lovely sunny day. Service is divine – the bill not so much!

In the nineteenth century, churches closed at noon, so one always had to visit in the mornings. I did not visit St George's Anglican Church as I hadn't 'married' Alex and Arabella in Italy at that point in my plotting. It wasn't until 1889 that St George became 'the English Church in Venice' but I needed a church, and this one fitted the story. It is a fairly non-descript building and apparently hardly ever open.

Venice, these days, is an expensive place to visit during Carnival, which takes place in February. Carnival traces its origins back to the Middle Ages, until it was officially abolished in 1707. It reappeared gradually in the nineteenth century but only for short periods and mainly for private parties. I have taken some artistic licence – Effie Gray does however describe Carnival balls in 1850 and going to the Cavalchina – the famous masked ball which finishes the festivities. All of the characters in the book's Venetian Society are fictional.

In London, Ushington House is loosely based on Spencer House in St James's – not far from where I write my books in the London Library. Built by the Spencer family in 1756, it is one of the few houses still owned by the same family. It is currently on a long lease to the Rothschilds, who use it as offices, but Jacob Rothschild funded the restoration of the state rooms and garden to their original appearance and tours are available on Sundays. I also used the Wallace Collection for inspiration.

Marlborough House is now the home of the Commonwealth offices but was once the royal residence of

Edward VII when he was Prince of Wales. His circle was known for its decadence and he was known for his mistresses such as Lily Langtry who appears with him in the book. Louisa, Duchess of Manchester, was also part of his circle – her marriage was a disaster and she was known to help socialites move up the social ladder for a fee. Her affair Lord Hartington was also well-known. After her husband's death in 1890 she married Hartington, by then the Duke of Devonshire, earning the nickname the 'Double Duchess.'

The women's rights movement and the subject of slavery feature in the book. Here are some key facts pertinent to the book. In 1854, a married woman's body belonged to her husband. In 1857, men could divorce women on the grounds of adultery, but a woman could not divorce her husband on the same charge. Insanity after marriage however did not invalidate the marriage. Up until 1891, a husband could still imprison his wife in her own home.

In 1866, a group of women organised a petition demanding that some women should have the same political rights as men. Henry Fawcett and John Stuart Mill were politicians who supported universal suffrage. 1867 saw the foundation of the Manchester National Society for Women's Suffrage (MNSWS) and was regarded as the start of the women's suffrage campaign. The 1882 Married Women's Act allowed women to own and control property in their own right for the first time. By 1897, seventeen women's groups came together under the umbrella of the National Union of Women's Suffrage (NUWSS) led by Millicent Fawcett, wife of Henry.

Regarding slavery, it was abolished throughout the British Empire in 1833 and was outlawed by the Thirteenth Amendment to the United States Constitution in 1865. The importation of slaves had been banned in 1807 by Congress, but this did not stop the illegal trade continuing. The *Clotilda* was the last-known slave ship to transport enslaved Africans to the United States. It arrived in Mobile Bay, Alabama, in 1860 with one hundred and ten men, women, and children on board. The ship was intentionally sunk to hide the evidence of the illegal voyage, and although the federal government prosecuted the captain and his financial backer, the case was dismissed for lack of this crucial evidence. The wreck of the ship was found in 2019. Hannah Durkin's book *The Survivors of the Clotilda* is an evocative read. John Burton and his family are entirely fictional but based on the stories of illegal slavers such as this.

The role of the asylum obviously plays a huge part in this book, and it is a very disturbing history. It is also a well-known trope of Victorian literature past and present – the mad woman in the attic is both terrifying and depressing. In the 1880s, when my book is set, a woman could still be committed far too easily to an asylum by her husband or family. Private asylums such as Ticehurst were more likely to admit women on flimsy evidence or on the signatures of well-paid doctors known as 'mad doctors,' i.e., those willing to certify a woman as insane.

For hysterical women and their families, the asylum offered a convenient and socially acceptable excuse for inappropriate, potentially scandalous behaviour. Rather than being viewed as a bad and immoral woman, honour and reputation could be maintained by the diagnosis of a medical condition and commitment to an asylum.

Many admissions to Ticehurst were sent there after being diagnosed with gynaecological disorders, as well as conditions tied to their stubborn refusal to conform. Hysteria, 'the daughters' disease', was depicted as a condition which particularly afflicted young well-to-do women, who would throw their households and family life into confusion with their so-called irrational behaviour and attention-seeking displays.

Ticehurst House Hospital was opened as a private lunatic asylum in Ticehurst, East Sussex, in 1792. The clientele was increasingly upper class as the nineteenth century progressed. In the 1820s, a prospectus was issued with illustrations of the asylum and grounds, which included a pagoda, a Gothic summer house, and a lake. The photographs dating back to the late nineteenth century show comfortable drawing rooms and scenic gardens – see the Wellcome Collection archives for the lovely surroundings Arabella was kept. Catherine Corbeau, Sir Charles's mother, was not so well looked after, as Ticehurst was certainly not the norm.

And so, to Ravenscourt. I do like to use real buildings when I write, and when I first thought of how my house would look, I googled Victorian Gothic houses and up popped Tyntesfield, a National Trust property outside Bristol built in 1863 by William Gibbs, a merchant. Visiting there in June 2025 provided me with so much inspiration – the Glass House for example was destroyed in a storm in 1916. The hall is wonderfully atmospheric, with its carved lantern roof and galleried stairs, and I could almost imagine Arabella and Mary looking down at me. The medicine cabinet in the ensuite bathroom of Lady Blanche Gibbs' bedroom (Alex's in the book) was a wonderful find, especially as it contained both opium and poison; the stag heads in the Billiard Room provided more drama; and I was also inspired by many of the beautiful portraits in the house. It was just the most perfect model for Ravenscourt.

Acknowledgements

It takes a great team to get my books into shape, and I am so lucky and thankful to have the following people in mine: my editor extraordinaire Katie Seaman; my meticulous proofreader Mark Swift (with added thanks to his wife Kathryn for all her support too); my publishing guru and fabulous friend Karen Stanley from Mabel and Stanley Publishing; and my marketing expert Dani Butler of Build the Buzz.

Writing can be a solitary process, and I am grateful for my two wonderful groups: The Mabel and Stanley Writing and Publishing Community, in particular Paula Russell and Jackie Sansom; and Your Author Group run by the amazing Lesley Sainty, with my three amigos Lee-Anne McAulay, Natalie Shaw, and Barry Lynch.

Although this book is not set in the Tower of London, I couldn't be without my Tower Support team who are just the best supporters of all my writing ventures: my Tower Twin Victoria Carrington, Julie Ttoffali, Holly and Nathan Bridgeman, Roy Booth, Sarah Lawson, Sarah Lambert, Laura Fairleigh, Stephen Jolly, Gary Leighton, Phoebe and Craig Joyce, and Jose Santonja.

I have the most amazing friends who are all just the bee's knees: Chris, Jaz, and Mickayla Skaife; Lindsey Fitzharris and Ade Teale; Emma Rainbow and Ian Madgin; Kitty and Andy Cowan; Alan Beeson (with huge thanks for the website overhaul); Darren Dadabhay and Colin Delvin; Caroline Latty and Sarah Wicket; Julie Sullivan, Stacey Thomas, Debbie Smith, Barry Wellington (my beloved history teacher); and old school friends Ruth Huntsman and Elizabeth Jose.

When I moved to Whitstable seven years ago, I could not imagine the fantastic new friends and neighbours

I would gain in my life: Hannah Berry and Simon Norton and of course Amelia, Rosie, and Socks; Hayley Turner; Izzy and Roger Jobson; Ken Baker, Alison and Tom Baily; James Edward-Hughes (we will always have Rochester!) and Josh Luun; Jackie Keane and Hannah Finnegan; and Marnie Summerfield Smith (although we met in York!).

Libraries have always played a huge part in my life from a very early age, and they are just an amazing resource for which we should all be thankful! I just want to give a shout-out to a few that have helped and supported me either for a long time or over this past year with my debut novel *Tower of Vengeance*. My local library – Swalecliffe Library – may be small but it is mighty in my eyes. Librarian, Sally Todd, has been so supportive and gave me some useful leads and contacts, and the Thursday Talk club were so welcoming to this debut author. In London, Shoe Lane Library and Sona Kalenderian hosted my very first author talk, and I will forever be grateful. I do all my writing in the London Library in the writing room called the Study – what an inspirational place, and I sit amongst the ghosts of literary genius. Also, I must give a shout out to Celine and the team at Dr Johnson's House for also hosting an author talk for me (which can be found on YouTube!) and for all round support.

Ravenscourt the house does not exist, but it was based on the National Trust property, Tyntesfield, and I spent a lovely day there with the best staff and volunteers who just gave me so much time and even more inspiration – so a shout-out to them and of course their scones.

I cannot forget my family – each and every one of you are truly loved, in particular the best brother-in-law, David Stonier, and of course, my darling mum, Jackie, and my big sis, Kathryn – we three against the world.

I mustn't forget Belle and Rudy, my gorgeous cats, as apparently, they were not amused at being omitted last time …

Lastly, this one is for Linda Grant and Judith Hudson, who do all the beta reading, listen to countless plot conundrums, and have the hardship of drinking numerous cocktails with me. Your feedback is always spot-on, but your friendship is the greatest gift.

About the Author

Samantha Ward-Smith writes historical fiction steeped in shadows, secrets, and the echoes of the past.

She holds an MA in Renaissance Studies and a PhD in English from Birbeck, University of London.

Her debut novel *Tower of Vengeance* was published in 2025.

Samantha lives in Whitstable with her two cats Belle and Rudy. She loves ravens, castles, and travelling as long as she has a case full of books to read. Find out more about Samantha on her website:

www.samanthawardsmithwriter.com

Tower of Vengeance

Tower of London: 1214

Maude de Mandeville is dying. Murdered by a poisoned egg for rejecting King John's advances. As she stands before Death, she makes a pact with the Devil to avenge her murder and return as a ghost to protect her only son with the help of her inherited witch's powers.

Available now on Amazon, and to order at all good bookshops.

"Everything you would hope for in a book of love and vengeance"

Christopher Skaife, author of 'The Ravenmaster'